THE ECHO OF A
THOUSAND VOICES

THE FORGOTTEN ONES - BOOK THREE

JILLIAN WEBSTER

ALSO BY JILLIAN WEBSTER

Scared to Life: A Memoir

The Weight of a Thousand Oceans: The Forgotten Ones - Book One

The Burn of a Thousand Suns: The Forgotten Ones - Book Two

This is a work of fiction. All characters, organizations, and events portrayed in this novel are either products of the author's imagination or are used fictitiously.

THE ECHO OF A THOUSAND VOICES: THE FORGOTTEN ONES - BOOK THREE
Copyright © 2022 by Jillian Webster

www.jillianwebster.com

Cover design by Murphy Rae
www.murphyrae.net

978-1-7350256-9-8

First Edition

AUTHOR'S NOTE

This is a work of fiction. This story takes place in the
northern lands of North America, but they are not as we
know them today. The oceans have risen hundreds of feet,
and the coastline and climate have changed. Some
geography and places have been altered, while others
invented entirely.

He aha te mea nui o te ao?
He tāngata, he tāngata, he tāngata.

What is the most important thing in the world?
It is people, it is people, it is people.

- Māori Whakataukī (proverb)

PROLOGUE

Maia wavers in the middle of a crowded street, lost in a sea of strangers. Eyes glazed, she desperately searches the faces as they pass. Scouring left to right. Right to left.

Not him.

Not him.

Not him.

The countless people shuffling past take no notice of her. Their shoulders brush against hers, some harder than others. A man pushing his way through the horde knocks into her and she stumbles back. "Sorry," he mumbles over his shoulder. She blinks and regains her footing.

The flashing lights along the side of the road illuminate large signs, advertising things that don't matter. She thought they would matter.

Why don't they matter?

Gazing up at the dark sky, Maia locates a single flickering star. The constellations she has grown to love so fiercely have all but disappeared, devoured by the hungry lights of this large metropolis. *Light pollution*, she was told in orientation, right before being chastised by an annoyed instructor to *stop asking so many questions*.

It is Leucothea Day. Today, the people of this massive city have piled out from behind the closed curtains and locked doors of their private homes to celebrate "the greatest civilization on Earth." They've filled the streets, laughing and cheering and waving little black flags with a single white star in the middle—symbolizing Leucothea as a beacon of light in a dark world. Enormous signs with bold letters plaster the city, repeating the same slogan Maia has heard repeatedly from the moment she arrived ... or at least from the moment she awoke:

Leucothea has saved you.

The festival is coming to a close now that the early-autumn sun has finally dipped below the horizon enough to give the people the darkness they crave. The heaving crowds make their way toward Leucothea Square, each holding a candle to be lit as their beloved leader delivers his awe-inspiring speech, broadcasted on screens across the city. Then Leucothea's citizens will cheer the fact that they are *in here* and no longer *out there*. And the echo of thousands will be heard across the Arctic.

They have been saved. Protected. Walled in.

Maia continues searching the faces passing by on either side in a blur.

Where is he? Is he here? He has to be here somewhere.

One after the next, the people pass; an endless parade of bodies in varying colors, shapes, and sizes. So many faces and they all look so different—the shape of their eyes, the length of their noses, the shade of their skin. Pink and freckled. Rich olive. Deep ebony. Long hair. Short hair. Curly, straight, dark, light. They are all so unique. So diverse.

Yet, not a single face belongs to the man she seeks.

2

These are the people Maia has always dreamed of meeting. So many late nights in New Zealand she would stare at the moon, imagining people gathering here from all over the world, It is one of the last remaining civilizations on Earth. The success of this city marks a "New Dawn" for an almost extinct humanity. This is the beginning of everything. They are so lucky. *They are a part of history.*

Yet, none of this matters. She thought it would matter.

Why doesn't it matter?

A man stands by the curb, his back toward her. His hair is short, dark—*curly.*

"*Lucas.*" Maia pushes her way through the bodies. "Sorry. Sorry," she mumbles as she weaves her way through.

Orientation was so rigorous with training each migrant on how to behave, particularly when in crowds—most people would have never been in one before arriving. If you bump into another person, you must say, "sorry." You are also supposed to stand "in a line" and "wait your turn." You must *always* look both ways before crossing any street. The rules seemed endless. But if one is granted entry inside Leucothea, they will be a contributing member of a grand and privileged society. Always obey the rules. Always work as hard as you can. Always think of Leucothea before yourself.

Leucothea has saved you.

"Hey! *Watchit!*"

"Sorry," Maia mumbles. "Sorry—*Lucas?*"

A woman next to her laughs a little too loud, and Maia recoils like a wild animal. The woman stops, her smile fading as she looks down her pointed nose at Maia's baggy and faded clothing, donated to her as a new migrant. Her eyes linger on the monitoring contraption secured around

Maia's wrist, the small bulb on the side lit green. She tosses her hair as she turns away.

Maia wraps her hand around the flashing beacon of her alien status.

I am 'them.'

She pulls her sleeve over the device and continues to weave through the tangled web of people—a wild mix of strangers bathed in bizarre lights and foreign smells. What is that smell? Maia can't place it.

She stops as the man next to the curb turns toward her, laughing. No, it's not Lucas. She sighs, hanging her head. And no, this isn't a smell. It's actually the *lack* of a smell— the only scent that matters to Maia. The one sweet aroma she craves more than anything: the rich essence of dirt —*earth*. It's the lack of her beloved sounds too. There are no chirping crickets or trilling birds calling from their perches between branches. No ocean waves lapping against the shore. No soothing whispers from the trees.

Mother. Mother. Mother.

No, not here. Very few trees line these streets. Maia and the deafening crowd around her are surrounded by a jungle of brick and stone and towers of shining glass, reflecting flashing lights in a hypnotic neon glow.

As Maia steps onto the sidewalk, she catches her reflection in the blackened window of a storefront. Taken aback, she wanders to the glass, her hand reaching to the stranger on the other side. She barely recognizes herself. Her eyes— they are empty. She tilts her gaze. *She* is empty. Fed, yet somehow starving.

The only shimmer in her eyes now comes from the reflection of artificial lights. So many strange and wonderful lights. Cut off from the one thing that feeds her soul, the real glimmer behind her eyes has faded. Her powers diminished.

She doesn't dare ignite a single candle. *They* are always watching.

Give it time, a caseworker had told Maia, completely unaware of the real cause of her suffering. *There's an adjustment period for all migrants. It's okay. You are safe now. You are protected. Leucothea has saved you.*

Has Leucothea saved her? Yes. Yes, Leucothea has saved her.

Has it?

Where is Lucas? And why, with every stranger that she passes on this busy city street, is she always looking for Miguel? He's not here; she knows he's not. But she is always searching. Searching. Searching.

Hello, little bird.

Every day, standing at her assigned job next to something called a "conveyer belt," Maia sifts through the items collected by the armies of S&R—*Search and Rescue*—Crews. She pauses and looks around. Is he here? Is either one of them here? Why can't her caseworker locate Lucas? Miguel promised he would come.

And yet, Maia is alone.

Ache. Ache. Ache.

And so, the items pass by in an endless procession on the belt. Toothbrush—unused. She swipes it and tosses it into the green hygiene bin behind her marked "Citizens." Used toothbrushes go in the red hygiene bins to be washed and used by a migrant—a migrant like her. Everything is equal, unless you're a migrant. Keep your head down. Work hard to fulfill your contract. Be a good worker, and you can graduate to citizenship. Then they will remove your monitoring bracelet.

They even give you flowers.

A pencil. She grabs it as it passes, tossing it in another bin behind her.

A contraption used to open cans. Swipe. Toss.

Shoe. Swipe. Toss.

An old device: flat and rectangular with a glass top. Grab. Toss. That one goes into a bin for the teams working on reviving their ancestor's old technology. Simple things with on/off buttons that feed off electricity are pretty abundant in this city—although Maia still doesn't understand where all this electricity is coming from. Lights, central heating ... they even have televisions. They only play the news and an old movie on Friday nights, which is the highlight of the week for most. Contraptions that require something called "the web" still remain dark.

A sweater passes on the belt—good condition. Swipe. Toss.

A package of unused plastic cups. Swipe. Toss.

Box of cutlery. Swipe. Toss.

Today's shipment of collected items from the S&R Crews is pretty empty. They have to travel farther and farther these days to find anything useful. But there are enough of them out there that Maia and the other workers assigned to this warehouse get shipments every few days to sort and sift for the supply warehouses. There is much work to be done. There are a lot of people in this city who need things ... things that are just ripe for the taking *out there*. But those things need to be sorted and rationed. Maia's job is important. She is a valued member of society. Very useful; she is very useful.

A man coughs behind her. Maia stops, glancing over her shoulder.

Is it Lucas?

No.

She only sees Lucas in her dreams. It's the same dream, the same vision that started back when she was hiding in the storage closet in the bowels of that ship—*his* ship. The ship where they met. The ship where she would have starved to death if it wasn't for him. The ship he'd still be on if it wasn't for her. The two of them risked everything to get to this city that called out to her from the shores of New Zealand so long ago.

It takes everything inside her not to constantly question why.

Every night her dreams are the same: wandering the soiled alleyways of a drowned city, the water sucked dry from the sky. She steps over a flopping fish, suffocating in a puddle in the street, and then right on cue, the curly redheaded child peeks out from behind the buildings. Her giggles echo off the dripping brick. Unable to resist, Maia follows the child until they reach her old New Zealand cabin, tucked between the buildings at the end of a long corridor. Only now, as she wanders down the empty streets, the gray skies release a fluffy white snow. Drifting like tiny feathers, the flakes float in the air but never land.

Up the cabin stairs Maia goes, the old wood groaning with every step. She passes the two rocking chairs made by her grandfather and then nudges open the front door. The small child stands at the living room fireplace next to him —*Lucas?* His curls are gone, his hair shaved short. He is obscured ... out of focus, his back always toward her. The child reaches for him, and he turns to look at her. Just as Maia is about to make out his features, she awakens.

After all this time, she never once sees his face. Never once sees the child's face. She yearns for nothing more than to see them, often screaming into her pillow upon awakening. This child ... Is it her? Like the little girl with two different-colored eyes from the pond outside Miguel's cabin? And Lucas—he's different in her dreams. Something about him is different. Sometimes Maia can't even be sure it's him. Why would he visit her dreams so relentlessly but not allow her to see him?

Where is he?

ONE

The woman with no soul has spoken again. Her voice is robotic, void of emotion. After what seems like hours of blissful silence, her voice blares through the ether. "Welcome. *Bienvenido. Bienvenue. Willkommen.*" On and on she goes, speaking one word at a time—most of which Maia does not understand—and then there is silence.

Lying on an old mattress on the floor, Maia opens her eyes to a small brick room painted in a blinding, glossy white. The small space is empty, save for a metallic toilet in the corner. The only door in the room has no handle, just a small rectangular window toward the top and another along the base—both closed. A sliver of windows near the ceiling is the room's only source of light.

Every time Maia awakens, mainly to the voice from above, she believes herself to be dreaming, or awakening from one dream into another. In and out of blackened slumbers, she has dreams upon dreams upon dreams—faraway worlds in her mind.

But she *must* be dreaming. She knows this because when

she *actually* wakes, she will be curled up in her little umiak with Lucas by her side, drifting into the city of Leucothea. This is the last thing she remembers: holding Lucas's head against her, reaching for a searchlight so bright that it burned her eyes.

And then, there was darkness.

"Welcome. *Bienvenido. Bienvenue. Willkommen. Bem-vindo. Välkommen.*"

"*Shhh!*" Maia grumbles. Holding her pounding head, she rolls over on the mattress, its groaning springs digging into her bones.

The woman goes silent.

Maia turns onto her side and sighs. She is *not* dreaming. Rolling off her mattress onto the cold floor, she reaches with a trembling hand for a small jar of water left next to the door, desperately gulping its limited contents without stopping for breath. The cool water is like heaven.

She slams down the jar and wipes her mouth with the back of her hand, noticing for the first time a black contraption secured around her wrist. It's thick, like a large plastic watch with no face. A red light emanates from a small circular bulb on the side.

"Welcome. *Bienvenido. Bienvenue...*"

"Hello?! *Lucas*?" Maia calls out, tapping the red light.

A sign next to the door reads:

*Do not tamper with the device around your wrist. Damaging the bracelet in any way will result in your immediate removal from Leucothea. There will be no permission for reentry.

She *is* in Leucothea. Maia looks again at the bracelet. *What on Earth?*

Bracelet. She glances at her other wrist. Lucas and Miguel's braided bracelet—it's gone. Her heart pounding, she slowly reaches up to her chest. She fumbles around her neck in a panic, digging at her skin, praying her fingers catch on a necklace.

"No..." she whispers. "Please, *no*."

Her pounamu, her beloved greenstone necklace carved by her mother. *Gone.*

"*No!*" Her bellow echoes in the small space. "*Please!* Can anyone hear me? Hello?!" She lifts to her feet and throws herself against the door, banging her fists against it.

"*Willkommen. Bem-vindo. Välkommen*," the woman with no soul continues.

Maia follows the sound of the voice. It's coming from a little black box in the corner. A small device hangs from the ceiling next to it—it looks like an old camera. Like her bracelet, it has a small red bulb lit up. Maia crawls back to the old mattress as the speakers blare, burying her head under her arms. "Please ... *stop*."

A metallic click sounds from behind, and Maia flips around on her bed. The small window at the bottom of the door slides open to a mesh screen.

"Do you speak English?" a woman from the other side asks.

"Yes..."

"Can you read?"

"Yes."

The screen opens, and a glass jar filled with a white substance slides across the glossy floor. The woman tosses in a clipboard with a paper attached before closing the screen. "Soup and a contract. Please take your time with the food if it has been a while since you've eaten. If you need to throw up, use the toilet in the corner. Read the contract. Someone will be back shortly." The window slides shut.

Maia crawls over to the jar. The glass is still warm. She unscrews the lid and lifts the vessel beneath her nose. It certainly *smells* like food. She dips her pinky in and gathers a small dollop on her finger, touching it to the tip of her tongue.

Definitely food.

She reads the paper:

Welcome to Leucothea!

Congratulations on making it safely to our haven. Please read the following contract. A guardian will come back shortly and will ask for a simple "yes" or "no." Please reply with "yes" ONLY IF YOU AGREE TO EVERYTHING YOU HAVE READ. This is not an opportunity for barter. Should you choose not to accept the conditions below, we will escort you outside our gates to be on your way. You will not be allowed reentry.

1. *I understand that I am at Leucothea's Migrant Facility outside the city's inner walls. I have not yet been granted entry. I do not have a "right" to be here. I am a guest.*
2. *I will be given food, lodging, clothing, and medical care (if applicable) while residing at this facility. I agree to pay for these services and items if I am allowed entry into Leucothea.*
3. *I vow to cause no harm to any person or thing. Breaking this rule will result in immediate removal from Leucothea, and I will be banned for life.*
4. *I accept that I must attend a two-week intensive course to help me navigate living in a world of the future. I agree to obey all rules outlined in orientation without question. A final exit interview will assess whether or not I have learned the skills required to be a contributing member of society. The*

fee for this will be included in my contract, to be paid off over a set course of time once permitted entry into Leucothea.

5. *Should I be granted entry, a guardian will be appointed to me. This person will assess my progress and select a work assignment where I will be most valued in the magnificent city of Leucothea.*

6. *Once my contract has been fulfilled, I may be granted citizenship in Leucothea, free to live and explore a life like that of our ancestors in the greatest city on Earth.*

Congratulations. Leucothea has saved you.

Maia holds the paper before her. *Saved* her?

"Hello?" she calls out. She reads the list again.

The door's small window slides open to the screen. "Yes, or no?" asks the woman on the other side.

Maia hesitates, looking over the list. Does she have a choice?

"*Hello*? Yes, or no?"

"Yes."

The door's metallic latch clicks, and it swings open. Two armed guards stand on the other side, a man and a woman dressed in black. Their uniforms have silver buttons up the front and a white, five-pointed star embroidered on the right chest pocket. They have guns, but they do not point them at her. "Come with us," the woman says with a smile that does not reach her eyes.

Maia stands, slowly backing into the wall. The woman maintains her smile, motioning for Maia to come forward. "It's okay," she drawls in a soothing voice.

"I came with a man—"

"We separate all travelers upon arrival. Men and women are held and assessed independently for their safety."

Still hesitant, Maia shuffles forward. Why doesn't she remember arriving here? "I was wearing a neck—"

"Come on, we don't have all day," the woman snaps. "We'll bring you to the showers first, and then you will meet with your guardian. You may ask questions then."

Maia steps into the hallway. Her legs are incredibly weak and she is *desperately* thirsty. Despite her hunger, she didn't dare eat her soup. As she follows the woman, the male trails quietly behind them. Closed doors line the hall, and sparsely placed single bulbs hang from the ceiling, illuminating the corridor in dim cones of light.

Maia has so many questions. She's in a migrant building? She's in Leucothea but outside the city gates? Where is Lucas? Someone took her pounamu.

The woman pulls a device from her belt. It's a talkie-walkie ... or a talker-walker? It's the same type of radio they used in New Portland. Maia smiles from the memory. She'd often forget the name, and Miguel, always by her side, would correct her with an amused grin.

Ache. Ache. Ache.

"We're bringing arrival four eight two nine seven to the showers now," the woman says into the radio.

Is it a walkie-talkie? No, that's not it.

"ETA entrance interview fifteen minutes," the woman continues into the radio. She turns and smiles at Maia, reaching for her.

Maia recoils.

"It's okay." The woman grabs Maia's arm and guides her toward a door with the word *Showers* printed on a sign. "You are safe. We aren't going to hurt you."

The two women step inside the room. A handful of

showers separated by curtains line the left wall, with a small metal bench outside each. Most of the faucets are already on, releasing heavy clouds of swirling mist. Black dirt runs in streams from the feet behind the curtains, emptying down a drain in the middle of the room.

"This is your shower here." Still clutching Maia's arm, the woman guides her to a space in the corner with clothing hanging on the wall beside it. She hands Maia a bag. "Put your dirty items in here. We'll get them cleaned up for you. Until then, wear the clean clothes we have left on the hook there." She steps inside the shower. "This knob here will make the water turn on," she says slowly, as if speaking to a child. "Turn the knob *all the way* to get really hot water, or just *halfway* to get warm water. Make sure to turn it *all the way* off when you're finished. Okay?"

"Sure, I understand," Maia says.

"It's okay if your bracelet gets wet. Oh, and there is a bar of soap just here on the wall. You use this to clean the dirt from your skin and hair. Do you understand?"

Maia nods.

"Please do this as quickly as possible, as we have a guardian waiting to meet you."

"Thank you," Maia says.

The guard looks at her, and she smiles. "You have manners. How refreshing," she says, and then she steps from the room.

Maia strips down behind the curtain, hanging her dirty clothes over its rod. She turns the faucet *all the way*, amazed at the cascade of clean water shooting out. She slowly steps beneath it. The steaming hot shower sends chills down her skin and she stands beneath the rush, gulping down as much as she can without making herself sick. It's a learned skill, holding back when you are so thirsty. Just a little at a time.

Lathering up the soap, she washes the layers of grime from her skin, running her fingers through her head of long crimson curls. Like the other women, the black dirt from her feet escapes in a torrent down the drain.

Afterward, Maia slides into the clothing they've supplied. The fabric is incredibly worn, some parts so thin the fibers nearly pull apart, but it is all so *clean*. Her trouser waistband has strings inside that she can draw to tighten. She has to pull quite a bit to keep the pants on, but the fabric is so soft. She buttons her oversized shirt and rolls up the sleeves, then slides her boots back on, grateful no one has taken them. These are now her only possession, a refurbished gift from the tribe. She shoves her dirty clothes into the bag they've given her. The number *48297* has been written on the front.

Maia steps out of the shower room with her bag in hand and quietly follows her guard, the male still trailing behind. The woman leads them along another narrow hallway, up a set of metallic stairs, then down a long corridor until she finally stops, knocking on a door.

"Come in!" another woman's voice sounds from inside.

The guard opens the door and leads Maia in, taking her bag of clothes.

Inside the room, a blonde, middle-aged woman sits behind a wooden desk much too large for the small space. She clasps her hands before her, bookended by tall columns of files. Not a single inch of her workspace is empty. There are stacked papers everywhere, filling the bookshelves lining the walls and slouching in piles on the floor.

"Hello, please come in." The woman stands, motioning to a chair opposite her. "Sit."

Uneasy, Maia does as she's told. Her armed guards stand close behind her.

"My name is Rebecca," the woman behind the desk says. "What is your name?"

"Maia."

"Maia..." Rebecca squints, leaning across her desk. "Your eyes are different colors."

Maia nods but says nothing.

Rebecca sits back. "I didn't know that was possible." She looks at the guards behind Maia. "Did you?" She glances between them. "No, me either." She turns her attention to Maia again. "And where do you come from?"

"New Zealand," Maia replies, her knee bouncing.

"My, my! You've come so far! You must be exhausted—"

"I'm sorry," Maia cuts in, "but I came with a man. His name is Lucas. Please, do you know where he is? Is he okay? He was very sick."

Rebecca stares at her, a crease between her brow. "All travelers are separated upon arrival," she says after a moment. "We need to assess each person's mental and physical health independent of one another. We find this is best in helping people learn how to integrate into the city— fewer distractions. It's a huge adjustment going from the dark world *out there* to the haven we have in here. But don't worry, we have a Migrant Services Building inside Leucothea that reunites travelers with their loved ones *if* they're allowed inside."

"And if they're not?"

Rebecca smiles. "Most people are. No one comes here by accident. However, some take longer than others to learn the rules."

"Rules?"

"Yes, learning to live by the rules of time and being a

17

contributing member of a large society. Working with electricity and navigating city streets with lights and moving
vehicles. This can be a huge adjustment for many, especially
those who've lived in a hunter-gatherer lifestyle, or those
who've spent most of their lives alone."

"I suppose that makes sense."

"Is there anything else before we get started?"

"Yes," Maia whispers. She places her hand against the
bare skin of her neck. "I was wearing a necklace with a
greenstone carving. I had a bracelet too."

"There's a Lost and Found service on the first floor. You
can file a report with them about your missing items. If they
are found, someone will get them back to you before you
leave."

If? Maia's heart sinks. "Right."

"Any other questions?"

"No. Actually, yes. How big is Leucothea?"

"We have nearly fifty-thousand people from all over the
world."

Maia covers her mouth.

"But not all of those people are in the city. We have civil-
ians who grow our food outside the gates, and others who
take care of our waste or keep our electricity running
smoothly. We have a massive fire brigade always on the
move against wildfires. We also have the highly regarded
Search and Rescue Crews that travel outside of Leucothea
on missions to collect supplies, tools, clothing, spare parts,
and building equipment—this one is huge. Our magnificent
city is growing so fast, and we need to keep up with demand.
There's still so much *out there* that we can use."

Maia nods. No wonder it was so hard for her and Lucas
to find supplies.

"You'll learn all about this in your classes over the next

few weeks. But first, I need to ask you a few questions before we can allocate a spot for you."

"Okay."

"Now, Maia, I need you to be completely honest with every question I ask. Do you understand?"

"I do."

"If we discover at *any time* that you have lied to us about *anything*, we will immediately remove you from our city, and you will be banned for life—without your partner or family." She leans toward Maia, once again clasping her hands before her. "Do you understand how serious this is?"

"Of course," Maia says. "I understand."

"Okay, good. Let's begin." Rebecca slides open a drawer beside her and pulls out a yellow folder. After scribbling Maia's migrant number across the front, she opens it and clears her throat. "Okay, first question. Have you ever killed another person?"

TWO

Maia stares up at the underside of the wooden bunk. The timber is rough, slivered, like the bed had been quickly thrown together from the offcuts of another project. The woman lying on top tosses on her mattress, shaking the bunk. She doesn't speak English, or maybe she just doesn't want to. When Maia settled into their shared quarters earlier, she tried to smile, make eye contact, say hello ... but her new roommate wouldn't look at her.

It's too bad, such a small space to be sharing with a complete stranger.

After Maia passed her entry interview, Rebecca led her to a different part of the Migrant Facility, separated by a series of locked metallic doors with loud buzzers. This part of the building definitely has better lighting ... more windows, nicer carpet. It's a little cozier than the bare confines Maia was in before, although she wouldn't necessarily call this room *cozy*. Just a bunk bed and a small desk nestled up to a window overlooking a cement courtyard, enclosed, of course, by more walls.

This is apparently where the students reside, migrants who have been given the opportunity of being granted entry into Leucothea *if* they work hard enough. But first, they must prove they can integrate smoothly into society.

Maia continues staring at the bed's slats above, reading a sentence someone had etched into the wood. Clearly, *they* didn't know the person who had slept in this bed before Maia had ... *opinions*.

Or maybe they did.

Scratched into the wood is a sentence with letters no wider than a pencil:

"Leucothea will *destroy* you."

Maia looks up at the sentence, reading it over and over again. The letters of "destroy" have been etched into the wood much deeper than the rest, like the person writing it had gone mad.

Maia's conversation with Rebecca felt much more like an interrogation than an interview. She sighs. Reaching up to the slivered wood, she traces the remnants of another person's misery with the tip of her finger. There are no smiling faces or rainbows or *Leucothea has saved you* in this bed.

No. It's just, "Leucothea will *destroy* you."

That interview was so intense. It was like Rebecca was after something ... prying at Maia to get her to break. There were so many questions.

There were so many lies.

"Have you ever killed another person?"

Maia swallows hard and her cheeks flush. "*No.*" Her response is loud—defensive.

Rebecca looks at her with slitted eyes. Her features soften, and she smiles. "No need to get upset, Maia. Unless you have something to hide. *Do* you have something to hide?"

Lucas will be waiting for her on the other side. Miguel swore he'll come, after the first snowfall of her second winter. He *swore* he'd come.

"No, of course not," Maia says. "Nothing to hide."

Rebecca leans back in her chair, eyeing Maia. "You came to Leucothea in some sort of ... *canoe*."

Maia bites her tongue. *It's called an umiak.*

"Maia? Where did you get that canoe from?"

Tema *hated* Leucothea, although she never told Maia why. It would be the ultimate betrayal to discuss any details of the tribe with the authorities here. "Lucas and I found it —abandoned ... on the side of ... the road." Her heart pounds. *Road*? Why didn't she say river?

"How did you get *all the way* from New Zealand to North America?"

"I came on a ship."

"A ship?" Rebecca leans forward. "What *sort* of ship?"

Maia thinks back to Lucas standing across from her in the storage closet of his boat. They barely knew each other. They had only just started talking. That was *before*. Before everything had changed so drastically for the two of them. Before they became stranded in the middle of the Pacific Ocean among endless mountains of plastic. *People like us*, he had whispered as they hid among the crates, *we follow our own rules. Our ship is banned from Leucothea.*

Maia racks her brain for a quick answer. What would Lucas be saying in his own entry interview? She clears her throat. "Some people my father knew were sailing to North

America. They allowed me to come along." She's not *technically* lying on that one.

"Have you or the man you were with ever stolen from living people?"

Lucas has ... from Jake, on the ship that rescued them. *I stole that knife, he told her back in LA. And the waterproof torch. I felt justified because it was Jake, and he was such an asshole.*

"No—never," Maia says with a contrived smile.

Rebecca inhales, repositioning herself on her seat. She scans the paper before her, exhaling a long breath from her nose. "Have you..." Her voice trails as she examines the questions, her fingers drumming the wooden desk. "Have you ever caused extreme grief or harm to another person?" She peers up at her.

Maia's mouth dries. Memories from the past year come flooding back to her: ordering the stray German Shepherd she had named Charlie to kill that man while she stood over him and ... *smiled.*

You were going to kill us, Maia had said as the man's life hung on a thread.

No! No, we just wanted your packs!

Same thing, Maia replied, and then she snapped her fingers, ordering Charlie to lunge at his neck.

Choking. Gasping. Gurgling.

She recalls the chaos of the mob in British Columbia running between the trees, screaming in terror, their bodies engulfed in flames. Their one-eyed leader had just been smashed under a burning semi, his blood spilling from beneath.

All death and destruction caused by Maia's hands and Maia's hands alone.

More memories: Maia slamming a massive pine tree into

three men, crushing them to death against the forest floor. Maia ordering the old alpha wolf on another man ... and then walking away with his gun while her pack of wolves tore him limb from limb.

She shakes the images from her mind. "No. No, of course not. I could *never*..." She bites her nail.

Stop.

She grips her hands in her lap.

The interview was long and tedious, with Rebecca asking the same round of questions on repeat but wording them a little differently. The entire time, she watched Maia with a tilted gaze, scribbling little notes as Maia stuttered and mumbled and looked around nervously.

That seemed like more than just an entry interview. It was like Rebecca was merely waiting for Maia to confirm what she already knew.

Maia asked if there was any way she could see Lucas but was met with a clear and definitive *no*. Maia had so many questions, but in the end, only one was answered:

"Why don't I remember arriving here?"

"We shot you with a tranquilizer bead—both you and your friend. It was tiny. You wouldn't have even known it hit you."

"Why?"

"It's for everyone's safety—more so ours than yours. We require every arrival to drop their things at the gates and separate, but we couldn't ask that of you. You were floating in on a boat, somewhat hysterical, from what I'm told. They didn't know what you may have had hidden in that canoe or what your intentions were."

"He was really sick, my friend. He injured his leg on the rapids. It became infected. His heart ... that tranquilizer could have ... are you sure—" Maia looks at Rebecca through her tears, struggling to hold herself together.

"Maia, I know this is hard for you at the moment, but I need you to focus. Your friend should be perfectly fine."

"*Should*? Why don't you know?"

"I am in charge of the women arrivals. The men's building is located elsewhere. I don't have details of their migrants, but I can assure you that everyone working in these buildings has your best interests at heart. You will be reunited when you *both* prove to us that you can live as contributing members of this society. *Or* when you prove that you cannot. If that is the case, we will escort you away from our walls, and you will be free to find him again ... *out there*. I wouldn't recommend that. Look, the best thing you can do to be reunited with ... Lucas?"

Maia nods.

"Right. The best thing you can do to be reunited with Lucas as quickly as possible is to give this orientation your *all*."

Maia sighs, glancing away.

"Maia, I am trying to help you. Help *me* help *you*. Do your very best in these classes, and then we can release you to the other side. Okay?"

Maia looks back at her. If being a good student is what will get her inside those walls, then that's exactly what she'll be. "Okay."

THREE

The next few weeks pass in a blur. The Migrant Facility's orientation classes last all day, with Maia and eight other women crammed in a small classroom lined with posters of smiling people working in some sort of utopia favoring blue skies and rainbows. Leucothea's government, "The New System," apparently leaves people delighted while walking around green pastures hand in hand. Every poster says the same thing:

Leucothea has saved you.

A framed portrait of Leucothea's leader, President Augustus, is hung at the front of the class, next to a large black flag with a white five-pointed star in the middle. The president looks like the sort of man people would adore. With a thick head of white hair and a welcoming smile, he appears to exude power.

Their instructor, Miss Mary, has the opposite appeal—like she's desperate for control and wouldn't hesitate to use brute force to command it. Her sleek gray hair is pulled into a tight bun on top of her head, and her grimace is as unsettling as her grin. It's as if she was born to scowl.

The first thing Miss Mary wanted to know was who was educated and who had experience with electricity. Most of the women could read and write a little, but their knowledge was limited. Only Maia and one other woman, Dawn, could be considered well read. Maia was the only one who had any experience with electricity—in New Portland—but even that was short lived. She, Lucas, and Miguel had only spent a single night in that home.

Unfortunately, Maia's mute roommate only lasted a day. After refusing to speak or participate, she was asked to leave the class. When Maia climbed into bed later that night, the bunk above her was empty. And empty it remained for the rest of Maia's stay.

Every afternoon, after a morning of intense coursework, Miss Mary took the women to a large gymnasium divided into zones called "learning modules," where the women could practice the skills that may grant them entry into the city of lights.

Some of the modules seemed so simple, like turning different devices off and on. Others involved working with running water, washing machines, dishwashers, and showers. Alarm clocks and clocks in general, were an entire module by themselves. Living according to time is very important in a thriving society.

There was also a kitchen segment, where they were taught how to cook the food that will be supplied to them in the city: working an electric stove, an oven, and a microwave, which heated their meals in a matter of seconds with an invisible fire. *Like magic.*

Many of the lessons seemed to drag as the instructors spoke to the women slowly, with loud voices, as if they were simple-minded barbarians. During one of Maia's brief check-in sessions with Rebecca, she complained that the women were being treated like savages. This made Rebecca laugh. "Maia, some of them *are*. It's best if we start with the very basics with every migrant."

A few skills took the women a little longer to learn, even Maia. Like how to manage the Leucothean coins they will earn from their work assignments, after the fees for their orientation, set-up supplies, basic food, clothing, housing, and probationary period are taken out. This was called "budgeting," and it took all day for the women to gather the basics. They may spend their leftover money on extra supplies, which could range from tea or spices at home, to going out for meals, or buying new clothing. Maia did all right with this, but the women who could barely read or write had a much harder time.

The traffic module was the most overwhelming to Maia, much more than she could have anticipated. Miss Mary had informed the women about the process in class, but after spending an entire lifetime in darkness, nothing could have possibly prepared them for the lights and sounds of a busy city street at night.

As Maia stepped inside the pitch-black room, the door behind her clicked shut, startling her. She took a deep breath and steeled herself, knowing Miss Mary and the rest of the women would be watching from behind a large glass window along the outside wall.

First, four street lights flickered on, one after the next, lining the cement road inside the module. There was a small curb and sidewalk along either side, with cityscape painted on the walls. Maia smiled, the lit lamps reminding her so much of New Portland. It was just as magical as she remembered.

And then it began. A honking horn blasted from a speaker on Maia's left. She couldn't help but flinch. Foot traffic—countless heels clicking against cement—blared from the speakers on her right. Banging hammers, a man yelling, and a high-pitched siren assaulted Maia from every angle. Another loud car horn, and another. A baby crying. Coughing. Thumping music. The noises exploded from the speakers along the walls, and she grimaced from the onslaught, forcing herself not to cover her ears.

"Maia," Miss Mary's soothing voice sounded over the clamor. "Are you doing all right?"

Maia nodded, standing up straight, struggling to find her breath.

"Maia? I need you to cross the street."

The pole on the other side of the makeshift road had a small box on top, with a bright white symbol of a person walking mid-stride. Maia had been taught about this in class. *Walk.* As she stepped out onto the street, the sign changed to a flashing red hand.

Red means *stop.*

Panicked, Maia froze in the middle of the road, glancing around as the city noises continued to clash from the speakers. The sounds—they were so aggressive. Threatening. She couldn't think.

Miss Mary's voice called through the speakers. "Flashing red means you can keep going if you're already in the middle of the street. But you didn't look both ways!"

Maia obligingly looked to either side of her. Obviously, no cars were coming, but she was being tested. A loud *screech* sounded, and Maia covered her ears as a car horn blasted above the noises.

"Maia! Don't just stand in the middle of the road! You could be hit by a car! Move, move, move!"

Maia ran to the other side, still holding her ears, and the sounds stopped at once.

"Students, let us all pay attention to Maia's mistakes. You may cross the street if the walking symbol is white. *Keep walking* if it begins to flash red, but don't *begin* to cross if it's already flashing. Do not cross if it's completely red. Do we all understand? We've been through this. And always look both ways first!"

Maia nodded.

"Maia, the next time you cross without looking, it will be an automatic fail. *Always look both ways*, ladies, no matter what! I cannot stress this enough. There are moving vehicles *everywhere* in this city."

Maia waited on the fake city's curb, barely making out the faces on the other side of the glass, watching her with wide eyes.

Miss Mary spoke again into the microphone. "Okay, you may head out now and give someone else a try."

Over the next week, the women learn about Leucothea's history. Once a reputable and thriving commune during the turbulent times of The End, the city was the prime location to grow the booming metropolis it has since become. It has an incredible built-in infrastructure with running water and a wastewater treatment system, and it has all been done with renewable electricity. High up on a cliff and once considered inland, it has been safe from the rising ocean waters. The region is still cold in the winter and warm in the summer, versus so much of the planet that has become so hot that it is uninhabitable.

Unfortunately, the city could only support so many people before its infrastructure became stressed. The systems put in place began to break down, fall apart. So, a new government, The New System, took over and solved the city's apparent woes.

The metropolis is like a well-oiled machine. Now double walled for the people's safety— the second wall newly constructed—the massive cement structures are constantly patrolled by an army and a fire brigade. With the use of clean electricity and warehouses filled to the brim with everyday items that the S&R Crews are constantly restocking, it is like they are living in the world of their ancestors. Yes, a few things are in short supply but high demand, and those things must be rationed, but as more and more people are granted entry into the city, they will eventually have the workforce and resources to begin manufacturing those items themselves.

"The New System has big plans for our future, ladies, *big* plans," Miss Mary says with a wide grin. "It is a privilege and an honor to play such an important role in the future of mankind!"

The food they have been eating, although Maia wouldn't call it "food," is a conglomeration of a colorless goo made from fruit, vegetables, and grains grown in vast warehouses filled with artificial lights. Manufactured and packaged outside of the city, the bulk of the meals rationed to Leucothea's migrants have been freeze-dried or dehydrated, especially for the long and dark winter months. Although, the women have been told that once they finish their contracts and become citizens, they will earn more money, and their meal options will improve as well.

The animals born and bred to be eaten are unnatural to the Arctic, so they, too, have been crammed into warehouses with artificial lights.

"Now, I want you to know, this is for your own good. The natural animals living in the Arctic are too toxic to eat. Hunting is prohibited! The pollutants of the world have been gathering in the poles for hundreds of years. Long before The End, the Indigenous peoples of the Arctic were the most poisoned people on Earth. This is *not* the case for the people of Leucothea." Miss Mary pauses for effect.

Maia looks up. She has learned to give Miss Mary the full attention she demands, lest she pay the price.

"Ladies, you are *so lucky*," the old instructor says, clasping her hands before her, "to be fed our nourishing food and to be taken care of like this. No more scavenging toxic foods or going hungry!"

Their final week of orientation has been dedicated to respecting law and order.

"There is no crime in Leucothea! Zero! None!" Miss Mary holds up a large photo. "Now, pay attention! We call this a 'drone.' You will see these flying around the city, but do not worry! They are not to be feared! They will *not* harm you! They are simply keeping an eye on things, ensuring every inhabitant of our magnificent city is safe and protected. You all know how horrific life is *out there*. If you are allowed inside our gates, you will have made it to the good life. *Never again* will you have to look over your shoulder in fear of bounders!"

The woman sitting in front of Maia, Dawn, turns around to face her. Maia likes Dawn. She's the only other person in here who has read as many books as she. The two have become quick friends over the past week, often chatting over breaks and mealtimes about the books they've read and their journeys here—although they have both kept those details light.

Dawn leans in, whispering, "Have you ever read the book *1984*?"

Uncomfortable, Maia glances between Dawn and Miss Mary. Talking during lectures is *not* allowed.

Miss Mary clears her throat, and Dawn faces forward. "Sorry," she mumbles.

Miss Mary eyes her. "By now, you all should fully understand your bracelets will remain on your wrists for a short probationary period, which is different for everyone depending on their contracts." She glares between Dawn and Maia. "This is normally between one and two years, as you pay your way into the city and prove yourself to be trustworthy. This is only fair; everyone has had to do it."

"Even you, Miss Mary?" another woman asks.

Miss Mary smiles. "Even me." She walks between the aisles of desks. "Now, the light on your bracelet will be switched to green on graduation day so that the citizens of Leucothea will know you are in good standing. But, should you break any of the rules outlined in orientation, the green light on your bracelet will be switched to red, prolonging your probation. Now, everyone makes mistakes. In most cases, a migrant will be allowed two mishaps, depending on the severity of the crime. But three offenses result in permanent expulsion, so always be on your best behavior!

"Once you have been granted citizenship, you will be given a ceremony, your bracelet will be removed, and you will understand that all those newcomers entering our paradise should also be watched. The safety of our people is of the utmost importance. Leucothea will always protect you."

Maia raises her hand.

"Maia?"

"Yes, you've told us this city and most of the vehicles are running off renewable sources?"

"Yes."

"What are those exactly?"

Miss Mary laughs. "Excuse me?" She frowns, looking around the room. "That's a strange question."

"It's just ... in a landscape as harsh as this, with long periods of darkness, a city this large couldn't possibly work off solar alone. Same with the wind. How—"

"*Maia!*" Miss Mary slams her hand onto her desk, startling the class. "Running a city such as this is an incredibly complex endeavor! I can assure you that the New System has nothing but our best interests at heart. Leucothea has electricity unlike anywhere else in the world, and it has always been done with *clean* energy."

Maia quickly nods.

Miss Mary straightens her top, lifting her chin. The room is eerily silent. She walks over to her drawer and pulls out the women's files, searching through them until she finds what she is looking for. She selects a single folder, eyeing Maia, and aggressively writes something inside. After placing the papers back into the drawer, she smiles at the class—everyone except Maia—and continues with her lesson.

Maia looks down at her bracelet and its bright red light, swallowing hard.

The class goes on to learn that the Search and Rescue Crews, like Leucothea's growing army, are celebrated heroes. Every day, the men and women of these troops risk their lives so that the people inside Leucothea can live *the good life*. With the warehouses so well stocked, the S&R Crews' biggest mission as of late has been finding more building supplies and mapping where the old manufacturing warehouses are so they can stock up. Recently, there have been reports of fighting with another—*much smaller*, according to Miss Mary—Arctic city in Canada called Asiaq Bay. Apparently, this city wants to take what the S&R Crews have rightfully scavenged, so a few of Leucothea's heavily armed soldiers now join them. Maia wonders why she's never seen one of Leucothea's massive solar powered trucks out on her travels, but then again, she, Lucas, and Miguel were always so careful to stick to the back roads and trails as much as possible.

Maia raises her hand, despite herself.

Miss Mary sighs. "*Another* question, Maia?"

"I'm sorry, but ... what about the people ... *out there*?"

"What do you mean?"

"Well, you call them 'Search and *Rescue*—'"

"*We*, Maia. You need to say 'we' if you want to become one of us."

"Okay ... *we* ... call them 'Search and Rescue.' Are these teams also bringing back people who are stuck out there? Helping them? Maybe those they come across who are alone or in a bad way?"

Miss Mary sighs. "They can't. They are under strict instructions to leave the people *out there* 'as is,' let nature take care of nature. Some of those people are incredibly dangerous, as you know. Also, the crews simply don't have the space. Anytime they find the supplies our city needs, they need to use every square inch of their trucks to load up."

"But..."

Miss Mary crosses her arms.

Maia is on the verge of overstepping her boundaries, but she doesn't care. "I'm sorry, but why call the crews 'Search and *Rescue*,' then? Who are they rescuing?"

Miss Mary's arms fall to her sides, and her hardened features soften. "*Us*."

FOUR

The big day of graduation has arrived. Maia lies in her bunk for the last time, staring up at the words carved into the wood and slowly tracing each letter with the tip of her finger. Whoever carved this ... Did she make it in? Or did Leucothea *destroy* her?

There was no class this morning. It is done. Yesterday's final exams lasted from morning till night. Miss Mary, Rebecca, and other assorted guardians stood along the sidelines of the gymnasium with their clipboards in hand, marking notes as each migrant demonstrated her skills, proving once and for all that she was willing and able to integrate into the high society of Leucothea. Now, each woman, after having spent her entire life preparing her homegrown vegetables or freshly caught meat over a fire, will be able to heat her processed and rationed meal in a microwave.

This morning at breakfast, the once quiet and reserved women of Maia's class were excited. Smiling. Giddy. But Maia sat alone at her little table, biting her nails. Worried. Dawn never showed for breakfast. She wasn't at the exams yesterday either. She had been asking more and more questions lately, voicing the concerns Maia also had but didn't dare say. Every question Dawn asked only seemed to further agitate Miss Mary. Maia decided early on to keep her head down—just get through this orientation to get to the other side of those gates.

But where was Dawn? And did keeping her mouth shut make Maia smart ... or a coward?

For the last time, Maia traces the words on the underside of the bunk: *D-E-S-T-R-O-Y*. Today, Maia and the other women will be allowed inside Leucothea's massive inner walls. Today, they begin a new life, a life like their ancestors. They have been prepped, educated, cleaned, fed, and will now be driven to their very own homes, called "apartments," in a particular area of the city allocated for migrants. Most of the women will already have roommates inside those apartments, but should they have loved ones within the city, they may apply at the Migrant Services Building for different housing.

Today, the women will have a chance to reunite with their loved ones. Maia thinks of seeing Lucas again and she holds her hand against her mouth, tears filling her eyes. Those last days in their umiak were so dark. Lucas was clinging to the last of his life, while Maia desperately clung to the last of Lucas.

I want to thank you again, Maia, Lucas gasped between breaths, *for saving me back on that pirate ship. You saved me.*

Maia quietly sobs, envisioning his gorgeous face, so pale. So sick. Pleading with him as she held him, *Just hold on, okay? You can do this. Just don't let go...*

And then he finally whispered the words aloud that they both knew but didn't have the courage to say, *I fought to keep you as my own even though I knew that maybe ... maybe you would have been happier ... with ... my brother.*

Maia draws a sharp breath and sits up in her bunk, wiping her eyes. His words have not ceased echoing in her memory since that early morning on the river. Looking back, it's easy to see they both knew it was over. They knew before leaving the tribe, but they both stubbornly held on because they had been through so much. And for so long, it seemed, they were all they had. It wasn't just that Maia had saved Lucas, but he had saved her as well, in a thousand different ways. But Miguel was right ... they were no longer *in love*. Maia had grown so tired of Lucas doing everything he could to protect her, but in the end, she was equally guilty of doing the same.

And so, neither was willing to let go, watching in horror as their relationship slowly crumbled beneath the weight of something far greater than them. Guilt clenches at her chest. She would have given anything to be with Miguel, but she wouldn't have him at the expense of Lucas. And now ... now she may pay for that decision for the rest of her life.

Maia stands, preparing herself. It is time. She is about to leave the gated and locked Migrant Facility to begin a new life in Leucothea, the city that has called to her for her entire life. She is so *close*.

Miss Mary knocks on her door, peeking her head in. "Ready?"

Maia nods and joins the women in the hallway, dutifully following at the back of the line. Not a word is spoken as Miss Mary leads the group down a narrow corridor separated by locked doors and buzzers.

Eventually, they reach the building's front entrance. The lobby walls are lined with utopian-inspired paintings while large Leucothean flags drape from the ceiling. The two glass doors leading outside have been left wide open—a rare sight to see—with a nearly blinding white sunlight flooding the carpet.

Maia glances at her classmates in line before her, and she bites her nail. Why are these women walking so slow? She yearns for that sun. That fresh outdoor air. Blue skies. She has been cooped up inside here for weeks.

A few armed guards make their way past the line of women. As they approach, Maia notices a migrant walking between them, her head down...

Dawn.

Her face is red and puffy. She is sniffling, and her hardened eyes are downcast. Angry.

Despite herself, Maia reaches for her.

Dawn looks up in surprise. "Maia!" She clutches Maia's hands.

"Keep moving!" The guard behind Dawn shoves her, but the two women maintain their grasps.

"What's happening?!" Maia whispers, gripping Dawn's hands as the guards work on pulling them apart. "Where are they taking you?"

"Maia?" Miss Mary yells.

Maia glances over her shoulder. The instructor has turned from the line and is hurriedly approaching.

"Maia!" Dawn screeches as the guards force them apart.

"Keep moving, ladies!" Miss Mary smiles at the women, who've all turned to watch the spectacle Dawn and Maia are making. "Freedom is just through those doors!" she says with exaggerated claps. The women turn away and continue toward the exit as Miss Mary throws her arms around Maia, shoving the guard away from her.

He quickly joins his comrade, and they drag a screaming Dawn toward the hallway.

Maia watches, horrified, but her voice is wedged in her throat, her feet frozen in place. Miss Mary stands by her side, her arms wrapped tightly around her.

Dawn and the guards disappear around the corner, and a loud buzzer sounds. A door slams shut, muffling Dawn's screams from the other side.

"Maia?" Miss Mary's smiling face comes into focus, blocking Maia's view. "You have come so far. *Look.*" She grabs Maia's shoulders, turning her toward the open glass doors. "*Freedom*," she whispers in her ear.

Maia briefly glances back at the empty lobby. She has so many questions but doesn't dare speak a word. She peers toward the open glass doors where the final two women stand next to Rebecca, who has a small black box in her hands. The first woman holds out her wrist, and Rebecca places the device against her bracelet. After a moment, the box beeps, and the red light on the migrant's bracelet turns green. "Congratulations," Rebecca says with a smile.

The woman jumps up and down, hugging her classmate behind her, and then she disappears into the light.

Maia sighs. She *has* read *1984*. She was young, probably too young to fully grasp its message. But Dawn's question from class wasn't lost on her. Of course there are worrying things about this city. The contract Maia signed at her exit interview left her with a nervous pit in her stomach, although she couldn't place why. There wasn't anything in there that hadn't already been discussed in class ... Was there?

No, it was pretty simple. Every migrant needs to work in their allocated job to pay off everything initially given to them. Probation lasts until one proves their loyalty. But something still felt *off* ... tugging at Maia's conscience. She was required to pledge her allegiance to Leucothea aloud, repeating the words called out by Rebecca to a large cloth flag pinned to a wall beside a picture of their smiling president.

The white-starred banners plastering these halls may be black, but there are red flags all over this place.

Yet, Maia is about to enter a city of lights in a dark world. This is *the good life*. They have a hospital to care for the injured and sick. They have a university. Electricity. She will never go to bed hungry. Or thirsty. And there is no crime? What would that sort of security feel like? Maia can't imagine.

She would be lying if she said she wasn't excited—thrilled even. She has always dreamed about living a life like this. Besides, she has no other option but to keep moving forward. Lucas will be on the other side of those walls, somewhere in that city, waiting for her. They will always be a part of each other's lives ... good friends. And Miguel will come. He swore he would find his way back to her. He *swore* it.

Maia glances back one last time. Dawn is gone—her chance of living in Leucothea shattered forever. There is nothing Maia can do for her. She gazes at the open glass doors leading to freedom. Leading to Lucas. To Miguel. She inhales, and she places her first foot forward.

"Good girl," Miss Mary whispers, ushering Maia toward the light.

She meets Rebecca at the doors and holds out her wrist, butterflies tumbling inside her gut.

"Maia," Rebecca says with a smile. She places the contraption on Maia's monitoring device, and a beep sounds. The light on her bracelet turns green and she grins.

Green means *go*.

"Before you head out, I have something for you."

Rebecca hands her a small piece of paper with a hand-drawn map. "The Migrant Services Building. Good luck finding Lucas."

"Thank you, Rebecca," Maia says, and the two women hug.

Piling into an electric van, the migrants inside are giddy. The woman beside Maia grabs her hands. "This is it!"

"Now, remember what we taught you, ladies. Safety first!" Miss Mary calls from the driver's seat.

The women dutifully buckle their safety belts. *Click, click, click.*

The electric van slowly glides forward, and the women snicker and giggle. None of them have ever been inside a moving vehicle. "It's like a dream!" the woman beside Maia whispers.

The van stops at a gate, surrounded on either side by tall chain-link fencing with barbed wire snaked along the top. Maia looks back at the block of brick buildings. Three stories tall with numerous tiny windows, they are much bigger than Maia could have imagined from the inside. They look like an old jail.

A guard at the gates peers inside Miss Mary's open window.

"Show him your bracelets," Miss Mary says from over her shoulder.

The women lift their wrists, and the guard eyes them all. He nods and steps away from the van, speaking into his radio. The gate opens, and the van lurches forward. Some of the women squeal, holding on to the seats and each other. Miss Mary smiles with pride.

Their van drives through what looks like scorched dead-land: massive brown fields of dirt raked into lines, with tall brick search towers in the middle. Anyone escaping the Migrant Facility would be spotted in an instant.

After about five minutes of driving, Miss Mary calls out, "Here we are!"

The women push to look out the windows. They are approaching an immense cement barrier lined with search-lights—Leucothea's inner wall. Armed guards are everywhere: inside the towers, walking up and down the street, and stalking across the grounds. The van stops at the wall's imposing metal gate. Above it is a sign, its sprawling letters lit up in lights:

Welcome to Leucothea.

Maia's eyes well with tears. What a journey it has been to get here. So many goodbyes. So much loss. Heartache. Danger. All while following a pull in her heart that she barely understood.

Another guard approaches with her assault rifle in hand, and Miss Mary rolls down her window to let the guard check inside. The women lift their wrists, showing off their green lights. The guard nods. Stepping back, she speaks into her radio, and the massive gate slowly opens. The van glides through, the women plastered to the glass.

Maia twists in her seat, peering out the back window as the gate slides shut. Two soldiers with machine guns walk across the road. She faces forward again, sighing in relief.

They are in.

FIVE

Traveling down the city street at dusk, it all seems a little anticlimactic—just a simple road lined with enormous warehouses behind chain-link fencing and the occasional patrolling guard.

But as Miss Mary drives on, the skies darken and the streetlamps flicker on, illuminating the large metropolis in hues of gold. The women around Maia gasp, and she can't help but join. Unlike New Portland, where they only had working lights around the village square, this city seems to have them *everywhere*.

The warehouses are soon replaced by homes, and then high-rises, storefronts, and restaurants. As the skies darken, the glimmering city seems to blossom before them in an explosion of light, and the murmuring women inside the van are silenced in awe. Their mouths agape, they stare out the windows with wide eyes and quivering chins. They gasp and they point, twisting in their seats and craning their necks.

There are people everywhere—walking down sidewalks and crossing the streets, sitting in vehicles pulling up beside them when the lights draped across the road switch from green to yellow to red. They fill glittering shops stacked with unbroken things and stand outside crowded restaurants, bathed in their signs' neon hue. Everywhere Maia looks, there is life. There is *light*. The woman next to her begins to sob.

Tiny trees line a few of the sidewalks, enclosed by small, white picket fences and more cement. Maia holds her hand against the window, her breath fogging the glass. The trees —she yearns to touch one. If she did, would it still reach back? Would it whisper? She cannot hear them from inside this van.

"It's like a dream," the crying woman beside Maia whispers, barely able to catch her breath. "It's all so ... *magical*."

Signs for Leucothea Day plaster the streets and the lampposts and the billboards on buildings. It is only a week away. Maia and the other women learned about this festival early on in class. It only happens once a year. They are *so lucky*. Now that they have passed orientation, they will be free to celebrate with the citizens in the city.

Miss Mary pulls the van down a narrow street. The buildings around here all look the same: two-story, brick, small windows. They are much more rundown than the rest of the city.

"This is where you ladies will be living," Miss Mary says from over her shoulder. She stops the van along the side of the road. "Maia, this is you. I'll introduce you to your roommate, Renee. She'll show you around. But we need to make this quick. I've got quite a few stops to make tonight."

The women pile from the van to let Maia out, and she looks around, unsure. What is that scent? She's never smelled it before. It's unnatural—strange.

A man is leaning against the streetlamp across the road,

his arms crossed, watching her. *Is* he watching her? His dark hair is slick, tied back. His glare is intense, a sinister smile tugging at his mouth. She's never seen him before, but the way he's looking at her ... it's almost as if he *recognizes* her.

No, that's crazy.

"Come, come," Miss Mary says, tugging at Maia's arm, and they turn away from the street.

As Maia is led up a weed-infested path to one of the buildings, she briefly looks back, but the man has disappeared from the light. A chill runs down her spine, surprising her.

The two women walk up a set of corrugated metal steps to the apartment's second floor. As Miss Mary knocks on the door, a drone slowly flies past. Maia steps to the railing, watching it hover above the buildings. It's so surreal to see one in real life. It lowers itself before her, so close she can nearly touch it. Like a mechanical bumblebee, its propeller-like wings hum to keep it in flight.

The door behind her opens. "Maia, this is your roommate, Renee," Miss Mary says.

Maia turns to find a young woman in the doorway with shoulder-length blonde hair and a thick fringe. Her striking green eyes have a thin line of black paint around them. *Makeup.* "So nice to finally meet you, Maia," Renee says with a smile.

"So, you'll take it from here? I've got a lot of drop-offs to do," Miss Mary says to Renee.

"Yes, of course. I got all her information in the mail this afternoon. I'll help get her settled."

"Thank you," Miss Mary says, then she quickly disappears down the stairs.

"Come in!" Renee says. "Welcome to your new home."

"Thank you," Maia says, her voice nearly a whisper. She

steps inside the tiny apartment to the living room, where a sagging couch covered by a blanket and a white plastic outdoor chair have been placed around a makeshift coffee table made of plyboard and bricks, A dark television sits along the opposite wall, next to a single lamp and a window with no curtains. The other side of the living space has a small kitchen and a table with two mismatched wooden chairs.

"Your bedroom is through the door next to the television. My room and a bathroom are just down the hallway on the opposite side."

Maia nods.

Home. This is her home? It doesn't feel like her home.

"It's a lot to take in, I know. You'll find the basics in your room. Enough clothing to get you started. A mattress, clock, and closet. As you work and save your money, you'll start to accumulate more belongings. There are events called "Migrant Sales," where the citizens sell their unwanted things for super cheap. I'd be happy to take you to one once you get settled and get a few paydays under your belt."

A small shelf next to the sink has an assortment of glass jars on top, filled with dried leaves.

"Is that tea?" Maia asks.

"Sure is,'" Renee says. "Would you like a cup?"

"I'd love one."

"Perfect. We can sit down and I'll explain your job to you. You'll be a sifter. It's actually a really great assignment," Renee says as she heads to the kitchen. "It's clean ... easy. You'd be surprised at how dirty some of the migrant jobs are." She pulls a jar from the shelf and fills a kettle with water. "You had high marks on honesty and loyalty, so you get to sort through the supplies found from the S&R Crews to be rationed to those in the city based on need. The warehouses where you'll be working have heat in the winter and cool air for the hot summers..."

As Renee keeps talking, Maia wanders around the tiny living room. The blackened television is covered in dust, a metal tool clamped to its broken dial. The lamp in the corner has a large hole in its shade, filled with a spider's web. She lifts the corner of the blanket from the couch. The cushions beneath are tattered and stained. A hole has worn through the center of one, now stuffed with a towel.

Another drone hovers near the window, startling her before quickly flying off.

Catching Maia's reaction, Renee laughs from the kitchen. "Oh, you'll get used to those. Noisy little buggers, always flying around, but they keep us safe. I actually find their presence comforting."

Maia pulls the paper map from her pocket. The Migrant Services Building won't be open anymore tonight; she'll have to go after work tomorrow.

Seems like such a long time to wait to find Lucas.

She looks around the small apartment and the strange woman in the kitchen, talking away. When Miss Mary introduced them, Renee said, "finally."

So nice to finally meet you, Maia.

So odd. Maia only just graduated this morning.

Another drone zips past the window.

"Hope you'll make yourself at home..." Renee continues from the kitchen.

Home. Is this her home?

This is her home.

Pushing open the cracked glass doors of the Migrant Services Building, Maia steps into a packed room filled with rows of chairs—every single one of them full. The people inside this building do not look like those walking around the city streets. These people look ... hardened. Scared. Sad.

Maia weaves her way to a counter with a large man behind the glass. He's ... *enormous*. His bone structure has been swallowed beneath bloated rolls of skin. He looks at her, annoyed, then slowly shakes his head. A woman behind Maia clears her throat.

Maia turns to find a line of people looking at her with their heads tilted, arms crossed. "Right ... Sorry," Maia says, and she walks to the back of the line.

And then, she waits. The anticipation is killing her. Just a little while longer, and someone will tell her where she can find Lucas. Shifting from foot to foot, she crosses her arms and joins the migrants around her with sporadic, frustrated sighs. She watches the clock on the wall as its hands slowly *tick*, *tick*, *tick*, and she finally understands all those references of time she had spent her entire life reading about but never fully grasping—until now.

Finally, it is her turn. The man behind the glass motions her forward.

"State your migrant number."

"Four eight two nine seven."

The man yells over his shoulder to a worker behind him, "Four eight two nine seven!"

The worker runs off.

"He'll be grabbing your file. What can I do for you?"

"I'm looking for the man I traveled here with. We arrived about two and a half weeks ago. His name is Lucas."

"Don't need a name, just a number."

She blinks.

"Do you have his migrant number?"

"Oh ... *no*. No, I don't. I'm sorry."

The man lets out an exaggerated sigh. "Fine. It might be connected to your file. Anything else I can do while we wait?"

"No, that is all. Actually, are we allowed visitors ... from *out there*?"

The man huffs. "It can be arranged for some, but not while you're on probation."

Maia quickly does the math in her head. Miguel said he'd come around the first snowfall of her second winter here. It's still autumn, so that's a little over a year from now. As long as she doesn't mess anything up and prolong her probation, all should be fine.

"Anything else?"

"Yes. My necklace has been missing since I arrived."

"You should have filed that with Lost and Found at the Migrant Facility Building where you had your training."

"I did. They didn't have it."

"Well, we certainly won't have it here."

Her heart sinks. "Right."

The worker comes back with Maia's file. It looks smaller from the last time she saw it in Rebecca's hands. The man flips it open to a single sheet inside. *Definitely* smaller. "Sorry, but there is no mention here that you arrived with another traveler."

"*What*?!" Maia screeches, and the man looks up at her, unfazed. "That's not true! I did! His name—"

"You were probably just released before he was, so his file hasn't been attached to yours yet. Until that happens, there is no way we can track him to you, especially if you don't have a number."

"I didn't know. I didn't ... know." Why didn't Rebecca tell her? "What can I do?"

"All migrants, *if* they are allowed into the city, are released within a week of each other. We don't have the time or resources to keep anyone longer."

"What if he's at the hospital?"

"It would be linked in your file. All migrants are given numbers that are linked with each other. Best you can do is come back and check. If we don't have any information within a week, then it's because we don't have him in our system."

"What does that mean?"

"It means he wasn't allowed in."

"But—"

"NEXT!"

The following week passes in a blur. Maia knows she should be working hard at her new job sorting supplies, but all she can think about is Lucas. She searches for him in every face that passes, checking over her shoulder every moment at work. Every morning, she wakes up hoping that today is the day they will finally link her number with his.

Maia goes back to the Migrant Services Building every day after work for a week, and every day it is the same, her hope shattering into even tinier pieces. Leucothea Day approaches, and the offices are closed. Renee tried to get Maia to join in the celebrations, but she couldn't concentrate. Eventually, she ended up leaving Renee with a few other migrant friends so she could stand in the middle of one of the busiest streets in Leucothea. Surrounded by a city in revelry and the echoes of cheering, Maia never felt so alone. Desperate, she searched the faces until the streets were empty.

The next day after work, Maia again stands in line, staring at the clock. This is her last chance. If they don't have their numbers linked by now, they never will. And then what? If Lucas is *out there*, she'll leave.

Will she?

If a migrant leaves Leucothea under probation, they are not allowed back in. What if Miguel comes for her and she's not here? It may be her only chance to reunite with him. She could go back to the tribe. But then what was all this for? She couldn't possibly live in here if Lucas is stuck *out there*. But also, there's the harsh reality that she could leave Leucothea to look for him and never find him.

"Next!"

Maia approaches the glass to a woman on the other side. *Annie* is written on her name badge.

"Four eight two nine seven," Maia says, her voice trembling.

Annie calls out the number to the worker behind her. "Are you okay, ma'am?" she asks.

"I'm just ... *nervous*. I really need to find my friend."

The worker brings back Maia's file, and Annie flips it open. She lifts her brow as she reads the paper, and then she peers up at Maia.

Maia tries to read her face, waiting for a smile.

Please smile.

But she is met with a look of pity instead. Annie glances around nervously. "Come with me," she finally says, pushing back her chair.

Maia's heart pounds. Is he here? Why would they not just tell her at the desk? Is Maia in trouble? Did she let something important slide by on the conveyor belt at work?

Annie lifts the countertop and holds it open for Maia to step through, then leads her down a hallway behind the offices. She opens a door to a small room with a table and two chairs inside.

"Please, sit down," Annie says. "I'll be right back."

Maia walks into the room. Taking a seat, she bites her nail, looking around. Whatever this is, it isn't good. She's in trouble, or maybe Lucas is. Perhaps he wasn't allowed in, or he's recovering at the hospital? If he's *out there*, she'll leave. She'll rip off this monitoring bracelet right now, and she'll go find him—bounders and all.

Annie comes back with a small white container the size of a shoebox in her hand. She pauses at the door as she closes it, her back toward Maia, and the latch clicks into place. As she turns to face Maia, a palpable sadness has seeped behind her gaze, and she sets the box on the table.

Maia glances between the box and Annie. "Do you ... do you know where he is?"

"Maia, I'm so sorry."

Maia stands, knocking her chair backward. "Why?" Why is this woman apologizing? "Why are you apologizing?"

"The man you arrived with..."

Why does this woman keep shaking her head? What is that look on her face?

"...was deceased upon arrival."

Remorse.

"*What*?" Maia whispers, covering her mouth.

"I'm *so* sorry."

"What?! No. I don't believe it." Maia stares at her. This is a mistake. Surely, this is a mistake. "You're *wrong*! Look again in my file. Something isn't right—that file is *significantly* smaller than before. You're missing something. Look again. *Please*, look again!"

"He's been cremated," Annie continues, her voice soft. "And these are his—"

"*What*?!" Maia screams, backing into the wall. "No! You're wrong," she gasps, heaving for air. She grips at her chest—can't breathe. She can't take in a breath. She can't *breathe*!

"We are not wrong. This is the man you arrived here with."

Maia laughs through her tears. "That's not Lucas!" She points at the box. "*That* is *not* Lucas. No, I don't believe it."

Annie looks at her and sighs. "I'm *really* sorry."

Maia glares at her, her mouth open. It feels as though her heart has just stopped. She clutches at her chest, turning in place. Annie starts to say something with her hand held out, but Maia can no longer hear her. Is she still breathing? She's not breathing. The room is spinning, closing in on her. She presses her back against the wall, gasping, and the earth begins to tremble.

Annie looks around in a panic.

Doubling over, Maia unleashes an agonizing wail, and the earth shakes harder. Annie grabs her and forces her under the table. Maia collapses to the ground with her cheek against the carpet, and she closes her eyes, focusing on her breath. The ground stills. Annie's sigh of relief echoes beneath the table.

If only Maia could go back to that little umiak. Back to that moment where Lucas said he wanted to be with her *more than anything*. If only she could just go back to that moment. Turn around. She could turn it all around.

"You're wrong," Maia says into the carpet. "He was *alive*. He was still alive when we arrived." She lifts herself from the ground, surprised at how hollow she suddenly feels. Her body is weightless. No—empty. *Gutted*. Wiping the tears from her eyes, she whispers, "I really think you've made a mistake."

"That man," the woman speaks soft and slow. "The *only* man in the boat with you when you arrived at our gates, was dead."

"He *wasn't*. I know you think I'm crazy, but I cradled him in my arms and he groaned. I *heard* it…"

"Sometimes, when moving the body of the dead, air can escape the lungs, and it can *sound*—"

Maia lifts her hand. "He was *alive*."

Annie looks down. "Well," she says quietly. "He's not anymore."

"Are you … are you *sure*?" Maia whispers between her gasps. "You don't understand. This man … this man is a *good* man." She smiles. "He's my Brazilian pirate." She looks at Annie expectantly, as if saying those words will somehow help her register that she's made a mistake. "He would do anything to protect me. He is a *good man*."

Annie looks up at Maia. "It's all there in your file. I'm really sorry."

Maia falls back onto the ground, sobbing. Her cries are so loud in the small space beneath the table.

Annie backs away on the floor. "I'll grab you some tissues." Weary, she climbs to her feet.

"Why did it take so long?" Maia mumbles into the carpet.

"Excuse me?"

"If he was deceased upon arrival, why did no one tell me? I've been here nearly a month. I've been coming to this building every day for over a week."

"I'm sorry, I don't know. The paperwork must've gotten lost or something."

Maia wails, curling into herself.

"Please, excuse me." Annie quickly exits the room, leaving Maia in a quivering ball beneath her little box of ashes.

———

Maia walks back to her apartment in a daze. Her home. Is that her home?

That's not her home.

She looks down at the white box in her hands. Is this Lucas? This isn't Lucas. It *can't* be. Denial is a stage of grief. But she's not in denial—this *isn't* Lucas.

Or is it?

The city scenery surrounding her is so much like the simulation in class: lights flashing in a dark night as Maia wanders through an endless sea of noise. Just like orientation, Maia does not look both ways before stepping onto the street. But unlike orientation, this time, she knows better.

She simply doesn't care.

A loud screeching of tires and a car horn blast behind her. A man starts to yell ... something about her being a bounder. She peers across the road at the box on top of the pole. The hand symbol is the bright, electric color of red.

Red means *stop*.

Where was that message before? Before she left the shores of New Zealand on this ridiculous quest and started destroying people's lives? She keeps walking, devastated when she steps onto the curb on the other side of the road.

She turns to face the car, still idling in the middle of the street. The man sticks his hand out the window and lifts his middle finger. His tires squeal against the pavement, and he peels off down the road. Maia glares at the red lights on the back of his car, filled with resentment.

Yes, she is on the other side. After all that danger, all that risk, all that *loss* ... and she has reached the other side of the road, on the other side of the wall, on the other side of the world.

She has finally made it.

Her dreams have come true, but all she can see is a nightmare.

SIX

Walking down the narrow city alley, Maia reaches out to the white flakes flickering from a swirling gray sky. It has become colder in her dreams, noticeable only by the puffs of air exhaling from her mouth. The remnants of water dripping down the buildings have frozen in place, like veins of glass stretched across the brick.

The snow falls heavier as she approaches her cabin, blurring the city's sharp edges into a silver haze. She keeps her hand reaching out. So close. She is *so close* to them. She wants to run, but like torture, her feet shuffle against the pavement as if filled with lead.

Up the creaking steps she goes, past the old rocking chairs, now covered in a thin layer of white. Stepping across the threshold, she finds the small child and man once again by the fireplace, their backs toward her. Something about the man is different. Is it Lucas? She reaches for him, yearning to touch him. *Is* it him?

As he turns toward her, a loud, repetitive beep screeches into her dream, yanking her back into the harsh reality of her tiny bedroom. She grabs her pillow, screaming into it.

Every night it is the same.

The numbers on her bedside clock flash four thirty, illuminating the small space in a strange shade of red. Every morning, the little device proudly introduced to her at orientation wakes her up far too early, jolting her out of the natural rhythms of her body. Ripping her from the only place she yearns to be. She whacks it off the table.

After finding out about Lucas's death, Maia spent weeks crying herself to sleep. She'd fall asleep crying, wake up crying, always curled around the little box of ashes that she couldn't fully believe was him. Trapped, she mourned his loss while refusing to believe he was actually gone. He *couldn't* be; some part of her could still feel him, still feel his life tied to hers. Maybe they were wrong. Her file was so much smaller than it was before.

She tried going back to the building to ask for another caseworker to search the files but was met with the brute force of two security guards and the very grave threat that should she return, it would be logged into the system as her first offense, switching her bracelet to a flashing red.

Her case has been closed. There's nothing more they can do. Don't bother coming back.

And so, Maia drifted into a deadened, mind-numbing fog. Weeks turned into months as she volunteered to work overtime—her job as a sifter such a blessed distraction.

Swipe. Toss. Swipe. Swipe. Toss.

Items Maia and Lucas had risked their very lives for on the streets of LA pass by in an endless parade, placed faithfully into their allotted bins by Maia, ready to be handed to the outstretched hands of this city's greedy citizens.

More, more, MORE. They always want *MORE*.

It feels strange to be surrounded by so much that is dead. The packaged food the migrants eat is processed and dead. The brick and glass and metal ... all dead. With no natural surroundings, the disconnection Maia feels is palpable. Every day she remains separated from the trees—from nature—is another day she slips further away from herself. It is like she is slowly starving to death. No amount of water can satisfy her thirst; no food can satiate her hunger.

On top of that, Maia has a constant, nagging feeling that she is being watched. Of course, they all are. The New System has been transparent in this regard. The cameras on the drones and the streetlamps ensure their safety.

But it's more than that. Everywhere Maia goes, it feels as if there are eyes on her. Not like in nature, where she was surrounded by trees, by her family. This is different, more sinister. She's never felt anything like it. The drones seem to follow her, linger in the sky whenever she stops. And there is this man—the same man she noticed her first night in the city with the shoulder-length, pin-straight black hair pulled into a low ponytail. The same creepy, almost resentful look in his eyes. She sees him everywhere: sitting at the other end of the bar or standing just around the corner at a shop, glaring at her while pretending to read the paper. More often than not, he is leaning against the streetlamp on the corner of her road.

I think he's our neighbor, Renee told her with a shrug. *Honestly, Maia, you need to lighten up. Leucothea is big, but it's not that big. It's not uncommon to run into the same people.*

But it's not like that. She *knows* he's following her. Yet, everyone she has grown to trust is telling her she's being paranoid. Is everyone else sane, and Maia has lost it?

Give it time, she was told by a coworker. *It takes a while for every migrant to adjust. This is normal.*

Is it normal? Is *any* of this normal?

And what about Maia's tiger? The thought of him crushes her. Where is he now? Is he safe? Sometimes, when returning home at night, Maia will walk along the border of the city's wall, wondering if he's sitting out there somewhere on the other side. She'll stare up at the imposing cement structure—this city's protection; this city's jail—holding her hand against the cool stone. Technically, she is free to leave at any time, but then what? She could go back to Tema, back to Miguel, but he said he would come here. The last thing she wants to do is leave when he may be on the other side, fighting to get in.

Besides, she *can't* leave, because then all that loss and heartache would have been for nothing. She came here for a *reason*. She doesn't know what that is yet, but there must be a reason she is here. There has to be.

And so, Maia oscillates between mourning the loss of Lucas, worrying about her tiger, and missing Miguel so much she can't breathe. He is like a weight she can't shake. What is he doing right now? Is he still with Shinesho and Chayanne and the tribe? Is he still coming to Leucothea? His face—it's been so long that she's starting to forget what he looks like. Was his dimple on the right or left side? His laugh ... She's replayed it so many times in her mind that she fears it has become lost in the haziness of her memories. Like she's rehashed it one too many times, and it has now become distorted.

And Lucas—she needs to tell Miguel about Lucas. She placed a request at the Migrant Services Building to leave, just for a little while, so she can mourn her loss with the people she loves.

Not while you're on probation.

Maia's not so sure this is true either. No one ever leaves

this city besides the S&R Crews. *Ever*. Besides, why would you want to leave such a magnificent place for *out there*?

And her powers. Slipping, slipping, slipping away. Last night, Maia hid in their tiny bathroom with a candle, curled up in the dark bathtub with the shower curtain drawn. She closed her eyes, igniting a small flame on the wick, but it was so difficult. Took so long. And in the end, the process only dredged up painful memories of the life she once had. The fires she used to start, illuminating the faces of the people she once loved.

So, the powerful woman she had become *out there* has suffocated behind these walls.

And she has allowed it.

The only saving grace of this new life is Maia's roommate, Renee. Every night, when Maia walks through her apartment door, Renee is there. The two of them get on so effortlessly. They often share dinner and stay up late into the night talking over their steaming cups of tea.

Renee traveled to Leucothea from the East Coast of the Old America with her best friend, Clara, and Clara's two younger brothers. Born and raised above the flooded streets of New York City, the four of them and their parents were self-proclaimed boat people, living in neighboring penthouses of an old high-rise.

But the rust ... the rust was overtaking everything. The safety brakes of the buildings' elevators had started deteriorating, sending the cumbersome boxes of metal plummeting story after story, smashing into the buildings' already compromised and decomposing floors like bombs.

Renee and Clara were in their boat outside one of the city's older skyscrapers while their parents were inside on a mission for supplies. An elevator line snapped, and it was the last straw for the wavering structure. The grenade of metal smashed into a floor so hard that the building caved, sending it toppling into another. Both buildings crumbled into the sea, with Renee's and Clara's parents trapped inside.

After that, the four orphans didn't trust anything. The once sturdy structures they had spent their entire lives in had become like ticking time bombs, the ground beneath their feet a risk to their very lives.

They had heard about Leucothea, seen old flyers around town. Slowly but surely, they made the journey here, but unfortunately, a sniffling Renee told Maia late one night, they lost Clara to a strange illness somewhere in Illinois. They stayed with her until she passed, and then they had no other choice but to bury her next to an old, dusty highway.

Loss is such a common denominator for the migrants of this city. And that's what every last one of them is: a migrant. Even those smug citizens looking down their noses were once scared refugees—lost souls who had to find a better life in a burning world. There are so few people in this city who haven't sacrificed to be here.

You never know the stories people belong to, Lucas once said. *The battles they've faced. The scars they carry.*

Leucothea is filled with fugitives plagued with scars—a glittering battleground of festering wounds.

And Maia is no different.

She finds it easy to open up to Renee, especially after Renee has told her so many of her own intimate details. And Renee seems to have endless questions. As soon as Maia answers one, Renee is ready and waiting, on the edge of her seat with another. How did Maia get here? What was it like in New Zealand? What does she dream about? What does she fear? Renee wants to know everything.

And Maia, relieved to be freed of the ghosts of her past, is happy to oblige. Her nightly chats with Renee have become like welcomed therapy sessions. She tells Renee about her life back in New Zealand—the devastating loss of her grandfather and her heart-wrenching goodbye with Huck at the docks. She opens up about her perilous journey across the Pacific. She tells Renee about the ship with Jake, Mario, and Claire that saved her and Lucas and then dropped them off in the flood zone of LA. Maia even opens up about her North American journey to Leucothea with Lucas and Miguel, and the nightmare that nearly broke them.

But Maia decides not to tell Renee *everything*. She doesn't tell her that there once was a time she could command the wind or that she could hear the whispers of the trees. She doesn't regale her with stories of igniting a fire with just a flick of her wrist. Or about the nurturing beauty and the heartless destruction silently lingering just beneath her surface. She doesn't confess that sometimes, when looking at the greedy faces of this city, she yearns more than anything to burn the entire metropolis to the ground.

She doesn't tell Renee that her guilt about Lucas's death is eating her alive, hardening her heart by the day. Or how she'd do *anything* to forget about Miguel and her tiger— both somewhere *out there* while she rots away in here. How the lack of anything natural or wild within these walls is stripping her down into a shell of who she once was.

Or how every day that passes, she finds fewer reasons to care.

No, Maia decides to keep these things to herself. Some things are better left unspoken. Like a gaping battle wound, she'll tightly bind her grief inside her.

She'll smother it with silence.

SEVEN

onths tick by in a monotonous blur as Maia continues to work long hours as a sifter, determined to pay off her contract before her second winter. She keeps her head down, barely noticing when the endless winter nights give way to ceaseless summer days. And then the Earth leans once again into darkness, shrouding the Arctic city in layers of frost and shadows.

Walking to the factory in the cold, early-morning hours, Maia stops as a migrant worker leans a ladder next to a lamppost. A string of Christmas lights is wound around his shoulder, trailing across the sidewalk. It's that time again. She should be thrilled, but the sight only fills her heart with grief.

It is her second winter in Leucothea, and nothing about her life looks how she imagined it would. She should have graduated from probation by now, but despite the hours she's put in, her managers at the warehouse have told her it will take some time yet to pay off her debts. Food prices have hiked dramatically, a result of a raging summer wildfire that swept through the lands where the city manufactures its food, so every migrant must work a little harder—*a little longer*—to pay their way into the city.

It is also well past this winter's first snowfall. Miguel is supposed to be here—he swore he would come, but every day that passes, Maia bleeds hope that she'll ever see him again.

She knows now how impossible it would be. She is walled in; Miguel can't just "visit." She could never imagine him sitting through two weeks of orientation for the woman who denied her love for him and then left him behind for a brother she barely knew. Knowing Miguel, he would have moved on with his life. He *should* have moved on with his life. And now Maia is doing everything in her power to do the same.

But it's not working.

The worker plugs in the cord, and the bulbs light up. Maia holds her hand against her chest as the memories she has tried so hard to suppress come flooding back to her: walking down Main Street in New Portland, holding on to Miguel's arm as she experienced the Christmas lights for the first time.

Ache. Ache. Ache.

She has been in Leucothea for nearly a year and a half, and she still has to shove the lingering pain of her old life back down inside her gut. The hard days are fewer and farther between, but moments like these—when she's completely caught off guard—are the moments that *gut* her.

She turns away from the lights, drawn to a scene unfolding inside the café next to her. Placing her hand against the glass, she watches as a man and woman sitting at a table sip their hot drinks. They are clearly citizens; there are no monitoring bracelets around their wrists. Their clothing looks so nice—so new. It actually fits them, unlike Maia's oversized and tattered migrant attire. The color of their pants hasn't faded at the knees. There are no patches sewn into the elbows of their shirts. There are still buttons on their jackets.

The woman on the other side of the glass looks so elegant, so self-assured with her chin up and her shoulders back. Maia stands up straight, lifting her chin. The woman takes a bite of what looks like a baked bread coated in sugar. The decadent smells wafting from beneath the café's glass doors cause Maia to salivate. This is the case with most restaurants that Maia passes to and from work, all establishments she cannot afford. She wonders what the food must taste like. It all looks so real, so unprocessed.

As Maia steps away from the glass, her hand falls to her side, and she looks down at her jacket. Only two buttons remain. The rest are long gone, leaving behind lonely patches of bare thread. She wraps her arms around herself, shivering from the morning's icy draft sneaking beneath her oversized coat.

One day, when she is a citizen, she will go to the university and get a better-paying job. And then she'll be able to wear clothes that fit and eat good food. *Real* food. This has always been the promise, and she is nearly there.

Sometimes, when a nice sweater passes on the conveyor belt at work, she wonders what would happen if she tried to take it. Would anyone even notice? Just *one* nice sweater. Just to feel the weight of its warmth. To look like one of *them*.

To be like one of them.

They say everyone is equal in this city, but that's not true. Somehow, Maia is always on the outside looking in.

It's another Saturday night, and Maia, Renee, and another woman from Maia's work, Aria, are out on the town. They've chosen one of the city's migrant clubs to spend the evening; a place with great dance music and cheap drinks. Everyone inside is wearing a tracking bracelet with a green light. Migrants with red lights are banned from most establishments.

Maia sips her beer, looking out the bar window, grateful that the warmer winter air has turned their snow into rain. She would be happy if it never snowed again. Between Miguel's broken promise and the dreams that still haunt her at night, snow has become a heartless reminder of everything she has lost.

"Apparently, our ancestors called The End 'The Anthropocene,'" Renee says to Aria.

"What does that mean?" Aria asks.

"Something about the age where human activity destroyed the planet."

"I heard they called it 'The Eremocine,'" Aria says, and she takes another swig of her beer.

"Eremocine? What does that mean?"

"The Age of Loneliness."

Maia downs the last of her drink and slams the glass against the table. "And how is *this* any different?"

The women look at her, eyes wide, and the three share an awkward laugh. "Let's go dance," Maia says, pushing back her stool.

They head into an enormous warehouse at the back of the club, where beams of multicolored lights flash across a sea of bobbing heads. Maia smiles, watching the mass of bodies dance to music louder than anything she ever thought possible. But like a drug, the beat soothes her aching heart. She closes her eyes, feeling it reverberate inside her chest.

Thrilled, she grabs Renee's hand, and the three women join the crowd. They whip their heads, throwing their hands in the air and shaking their hips. The atmosphere is euphoric. The lights. The bass. The rhythmic, pulsing beat. It's as if the music has become water, and they are swimming in an ocean.

Renee holds Maia's hand, spinning her around. Maia stops mid-twirl, catching the eyes of a man across the dance floor. He is *gorgeous*, with almond-shaped eyes and dark brown skin. She flashes him a seductive gaze, and he smiles.

The two weave their way through the heaving crowd, meeting in the middle. As she looks up at him in the hypnotic flashes of light, he grabs her hand and pulls her into him. She wraps her arms around his neck, and they interlink their legs, pressing against one another to the beat. Without hesitating, he grabs her face and kisses her.

This is not the first man to kiss Maia in the middle of a dance floor. The bars of this city have become the balm to her emptiness, the men an elixir to soothe her ache. The first time a migrant kissed Maia, it felt so bizarre. She had never kissed a stranger before. It felt empty ... and exhilarating.

It has since become the only thing to take away the sting of loneliness. Despite her best intentions, Maia has found herself drawn to these places called "clubs" more and more, where the glittering lights bathe crowded rooms of intoxicating strangers, all more than happy to take Maia's mind off the love she has lost.

As she continues to make out with the beautiful man in the middle of the club, a migrant with long dreadlocks brushes past them—tall, broad shoulders.

Maia pushes away. "Oh my God," she breathes.

The man she had been kissing laughs, and he reaches for her. "Hey, now. Where do you think you're going?"

She swats at his hands, watching as the back of the migrant's head disappears into the crowd.

Could it be?

She follows. "Sorry, sorry, sorry," she mumbles as she pushes through the people. She stops and stands on her toes. He's near the bar, waiting to order a drink.

As she approaches him, her heart thrashes beneath her chest. She takes a steadying breath, then reaches up with a trembling hand and grabs his shoulder. He turns to face her. Gazing up at the stranger's blue eyes in the pulsating lights, she suddenly finds it hard to breathe.

Not him. *Of course* it's not him.

He looks her up and down with a cheeky grin. "Well, hello there."

She backs up, shaking her head as the flashing lights and the crowd of strangers close in on her. This music is too loud. She has to get out of here. She barrels toward the exit, shoving the patrons and spilling their drinks. They yell and curse at her back.

As she runs out into the cool night, she smashes into a couple passing by. "*Sorry,*" she slurs. Her last beer has hit her hard, and she wavers on her feet.

She spots her stalker sitting on a bench across the street, *glaring* at her. She rolls her eyes. How many times has she thought about saying something to this man? There have been many. But something about him makes her skin crawl. When he's around, her hair stands on end. There's something deeply disturbing about him, and she hasn't dared approach him to find out what.

The man stands, taking a single step toward the curb.

Maia's gut twists, but she does not turn away. The traffic between them is heavy—too heavy—and there's not a crosswalk in sight. The two stare at one another from across the whooshing stream of speeding cars.

Ugh. Maia can't take this anymore. She has to get out of this godforsaken city—*now.* She slowly backs away from the street, and then she *runs.*

Yes. She'll leave tonight—she'll leave right now. She'll make peace with her powers and she'll live in the trees. She doesn't need *supplies.* The wolves will help her! So will her tiger. Surely, he'll still be out there, waiting for her somewhere. It hasn't been *that* long. She'll go back to the tribe, to Chayanne and Tema. To Miguel. She has to see him again. Now. She can't wait another day.

Running down the city streets, Maia suddenly feels elated. Her feet splash in and out of puddles, and the cool night air kisses her cheeks. This is good. She's going to see Miguel again! She's no longer going to sit here and rot and wait for a day that may never come. She's going to take matters into her own hands.

The hum of a drone follows above. She glares at it from over her shoulder. *Again* with the drones. She has repeatedly complained to Renee and countless caseworkers at the Migrant Services Building—to anyone who will listen—that there is *always* a drone following her. But no one will take her seriously.

Approaching another busy road, the crosswalk's symbol is red. Red means stop.

Screw red.

She races across the street, past swerving cars and honking horns, and slips down a dark alley. The drone follows. She meets a large cement barricade, skidding to a stop. There's an exit gate around this neighborhood somewhere, she knows there is. She'll plead with the guards. They *have* to let her out; she's free to leave whenever she wants.

She turns and sprints back toward the road, and the drone follows. She races down another street. No gate—just another massive cement wall. She turns and runs down another. And another. *Another*. Every road she travels, she meets another wall.

Guarded.

Trapped.

Standing before the immense structure, she considers climbing it. She once ran up the side of a tree as if gravity had no bearing on her. Can she do the same now? It would involve using her powers and there's a drone above, recording her every move. But then she'll just drop to the other side and run ... *right*? There'll be another wall beyond that. But she used to be unstoppable—powerful beyond measure. She couldn't have changed that much.

Steeling herself, she backs up and runs to the colossal barrier, jumping. Her palms slap the cement and she slides back to the ground. She bangs her fists against the wall, screaming into it. The drone is still behind her. Its motor's incessant buzz is so *grating*, setting her nerves on end.

Her temper flairs. She is *so sick* of being followed. Why won't anyone listen to her?! She turns to face the small hovercraft, its camera's red bulb lit. Watching. *Recording*. Her jaw clenches, her fists white-knuckled as her fingers dig into her palms.

You want a show?

Maia looks around the cracked pavement and finds a large stone. Without thinking, she whips it at the drone. It hits the body, sending it spiraling toward the ground. She covers her mouth, holding her breath. It corrects its course mid-air and lifts higher into the sky.

She tips her head back, sighing in relief.

And then she smiles.

How *exhilarating*.

The drone flicks on its searchlight, shining it in her face. She glares at the small aircraft, refusing to shield her eyes. Its alarm bell begins to sound—a high-pitched siren to alert backup. Another drone flies down the alleyway toward them. It, too, has its alarm blasting on repeat. More will be coming.

Maia runs back down the alleyway toward the road. The two drones follow with their sirens blaring, their search-lights flooded across her. Clusters of people standing along the streets stop and watch, jumping out of Maia's way as she races down the sidewalk.

She turns behind one of the large brick buildings to a loading zone and searches for another rock. She swipes one from the wet cement, chucking it at one of the drones as it flies around the corner. She misses. "Why do you keep *following* me?!" she screams. "What do you *WANT*?!"

Both drones now hover above with their lights on her face. The rain has started again—a light, misty haze. Maia blinks against it. Her breath heaving in clouds, she tries to calm her temper but to no avail. The drones lower them-selves closer. She could swear they are *taunting* her.

She looks around, spotting a pile of busted bricks against the building. She picks up a sharp corner from the mound. It sits heavy in her hand. This time she won't miss. She throws the brick as hard as she can, and it slams into the first drone's propeller, sending it spiraling to the ground. It smashes to pieces, metal parts scattering across the pave-ment. Its searchlight flickers until it dies.

Maia covers her mouth, her eyes wide.

The second drone's alarm continues to ring as it shines its light across the wreckage. Maia quickly runs across the loading zone down another dark alley and slides between two dumpsters. The drone flies past, with another two now following behind it. They hover at the dead end for a moment, their searchlights in beams across the wet brick. Then they lift into the sky and disappear over the buildings.

They don't need to follow her anymore. They know exactly who she is.

Maia waits, hanging her head between her knees as reality seeps in like the freezing rain into her clothes. She wanders into the middle of the dark alley, shivering and peering up at the sky. Footsteps sound behind her, and she whips around.

It's Renee. "Maia, what on *Earth*? What are you doing?"

Maia folds forward with her hands on her knees. "How did you find me?"

"A couple on the street told me you ran back here," Renee says, unamused, and she hands Maia her coat. "I sent Aria home. I'm pretty sure she thinks you're crazy."

Maia stands, breathless, and she swipes her jacket from Renee. "She wouldn't be wrong. Can we go home now?"

———

Later that night, Maia joins Renee in the living room with two mugs of tea and fills her in on what happened with the drones. Renee holds her steaming cup before her but, wide-eyed and horrified, she forgets to drink it. She only stares at Maia, mouth agape, saying nothing. There isn't anything she can say. Maia has destroyed one of Leucothea's precious drones, which is the same offense as assaulting a police officer. She is in serious trouble.

"Oh, Maia," Renee finally says. "What were you thinking?"

"I wasn't. I lost my temper and the next thing I knew, I was standing next to a pile of parts."

Sitting in silence, they both watch as the green light on Maia's bracelet switches to a flashing red. After all that time, all that hard work. Maia was nearly finished with her contract. She and Renee look at one another, Renee's face contorted with worry. It is done. Maia will be getting a visit from the authorities tomorrow.

"What happened?" Renee whispers. "You were having such a good time and then what? You completely lost it."

"I thought I saw Miguel."

"Miguel." Renee rolls her eyes. "Maia, we've *talked* about this."

"I know."

"If he were going to stick to his promise, he would be here by now."

"That's not true—"

"It's time you move on from this. If Miguel does come, it could be tomorrow or it could be five years from now. Hell, it could *never* happen! You know that, right?"

Maia clenches her jaw, shaking her head.

"You've had such a treacherous journey to get here, and you've made it! You're here! You've been here for over a year, but you keep looking behind you, *torturing* yourself. You could be making a better life for yourself, but you've got one foot firmly planted in your past. Lucas is gone. Miguel is God-only-knows where. And now look what you've done! At best, you've prolonged your probation—*big time*. At worst, you'll be kicked out!"

"I know."

"So, enough already. What happened between you and Miguel and Lucas is long in the past. You want forgiveness from them, but you're never going to get it. You have to forgive *yourself* and move on."

Maia looks down at her flashing red bracelet. "I don't ... I don't know how to do that," she says quietly.

"Maia, you can't help who you fall in love with, and whoever disagrees with that is a damned fool. You were trying to do what you thought was right. You can't beat yourself up for that. You made a choice to stay with Lucas, and Lucas made his *own* choice to be with you. He *chose* to come here with you. His death is not your fault."

"I know."

"Really? I don't think you do."

Maia glares at their faded carpet, lost for words.

Renee stands. "I'm going to bed, and you should too. You're going to have to answer some serious questions tomorrow." She walks toward the hallway and stops, turning around. "Maia?"

Maia looks up at her.

She tilts her gaze and sighs. "At some point, you're going to have to stop apologizing for who you are."

EIGHT

In the black of night, the shouting begins. Men's voices boom through the cheap apartment walls as footsteps stomp up the metal staircase, and then fists pound the front door like jackhammers.

Disorientated and afraid, Maia stumbles across the dark living room, banging her shin against the ragged plyboard coffee table. She opens the front door to four brooding men with batons on their belts and guns in their hands and a bright white star on each of their uniforms. A handful of drones hover behind them in the sky. Maia holds out her hand, squinting against their lights.

The officers push past her. They're so *large* as they file inside the tiny apartment. She turns to face them, a sickening feeling churning inside her gut.

"Maia?" Renee calls from the hallway.

As Renee rushes into the living room, one of the men yanks her back by her collar and throws her against the wall. "Go back to bed," he growls.

"Maia?" she whimpers on her hands and knees.

"It's okay, Renee," Maia says, her voice quivering. "Go back to your room."

Renee stands. Terrified, she glances between the officers, her brow deeply creased. And then she turns and disappears into the dark hallway, leaving Maia surrounded by thugs in black clothing.

The towering men begin circling Maia—an intimidation tactic she tries not to show is working. She stands up straight and holds her head high as one of them lowers his face just inches from hers.

"So, you've decided to assault a drone, have you?"

"*Assault*?" Maia whispers. She swallows hard, summoning her courage.

The men tighten their circle, and Maia holds her hands to stop them from trembling.

Another officer leans in behind her, startling her. "Did you know," he sneers, and she whirls toward him, "that your little discrepancy earlier is actually *three*? Assaulting a drone, *destroying* a drone, *and* public intoxication." He smiles. "The first two are major offenses."

Maia closes her eyes, filled with dread. She knew when she threw those stones that she would get in trouble, but it never occurred to her in her drunken rage that every stone was a separate offense.

"Your court date is in two weeks," another says beside her. "And you can rest assured that you will be held accountable for every single one of your crimes to the fullest extent of the law."

Maia doesn't dare ask what that means, but she knows it will haunt her every day until her sentencing.

"You will also have a drone following you everywhere you go, so don't try anything *stupid*," another spits from behind.

Maia turns toward him. She has to bite her tongue to not tell this goon that a drone following her every move would be *just another day in paradise.*

One of the officers grabs her chin, and she fights the urge to slap him. "Ungrateful *bounder*," he seethes, and the men turn to leave.

She holds on to her composure until the front door slams closed, and then she collapses into a trembling heap on the floor.

Renee rushes out from the shadows and holds her, rocking her as she whispers the same question over and over and over again:

"What have I done? What have I done? What have I done?"

Early the following evening, Maia lies on top of her bed, staring at the cracks in the ceiling. After sitting through an excruciatingly quiet dinner with Renee, neither one able to take her eyes off the flashing red bulb on Maia's bracelet, Maia excused herself to her bedroom.

She's exhausted, but she knows she won't sleep. After the events of the past twenty-four hours, she's pretty sure she won't sleep again for a *long* time.

What was she thinking? How could she be so careless? What will happen to her now?

The questions echo on repeat with the same long tail of regrets. Should have kept her head down. Should have ignored the drones. Should have controlled her temper. Should have had one less drink. Should have forgotten about Miguel and Lucas and her tiger. Those ghosts from her past have done nothing but hold her down, shackle her beneath an ocean of regret.

And yet, she is the one still holding the tether.

She needs to get out of this apartment, get some air. She slips on her hat and tattered coat to go for a walk. Clanking down the rusted steps outside her building, she runs into her neighbor, Bud.

Bud isn't quite all there, but he is by far Maia's favorite person in this city besides Renee. He's unassuming. Simple. Honest. He works so hard and never complains about anything, despite the fact that he's getting on in age and could use a break. He always wears the same threadbare coat, and a stained baseball cap with something called "Bud Light" stitched across the front. The poor man walks with a horrific limp—an old battle wound from his travels here.

"Miss Maia! Hello, there!" He tips the front of his hat.

Maia hides her red bracelet behind her back. Bud would freak. "Coming home from your evening walk?" she asks, plastering a fake smile.

"Yup," he says with a nearly toothless grin. "Say, must be something pretty exciting happening with all these drones around! Aren't *ya* glad we're so protected?"

Maia maintains her smile. If only he knew. "Yes, Bud. Very glad."

"Okay, bye. You have a great night!"

"You too."

Wandering along the city streets, Maia walks in and out of the streetlamps' beams, past glittering shops and crowded restaurants. She feels torn. Her probationary period has been challenging, no doubt about it, but there is so much *promise* in the life awaiting her on the other side. She's gotten used to this city of lights. Grown accustomed to not having to worry about bounders, or where she'll find her next meal. She's forgotten about the near-maddening affliction of thirst. Living through another day has become expected, and if her life is in danger, there's a hospital with trained staff ready to take care of her. Sure, she's had to compromise a few freedoms, but feeling safe on a regular basis is such a beautiful way to live.

As much as Maia hopes that they kick her out so she can go back to the tribe, there is also a significant part of her that doesn't want to leave. She's always known that she belongs here, and despite the fact that things haven't turned out the way she had hoped, she isn't ready to give up. Not yet. Not after all she has lost.

Getting in trouble is the final straw to knock some sense into her. Renee is right; it is time for Maia to lay her old life to rest once and for all and move on. Maybe her powers were only there to help her get here. They are the *only* reason she has made it this far. And now, perhaps she no longer needs them. Now, she can live her life in Leucothea, finish her probation, and go to the university. She's always wanted to go to school. Now, she can live the life she has always dreamed of.

She looks around the winter streets lined with lamps wrapped in garland. A couple walks past, hand in hand with knitted hats and woolen coats. She sighs. Yes, this is what she'll do. She'll deal with the consequences of her actions, she'll put her head down and work, and before she knows it, *she'll* be the woman behind the glass, sitting in a nice café eating sweet bread.

A chill runs down her spine, and she glances over her shoulder. She's being watched, and not just by her drone. He's here somewhere—her stalker. She can feel his beady eyes on her.

He's across the street, leaning against a building. She glares at him and he stares back, defiant. Who *is* this man?

No, Maia—just ignore him. Put your head down and keep walking.

She shakes it off, deciding to head in the opposite direction. As she steps off the curb, someone grabs her arm, pulling her back. A woman's voice speaks. "Maia?"

She knows this voice. She turns to find Claire, the young doctor from the ship that saved her and Lucas when they were stranded in the Pacific. "*Claire*?!" Maia stares at her in disbelief.

"Maia! I thought that was you!"

The two women hug, and then Claire pulls away, looking Maia over with wide eyes. "You look so ... *different* from when I last saw you. Has your hair changed?"

Maia laughs, nervously tucking a curl behind her ear. "Yes, I guess it has, hasn't it?"

Claire stares at her, waiting for an explanation of how her head of wavy auburn hair has turned into scarlet ringlets.

"So, how are you?!" Maia asks, changing the subject. "I can't tell you how good it is to see you!"

"I'm well! I was planning on going back to my village, but Jake has put me in charge of the university up here, which is an opportunity beyond my wildest dreams, so I'm staying!"

"Jake? Jake from ... *the ship*? I had no idea he had that sort of power."

Claire stares blankly at Maia. "Are you ... *joking*?" She laughs incredulously.

Maia looks at her, unsure of how to answer.

The smile fades from Claire's face. "Honestly, Maia?"

She shakes her head. "Jake is the army general of *Leucothea*. He's President Augustus's right-hand man."

"*What*?"

"What do you mean?" Anger flashes across Claire's face. "How can you *not know*? There are like ... *murals* of him around the city."

Maia's cheeks flush. "I guess I've been a little distracted."

"Clearly," Claire says, raising her brow.

"And Mario? How is he?"

Claire sighs, and she looks around. "We have so much to catch up on. What are you doing right now? Do you want to grab a drink..." Her voice trails as she eyes the flashing red on Maia's wrist.

Maia covers her bracelet. "I ... I can't."

"Let's get a tea then."

"It can't be anywhere around here. They won't let me in."

"Yes, they will. I'll vouch for you."

"Can you do that?"

"I'm part of Jake's political party. I can do anything."

"*What*?"

Claire smiles. "Just, come on." She grabs Maia's hand and leads her to a quiet little café nestled between more shops Maia can't afford.

Walking through the glass doors, Maia is immediately uncomfortable. She hasn't gotten around to sewing the latest hole in her jacket, and she's down to a single button. The patrons inside look her up and down, their gaze lingering on her bracelet. Maia pulls her sleeve to cover it.

Claire leads them to a small circular table in the corner of the café. Maia is quick to sit, taking the chair with her back toward the people. She watches as Claire unlatches a long row of golden buttons down the front of her wool coat.

She slips it off and hangs it on her chair before taking her seat. "Get anything you'd like. It's on me," she says warmly.

Maia glances at the menu. One tea here costs the same as an entire bag at the Migrant Supply Store. "Oh, no. Thank you, but—"

"Maia, it's not an issue. Really."

Maia smiles. "Thank you." She orders a tea and Claire does the same, and then Claire proceeds to tell her that Mario went on a special mission and never returned.

"Oh, Claire, I'm so sorry."

"It's okay. Unfortunately, it's all part of it. No one goes on a mission without understanding the risks."

"So we've been told."

"And Lucas? What is he up to tonight?" Claire asks. She smiles wide, blowing before sipping her tea.

Maia looks up at her, tears surfacing. Claire is the first person in this city who knew Lucas. It's another blow to the gut Maia wasn't prepared for.

The smile drops from Claire's face. "Oh, Maia. Oh, I'm so sorry. He..." She shakes her head. "He didn't make it."

Maia can only look down. *Please don't ask why.*

Claire glances around anxiously. "Shall we get you something to eat? Are you hungry? They have the best little cakes here."

Maia forces a smile. "Only if you're having one."

"Sure! Why not?" Claire motions to the server. "Two of those divine little cake thingies, please."

The server nods and turns away.

"Now, tell me," Claire says. "What has happened with your monitoring device? Why is that godawful bracelet flashing red? I keep telling Jake we need a different system, but I suppose it works, doesn't it?" She takes a drink of her tea.

Maia can only look at her, lost for a response.

"Maia, *tell* me."

"I can't. I'm embarrassed."

"It's okay, you're safe with me. You can tell me."

Maia sucks in her lips, hesitating. "It's a long story, but basically, I was sick of the drones following me. So, I threw a rock at one."

Claire scrunches her face. "*Really*? Oh, Maia, those drones aren't following *you* specifically."

Maia sighs. *They are now.*

They share an uncomfortable moment of silence, and then Claire leans in. "Well, then it's fate that we've met tonight." She grabs Maia's hand across the table. "We're going to get you out of that bracelet."

"Can you do that?"

"I can't, but Jake can. He's incredibly powerful. If anyone can get you out of this mess, it's him."

"Wow," Maia says. "I would be so grateful."

"We can at least try, right? I mean, you've destroyed a *drone*. They're not going to just let you walk away, but even if Jake can lessen your sentence."

"I'll take any help I can get," Maia says.

"I bet Jake would like to see you. Actually, I know he would. Why don't I take you to him?"

"Really?" Maia bites her lip, thinking of the last time she saw Jake on his ship. They were in the flood zone of LA and he was trying to get her to go to Leucothea with them. It was right before she jumped off his boat like a raving lunatic to swim after Lucas. Jake was holding her, trying to get her to calm down. He wouldn't let her go. The way she glared at him caused him to stumble backward. He looked horrified. She can't be sure of what he saw, but it's pretty clear he witnessed ... *something.*

But he has authority in this city—the sort of authority Maia desperately needs to get herself out of this mess. She smiles at Claire. "I would love that. Thank you."

Stepping out of the café, Maia spots her stalker across the street, leaning against the building. Claire follows her gaze. When she turns around again, she carries a sympathetic smile.

"Do you know him?" Maia asks.

"No, I've never seen him before." Claire shrugs. "He's probably an undercover guard. You do have a flashing red beacon on you."

Maia sighs, rolling her eyes.

"Just don't make a scene, okay? I'm trying to help you. Don't make it hard for me."

This makes Maia laugh. "Fair enough."

"Promise?"

"I promise. I'll be a good girl."

"Okay, I'll come to your house first thing in the morning," Claire says.

"Oh, I can't. I have work."

"No, you don't," Claire says with a wink. "See you tomorrow." She hugs Maia and walks away.

Maia watches her, absently holding her monitoring bracelet across her chest. How quickly things can change. She looks down at the flashing red bulb on her wrist, dread swimming about her gut.

You will be held accountable for your crimes, bounder.

She peers over at her pursuer across the street. Yes, her bracelet may be flashing red, but this man was following her *long* before she destroyed that drone.

As she begins her journey home, the man lurks closely behind. She walks faster, zig-zagging between the people on the sidewalk, and he, too, picks up his pace. She spots a large gathering of people in an inner-city park across the street. A banner hangs across the entrance: *Christmas in the Park*. She runs toward it.

As she weaves through the mass of people bundled in scarves and sipping hot drinks, she glances over her shoulder. He's still there. Never once taking his eyes off hers, he pushes his way through the crowd.

This is impossible—it's not like she'll lose him. He knows where she lives. That's where she most often sees him, across her street, either beneath the lamppost or outside his black car, leaning against the door. Maybe she should talk to him in this crowd of people. It's safer this way. She'll ask him who he is, and why he has been following her.

She takes a deep breath and stops, turning toward him. He hesitates, surprised by her about-face, but then he smiles, making her skin crawl. He slowly snakes his way toward her, his glare like ice.

She lifts her chin, trying to hide the fact that her heart has jumped into her throat. As he approaches, he quickens his pace, ramming his shoulder into hers so hard that she slams into a woman behind her.

"Excuse me!" the woman yells.

"I'm so sorry," Maia gasps as she fumbles to her feet.

He peers back at her from over his shoulder, and then he turns away, disappearing into the crowd.

NINE

The following day, Maia stands on the edge of the tub, trying to get a better glimpse of herself in the small bathroom mirror. She has borrowed a top from Renee. Black, long sleeves. It was a steal from a Migrant Sale—barely worn, and it actually fits. Her baggy pants are another story. The darker denim is faded and stretched at the knees, and the hems are missing from the bottoms, the fabric frayed. But this is the best she has.

She jumps to the ground, stepping closer to the mirror. She smiles at herself, practicing her greeting for the hundredth time. "Hello, Jake. Thank you for meeting with me."

She is so *nervous*. Claire was annoyed with her for not knowing about Jake's status, but no one on the ship told them who he was. In fact, they downplayed it. Made him look like another traveler like them.

She and Lucas didn't exactly make the best impression either. Neither of them tried to be friendly with him, despite the fact that his ship had rescued them. For some reason,

Lucas hated him—told Maia to steer clear. Maybe he was threatened. Jake was arrogant and handsome, and he was not subtle about his attraction to Maia.

A knock sounds from the front door, and Maia answers to another man in uniform. This one seems much friendlier, which is a welcomed relief.

"Ma'am." He nods with a smile. "My name is Orson. I'm your driver. Claire is waiting for you in the car."

A driver? Maia assumed Claire would be driving them. She grabs her coat and follows him to the front of her apartment building where the shiniest black car she's ever seen is waiting out front. It looks as if it has been melted and stretched long. She glances across the street—her stalker is gone.

Orson waits for her at the open door.

"Thank you," she says, climbing in next to Claire.

Claire looks stunning. She's put on makeup, accentuating her high cheekbones and dark eyes. Her long black hair has been curled in loose waves, and she has a bright yellow scarf tucked into her black woolen coat. "Maia. So lovely to see you again," she says, her eyes raking over Maia's clothing. "Would you like some water? Jake is high on a cliff between the inner and outer city walls, so we've got a little drive ahead of us."

"Between the walls? I didn't realize there was much land there."

"Depends on where you are. The walls' entry and exit gates are relatively close together, situated near the city. But a portion of the outer wall extends quite far into the woods behind Leucothea. Only a few of the New System's most highly regarded government officials live back there."

Claire seems different this morning. There's an air of

superiority about her. She seems ... distant. "So, water?" she asks, looking at Maia.

"No, I'm okay. Thank you."

After Orson brings them through a checkpoint at the inner-city gates, he takes a sharp left. A few minutes later, they are cruising down a narrow, winding road in the woods. Maia leans against her door, craning her neck at the window, her heart *reeling*.

They are surrounded by a wall of green. After a year and a half of being locked up in a concrete jungle of artificial lights, seeing this many trees again has unleashed a devastating tsunami of buried emotions. It's like being reunited with a long-lost love, and Maia struggles to hold herself together.

Thankfully, Claire doesn't notice. She absently looks out her window, flipping her hand and talking nonstop about the university. The New System. *Jake*.

Maia peers at her from over her shoulder. Having spent a majority of her life around only one man, she has become the ultimate observer of people since leaving the shores of New Zealand, fascinated at how much someone can communicate without using words. She watches Claire as she talks about Jake. The way she says his name and the way she smiles when she says it, it is clear she has strong feelings for the man.

Maia tries to focus on what Claire is saying, but the trees ... there are so many trees. Despite herself, she turns back toward the window, back toward her family, her source of life. Do they still whisper? She's stuck behind this glass, but she has to know ... Can she still hear them?

"New System isn't perfect, but well, it's hard to fault it compared to life *out there*..." Claire continues.

"I'm sorry," Maia says, turning around again. "Can I make this window go down?"

"Just that button there. Hold it down."

Maia presses the button and the glass disappears into the door. She closes her eyes, breathing in the fresh mountain air.

Oh, how I've missed you.

She wants to ask Orson to stop. Can she do that? What she wouldn't give to get out. Claire keeps talking—*New System this, Jake that*—while Maia is using every ounce of constraint she has to not jump from the vehicle and run into the trees. She leans farther out the open window, gasping.

She can still hear them. The trees—all of them ... they are still whispering.

Mother. Mother. Mother.

She bites her lip, holding back her tears as she grips the window's ledge. She inches her head out a little more, inhaling the intoxicating scent of pine. She yearns for them. Just to touch one ... just one tree. She inches out a little more. It has been *so long...*

"*Maia!*" Claire yanks on Maia's coat.

Maia sits back inside the car, embarrassed.

Claire looks surprised. "Maybe put that window up. Can't have you looking like a wild animal," she says with nervous laughter. She leans across the seat, the leather groaning against itself, and she smooths back Maia's windblown hair.

The car slows as they pull up to an ornate wrought-iron fence. An armed guard steps from a building larger than Maia and Renee's entire apartment. He nods at Orson, and the gates open. The car eases through and slowly travels down a long gravel driveway surrounded by sprawling trimmed lawns and evergreen hedges.

Maia's heart continues to pound, but for different reasons from before. She is out of her element. She should have borrowed money from Renee to buy nicer pants. She didn't have time to sew the hole in her jacket. This is her one opportunity to fix this mess, and suddenly she feels ill-prepared. She was expecting "Jake from the ship." Even though Claire told her he had positioned himself as a man of great power, she didn't fully understand what that meant ... until now.

The road leads them to a lavish brick estate on a cliff overlooking Leucothea and the ocean. The house reminds Maia so much of the home where they stayed in New Portland, but this one is three times the size. It's like a *castle*.

It is the most beautiful home Maia has ever seen.

The car pulls along a circle drive before the mansion's front steps leading to a two-story, glass-door entry with granite balustrades. There are four guards dressed in black standing outside. Their stance is wide, their hands clasped behind their backs.

The car comes to a stop, and Maia searches for the door handle.

Claire swipes at her wrist. "No!" she whispers. "Let them do it for you."

Maia sits back and waits. Orson opens her door, and he offers his hand. "Ma'am."

As Maia steps outside the car, she looks up to thank him, but his eyes are fixated on her bracelet.

Another man helps Claire from the other side. She walks before Maia and motions for her to follow. "Come," she says with a proud smile.

The guards open the two front doors for the women, and they step inside a lofty foyer beneath a tiered crystal chandelier. Maia's heart beats faster.

Claire leads Maia down a long hallway lined with floor-to-ceiling windows on one side. They walk past an office with the doors left open. A few guards with guns strapped to their hips are inside, talking quietly around a desk. Maia swallows hard, and they continue on.

Claire stops at the end of the hallway, knocking on a door. There is a buzzing sound, and she positions herself in front of Maia before opening it. Maia peers in over Claire's shoulder. It's another office, filled with more cathedral windows between immense wooden shelving packed with books.

"Claire," a man's voice rings from inside.

"Good morning, Jake," Claire says, and she steps to the side.

A rush of emotions fills Maia as she sees Jake again, like seeing a ghost from a past life. He is sitting behind a grand mahogany desk. Behind him, a wall of windows overlooks the ocean. His trimmed dark hair and short beard are speckled with gray, and Maia wonders about his age. He can't be older than his late thirties. His salt-and-pepper hair makes his brown eyes appear nearly black. Despite having made up her mind about him a long time ago, she is surprised at how attractive she finds him.

He stands, smoothing his pressed suit—one clearly tailored to fit him. A small porcelain cup of black liquid sits in a saucer on the desk. Maia assumes it to be coffee. She's never had it before—she can't afford it—but she knows the smell from the shops.

Jake walks around his desk and stops before her, carrying the scent of warm spice. "Maia. It is so good to see you again." The way he's speaking, it's more refined than before. He's carrying himself differently as well. It's like he's another person.

"Jake, hello." Maia reaches out her hand.

He takes it, holding it tightly between his as he looks her up and down. She's confused by his expression. It's like he's fascinated by her and repulsed at the same time. He studies her bracelet. Shaking his head, he chuckles. "Flashing red. *Why* does this not surprise me?" He gazes at her. *This* look is undeniable—attraction. Maia's heart pounds harder.

He continues to survey the state of her. Finally, he says, "You look different ... I can't place why. It couldn't have been that long since we last saw each other. Two and a half years, maybe?"

"Something like that."

"Still causing trouble, I see? Jumping off ships?" He leans in close. "*Stealing* from people?" he says under his breath.

He knows. Maia swallows.

Jake starts to laugh, and Claire follows suit. She sounds nervous. He drops Maia's hand and steps around his desk, leaning back on his leather chair. He lifts the small cup from the saucer. Sipping, he stares at Maia.

She stands unmoving, unsure of what to do.

He sets the cup down, and it clinks loudly in the porcelain dish. "It's okay," he says. "I know that was Lucas who stole from me and not you. Please, sit." He motions toward the chairs, and Claire lowers herself into the seat next to Maia.

"Not you," he says.

She freezes, then stands.

"Leave us," he says, still staring at Maia. He looks at Claire, raising his brow.

Wounded, Claire smiles. "Of course," she says, and she shoots Maia a look.

Maia knows that one too: *resentment.*

Claire and the guards exit the room, leaving Jake and Maia alone. She sits on the edge of her seat, looking around. This room is exquisite. What she wouldn't give to have access to all these books.

Jake stares at her for a long time without speaking. Is he waiting for her to say something?

"Maia." He tilts his gaze. "You look *so good*."

Chills run down her spine. Her gut instinct about this man is confusing. She finds herself captivated by him. Curious, yet uncertain. There's something about him, something she noticed from the moment they met on his ship. Something alluring, yet ... *dangerous*.

"And so bad," he adds, shaking his head. "My city isn't treating you well?"

My city? Maia still doesn't speak.

"Although, you're not really helping yourself either, what with all the drinking and partying you've been doing."

How could he possibly—the drones. "Are you *spying* on me?" she asks.

He is quick to respond. "I don't need to spy on you, Maia. I know everything that happens in this city."

She holds her tongue.

Jake sighs, then takes another sip of his coffee. "Look, Claire has told me about your predicament. You've gotten yourself into a lot of trouble. Those drones are our police force. We can't have people thinking they can just throw shit at them."

"But no one saw what I did."

"I also see we've got you working as a sifter. That's a shit job, and you'll never get out of it."

"What do you mean?"

"The contract you've signed. And now the trouble you've

gotten yourself into ... You'll be upside down on your payments for life."

"Meaning?"

"Meaning, you'll be in debt to Leucothea forever. The amount it costs to house and feed you, plus now legal fees and the time and resources we'll need to replace the drone you've destroyed. Those parts are limited and incredibly hard to find. You'll never repay us doing the assignment you're doing."

"But I've been working overtime!"

"Doesn't matter. Apparently, you're good at your job. And you're educated—too educated. You're also feisty. Trouble. You ask too many questions. You stay up late, drink too much. They'll keep you right where you're at—overworked and underpaid."

Maia closes her eyes, her heart sinking.

"But..."

She looks up at him.

"I am a very powerful man. I can help you."

She stares at him, lost for words.

He smiles. "You're unsure about me. That's okay. Our time on the ship was very brief." His eyes narrow, calculating. "And it ended ... *strangely*."

He *did* see something.

Clearing his throat, he continues. "I'd like to have dinner with you. But not..." He surveys her clothing, her wrist. "Not yet. Let me see what I can do about your sentencing. And those clothes." He shudders. "I can't be seen with a woman who looks like a bounder."

Maia looks down at her clothing. This is the best outfit she has. She follows his gaze to her wrist, and she covers it with her sleeve. Shame has become a weight she can't shake.

"Thank you," she says quietly, wanting to crawl under his mahogany desk.

He smiles warmly. "You're welcome. It's nice to see you, Maia. I've..." He hesitates, then clasps his hands on his desk, leaning toward her. "I've been hoping I'd see you again."

Maia's heart skips, and she swallows. "You have?"

He nods once, his black eyes penetrating. "I have."

TEN

Ten days have passed, and not a word from Jake or Claire. Ten days, all of which Maia spent standing at her living room window while biting her nails, waiting for that stretched car to arrive. Waiting for someone to walk up her rusted outdoor stairs with a message. Waiting for something—anything. Every day that passed, she held on to hope that someone would pull through on *something*.

Jake seemed so sincere. Claire swore she would help.

But when her court date finally arrived, Maia had no other choice but to go with the police when they showed up at her door. She had a long and tearful goodbye with Renee, hoping she'd return but dreading the worst. And then Renee stood sniffling at their doorway as Maia's hands were cuffed behind her back, and she was thrown into a black van waiting on the street.

The courtroom was filled with souls like her. Some had monitoring bracelets that flashed red, while others emitted one continuous crimson glow. Whether their bracelets blinked or not, their faces looked the same. Hardened.

Hopeless. Crushed by the system that claims to have saved them. But maybe, like Maia, they, too, were their own worst enemies.

Maia's sentencing began. Standing before the judge, she was shamed for one discretion after the next as her guards stood beside her, gripping her arms and shaking their heads. Her heart was thumping so hard, she could see the fabric of her shirt quivering as she looked at her feet, the entire time thinking that surely, she must be dreaming. This wasn't happening. How did she go from a powerful and free woman in the wild, commanding the wind and sleeping with wolves, to a trembling, lost soul in handcuffs?

"You have destroyed..." the judge continued, "...shown nothing but malice for the justice of this city ... after being taken in, cared for, and fed..."

Maia focused on her breathing as the judge glared down through her bifocals, flooding her in a deluge of shame. "You will spend one week in the city jail until we have completed your paperwork, and then you will be taken to serve the rest of your sentence in the fields outside of Leucothea."

Maia gasped, looking up at the judge in shock.

"You are no longer a migrant. You are now a prisoner. Your monitoring bracelet will no longer flash a 'warning red' but will remain fully on as a 'prisoner red.' Your next court date is set for one year from today."

"A *year*?!" Maia screeched.

"One year," the judge said. And when she banged her gavel against its block, Maia's knees buckled.

"You will have a trial at that time," the judge continued as Maia stumbled to find her footing, the guards yanking at her arms, "with a selection of citizens who will vote on whether or not, *depending* on your behavior over the next year, we'll allow you back inside Leucothea for a second chance at probation."

Lightheaded, Maia wavered as the guards tightened their grips.

"Maia." The judge lowered her gaze, peering at her from over her glasses. "This doesn't have to be the end for you. You're young. Yes, you've messed up, but you can come back from this. Work hard to pay for your crime, and you may be allowed a second chance."

Maia nodded, looking at her feet, and the guards dragged her away.

———

Maia spends the next few days in complete silence on the stinking mattress of her tiny jail cell. She's back in a bunkbed, thinking about the words etched into the last one she slept in.

Leucothea will destroy *you.*

But whoever wrote those words was wrong. Leucothea didn't *destroy* anything. Maia has done that all on her own.

The jail has received a new shipment of prisoners, God only knows where from, so Maia has a new roommate. Apparently, she's been in the cell next to Maia this entire time, separated by a cement wall.

The woman hobbles in with her round, pasty-white belly sticking out from beneath her shirt, and announces her name as Bettina—but everyone calls her "Big Bets." Her blonde hair is so thin and wispy that it stands on end on top of her head, reminding Maia of an old troll doll she once found buried in dust back in New Zealand.

100

It's "lights out" in the jail and the women are supposed to be sleeping. Maia is lying on the cement floor with her legs against the wall, gazing at the moon through the room's small window.

After everything she has been through, she has *definitely* hit rock bottom. And she is done fighting. What's the use? Fighting has brought her nothing but trouble. So, she'll just slip down into that dark place deep inside her gut where she's buried all her ache.

And she'll *rot* there alongside it.

Big Bets is lying on the top bunk, staring at Maia.

Maia closes her eyes with an exaggerated sigh. "*What.*"

"I'm not sure why you lying on that cold floor when you gotta bed."

"The floor is fine," Maia mumbles.

"No, really. You wanna enjoy every last minute of that disgustin' old mattress, cause where they be sendin' you, you ain't gonna get much better than that floor for the next year, *at least.* Some people I hear ain't never gonna leave that place. Human slaves, they are."

Maia sits up, looking at her. "What are you talking about?"

Footsteps sound from the hallway. Big Bets lies down, shaking the creaky metal bunk. "*Shhh.*" She waves her hand over the edge.

A guard slowly walks past. He shines his light on Maia on the floor, then the lump of Big Bets' belly on the top bunk. He turns it off and keeps walking.

"Bets?" Maia whispers.

Big Bets flicks her hand over the side of the bunk. "Neva' you mind. Just a rumor is all. I shouldn't a said nothin'."

Maia sighs. *Whatever.* She lies back down again, looking

up at the moon. She closes one eye, covering the sliver with her thumb.

Big Bets sits up again, resting on her elbow. She peers down at Maia.

Maia watches her from the corner of her eye. "*What.*"

"It's just ... *why* you so skinny?! Migrants all gotta eat that same shit they make out in those warehouses. Keeps us alive, but there ain't nothin' in it. That's why we gotta eat so much of it. Some of us got real fat. But you ain't fat."

"Who knows."

"*Hmph*," Big Bets grunts, looking Maia up and down and clicking her tongue. "You don't look like you belong here. What'd you do, anyway? Why they sending you all the way out to the shit fields?"

Maia flops her head toward Big Bets. "I threw a rock at a drone. Destroyed it."

"*Ooooooo!*" Big Bets lies on her back, snorting and laughing and slapping her thighs.

"Quiet!" the guard yells from down the hall.

Big Bets pays him no mind. She laughs so hard that she starts kicking her feet, and Maia swears the entire bunk is going to buckle. "*Girl*," Big Bets says between snorts, "you skinny *and* stupid!"

This makes Maia laugh for the first time in weeks. She closes her eyes, pushing down the dread inside her gut. "You're right about that."

———

Days pass. Every time the guard walks past Maia's cell, she waits for him to stop and tell her it's time. Every time he passes, Maia's entire body tenses, she holds her breath, and she prepares herself to be led to a truck that will take her to a prison outside the city. The guard circles around so many times that when he actually does tell her it's time, Maia is so exhausted that she no longer cares.

"See ya around, Little M!" Big Bets says from the top bunk.

"Yeah, see you," Maia mumbles as the guards enter the cell. She holds her hands behind her back as they cuff them, and then they lead her out into the hall.

With a guard on either side, Maia walks past cell after cell filled with women, some with four or five prisoners to a single bunk. After passing through more locked doors with loud buzzers, Maia is led outside the jail to a gravel lot flooded by streetlights on the dark winter day. A large truck is waiting with its headlights on and back doors open. Three armed guards stand next to it, with a handful of prisoners already waiting on the benches inside.

Maia thought she would be more upset at this point, thought there would be tears, maybe pleading. But she has worked through all those emotions this past week and has accepted what is happening. She just has to get through another year.

Another year. Always waiting another year.

Approaching the truck, Maia is surprised when the men on either side of her yank her away. She glances between them, confused, as they escort her *beyond* the truck to a glossy, stretched-out black car at the back of the lot. Maia stares at it in shock. Every step they take feels like slow motion, the gravel crunching beneath their boots and their breath puffed in clouds, as the guards continue to lead Maia *away* from the truck and *toward* the car.

Two men step from the vehicle.

Jake's men.

One of them opens the back door, and a woman steps out. She has a yellow scarf around her head and large black glasses despite it being dark. She removes them.

Claire.

Maia sucks in a breath, struggling to hold her composure, and the guards jerk her to a stop. There is a clinking of keys as one of them unlocks her cuffs. Unbelieving, she holds her wrists against her chest. She still has her monitoring device on, but at least she's out of her cuffs.

"She's all yours," a guard says to Claire.

"Thank you," Claire says, slipping her glasses back on. She motions for Maia to climb into the car.

Maia rushes up to the vehicle, quickly ducking inside. Claire follows, along with Jake's men in front. Maia peers out her window as the guards walk away, one placing her cuffs in his back pocket. They disappear into the building as another two soldiers escort a woman out the door and into the truck.

Maia gapes back at Claire, speechless.

Claire takes off her glasses but she doesn't look at her. "I'm sorry it took us so long to get you out of there," she says at the window. "What we've done for you today is a privilege. It's not technically allowed."

Maia holds her hand against her mouth, and then she whispers, "Thank you, thank you so—"

"Don't thank me," Claire says, glancing at Maia. "Thank Jake. He did this."

"Did ... *what*?"

"He's working on getting you out of your sentence, but at this point, he has only been able to get you out of *jail*. You'll still have to wear that device with a red light, so you won't be allowed back in the city. You just need to stay put until we figure this out."

"Stay put? Where?"

Claire sighs. "Jake has a guest suite at the back of his property where you can stay. Hopefully, you won't need to be there long." The way she's talking, her words are bitter. "Just get some rest. Eat. *Shower*," she adds with a scowl.

Maia looks down at her filthy clothing. "Sorry. They didn't exactly care about hygiene in there."

"Let's just sit in silence for the rest of the ride, okay?"

Maia nods. She's not sure what she's done, but the friendly Claire that she barely knew seems to have gone.

On the car ride, Maia lays her head against the window, taking repeated deep breaths as they enter the long, winding road out of the city gates and into the woods. Into the *trees*. Tears stream down her face, and she has no strength left to stop them. She slaps her hand against the glass.

"I taught you how to operate the windows," Claire mumbles beside her.

"Out. Please ... let me out."

"You're *joking*."

Maia turns to her. "Please, I'm begging you."

Claire stares at her, horrified.

"Five minutes. Just give me five minutes in the woods."

"I ... I don't know."

"*Please*."

"If you run—"

"I swear to you, I'm not going to run. I've just been cooped up for *so long*," Maia's voice breaks. "*Please*!?" she shrieks.

A wave of compassion breaks Claire's hardened demeanor. She turns to the driver. "Orson, please pull over."

"I'm under strict instructions to bring you two straight back to Jake's."

"I'm going to throw up!" Maia screams.

Orson looks at her in his mirror. Maia covers her mouth and fakes a wretch.

"It's okay," Claire says. "I'm allowing it."

Orson pulls the car to the side of the road. With the wheels still rolling to a stop, Maia whips open her door, tumbling onto the dirt. Choking back a sob, she climbs to her feet and stumbles into the woods.

"Maia?!" Claire screams from inside the car, the door still open.

Maia whips around. "Five minutes!" she yells, walking backward. And then, she *runs*. She races between the trees with the last dregs of her strength, and their soothing whispers wash over her.

Mother.

Mother.

Mother.

She kicks off her boots, feeling the cool dirt between her toes for the first time since stepping into her umiak with Lucas so long ago. The heartbeat of the Earth—hundreds of miles of root systems coursing beneath every step—thumps in her ears with her own rapid pulse. She inhales the fresh mountain air—the exhalation of every tree. And then sobbing like a child, she falls at the base of a spruce, burying her face into the ground.

Lost. So, so lost.

Twigs snap, and Maia whirls around. Jake's men stand behind her with guns pointed.

Claire steps between them, her face contorted with alarm. "Put your guns down," she says quietly, and they lower their weapons. She crouches next to Maia, tenderly wiping the dirt stuck to Maia's tears.

"Lost," Maia whispers. "I've lost everything ... everyone ... *myself*."

"Maia," Claire says. "We're going to take care of you. We're going to fix this. Okay? We'll fix this." She pulls Maia into her, holding her as she weeps.

ELEVEN

L ying under the Christmas tree, Maia peers up at the crisscrossing of branches and the glittering lights. She swore she would never get used to it— electricity—but as with most things in life, the mind can become numb. The novelty wears off.

She got used to it. Became indifferent. Lost in a sea of lights.

She reaches to a silver ornament. So fragile. She wonders how far it traveled to be here, whose family home it was plucked from. Despite its frailty, this one did not break. She holds it between her fingertips, twisting it so it swirls. The glitter sparkles against the lights.

She crawls out from under the tree, gazing around. Somehow, she has made her way back into a one-room cottage, although this is called a "guest suite," and it is significantly nicer than her old cabin back home. The front door opens to a small kitchen and a white wooden dining table off to the side. The back of the suite has a sitting room: two armchairs in front of a fireplace covered in garland, and there's a Christmas tree in the corner. A plush bed is against the opposite wall with bedside tables and pillows upon pillows upon pillows. The suite's back wall is all windows and two glass doors leading out to a patio and a small yard surrounded by trees.

She has been here for over a week now, and despite the time being painful, it has also been surprisingly beautiful. She arrived here broken, but instead of fighting against it ... she *allowed* it. Sat with it. Listened to it. And now she feels like she has crossed over to the other side of it.

She has come all this way, fought for years to get to this seemingly mythical place in the Old Arctic. She has followed her heart, a gut instinct that she still struggles to believe was wrong. She risked her life; she risked *other people's* lives; she risked everything she had.

And then she lost it all.

She walked through the danger and the decay, away from love and in and out of people's lives, and then she stumbled into this new existence in the city of lights holding tightly to every last broken fragment of her old life. She gathered its fractured pieces into her arms and carried them around with her everywhere she went.

She gripped them till her fingers bled.

Wouldn't let go. *Couldn't* let go.

This past week, Maia has slept—*a lot*. She has eaten—*a lot*. Good food. *Real* food. Unprocessed, living fruits and vegetables. Every few days, a small shipment of groceries from the main house is delivered to her doorstep, and she spends hours cooking, attempting to recreate the meals she used to admire from the other side of the restaurants' windows. The decadent smells fill her small guest suite. The food soothes her soul.

Being mid-December, it is dark outside around the clock, which is perfect for a holiday with so many twinkling lights. Maia lies around all day, moving from her bed to her armchair to her kitchen table. She reads books next to the fire, pausing every few pages to glance up at her glittering Christmas tree. And then she steps outside the back of her little suite to walk around the ice-cold grass in her bare feet, reconnecting to the earth. Reconnecting, little by little, to *herself*. To the power inside that is still there but dimmed significantly. She doesn't dare try anything with her powers. Not here—not yet. The bracelet on her wrist is still red. She's still being monitored. Tracked. Like the city of Leucothea, there are cameras all over Jake's property. Drones sporadically zipping across lawns.

Claire has stopped by a few times to check on her. She even went to Maia's old apartment to collect a few of her belongings—Lucas's ashes in particular. Each time Claire has come by, she has kept her visit brief. She is friendly but not warm. Distant. Maia knows that Claire has strong feelings for Jake, and now Maia is staying on his property. Claire must feel threatened. Maia would love to tell her not to worry, but she can't.

This entire time, Maia has still not seen or heard from Jake. She has no idea why he's being so kind or what his intentions are. She and Lucas had believed him to be such an asshole—Lucas *hated* him. But Jake has gone above and beyond to help Maia. To save her even. She is more curious than ever about this distant man living in the mansion on the other side of the property, but Claire has told Maia that her future is still uncertain, to stay put and rest. So, that's exactly what she'll do.

This time has been good for her. Every day that passes, she arrives at an even stronger resolve in her heart to move forward and let her past go. She has been saved from a treacherous sentence at a forced labor camp. This is her second chance, and she is determined not to ruin it. She thought she came to Leucothea to make a stand, to fight for something bigger than herself. But with the loss she has suffered, the life she can now live moving forward *is* greater than herself. She has battled her way across a deserted and broken planet to live in the greatest civilization on Earth. There is so much *power* in numbers. The relatively few humans left behind have been gathering together for decades in this magical place in the Old Arctic to make this life possible.

It is a *privilege* to be here. Maia can see that now. She is ready to let go of the broken pieces of her past.

She is ready to live.

———

Sitting by the fire, Maia is transfixed by the flames. Lost in her own world, her mind wanders to the one person she's still desperately trying to forget. Miguel's laugh has disappeared from her memory, but she can still see his smile.

A knock sounds from the front door. Maia flips off her blanket and runs to open it. There is no one there, but one of Jake's black cars is pulling out of her driveway. A package with a card on top has been left on her stoop. She grabs it and closes the door, setting the box on the kitchen table. She opens the card to a small piece of paper inside with a single sentence:

Join me for dinner?
J

Her heart flutters. An invite from Jake. She sets the paper aside and opens the package. The inside is filled with

JILLIAN WEBSTER

a shiny black cloth. She slowly lifts it from the box. It's a ... *dress*. Beneath it is a pair of strappy gold shoes. She's seen other women in the city wearing these, has come across them in countless closets, but she's never once tried them on. She holds one up by its strap. The heels are high, like stilts.

She gathers the dress in her arms, rubbing it against her cheek. The fabric is so soft. Is this satin? She runs to a large mirror on the wall and holds the skinny straps to her shoulders. The dress drapes to the carpet. Like a fairytale.

Later that evening, after Maia has showered and dressed, she ties her hair off her neck, and a few curls fall, kissing her temples. She is surprised at how much she wants to impress this man. His kindness has been overwhelming.

Gazing at herself in the mirror, she twists in her black satin, floor-length dress, admiring how the draping fabric exposes the long curvature of her back. She lifts her chin, stands up straight. She has never seen herself like this before. If it weren't for her hideous monitoring bracelet, she would look like the elite of Leucothea. She looks ... *beautiful*.

Sitting at the kitchen table, she straps the shoes to her feet. When she stands, she is surprised at how much pressure there is on the ball of her foot. She steps forward, wavering like a toddler just learning to walk, and falls to the carpet. Laughing, she climbs to her feet and tries again. She can stand in these things, but she can't walk.

Holding the back of a chair for balance, Maia looks at her reflection. She's so *tall* in these shoes; she actually kind of loves them. If only Miguel could see her now.

It is small, like you.

The old ache flutters. She shoves it back down.

Three knocks sound at the front door. Maia quickly slips off her shoes and runs to open it, heels in hand, to find

112

Orson, Jake's driver. He is dressed in a suit and tie, and a woman's woolen coat is draped across his arm. He looks her up and down in surprise, then quickly averts his eyes, clearing his throat. "Ma'am, I've come to take you to dinner."

"Uh ... okay." She peers at the shoes in her hands. She'll have to carry them.

She steps barefoot into the cold night. Orson looks at her, unsure, and she shrugs. He suppresses his smile, then holds up the coat. She turns, and he drapes it across her shoulders. The thick wool is deliciously heavy. The fabric on the inside is so soft and cool. And, it has *all* its buttons. She hugs it to her body.

"Please, come with me," Orson says. He walks across the gravel and opens the car door, glancing away as Maia wavers on the sharp rocks beneath her bare feet. She gathers her dress and climbs into the car, and he gently closes the door, chuckling as he walks to the driver's side.

As they drive down the long gravel road to the main house, Maia's nerves prickle. Is this what they used to call *a date*? Her mouth dries. With *Jake*? With Jake, the asshole from the ship that saved them but is now the army general of one of the most powerful civilizations in the world? Butterflies flutter inside her gut, mixed with a strange urge to want to be back under that tree in the woods, rubbing dirt into her face. Is this *her*? The soul of the Earth having dinner in mansions with powerful men?

It could be.

For years now, Maia's life has been a constant, uphill battle. Struggle. Danger and hardship and death ... And for what?

Pain. Heartache. Loss.

She inhales, shaking it off.

Just have fun, Maia, for once in your life.

The car pulls around to the entrance of Jake's home. White Christmas lights line the balustrades, the windows, the doors. Twinkle lights are everywhere. Maia quickly straps on her high heels, almost giddy. Orson opens her door and she holds his hand as she steps out, looking up at the glittering castle towering above them. It's like a scene from one of her books. Minus the bracelet.

Somehow, Maia needs to walk from this car and up the steps to get inside. She wavers, and Orson holds out his arm. She looks at him in surprise, and he nods, his smile tender. She links her arm through his, and together they slowly make their way up the steps.

As Orson opens the front door, they are bathed in a cloud of warmth and the decadent smells of roasting meat. Baking bread. Something rich and chocolatey. They step inside, and Orson slips off Maia's coat. She looks around, exhaling a nervous breath through pursed lips. Her heart is *pounding*.

Orson once again offers his arm, and they walk down a cathedral-ceilinged hallway to a great room at the back of the house with windows three stories high and a Christmas tree nearly as tall.

A woman approaches, holding a tray with a glass of sparkling, fizzy liquid on top. Maia looks at it, uncertain.

"Champagne, miss."

Maia's eyes widen, and she carefully lifts the skinny glass, bringing it to her lips. The champagne tickles her nose, and she can't help but smile. She sips, surprised at the explosion of bubbles inside her mouth.

"You look ... *incredible*."

Maia turns to find Jake leaning against the entryway on the other side of the great room. The way he looks at her steals her breath. He is *strikingly* handsome, dressed in a dark suit, the buttons of his white shirt undone at the top.

She smiles, turning toward him, her heart tumbling beneath her chest. She's still so unsure about this man, yet ... his presence is intoxicating. "Hello, Jake," she says softly.

"From rags to riches," he says as he walks toward her, and Maia's cheeks flush. He holds out his arm, motioning for her to join him. "Come, I'll show you around."

She steps forward, wobbly on her feet, and bites her lip.

Jake laughs, and she can't help but join him. "Just take them off, Maia. Those things are ridiculous. I can't believe anyone ever thought it was a good idea to bring them back."

"Thank God," she says, and she kicks off each shoe.

"You look better without them anyway," he says with a wink. "Do you like the dress? You look stunning."

Maia stands before him. "Jake, I want to thank you for everything you've done for me. You've been so kind, taking me in and getting me out of that horrific mess. I can't begin to tell you how grateful I am."

"I had to help you. That's no life to live."

She turns away, blinking fast. After a moment, she links her arm with his, and she looks up at him. "Yes."

"Yes?" He holds her in his gaze.

"Yes," she says with a smile. "I love the dress. Thank you."

Later that night, Maia and Jake sit next to each other at the end of a long dining table after a candlelit dinner. It was the most incredible meal Maia had ever tasted. At one point, the table was filled with platters of roast duck, savory vegetables cooked in spices and butter, and a selection of green salads.

They finished with something called "chocolate mousse." It was so heavenly, Maia was pretty sure she never once opened her eyes while eating it.

After a few glasses of champagne, Maia and Jake have finally lowered their guards, and they've surprisingly shared a lot of laughs. Jake is no longer acting like he rules the world, and Maia is no longer trying to sit up so straight in her backless satin dress.

She gazes at Jake as he talks. Maybe she was wrong about him. It seems her life has become a cruel accumulation of lessons, all proving the harsh reality that she has been wrong about most things, most of the time. She was wrong about Lucas being the love of her life. She was wrong about leaving Miguel on the shores of that river. She was wrong about Leucothea ... in so many ways. Is it so crazy to think she may have also been wrong about Jake?

Besides, it would be so convenient right now.

"I have something for you," Jake says, reaching into his jacket.

Maia sets down her glass. "Another surprise? A girl could get used to this."

He looks at her very seriously. "Please ... *do*."

The smile slides from her face. "What is it?"

He grabs her hand and flips open her palm, placing a small black box inside.

"What is this?" she asks, her nerves fluttering.

"Place it," Jake says, "here." He points to a small circular indent on her monitoring bracelet.

Maia stares at him, speechless.

"Go on," he says, but he does not smile. "This way, you have saved *yourself*."

Maia places the box on her bracelet. She waits, but nothing happens. "Jake—"

"Just keep holding. Our technology is still a little slow," he says, intently observing the bracelet.

Maia watches him, then looks down at her monitoring device as the bright red bulb fades to black. She gasps, and then the entire bracelet unlatches at its hinge. "*Jake...*" she whispers, the loose band blurring behind her tears.

He slides the bracelet off and sets it on the table. Maia stares at it, absently rubbing her naked wrist. He grabs her hand, holding it within his. "Maia, you are *free*. I want you to take as long as you need in my guest suite. You may use my driver to come and go as you please. When you are ready, we will look for a job and a home that suits you. Maybe sign you up for some classes at the university? But please, don't worry about any of that now. Just relax. There are some great hiking trails around here. Claire said you missed the woods? Spend as much time here as you need."

Maia's chin quivers, and she looks away. "Why are you doing this?" she whispers, gazing up at him.

He sits back. The way he's looking at her, he almost seems ... *vulnerable*.

"What is it?" she asks.

"I'm not sure where to begin, so I'll just lay it all out on the table."

"Lay what..."

"I'm incredibly attracted to you, Maia—not just your looks, but to everything about you. I was drawn to you from the moment I met you in the kitchen of my ship, but I couldn't ever talk to you because ... well, Lucas and I didn't exactly get along."

Maia can't hold back her smile. "No."

"I was relieved when Claire told me a few months ago that you had survived the journey up here and were now living in the city. But then she told me everything you had been through, about Lucas's death, and how much trouble you had gotten into. You were struggling, working long hours, making next to nothing. That's no life to live. I saw you were sinking, and I knew I could help."

Maia looks down at her naked wrist.

"But it's more than that," he says, and Maia looks up at him in surprise. "I want to show you how truly *amazing* life up here can be. I want to get to know you. I think you might be the most incredible woman I have ever met."

"But ... you hardly know me."

"I know a little, and the little I know makes me want to know more. I like your honesty. I like the fact that you're a bit of a fireball. You're intelligent. These things are frustratingly rare. I find most people awfully boring." He sits back with his elbow on the table, resting his chin on his fist. "I know there's something special about you, Maia. I can tell. I'm an excellent reader of people."

Maia sighs, feeling overwhelmed. She used to think the same about herself. She's been unsure about this man from the moment they met, yet ... he seems so genuine.

"Look," Jake says, and he leans forward, still holding Maia's hand within his own. "I know you've been through a lot, so we can take it slow. No pressure, okay? You continue to stay in my guest suite. I'll remain in the main house. If you or I decide at any point that we'd rather be friends, well, then you get to be friends with one of the most powerful men in the world."

"In the *world*, Jake?" Maia laughs. "You think pretty highly of yourself, don't you?"

He sits back with an amused grin. "That right there." He points at her. "You're not afraid of me. I like that."

"*Afraid* of you? *Should* I be?"

He shrugs with a cocky grin. "Probably."

TWELVE

Maia's boot sinks into the soft new layer of snow, and she steps across another beam of moonlight cutting through the thick forest.

After a blizzard has covered the lands in a silent blanket of white, Jake has insisted on taking Maia hiking for their first official date. She tried to nonchalantly suggest something different, but he wanted to show her something. In a land that had once seen snow most of the year, it now only witnesses it sporadically during its darkest winter months. And when it happens, people everywhere in the city stop what they are doing to honor the frozen crystals drifting from the skies of a burning world.

Wrapped in heavy coats, mittens, hats, and scarves, Maia and Jake head out into the quiet white lands, hiking deeper into the woods behind his sprawling property. Her breath in clouds, Maia uses every last ounce of strength to remain constrained. Despite convincing herself that she has made peace with this new chapter of her life, she hasn't been able to spend any time alone in the woods. Too painful—like being torn between worlds.

She gazes around, sensing the life surrounding her in the trees. Their whispers, like the powers she had once harnessed on a regular basis, have dimmed significantly. They are so quiet, now a soft murmur versus a resounding chorus, but she can still hear them. She yearns to touch one, just one tree, but she doesn't dare. Not here. Not now.

If she reaches for a branch, would it still reach back?

Keep it together, Maia. Just keep it together.

She peers up. The massive pines impale the sky like daggers, their branches coated in a thick layer of white— just like her old dreams. Above them, her beloved constellations once again flicker across the sky. She thought she would be thrilled to see them after so long in the city, but instead, it only breaks her heart, reminding her of all those nights she used to lie next to the fire with Lucas and Miguel.

It seems like another lifetime.

A shadow flickers across the frozen ground, and a great horned owl lands on a branch above. She gazes up at him, her hand at her chest, and he glares down at her with piercing yellow eyes. It is like he knows, and looking up at him, she knows too.

"Maia?" Jake's voice breaks her trance. Just ahead of her on the trail, he looks so handsome in his winter gear. "Everything okay?"

"Yes, I'm here. Sorry."

"We're nearly there." He hikes back through the snow to grab her hand, and they walk side by side through the woods.

Maia looks down at their mittens wrapped around each other. Is this really happening? Maia is dating Jake.

Is that so bad?

Lucas would think so. So would Claire. Miguel. Tema.

Stop. She shakes the thought from her mind.

Jake leads her to the edge of a cliff. Below them, his incredible mansion is lit up in an array of white lights. Below that, tiered along the land overlooking the ocean, lies the glittering city of Leucothea. It is all so magnificent, yet, so strange to see such a large metropolis boxed in by complete blackness.

From up here, it looks just like their flag. A beacon of light in a dark world.

"Jake, this is so ... *beautiful.*"

He turns to look at her, his brooding features softened. "Yeah," he says with a smile, his breath in clouds. "I think so too."

That smile. Somehow, this man is getting in ... slipping past Maia's carefully constructed walls.

"I'm so proud of this city and everything we are doing. Just you wait, Maia. I'm going to show you. I think—no, I *know*..." His smile fades as his gaze drifts to her lips, and her breath catches as he slowly leans in. He places his hand against her cheek, his nose touching hers. "You and I..." he breathes, hesitating.

Maia waits, surprised to see a man of such power reduced to boyish nerves. But he doesn't speak. His lips softly graze against hers, and then he kisses her for the first time, standing in the drifting snow high above the glittering sea of lights.

The month of December has been an absolute dream. No, it has gone *far beyond* Maia's *wildest* dreams.

Dating Jake has been an intoxicating whirlwind of wining and dining, limos, and nights out on the town. There isn't a day that passes that he doesn't treat Maia to some sort of gift or surprise. After their hike in the snow, he insisted Maia get new clothes. So, Orson took her to the massive warehouses at the back of the city, and she filled her arms with clothing and dresses and shoes faithfully stocked by the S&R Crews. She even found a few more pairs of high heels. It only took a few sessions of walking around in the privacy of her guest suite to get the hang of them.

With all their extravagant evenings out and Jake's elevated status in the city, it doesn't take long for him and Maia to become Leucothea's newest obsession. More and more, as they are seen stepping from their limo dressed in their finest clothes to eat at the most luxurious restaurants, there are media photographers waiting to snap their photos.

The first few times this happened, the array of flashing lights was overwhelming to Maia. But Jake simply pulled her into him and held her tight, whispering, "Don't be afraid. I won't let anything happen to you."

She gazed up at him, beaming, and the photographers went *wild*.

Now the people of Leucothea know who Maia is. No one is slamming into her as if she were invisible. They no longer call her a bounder while looking down at her with disgust. They treat her with respect—adoration, even. They hold open her doors. They smile and nod as she passes.

Since Jake's work keeps him extremely busy during the day, Maia has spent most mornings cooking. Jake has even sent over his private chef, who has been giving her lessons. Cooking with all these available oils and spices feels like magic, and it all tastes so *good*. She's been thinking about going to the university to become a chef, maybe opening up her own restaurant someday.

Most afternoons, she's helped herself to the plethora of books in Jake's library, devouring the stories cover to cover.

She's also had Orson take her into the city a few nights a week to catch up with Renee when she gets out of work.

Every time Maia walks up those rusted metal steps to her old apartment, she peers over her shoulder for her stalker, expecting to see him standing beneath the street-lamp or loitering on the corner—but he's gone.

Maia and Jake have also discovered a mutual love for chess, which they play almost every night after dinner in Jake's living room. It's an old pastime Maia used to enjoy with her grandfather, so she jumped at the opportunity to play again. The game also brings out her competitive side, which Jake seems to adore. He'll often lean back with his fist at his chin, watching her with those piercing dark eyes—almost as if he's studying her. Maia doesn't mind. "Watch and learn," she had told him one night, and he threw his head back laughing. The feistier she gets, the wider he grins.

Their conversations are effortless, free-flowing—albeit surface. There is still so much about Jake that Maia doesn't know. Any time she has tried asking him more detailed questions about his work, he's changed the subject. He doesn't have an accent like Lucas and Miguel. Neither does Claire, even though they are both supposedly from South America. So, where is he from? What does he fear? "So many questions," he responded with a wink. "You should try a bite of my dessert."

And so, their perfect whirlwind romance comes slightly tainted. They are drawn to each other, without a doubt. Want to spend all the time in the world together. Maia craves his touch, and his kisses are divine. But they are both guilty of holding back, hiding parts of who they are, and it seems they are both more than aware of this fact. The two are always watching each other. Trying to figure the other one out. Maia doesn't know what, but there's more to him—more than what he's willing to reveal.

There is something dark lingering beneath his surface.

And really, is Maia so different?

On a rainy afternoon, Maia visits her new favorite café, the one where Claire brought her a few months back. Once again, the patrons turn to look at her as she steps inside, but for different reasons than they did before. They are no longer sizing her up, judging her to be *less than*. She lifts her chin, and the people's heads follow as the server leads her to a table next to the window. He comes back immediately, placing a sugary bread before her.

A few migrants with monitoring bracelets pass on the sidewalk, pausing as they notice her sitting there with her hot tea and her steaming sweet bread fresh from the oven, and then they quickly continue on. Maia sets down her fork as it dawns on her...

She has become the woman on the other side of the glass.

Sipping her tea, she peers over her shoulder at the television in the corner. It's playing the news—always playing the news. Jake's name is mentioned more and more these days, and the message is always the same: the world *out there* is bad. This city needs more protection. Jake is a man of the people. Just keep your faith in Leucothea. You are safe here. *Leucothea has saved you.*

Maia gazes around the glossy, whitewashed café. Leucothea *has* saved her. Life was so dark and hard for so long, but not anymore. Jake was right—this is the good life.

It's only at night, when Maia is alone in her bed, that *they* still haunt her, reaching into her subconscious and ripping her from the cushy illusion of her life. Every night, the mysterious man and child await her in her old cabin in a drowned Leucothea. Every night, they call her to them, and she is powerless to refuse. And then, every morning, she wakes up screaming into her pillow. The emptiness they leave behind is excruciating. Hollowing her to the bone, these nightmares leave her gasping for a breath that will never fill her.

———

Jake and Maia step from his front doors hand in hand to head out for another night on the town. Once again, he looks striking in a dark suit and bow tie, while Maia is wearing her favorite black satin dress from their first dinner together.

Tonight is a celebration. Jake has pushed through Maia's paperwork, and she is now officially a citizen of Leucothea —just in time for New Years. He is taking her to one of Leucothea's finest restaurants. Located at the top of a high-rise, it has spectacular views overlooking the city.

Claire walks up the steps toward them. She and Jake address one another, but she says nothing to Maia.

Maia has given up trying to make eye contact or smiling. If Claire *is* looking at Maia, it's not a look she wants to see. Claire's aloofness has gone from cool and distant to down-right resentful. She is in love with Jake, and now Maia has ruined everything.

Later that night, sitting at an intimate candlelit table nestled against floor-to-ceiling windows, Maia gazes across the city with her chin on her fist. "I've spent my entire life in darkness. And now here I am, in a city of lights. Sometimes I still can't believe it."

"Anything is possible when you have this many people from all over the world gathered together. It's *power*: power of numbers, power to resurrect the technology of our ancestors, power of human minds and ideas and talents. It's quite simple, really. More people equals more power."

"Power over what? The world is empty."

"Oh, there are a few other civilizations up here in the Old Arctic. Two in particular that have become increasingly dangerous."

Maia arches her brow. "Really?"

"Yes, we aren't the only city that's been growing over the decades. There's one in the Old Russia that has become more of a threat in recent years. Another one to the east of us in the Old Canada called Asiaq Bay. Our precious Leucothea is sandwiched right between them."

"A *threat*? How so?"

"There are a lot of precious resources up here that need to be protected. Everything our S&R Crews have collected, our massive warehouses, our greenhouses, our electricity. Those cities have been threatening us for years, so I've been preparing our armies. Pretty soon, we will inform the people. Those other cities must be subdued. They want what we have, and they will take everything if we let them. This all needs to be protected and by great force."

"What does our president think of this?"

"President Augustus leaves it to me to take care of these issues—he trusts my judgment. I am the army general. It is my solemn duty to protect Leucothea."

Maia tilts her gaze. "So, what will you do?"

"Ah, Maia. You'll soon find out, but not yet. You just have to trust that I am a man of my people. I will do everything I can to defend what we have. This is a haven in a dark world. We have everything we could ever need. Imagine if we weren't prepared, and those other cities came in and took what is ours."

"That would be awful."

"This city and everything we are doing up here is history in the making. This is the beginning of a new humanity. This is what our children's children will read about in history books: the choices *we* made, the life *we* created. We can do anything. Claire and I have organized teams at the university to document and protect our history. I promise you, by the time you and I are old and gray, the world will forever know my name."

Maia watches him as he takes another bite of steak. He's not wrong; a city of this caliber would need to be protected. She, Lucas, and Miguel had to fight their entire journey up here just to defend their tiny backpacks. But, something in her gut is *screaming* at her.

She looks around, taking in the lighting, the music playing over the speakers, a server walking past with glasses filled with ice. "Jake, the electricity of this city..."

"You mean the enormous power making all of this possible?"

"Where does it come from?"

Jake smiles. "Renewable sources, of course."

"*Like*..."

"Oh, hell, I don't know. That's not my forte. I'm the war hero."

"You *are*?"

Anger flashes across his face. "I *will* be."

Maia swallows. *There it is.*

Jake sighs. "Maia, renewable sources. Wind, hydro, solar." He waves his hand dismissively.

Maia knows she's poking a sleeping bear, but she doesn't care. "Solar, Jake? There's no sun."

"Maia, you know what? That is a great question. A great question for you to discuss with your *guardian*, Rebecca. She takes care of all this minutia."

"I don't have a guardian anymore. I'm a citizen."

"Keep asking silly questions, and maybe that will change." He winks, then shoves another piece of steak in his mouth.

Maia sets down her fork.

He stops chewing and looks up at her. "I'm *kidding*! Maia, you know I'm kidding. Anyway, let's not ruin this romantic night with boring talk. I was joking. Too soon to joke?" He smiles.

Maia is uneasy. "No, of course not. I can take a joke."

Back at the house, Maia sits on the couch, looking up at the Christmas tree. Is this city of lights some sort of grand illusion?

Jake walks into the room, holding a small box with a red bow on top.

"*Jake*."

He sits next to her, handing her the package. "Happy New Year, Maia."

"I can't accept this. I don't have anything for you."

"Oh, don't worry about that. You've already given me the greatest gift." He lifts her chin. "Your company."

Maia smiles. "That's a little too corny, even for you."

He laughs. "You're right. You know me too well. But in all honesty, I have really enjoyed this last month together. I'm looking forward to having you around here ... *more*."

Maia looks into his dark eyes. The way he said that ... It was so peculiar. Sometimes it's like he's speaking in code.

He nudges the box. "Open it."

Maia lIfts the lid and gasps.

Her pounamu. Her beloved koru greenstone carved by her mother. Maia is stunned. Its woven flax cord is gone, now replaced by a gold necklace.

"Its string was torn." Jake takes it out of the box and clasps it behind her neck. "So, I had this chain made for you. It'll be sturdier now, less likely to break."

Maia holds it against her chest. "How did you..." she breathes. "*Where* did you?"

"I have my ways."

"I thought I lost this."

He grabs a small mirror from the coffee table and holds it up for her.

She clutches the glass, staring at her neck. This is so *unreal.* "Jake," she says, her voice trembling, "you have no idea what this means to me."

He smiles, an undeniable gaze of affection behind his dark eyes.

Maia drops the mirror and kisses him, bathed in the glow of the tree's twinkling lights.

THIRTEEN

Maia shoves aside the wooden stool, a tendril of seaweed hanging off the back, and it groans loudly against the floor. The child's giggle echoes across the empty bar, her chubby feet pattering across small puddles. She runs out the front door. Maia follows.

Out in the barren city, Maia steps over a flopping fish. It's the same fish she crosses every night, its mouth and gills opening and closing as it suffocates against the wet cement. The redheaded child rushes across the street and down a narrow brick alley. It's the same alley she always runs down, and Maia follows as she always has.

As the two wander in and out of different passageways, the child's laughter echoes in waves. Maia turns a corner and is once again met with her New Zealand cabin, the child on the front porch, reaching for the doorknob. The door opens and she slips inside.

Maia walks toward the cabin, knowing they'll both be waiting for her. But something about tonight is different. As she steps through the puddles, the icy water bites her skin.

Her breath hangs heavy in the frigid air, and she shivers. Night after night, this dream is the same, yet, she's never *felt* the cold like this. Her long white gown catches against the rough cement. She's never noticed that either.

It begins to snow. Smiling, Maia holds out her hands, watching the flakes melt into her skin.

The child's laughter pulls her attention back to the cabin. She makes her way up the creaky wooden steps, past the rocking chairs layered with fresh snow, and pushes open the door. It groans until it hits the wall.

The child stands next to the man at the fireplace. His hair is short, his shoulders broad. He turns toward the child and Maia gasps. The side of his face ... She can start to make out his features. She *knows* that face...

The man offers his hand to the child, and she wraps her tiny fingers around his. She beams up at him with trust in her gaze. Affection. And then, for the first time, she turns around.

Maia draws a sharp breath. *The child's eyes.* This is not the same little girl she followed around the pond outside Miguel's cabin. That child was Maia; their eyes were the same. This little girl smiles, and her chubby cheeks round under two *blue* eyes.

She is holding an exotic wildflower Maia has never seen before. Its yellow petals haven't opened yet. Tightly coiled into themselves, they give the flower the look of a pinwheel. The child holds it out to Maia. "Mum."

The air is knocked from Maia's lungs. *What did she just say?*

Inside the cabin, it begins to snow.

Maia stumbles forward, reaching for the child. That face ... That gorgeous, innocent little face. She finally understands; she has always recognized that face as a *part* of her own, but not her own.

Maia pushes a chair aside, and the legs drag against the floor. Startled, the man looks up. He turns to face her, and she staggers backward. Her hand against her chest, she is breathless.

Just like the first time they met.

Just like the first time she saw him round the corner of his porch.

He smiles, dimple showing. "Hello, *little bird*."

Sitting next to the fireplace, Maia's eyes glaze over as she stares at the flames. Tears drip from her chin, but she doesn't make a sound.

Miguel. That man has always been *Miguel*. She wipes her cheeks, rubbing her hands on her robe. It was all so real. *He* was so real, standing so close she could nearly touch him. Her heart sinks, and she closes her eyes. With his dreadlocks gone, his brown eyes and the sharp lines of his jaw were accentuated.

He was more handsome than ever.

She folds onto her knees, holding her head in her hands. And that child was *her own*?

It was snowing inside that cabin.

Over and over again, Miguel's face flashes through her mind. Every time she sees it, her pain mixes with even more anger. His voice. She had forgotten the sound of his voice, much to her own horror. Now it's all she can hear, and it's more haunting than ever.

She is so *angry*. She had finally gotten used to the idea that she'd never see him again. She had laid him to rest. She had laid it *all* to rest and had moved on! This is her life now. This is all she's ever wanted. And she no longer has to fight *so damn hard* for *everything*. She's finally here, living in Leucothea with a large community of people, and her life is amazing.

For the most part.

As hard as Maia tries, she still can't ignore the distinct feeling that something isn't right. And too many questions are typically met with defiance by her charming beau up in that mansion.

Are Miguel and this child going to haunt Maia for the rest of her life? The fractured pieces, everything she's worked so hard to bury—they all rain down on her now. And they cut deep.

She walks to the floor-length mirror. She is finally free. She has started researching classes at the university next fall. Jake promised they'd find her a good job. She's about to start looking for her own place in the city. Jake has tried to insist that she stay up here, but she wants her independence. They'll continue to see each other, but she needs to find her own way.

She holds her hand against her pounamu. These last few days, she has constantly held it against her chest, still doubting that it's actually there. She's so *relieved* to have it back around her neck. Although, it's hard to ignore that it's on a gold chain and not a woven flax cord. It should be on flax. Can she find that up here?

It's also hard to ignore the timing of it all. Jake had apparently only learned about Maia's presence in Leucothea a few months ago after Claire ran into her on the street.

Maia has been in Leucothea for a year and a half.

Her pounamu has been missing since she arrived.

Springtime settles upon the city of Leucothea, and the sun once again illuminates the endless dark skies. Flowers unfurl from frosty grounds. Chirping birds flutter in the trees.

The change of seasons brings about another shift as well. Jake's work has kept him incredibly busy lately, so his and Maia's nightly dates have turned into once or twice a week. No longer distracted, Maia finds Jake's absence in her life has only strengthened her uncertainty about their relationship. She has decided the time has come to get her own place, so she has had Orson take her into the city more and more to look for apartments. Jake has not been subtle about his disappointment in this.

The romantic tension between them has also been growing by the day. Jake promised to take things slow, but they have been dating a few months now, and his patience is wearing thin. Despite their steamy kisses, Maia has refused to go any further.

Late last night, Jake walked her down his long driveway back to her guest suite. She knew he wanted to come inside, but she kissed him goodnight on her doorstep. As she was closing the door, he said, "I thought you weren't afraid of me."

She opened it again, facing him. "I'm not."

He shook his head, barely noticeable in the dark night. "Then why are you pushing me away?"

"I'm ... I'm not—"

"You are."

"I just ... I feel like I barely know you. I ask you questions, and you change the subject. You're holding back, and I won't give myself to a stranger."

He blew out a long breath. "Okay, what do you want to know?"

"Where are you *actually* from?"

He stared at her, considering. "Montana."

She leaned against the doorframe, her arms crossed. "So ... *not* South America."

He looked at his feet for a moment, then back up at her. "No."

"Why did you lie?"

"Sometimes it's necessary as a man in my position to withhold information when traveling."

"But we're not traveling anymore."

He nodded, his hands in his pockets. "I'm sorry I lied. I was planning on telling you once we started dating, but ... I need to keep the details of my life private at the beginning of relationships. There have been so many women ... So many *empty* dates. Surely, you understand. I don't want to reveal too much until I know it's safe. But you and I ... I believe we're moving beyond that now. So, I'll tell you anything you want to know."

"What—"

"Your turn, Maia," he cut in. "Tell me something."

She shrugged. "What would you like to know?"

He tilted his gaze. "You're hiding something—about yourself. Something ... *significant*."

She swallowed, grateful for the cover of darkness. "Well, those questions aren't exactly equal, are they?"

"*Maia*."

"I'm not hiding anything. You already know everything about me." She grimaced inwardly at her epic lie. But she couldn't. She just couldn't.

His response surprised her—broke her heart, actually.

He hung his head, briefly shaking it, and then he walked away.

"Jake?"

He turned around, pausing in the middle of the dark driveway, his figure highlighted in the moon's light. "You say it's me. But it's not me, Maia. It's *you*. You're the one who's holding back."

She stepped from the doorway. "What makes you think that?"

"Just ... a hunch," he said softly, and then he turned and walked away.

Maia watched him for a moment, and then she went inside.

After closing the door, she leaned her head against it. *Is she pushing him away? She wants to be with him—she does. But she can't. There is still so much she doesn't know about him, so much he doesn't know about her.*

And she can't ignore that deep down, she's just not sure anymore.

About any of it.

This morning, Maia has met Jake in the main house for breakfast. He seems edgy today. His mind is elsewhere, the furrow between his brow deep with concentration as he looks over scattered papers at the opposite end of the table.

Maia sets down her tea. "Jake, there was a woman I was in orientation with. Her name was Dawn. She was highly educated, asked a lot of questions."

He sips his coffee without looking up. "And?"

"And ... I don't think she was allowed into the city because of that. I actually don't think some of the most uneducated women in orientation were either. Where did they go?"

A server brings in a plate of breakfast for each of them: eggs, bacon, toast. Maia shoves hers away.

"So many people who arrive here can't read or write. The uneducated need to be put in certain jobs," Jake says with a shrug, scrutinizing his food. "Especially those who clearly wouldn't be able to acclimate to a city of the future. You know, with our technology. But they make for great minions." He picks up a piece of bacon, tears it with his teeth. "And there's a fine line with the educated. Some need to learn to keep quiet. Some ask too many questions." He shoots her a dry look.

She ignores it. "Minions?"

"Yes, Maia. *Minions*." He sits back in his chair, annoyed.

Here we go.

"Look around you," he says. "Who do you think grows and packages all the food you and thousands of others are gobbling down every single day? All these people want is more, *more*, MORE. Who do you think takes care of all that waste we throw away or are flushing down our working toilets—some of the only working toilets in the *world*? Who do you think goes into the dangerous world *out there* to collect all the supplies we have to ration to the greedy people in this city? Or works on the rigs to deliver all the electricity you're enjoying?"

"*Rigs*?" She's pushing him, but she doesn't care.

He glares at her, slowly chewing his food. "Maia, you're like a toddler. Enough with the questions." His laugh sounds irritated. Forced. "I know! Why don't you let Orson take you shopping? Pick Renee up and treat yourselves. Or go for a walk in the woods. I thought that would be the first thing you'd want to do with our new spring daylight." He takes another drink of his coffee.

"I guess I haven't been in the mood."

He sets down his cup, and it clinks loudly in the saucer. "Well, maybe I need to help *get* you in the mood."

Maia isn't sure what they are talking about anymore.

"I insist. Go. *Now*. Enjoy the few hours of daylight we have. Orson will take you wherever you'd like to go. You can tell me about it over dinner. You'll join me tonight."

Maia's temper flares. Since when have his invitations become orders? She pushes her chair back and stands from the table. "We'll see about that."

———

Alone in her backyard, Maia peers up at the tree line and sighs. Jake knows how much she loves the woods. It's come up repeatedly in conversation. And he's right; it's shocking she hasn't stepped foot inside them. But with all the cameras around, she hasn't dared take the risk. After so long away from nature, she doesn't trust herself. What if she can't hold back? What if she's caught on one of Jake's cameras using her powers? Or worse, what if she tries to use them but finds they are no longer there? She can't bear the thought.

But it's not only that. Denial is a fickle beast, one best left unquestioned and unprovoked. If she steps inside those woods, she knows she may be reminded of things she's fought very hard to forget. Of the woman she would be—the woman she *should* be—but is no longer. And that's *terrifying*.

But she can't hide from herself forever.

She glances over her shoulder as another drone zips across the lawn behind her, heading down the driveway toward Jake's mansion. She just needs to get far enough into the forest and away from his estate. There are acres upon acres of woods on these cliffs. She knows for a fact that he doesn't have cameras everywhere—mostly just along the perimeters, and they are easy to spot. She waits for the drone to disappear down the road. And then she *runs*.

Racing between the trees, she breathes in the rich scent of earth and smiles.

How I've missed you.

She runs harder—she runs as fast as she can. What is this feeling? It's like she can't get away quick enough. She glances up at the branches. There's a camera up there. Over there too.

She picks up her pace, using every last ounce of her strength to get as deep into the woods as she can. Weaving between the trunks, she feels the cool forest air kissing her skin, and she jumps over another fallen branch, her landing cushioned by a carpet of pine needles. Bathed in the echo of trilling birds, she breaks through beams of sun and flittering bugs. It's been so long since she's felt this alive, and she fights the urge to scream.

She doesn't need to use her powers. Just being in this wild forest is enough to set her soul on fire.

Stumbling into a clearing, she stops to catch her breath. A great pine has broken through the canopy, soaring high into the sky. She wanders up to it and places her hands against its bark, her heart *aching*. She can barely hear its whispers.

Glancing around, she searches the trees, scouring the branches for little black boxes with red lights on top. There's nothing. She blows out a sigh.

Finally alone.

Standing before the ancient tree, she places her forehead against it, feeling its life pulsing beneath her fingers. "I can still feel you," she whispers. "I'm sorry. I can still feel you."

She gazes up at the gentle giant, and the energy of the Earth appears, pulsing up and down the trunk. It wants to show her something.

"No, it's too dangerous," she breathes.

A branch slowly lowers itself before her, hovering like the open hand of a child. She shakes her head. *Too dangerous*. But it doesn't move. It patiently waits, breaking her heart. She glances over her shoulder, straining to listen for the hum of a drone, then inspects the forest again.

There is nothing. She is completely alone.

She looks back at the branch, reaching for her. Waiting for her.

She can't *not* take it.

Despite herself, she extends her hand, smiling with relief as the pine needles caress the tip of her finger. Touching this tree is like *breathing* again. The branch slowly wraps itself around her hand, and another lowers to the forest floor. She steps on top, and they lift her from the ground. More branches swing around like countless offering hands while others curve into a winding staircase. Together, they gently guide Maia toward the canopy.

At the top, the cool Arctic wind whips at her hair. Far off, great clouds of smoke plume from the horizon.

The Earth is always burning.

A raven soars overhead, showing Maia his view. He flies alongside the walls bordering Leucothea, lined with heavy artillery and pacing armed guards. Then he travels far beyond the city, outside its crews of firefighters and into the barren lands of the Old Arctic, revealing a dark terrain outside their beloved city of lights.

Maia covers her mouth. Scores of people have been crowded into shantytowns. Destitute. Dirty. Living in horrific conditions and eating toxic food. A gaunt woman with sunken cheeks sits on a stoop outside her tin hut, rocking a baby whose skin has become tinged blue from fertilizer. Fertilizer used to grow food for the elite of Leucothea.

The New System's minions.

There are thousands of them, living under the illusion that if they just work hard enough, they may someday join the city that will save them. Armed guards surround the encampments, controlling the masses with weapons and brute force. These people have signed a contract. These people *owe* Leucothea. Those who disobey often disappear in the middle of the night, pulled from their homes, sending a deadly message to their families left behind, quivering in terror.

Leucothea, this beacon of light in a dark world, has been built on the backs of slaves.

Far off in the distance, there are endless fields of burning oil. The machines pump up and down, up and down, one after the next. Burning, burning, *burning*. Vast slicks of spilled oil slither in streams across the horizon, with blackened animals in glossy coats crawling through the muck.

The precious lights of Leucothea are not being powered by clean resources but with oil. The Arctic once hid billions of barrels of it under its ice. Once everything fell apart, it was all there for the taking. And Leucothea wants it *all*.

Suddenly, Maia understands everything Jake and his New System have been working so hard to do. The growing city in Canada to the east and the vast metropolis in Russia to the west aren't threats. *Leucothea* is the threat, and the few remaining civilizations know it. They don't want to take

Leucothea's supplies; they have been pleading with it to *cease and desist*.

Leucothea has resurrected borders and war from the dead. It has been growing dangerous armies, constantly feeding its people lies:

The world out there is a terrible place. Those cities are a threat. We must protect Leucothea above all else.

As the raven soars, Maia can see vast armies preparing. *Jake's* armies. They are going to surround those other civilizations, not only robbing them of their precious resources, but of their *people*.

The more people we have, the more power.

Leucothea has risen from the ashes of a burning world and is now breeding the most dangerous thing on Earth.

A lie.

FOURTEEN

The tree tenderly wraps itself around a quivering Maia and gently lowers her back to the earth. As she steps onto the ground, she releases the last branch like the hand of an old friend, and it slowly repositions itself high above her head.

A slow, exaggerated clap sounds behind her, and Maia whirls around. Jake is leaning against a tree, shaking his head. The smile on his face makes her blood run cold. "Absolutely incredible, Maia. Thank you. I *knew* it."

"Jake." Maia looks around. "What..." She forces a smile. "What are you doing here?"

He approaches and she backs into the tree. Grabbing her shoulders, he leans in and says, "You have no idea how long I've been waiting to see that."

Feeling betrayed, Maia looks up at the old pine behind her. It would have known. The trees have always warned her, protected her from danger. It would have known she wasn't alone. How *could* it?

Its tender whispers wash over her. Because it had to. It *had* to show her.

"Maia?" Jake's voice draws her back to him. "Before you do or say anything, you should know we aren't alone. Guys?"

Dozens of men with guns step into the clearing, and Maia looks around, terrified.

"Don't be afraid," Jake whispers, still holding her. "I won't let anything happen to you."

She glares at him.

"Now, don't look at me like that," Jake says, tilting his head.

"You're a *liar*."

"I am *not*. Well..." He gazes skyward, nodding. "Okay, *some* things I lied about. But I never lied about how I feel about you."

"Screw you!" Maia screams, and Jake's men raise their guns. He lifts his hand, and they lower them. She looks at them, then back at Jake. "What are you going to do? *Shoot* me?"

"Maia, the last thing I want to do is hurt you. Those are tranquilizer guns. Well ... most of them anyway. Which, can you blame me? We both know you can have a *bit* of a temper." He raises his brow.

"It was all a lie, wasn't it? Every last bit of it," she whispers.

Jake's hardened demeanor softens. "Not all of it." He grabs her face and kisses her. She shoves him and he stumbles backward, glaring at her from over his shoulder. "I'm getting really *sick* of this game," he growls.

Maia glances between Jake and his men, her heart in her throat. Their guns are pointed, ready to fire. With Jake out of the way, at least a dozen red dots now scatter across her chest. Lightheaded, she's finding it hard to breathe. "How ... how..."

"More questions—I should have expected that," Jake says, and he approaches her. "Let's start from the beginning, shall we? Do you remember back on my ship outside of LA, Claire and I were trying to get you to calm down."

Maia closes her eyes. She knows exactly what he's going to say.

"You wanted another raft so you could go chase after your little *thief* boyfriend. I was holding you, and you looked at me. Do you remember?"

She peers up at him.

He grabs her shoulders and leans inches from her face. "You said, '*Let me go.*' And your eyes did this really *fucked up* thing, Maia. Something *far* beyond the scope of what any human eyes could do. And I knew. I knew from that very moment that you were powerful. It just took a really long time to get you to *crack*." He throws her to the ground. "Take her to my house—the main house, not the bunker. She and I need to have a chat."

Maia is sitting on the couch, wringing one hand inside the other. The men have placed her in cuffs—*just as a precaution*, Jake had said.

Jake is pacing the floor before her. There are guards with guns *everywhere*. Claire is here too, standing in the corner by a window with her arms crossed, refusing to make eye contact.

"I know there are a lot of men with guns around, but you need to understand," Jake says, stopping to look at her, "*nothing* will happen if you remain calm. Am I making myself clear?"

Maia glares at him.

"Maia? *Answer* me."

She nods once.

"Good." He rubs his chin, stopping at the window, and then he turns to face her. "Well, I think it goes without saying, this does not change how I feel about you. It doesn't change anything I've said. I still want to be with you."

Maia swallows the bile coming up from her throat. Her eyes cut to Claire, now scowling at her.

"But you know, we've got a few things to sort out." Jake drags a chair before her and sits, placing her knees between his. He leans in and opens his mouth to speak, but then shakes his head and stands. "No, no, I can't sit."

He paces the floor. "I knew you were coming. I knew for a *long* time. You," he says, wagging his finger at her with a wicked grin across his face, "you've got a fair bit of blood on your hands—*bravo*, by the way. But you also let a lot of men live, and those men have talked. Those men have talked to *my* men, told them these grand stories about this stunning —albeit crazy—redhead who could command the wind and the trees and the *wolves*?! Oh yes, they've been talking about you. You think I don't know about all those barricades leading up to our city? They're great, really. They weed out the weak, who would only suck off our system. Plus, they've given us some great supplies in exchange for some of our cheapest food and liquor." He stops, turning to look at her. "There've also been reports of tigers?"

Maia's stomach clenches. She fights a reaction.

"Yes, I thought they were extinct, but they seem to be doing quite well nowadays. I suppose our ancestors *loved* their exotic pets. We've got some strange creatures wandering the woods. Anyway, a few tigers have gathered around the walls of our city for some reason. I've actually gotten a new rug from one of them."

Maia looks up at him in horror.

"*There's* a reaction. Good, okay—something about tigers. You can tell me later." He nods at someone behind her, and they bring him a glass of water. He takes a sip, then holds it up to Maia. "Want some? We've already kissed, so we don't have to worry about germs." He winks.

There is something seriously wrong with this man.

"Okay, I hate seeing you so upset," Jake continues, "so I'll cut straight to the chase. I know you have powers, Maia. *Incredible* powers that will, without a doubt, make Leucothea the most powerful nation to have ever existed on the planet. I want you to join me as my partner—well, someday my wife—and we will run this nation together. President Augustus will be stepping down soon, and I will be taking his place. You will be the most powerful woman in the world, leading the most powerful *nation* in the world, next to me, the most powerful man in the world."

"*No.*"

"Wait—I'm not done. I may need you from time to time, to you know ... *deal* with things. But for the most part, you will live like a queen. You will be written into the history books as a goddess. You will never want for anything. Do you understand what I'm saying to you? I am literally offering you the world on a platter."

But she *is* the world.

"Soon, the entire Arctic will be ours—both north and south. It is the only livable land left on this planet, and I—and my offspring, thanks to you—will rule over it. We will continue to give our people the best lives they could possibly live. But, as you know, it will all need to be protected. This is where you come in." Jake sits before her. He leans in close, saying very quietly, "You belong here, Maia. You belong with *me*. I know this. *You* know this. *I* am the reason you have always felt called here."

Maia looks at him in shock. The only person she had ever spoken to about her dreams was Renee, and that was in the privacy of their living room. "You were spying on me."

He sits back in his chair and shrugs, fighting a smile. "Only a little."

"You…" Maia says, her voice quivering, "are *evil*."

Jake stands. Grabbing his chair, he chucks it across the room. It smashes against a window, shattering glass across the floor. Claire stands next to it with her hand over her mouth.

Jake closes his eyes, breathing deeply. "I … am saving … *thousands* of people's lives! I am saving their *children's* lives who would have never made it past the age of *one*! I am giving these people a life unlike anything found anywhere on Earth! How does this make *me* the bad guy?"

"You are building this civilization on the backs of slaves. Making them sign contracts they can't read, on terms they'll never be able to fulfill, forcing them to live in deplorable conditions outside the city gates, just so the people inside can live 'the good life.' This entire civilization is an *illusion*! You are lying to everyone and simultaneously destroying what little hope we have left for this planet!"

"Look around you! The mass extinction has already happened! It's *done*! This world is only going to get hotter. Half the Earth is *burning*. BURNING! It's always on fire! Yes, fossil fuels have contributed to that, but they have also significantly raised the standard of living for *centuries*! Global warming didn't wipe out humans—a *virus* did!"

"Yes! A virus unleashed by *global warming*!"

"Maia, in all those books you've read, have you ever educated yourself on the chaos theory? You can't predict the future, but you can give yourself a shot in life by controlling what happens *now*. Do you think just because most of the people are gone that the weather will suddenly calm?"

"Obviously, I don't think that."

"You think the oceans will suddenly fill with non-toxic fish? The endless pieces of 'disposable' plastic that our ancestors chucked away for hundreds of years will suddenly disappear?"

Maia's temper flairs, and the ground begins to tremble.

Jake stops pacing, twisting where he stands. "Are you ... are *you* doing this? You stop it, or I'll have you shot."

Maia inhales to calm herself, and the ground slowly stills. Jake's men eye each other nervously, and she suppresses her smile.

"I'm not going to fight with you," Jake says with a sigh. "The reality is, this planet has *always* been a dog-eat-dog world. Sure, some things were really good for *some* nations, but do you think any of that mattered to the billions of people around the world who were starving? When the wealthy countries continued to burn fossil fuels and the weather *really* turned on them, who do you think suffered the most? The poor. It has always been the way—survival of the fittest. Now is no exception. You are fooling yourself if you think otherwise."

"I will not help you," Maia says through her teeth, "extort ... *innocent* people, destroy the planet, and wage a war. This city is everything that is wrong with the world, all wrapped up in one glamorous lie."

"You are wrong. *My* city is the only good thing left on this crappy planet. People have never been happier since The End. You think you'll be some sort of hero by taking that away? You think the people will *thank* you for that, Maia? You think they'll *celebrate* the fact that you plunged them back into darkness? Back into high infant mortality? Back into starvation and sickness and crime?"

"There's got to be another way. There's always another way."

"Don't be ridiculous. Also, the people of Leucothea will side with me, I guarantee it—including those slaving away in the fields. Their lives may not be glamorous, but they are being fed and protected, which is far better than anything they had *out there*. They want strong leadership and protection, and that's exactly what I've given them." He stands before her, his hands on his hips. "Uncuff her."

Maia looks up at him, and the soldiers around the room glance at one another.

"NOW!"

A guard rushes up and unlocks her cuffs. He stumbles over his feet as he backs away.

"I'm going to give you a few days to think this over," Jake says. "I know you think you have some compelling arguments, but you really need to think about my offer. You and I ... We are *meant* to be together, Maia. You and I will rule the Arctic."

"You're delusional."

"You're angry." He reaches for her, and she slaps his hand away. He smiles. "And I don't blame you, but don't be stupid. Think it over. I trust you'll make the right decision."

Maia stands, her face inches from Jake's, and the guards lift their guns. "I want to go *home*," she growls.

"What home?" Jake scoffs. "You have no home."

She glares at him.

"Whatever. Have Orson take you wherever your little heart desires ... within the walls of Leucothea, of course."

A guard steps forward. "But, sir—"

"This woman is my *partner*, not my prisoner," Jake snaps.

Maia storms out of the room,

"Don't make me regret this!" Jake yells after her. "Maia?! You can't hide from me! I'm *everywhere*!"

FIFTEEN

Maia peers out of the car's back window as they travel down the dark and winding road. There are three pairs of headlights following closely behind them, with a new set joining at the back. A handful of drones are hovering in the sky, their spotlights flooding the inside of the car with a bright, inescapable light. Maia knows *he'll* be on the other side of their feeds, watching everything play out on a screen from somewhere deep inside his mansion.

An armed guard is sitting in the front seat. Maia and a nervous Orson make eye contact through his rearview mirror, but he is quick to look away. He'll be wondering the same thing she's wondering. Probably the same thing they are all wondering.

What is she thinking? Has she gone mad?

She drops her head in her hands. So hard to think straight. What just *happened*? Jake knows about her powers; he has known the entire time. He wants to use her to take over the Arctic. To enslave and control. To dominate. To *destroy*. She leans back, her head falling against the leather. She won't do it. She won't.

She twists in her seat, peering once again at the headlights behind them, then flips around. Her car is surrounded. And as long as she's inside, it will remain surrounded. The guard next to Orson has been slowly loading his gun, holding it up in the drones' light pouring through the windows. A lovely reminder.

What can she do? If she can just get to her old apartment and talk to Renee. Together, they can come up with a plan —*after* Maia locates the recording devices hidden inside. She looks down at her pack. In her state of panic, she ripped random clothing off hangers and shoved them in a bag. She grabbed Lucas's ashes and a knife from the kitchen, but that's all she has. She doesn't have the right supplies to navigate the wilderness outside of Leucothea. It took her and Lucas *months* to find what they needed for their travels.

She'll figure it out. There is always a way.

Jake said she can take her time to think about this. She'll spend the next few days planning an escape so she can warn the other cities. This will undoubtedly accelerate an already impending war, but it will at least give them a fighting chance to save themselves from a lifetime of horrors at the New System's hands.

But are Leucothea's soldiers not also innocent? They would be honored to fight for their city, believing it to be a cause worthy of dying for. It would be so easy to trust what the New System's leaders have been telling them. Jake has always broadcasted himself to be a man of the people. He believes this, and so do they. But they shouldn't have to die for that.

First things first. Maia just needs to get out of Leucothea

and away from Jake. Miguel's face flashes through her mind. All she wants to do is run to him, but she could never risk his life like that.

Orson pulls up to Maia's old apartment. The car barely comes to a stop before she whips open her door and races across the lawn. She glances over her shoulder as three more of Jake's cars line the street. One of his men has already stepped outside his open door. She stops dead in her tracks as her eyes meet his.

Her stalker.

The man who has been following Maia since she arrived, leaning against buildings and waiting on street corners, has just stepped out of one of Jake's cars. *Of course* he was one of Jake's men. Maia shakes her head as she glares at him, and he places his elbows on the car's open door, the gun in his hand glinting in the streetlight.

She runs to the side of the building and up the metal staircase. Three drones now hover in the sky. Bursting into her old apartment, she slams the door behind her, locking it.

Renee jumps from the couch. "*Maia!*" she screams, her hand at her chest. "Oh my God, you *scared* me!" She chuckles, but as she takes in Maia's frenzied state, her smile fades. "What's wrong?"

"*Shhh!*" Maia steps into the middle of the room. *Where to start?* She rips a picture off the wall, checking behind it. Nothing. And then another—nothing. One after the next, she tears the frames from their hooks, throwing them to the ground. There's nothing there.

"Are you crazy?! What are you doing?"

"*Shhh! Please!*" Maia pulls the blanket from the couch. She grabs the cushions and rips out their stuffing. Nothing.

"Maia, you're scaring me."

She falls to her hands and knees, searching beneath the kitchen table. Nothing. Opening the cupboards, she ransacks their contents, frantically hunting for something —*anything*—that looks out of place. *Nothing.* She scans the room. Does he have them in the walls?!

"Maia!"

Maia grabs Renee's shoulders, then puts a finger to her lips. She mouths, *He's listening.*

"Who?"

Jake.

Renee rolls her eyes. "Don't be silly. Did you two get in a fight?"

Maia looks around. Where can they talk? She flicks on the television, turns the volume up full blast.

Renee covers her ears. "Maia?!"

Maia grabs Renee's hand, pulling her to the bathroom. She slams the door behind her and turns on both the shower and the faucet.

"Maia, you're really—"

"Whispers, Renee!"

"You're freaking me out," Renee says aloud, ignoring Maia's plea. "Are you in trouble?"

"Jake has devices all around this place, recording everything we say," Maia whispers. "There is so much I need to tell you," she gasps, holding her head. "I don't know where to begin."

Renee crosses her arms. "Well? Spit it out."

"This city is dangerous. Everything they have been telling us is a lie. I'm going to leave, and you should come with me."

Renee blinks slowly. "Have you been drinking?"

Maia grabs her shoulders, shaking her. "Renee, this city isn't what you think it is. It's ... it's..." Lost for words, she takes a step back as it dawns on her: Renee isn't going to believe her.

Jake's voice rings through her memory. *The people of Leucothea will side with me, I guarantee it.*

"It's ... it's all a ... *lie*," Maia says slowly, reading Renee's steely face.

Renee rolls her eyes. "Maia," she says, annoyed. "Use your words. What do you mean?"

"They're burning oil ... destroying the Arctic ... starting a war ... the workers outside the city are ... slaves..."

Renee laughs.

Maia's deflated. She knows she sounds crazy. "I'm escaping, and you should come with," she says, her tone flat. This isn't going well.

Renee exhales a long breath through her nose. "You don't need to *escape*. Just go to the gates and leave."

"It's ... it's not like that."

"It is, actually. We are free to leave whenever we want. But you'll be on your own. There's no way I'm leaving. I'm nearly finished with my contract, and then I can move out of this shithole."

"They're lying to you."

"No, they're not! They are always telling us how important we are."

Maia holds Renee's face. "They're *lying* to you and you know it. You'll be stuck in that tracking bracelet forever. How long has it already been? And they keep extending your time!"

The hum of a motor sounds on the other side of the frosted bathroom window. The two women turn to find a drone just outside, and then the green bulb on Renee's monitoring bracelet turns to a flashing red. Renee stares at it, her mouth open. She peers up at Maia, her eyes filling with tears, and then her face contorts to rage. "*Maia*! What have you done?!"

"That isn't me!"

Renee shoves her, screaming, "No! I won't let you wreck this for me! Not *everyone* has a famous boyfriend who can save them!" She opens the door and runs into the living room, flicking off the television. "Get out of here! Go ruin someone else's life!" She picks up a pillow and chucks it at Maia.

"Renee, please!"

Renee charges, pushing Maia into the wall as tears stream down her face. She whips open the front door, shoving Maia with repeated forceful blows until she stumbles over the threshold.

"Please, don't do this!" Maia screams.

Renee kicks Maia's bag outside and slams the door closed. Maia drops her head against it, and she begs into the wood. "Renee, *please*? You are my only friend."

Renee slides down the other side, sobbing, and the deadbolt clicks shut.

Maia steps away from the door, stunned. A drone is hovering behind her, just outside the porch. She screams and reaches for it, but it flies off.

She looks around, her breath in clouds. A misty rain has coated the cold Arctic city, and it dawns on her that she is completely alone. She has no one to turn to. Nowhere to go.

As a citizen, she is apparently allowed to walk up to the gates and leave. She closes her eyes, and she knows—there's no way Jake's men will let her get that far. But she can't stay outside on this cold metal platform forever, and there's no way she'll go back to Jake's mansion. She'll have to start walking and hope the answer comes to her somewhere along the way. Jake said she could take her time to think about this. That she's his partner, not his prisoner. His men can't stop her from walking.

She lifts her pack onto her back and kisses the tips of her fingers, placing them against the door. Then she slinks down the dark steps along the side of the building, thankful no one ever bothered to fix the lights.

The streets, however, are brightly lit, and there are cameras *everywhere*. Maia peeks around the corner. Three of Jake's cars still line the street. That's just what she can see; there'll be more. She sneaks to the rear of the building—two more cars are waiting out back. She sighs, leaning against the brick. Trapped.

Footsteps sound down the metallic stairs, and she whirls around. *Bud*. She rushes up to him and grabs his coat, yanking him into the shadows.

"*Whoa!*" he yells with his hands in the air. "Oh, hey ... *Maia*! Oh, *HEY*!" he shouts, and Maia grimaces, *shushing* him. He doesn't notice. "You're like ... *really* famous now!" He covers his mouth, tapping her shoulder. "You're that army man's girlfriend! You looked real pretty on the news."

"*Shhh!* Thanks," Maia whispers. "Hey, can you do me a huge favor?"

"SURE!" Bud yells.

"*Shhh!*" Maia glances around, then back at Bud, who remains utterly oblivious to her state of panic. "Can I borrow your coat and hat?"

"Oh man, Maia ... I *donno*. It's real cold out here."

Maia looks around in a panic. "I'll trade you? I'll trade!" She drops her pack to the ground. What did she throw in here? She searches through the clothing. "So many nice things in here. Look!" She pulls out her black satin dress. *Definitely won't be needing this.*

"Oh shit, you was in the news in that. It was all every-body could talk about."

"Yes! Yes, you ... you can have it. You can *sell* it! That would be fun! Right? You could get a lot of coins for this! Buy yourself *ten* coats and hats."

Bud nods. He snatches the dress, burying his face in it. "It smells nice too," he mumbles.

"Yes, real nice," Maia whispers, putting her pack back on. "Can I have your coat and hat?"

"This is strange, but okay." He takes off his hat, and Maia slips it on. She quickly braids her hair as she peers over her shoulder and shoves the braid beneath the cap. Bud takes off his coat and she rips it from his hands. The zipper is broken, but the snaps still close. She puts it on over her backpack.

"It's really big on you," Bud says, shaking his head. "It don't look right."

"Okay, last favor, I swear," Maia whispers. "Can you go back inside?"

"*What*? I'm working the late shift. I don't wanna git in trouble."

"I know you don't, but I will ... What else can I do?" She anxiously peers between the shadows of the yard. "Oh, Bud, *please*?! I need this from you so badly."

"Are you okay? Is somebody tryin' to hurt you?"

"No, it's okay. I just need you to go inside for *five* minutes. Please? Can you do that for me?"

"Okay, I guess," he says, his shoulders slumped, and he turns away, holding tightly to her dress.

"Thank you, you're the best!" she whispers at his back. She looks around, checking for drones. They're still hovering above, but she's pretty sure they wouldn't have been able to view her little exchange with Bud in the shadows.

Maia inhales, preparing herself. This is ballsy—stupid even—but it just might work. It could, at the very least, buy her some time and get these thugs off her back. If she doesn't want to look suspicious, she'll have to walk straight out in front of the cars. Nice and slow. Head down, hat pulled over her face, limping—just like Bud. They know he lives here. They know he works the late shift. That he'll be walking out of his apartment right about now, like he does most nights.

And if they stop her, she'll play cool and act like she's going for a walk—nothing wrong with that. Jake made it very clear that she is not his prisoner.

She peeks around the corner. A stray cat is walking down the sidewalk, in and out of the streetlamps' cones of light. The cars still idle with their headlights off. She takes a deep breath, and then she steps into the light. Her arm hanging to the side, she tilts her right foot in, walking on its outside edge. It's cool enough to see her breath, so she focuses on exhaling nice and slow. Limping across the yard, she makes her way toward the path alongside the cars. A drone hums above. She keeps her head down.

Turning down the sidewalk, she shuffles past the first car. Nothing happens. She walks past the second car. Is this working?

This is working.

The window of the third car lowers as she passes, and she picks up her pace.

"Excuse me?" A man's voice calls from inside the vehicle.

She keeps walking. A car door slams shut behind her. And another. She keeps her focus on the ground, her heart hammering against her chest. Does she run? She glances over her shoulder to find two men stealthily approaching.

"Stop! *Now!*" one of them yells.

"I'm just going for a walk!" she says, and he lifts his gun. *Shit.*

She dives to the ground, rolling across the pavement, and then jumps to her feet, sprinting between two cars. "*Help!*" she screams. "Someone, *please—*" She glances over her shoulder, and another guard slams into her.

"Now!" someone shouts, and he smothers her face with a wet cloth.

She fights against his embrace, and her world fades to black.

SIXTEEN

When Maia opens her eyes, she is lying on the couch in Jake's great room. He comes into focus, sitting on a chair across from her. His fist is at his closed mouth, his dark eyes pinning her.

Holding her throbbing head, she sits up, surprised to find she's not in cuffs. Jake continues to watch her, saying nothing. What is that look on his face?

Disappointment.

There is a caramel liquor in the crystal glass in his hand. He takes a sip, his piercing eyes never once leaving hers. A few of his men stand around holding guns, but they do not point them at her. Claire is in her little corner with her arms crossed, looking out the window. The room is silent. Subdued.

"It's called chloroform," Jake says, startling Maia. "We've got stockrooms full of it. Along with stun guns. Tranquilizers. I told my guards to use the chloroform. It can make you feel sick, but it's the least painful option."

She lowers her feet to the ground, staring at him. It feels

like they are playing chess again, only now, she doesn't know whose move it is.

"Everyone out," Jake says, holding Maia in his gaze.

The men and Claire pile out of the room, leaving just the two of them, and it is silent for a while. Finally, he speaks. "We had a good time, didn't we? I mean, I certainly did."

Maia doesn't know how to answer that.

"Maia?"

She leans back, crossing her legs. "We did. But in the end, it was all ... *tainted*."

He nods, looking down. He lifts his glass to take a sip, then stops. "Bourbon?"

She shakes her head.

"No. No, it's whisky you want," he says, and he takes a drink. "I know. I know everything about you." He sets the glass on the table next to him. "I knew the minute you paddled up to our gates. Had my men looking out for you for quite some time. Truth be told, I've been watching you every day since. That's a *long* time to be watching another person." He leans forward, resting his elbows on his knees. "I became ... *addicted* ... to you."

For a moment, Maia forgets to breathe.

"I know about your dreams," he continues. "I know about your hopes and your fears—at least those you've been willing to admit out loud. Everything you told me over our candlelit dinners, I already knew. And I *know*, beyond a shadow of a doubt, that you and I are meant to be together."

She's heard this before; she's said it as well. And they've been wrong—every last one of them. "Jake," she says very quietly. "I think there may be something seriously wrong with you."

He laughs, and in this terrifying moment, Maia is grateful for his smile. "Yes, well..." He leans back. Reaching for his glass on the table, he twists it between his fingers. "I think I could say the same about you."

She looks away, and he continues. "I don't blame you for trying to run. In fact, I expected it. But now you can see exactly what will happen. I am far too powerful. And so are you, by the way, for me to just let you leave like that."

"I thought I was your partner, not your prisoner."

"Well, you're not exactly my partner anymore, are you?"

Maia says nothing.

"*Are you*, Maia?" There is a new look taking over his face. It's a look she's never seen on him before, and it scares her.

Resentment.

She shakes her head.

"Are you going to *think* about what I've offered you?" he asks. There is pleading in his voice.

"No."

"I can't believe—that's *crazy*. Are you absolutely sure you don't want to consider what I've offered you?"

"Yes, Jake. I will never change my mind. Will you? About Leucothea? About your war and your oil and your slaves?"

"Of course not."

"Well, then, there you have it. So, where does that leave us?"

Jake shrugs. "I can't let you leave. Surely, you must know that. Putting how I feel about you aside, you know too much. You're too powerful. I can't have my most precious war asset walk out the front door, just to join forces with my enemies."

"What makes those cities your enemies?"

"If they aren't for us, they're against us." The vulnerability behind his eyes has faded. They now glare at her, cold as ice. "And I'm a jealous man, Maia. If I can't have you, *no one* can."

She feels like she's going to vomit. She swallows hard,

trying to summon her strength, and she lifts her chin. "What does that mean? You're going to lock me up like an animal?"

"No. The thought makes me cringe."

"So, what then?"

"I'm going to give you a week to calm down. Change your mind."

"I won't—"

He lifts his hand. "You'll need to stay in the guest suite, of course. But unfortunately, I can't trust you. Not while you're so angry. You're not thinking clearly. So, I'll have to ... *encourage* you to stay."

"What does that mean? You're going to *hurt* me?"

"Probably not. At least not badly."

"I'm not afraid of you."

He grins. "I know. I've always loved that about you. So, instead, I will make you watch as I hurt those *close* to you. People don't have to die, but if you leave, they will. *Scores* of them."

Maia laughs and Jake looks at her, amused. "Everyone *close* to me?!" she yells. "I don't have anyone. I'm all alone." It's crushing to say it aloud.

"Oh, but Maia," he says quietly, tilting his head. "You do."

Her brow twitches.

He sighs. "You came here with Lucas."

"*And.*"

"And he had a brother, didn't he?"

Maia's breath quickens.

"A brother I led you to—you're welcome, by the way. You never once talked about either one of them with me over all our conversations. Why is that?"

She glares at him, biting back her retort.

"I know you cared very much for this brother—*loved* him, even? Quite the mess you made on your journey here. Why can't I ever remember his name?" He looks up at the ceiling, then shakes his head. "It'll come to me. But I know everything about him too. Where he lives ... What he's doing in this very moment. I even know about his new wife. They have a baby on the way, did you know that?"

Maia closes her eyes.

"No, you wouldn't. But I do. You wouldn't want to ruin that for him, *too*, now would you?"

Breathless, it feels like Jake has ripped her heart from her chest.

"Miguel—*that's* his name. I don't know why I have such a hard time remembering that. Probably because, like your old scumbag boyfriend, I never liked him either."

Don't say a word, Maia. Don't. Say. A. Word.

Jake stands, pacing before her. "Also, I recall you came here in a boat—a very specific boat made with caribou skin. *Someone* gave you that canoe—"

She snaps. "It's called an *umiak*."

"I don't give a shit what you call it. There are only a few places I can think of where you'd get a vessel of that caliber. Actually, I know of only *one* community that would make a boat like that. Maybe ... someplace in the Old Yukon Territory?"

Holding her breath, Maia fights her tears.

Jake crouches next to her and lifts her chin, forcing her to look at him. "I will burn that place to the ground. I will take every last one of them, even those sweet little children. The elderly, too, although I doubt they'd make the treacherous journey back here. What's that old lady's name? She's a spitfire like you. *Tema*?"

Maia holds her hand against her mouth, and the tears

begin to fall.

"Maia, I swear to you, I won't touch a hair on their heads, but I'm going to need you to reconsider your decision."

"Is this *really* what you want, Jake? *Threatening* me to keep me here?!" she screams.

"YOU LEAVE ME NO *CHOICE*!" He chucks his glass, and it shatters against the wall.

"Sir?" Two of Jake's men have entered the room. "Everything okay?"

Jake stands, glaring down at Maia. "Fine."

"You're evil," Maia says as she sobs.

"No, I'm *powerful*, and power requires certain decisions to be made. It has always been the way. I accept that. You, on the other hand, are a *waste*." He kneels beside her, caressing her cheek with curled fingers. She pulls away. "A waste of … whatever it is that you are." His eyes rake her over. "Doing nothing with those powers while you barhop and get drunk, making out with a different man every night like a little *slut*."

"*Fuck* you."

"Tempting." He laughs. "I certainly tried. Would be nice to sample what the locals are having."

She spits in his face, and he stands, annoyed. "Take her to the guest suite."

Two men gather Maia between them. Tears streak her face, but she does not make a sound. Claire has walked back into the room. Her usual expression of resentment has contorted to worry.

"Leave everything unlocked. Front gates too," Jake says as he wipes his cheek. He smears his hand across Maia's face, and then he walks away. "If she wants to leave, *let* her." His voice echoes down the hall. "We'll make sure she gets exactly what she's promised."

SEVENTEEN

Walking toward the cliff, Maia peers up at Jake's grand estate sprawling alongside her. It's late afternoon and she's still in her nightgown. She didn't bother putting on a coat. Or shoes. Her bare feet are numb after walking across the cold, wet grounds from her suite to Jake's home.

His mansion. Her prison.

It has been nearly a week since she tried to escape Jake's men in the dark night outside her apartment. Nearly a week since her only friend in this godforsaken land slammed the door in her face. And then Jake threatened to harm the only people left in this world that she loves, sealing her nightmare by handing her an ultimatum that could only ever have one outcome at its end.

And so, Maia has made her decision. It is the only way.

Stepping to the edge of the cliff, an icy wind whips at her face. She peers down at the ominous waves crashing below, rain spattering against her skin. It's cold, she knows it's cold, but she can't feel a thing. She can't feel anything anymore.

She gazes at the views she had once considered breathtaking—the endless gray sky vanishing into a silver ocean, and a fog-enveloped Leucothea draped across the cliff.

Leucothea. The mythical land she once believed held all her dreams. Flashbacks of her old vision cross her mind: standing on this very cliff overlooking Leucothea, wanting more than anything to smite the entire place. She would be lying if she said she hadn't thought about it this past week. *A lot.* How easy it would be to burn everything to the ground.

And she would burn herself alongside it.

But after much deliberation, this is not what she has decided to do. She peers behind her. A few of Jake's men are now standing on the lawn, watching her. They are always watching.

She was so sure. For so long she knew, despite all her heartache and loss, that this was where she was meant to be. Now look at her, a powerful war pawn of one of the most dangerous men on Earth. She thought her destiny would be heroic. She thought she came here to thrive. But like a moth to a flame, she has climbed straight into the arms of her worst nightmare.

How could she have been so blind? This entire time she has been in Leucothea, Jake has been watching her. Studying her. He has discovered her biggest weakness and has used it to back her into a corner. He knows everything about the people she loves, and he will not hesitate to destroy every last one of them if she doesn't give him exactly what he wants.

Checkmate.

There are no more moves. There is nowhere to run. Nowhere to hide. If Maia leaves, people will die. If she stays, *people will die.* The few remaining civilizations in the Arctic will be emptied, forced into a lifetime of slavery for a ravenous empire that will never be satisfied. Like a virus,

Leucothea will expand across the only stable land left on this planet. It will do precisely what civilizations have always done: destroy everything in its path in its unquenchable thirst for *more*.

The one thing guaranteeing Jake's success is Maia. With the calculated use of her powers, she will ensure Leucothea's dominion over the masses. She will be the spark to set the last of the world on fire. To set herself on fire.

Unless ... She peers over the edge.

She could disappear.

Jake would lose his war pawn. Tema and Miguel and Chayanne would be safe. Without her, this world would be a better place.

But she *is* the world.

Preparing herself, she watches as the stones beneath her toes tumble down the cliff's ragged boulders.

"Miss?"

She glances over her shoulder. Jake's men are nervously approaching with their hands held out. She turns back around, a sly smile across her face. She only needs to take one more step, and Jake will lose everything. Tipping back her chin, she closes her eyes.

"What happened to my girl?"

Maia opens her eyes to an apparition of Lucas standing beside her. "What happened to, 'There's always a way'?" he whispers.

She turns toward him, tears filling her eyes. Reaching out, she grazes her trembling fingers along his cheek. He seems so real. "Lucas, I'm *so sorry*."

He smiles. "Why are you sorry?"

"Your death. It's all my fault."

"Darling," he says. "Nothing could be further from the truth. The time you and I had was my destiny, a destiny *I chose*. And I would choose it again and again. But you ... you are not finished. This world *needs* you. You can't give up."

"I don't know what else to do. This is the only way to keep people from dying."

"You are wrong," he says solemnly, and he closes her eyes with the tips of his fingers.

The future just inches from Maia's feet flashes before her. She watches as she falls from the cliff, shattering everything she was always destined to become into a pointless, hollow void. Enraged with bitterness, Jake would still seek revenge on the people Maia once loved. Miguel, Chayanne, and Tema would mourn her death as they, along with the rest of the tribe, are escorted in chains from the burning grounds of their home. A great war would still ensue as Leucothea took over the Arctic. Scores of miserable people would still be forced into a lifetime of slavery. Scores of illuded people would still give away their power to the select few at the top who only ever had their own interests in mind.

Maia opens her eyes. She wouldn't be saving anyone by giving up. Her absence would only solidify humanity's dark future on Earth. "Lucas," she whispers. "What am I supposed to do?"

"You know what to do."

"I don't."

"You do," Lucas says, and he places his brow against hers.

Another vision—her and Jake's nightly chess games.

Always think of your opponent's next move, he had once told her, the candles on their table illuminating his dark eyes. *Keep your friends close, your enemies closer.*

"What did Jake do?" Lucas asks. Maia looks up at him, and he whispers, "He kept his enemies close."

Maia gasps as images flash of Jake obsessively watching her from the city's video feed all hours of the night, and anger surges through her veins like ice. He kept her close. He studied her, stalked her every move, did everything he could to seduce her. He manipulated every vulnerable aspect of her to take her as his own.

"It's not over, Maia," Lucas says. "You know what to do. You *know* it."

Maia turns toward Jake's men, still cautiously approaching from across the lawn. She holds out her hand, slowly shaking her head, and the men halt.

Jake's right. He *is* the reason she has always been called here. She has been drawn to him from the beginning, but not for the reason he is so arrogantly assured of.

It is not her destiny to help Leucothea thrive. It is her destiny to *destroy* it.

It begins to pour, and Maia stands in the deluge at the edge of the cliff. The men continue to surround her, but they keep their distance. Holding their guns before them, they appear nervous. Unsettled. Maia looks at them, annoyed by their blind allegiance. Cowards in black clothing, the lot of them, hiding behind their weapons.

She could wipe out every last one of them. In seconds, she could command the wind. It would rush across this land with a force unlike anything they've ever known and sweep them off the cliff like rag dolls.

It would be so easy.

But she's not going to do that. Not today, at least. No, she will play Jake at his own game. He may have backed her into a corner, but this is far from over. She will keep her enemies close until the time is right. And when that time comes, she will take him down. She will destroy all of it—even if that means she must perish alongside it.

She is the beauty and the destruction. She could never understand or accept her dark side before. Sitting next to the fire with Miguel by her side, she used to get so frustrated with what she judged as her apparent lack.

When I am the most powerful, there is a darkness that comes out of me, one that doesn't think twice about destruction or ending a life. I feel like I am constantly battling against two opposing sides of myself, and I'm exhausted.

Now, the time has come to embrace all that she is. She is nurturing, and she is destructive. This Earth is hers, and she will not allow herself to be bullied any longer.

Leucothea has become a deadly virus, lovingly nourished by the greedy hands of Jake and his New System. He may be the most powerful man in the world, but Maia knows his greatest weakness.

I became ... addicted ... to you.

She peers up at the house. Jake is standing at his office window, watching her as he always does with his arms crossed, his fist at his chin. She turns toward him, her eyes fluttering against the rain, and a peculiar grin spreads wide across her face.

EIGHTEEN

As Maia pads down the long corridor, water drips from her soaked nightgown onto the hardwood floor, leaving small puddles in her wake. A handful of guards cautiously follow, their guns pointed at her back.

Jake is expecting her, having watched as she entered his home after standing on his cliff in the rain. His office door at the end of the hallway, often closed, has been left wide open.

As she approaches, she finds him leaning against his desk with his arms crossed, waiting. She flashes him a coy smile, and his eyes narrow, a grin tugging his lip. He strides toward her with a tilted gaze, and they meet in the middle of his office, neither one speaking a word. Just like their games of chess, they are reading one another. Only this time, Maia knows exactly whose move it is.

She peers up into his dark eyes. "I've considered your offer," she finally says, her voice like a song.

"*And...*"

She lifts her chin. "I'll take it."

His gaze is intense, his smile wide. "Good girl."

Jake doesn't waste a second. The following day, he has Maia meet him in the middle of a large field. They are surrounded by dozens of armed men and a handful of hovering drones.

Jake begins to circle her, and Maia mirrors him. He smiles. "So," he says, clasping his hands behind his back.

"So," she says.

"You said you'll take my offer."

"And?"

"*And* ... I offered you a lot, Maia," he says quietly, stopping before her. "What exactly are you agreeing to?"

"You and I will be partners."

He arches his brow.

"*Business* partners—nothing more."

He lifts his chin. After a while, he says, "You'll change your mind, but ... fine."

"I won't. I *hate* you."

He laughs. "There's a fine line between love and hate. Could be fun." He winks.

"Not that fine," she growls.

He shrugs. "We'll see. Anything else?"

"I am no longer a 'guest' staying in your little suite. I want my own estate. If I'm to be treated like a goddess, I want to live like one."

"More than happy."

"And I don't want your cronies following me around anymore."

Jake shakes his head. "No can do. Your little change of heart, while welcomed, is ... *sudden*. I don't trust you."

Maia sighs. "You've already told me loud and clear what will happen if I leave."

He nods. "Fair point. Fine, the guards will go, but the drones will stay."

"Is that how you treat a goddess?"

"Just give it time. Once you prove your loyalty to me—to *Leucothea*—the drones will go. I promise."

"Your word means *nothing* to me."

"Maia." He grabs her hands. "At some point, you and I will get past this little ... disagreement."

"And what?" Maia laughs, ripping her hands from him. "We'll live happily ever after?" She walks away. "*Screw* you."

"We're not done yet," he says, his tone stopping her. "Show me," he says at her back. "Show me what you can do."

She was prepared for this. She knew the first thing he would want was a show. She'll have to downplay as much of her powers as she can without losing his interest, or his precarious trust. He has heard the rumors; he already knows she can command the wind and the trees. But he doesn't know about the fires, which she'll use to her advantage. The earthquakes are still a mystery, but one she has time to figure out. He is still preparing. She still has time.

Soon, he'll demand the other cities in the Arctic vacate and leave everything to Leucothea, including their people, who will be forced into a lifetime of slavery. They won't do it, which Jake is expecting. So, a war will ensue. He'll surround them with his military and Maia—an advantage unmatched by anything those other armies will have. But before he does that, he'll want to know exactly what sort of damage she can cause.

"Maia? Let's see it."

"Not with all these guns pointed at me," she says coolly over her shoulder.

He laughs. "Ah, but you see, I need some sort of insurance."

She turns to face him. "Are you *afraid*?"

"I'm aware. There's a difference."

"I'm not doing a thing until they lower them."

He peers at her, long and hard, and then he nods. The men lower their guns. He walks backward toward the edge of the field, not once taking his eyes off hers. She is surrounded. They are all watching, waiting. Jake mumbles to the officer next to him, who orders a line of soldiers to walk toward her.

Easy.

Maia closes her eyes, her nerves fluttering. It's been years since she's used her powers to harness the wind. Breathing deep, she pulls strength from the ground. The Earth's energy gathers at her feet, its icy hot current flooding up through her veins, and she smiles.

Lifting her hands toward the sky, she commands a gale-force wind to gather. It barrels across the ground and swirls into a twister above her. The gusts sweep a few curls across her cheeks, but the soldiers around her barely stay on their feet.

She sweeps her arms across her body, and the winds slam into the line of trembling men. They fly backward and tumble across the field, smashing into the trees at its edge. She lowers her hands, short of breath, and the wind dies to a faint breeze. The soldiers lie disorientated on the ground, moaning. A few are motionless.

Her entire body tingling, Maia tips her head back and sighs.

How exhilarating.

Jake's hands are clasped before his smile. "*Incredible.* What else have you got?"

"Depends on how much damage you want me to inflict." She lowers her chin, flashing him a mischievous grin. "Would you like me to kill *all* of your men?"

The soldiers eye each other, uneasy.

"What about the trees?" Jake asks.

"That results in death. I can't have a tree 'lightly' squash a man."

He nods, and a handful of men grab some fake dummies piled at the back of the field. They place them under a line of trees, then quickly scatter.

Maia inhales. Reaching above her, she grabs the air and falls to her knees, yanking down hard. A massive pine groans as it leans to the side, followed by a thunderous crack. Sporadic pops and snaps sound as the tree fractures layer by layer, a gaping zigzag tracing down the center of the trunk. Then the pine severs in half and slams into the earth with a thunderous boom, smashing the dummies beneath.

Maia leans on all fours, gasping. She's weak, out of practice. She tries not to let it show.

Jake stares with wide eyes at the obliterated mannequins, shaking his head. For a moment, he is speechless. "You ... you made the earth quake—back at the house," he finally says, still eyeing the fallen tree.

"I know nothing about that."

He glares at her. "*Don't* talk to me as if I'm stupid."

She stands, wiping the dirt from her hands. "It comes out when it wants. I can't control it. Besides, an earthquake would destroy everything. Is that really what you want? To turn those other cities full of precious supplies and humans and infrastructure into rubble?"

"If I need to, yes."

She rolls her neck and sighs. "It has only happened a few times in my life, and it came on its own accord. I wouldn't even know where to begin. Destroying things by making the earth shake has never been an interest of mine."

"Well, *make* it an interest."

Maia shrugs, looking bored. "Fine."

Jake looks around. "What else?" He grabs a man by his shirt and shoves him toward her. "Throw him across the field."

She shakes her head. "Doesn't work like that."

He marches up to her, standing so close his breath is hot on her face. "How *does* it work?"

She looks up at him, refusing to step back. "I can't pick things up and throw them. I can make the wind rise when I call it, but it's unspecific. Whatever or whoever stands in its way will be annihilated. I can command the trees. That's all I've got."

He smiles. "I don't believe you."

Meeting his glare, she stands her ground. She needs to keep her temper under control—make him believe she is on his side. But it could also bode well to keep him on his toes. Fear is a powerful emotion, and she is done being bullied by this man.

Now, it's *her* turn.

"Why are you smiling?" he says under his breath.

She tilts her head to the side, tapping each of his shirt buttons with the tip of her finger. "You're not afraid of me. I like that."

"*Afraid*. Of *you*? Do you not see all these men holding guns?"

"I see them."

"And you think *I* should be afraid of *you*."

She shrugs with a cocky grin. "Probably."

NINETEEN

Maia's eggs are burning.

Standing next to the stove with eyes glazed, she bites her nail. For weeks, there has been a nervous pit in her stomach that she can't shake—ever since she and Jake stood in the middle of that field and she told him he should be afraid of her. She knew it wasn't wise to threaten him, but she was *so sick* of him wagging his weapons and his authority in her face.

The one thing that really pisses him off is being told *no*—anything that threatens his ego, really.

She knew that; she simply didn't care.

Since then, she has been on her best behavior. But something still feels ... *off*.

Or is that the smoke? She pulls the burning eggs from the stovetop and throws the pan into the sink. She wasn't hungry anyway.

These past few weeks, Maia has put on the performance of her life: joining Jake in the city for dinner, smiling for the cameras, wearing the gowns, faking the adoration for the man she has grown to hate more with each passing day.

Their conversations are brief and forced, and the entire time she is actively trying not to jump from her seat and stab him with her butterknife. Sometimes, she thinks she may actually be fooling him. Other times, she catches him peering at her suspiciously from the corner of his eye.

Is she fooling him? Or is he playing the game right back, making her *believe* she is deceiving him?

There are layers to his heinousness.

In the afternoons Jake is away from the house, Maia tries to work on making the earth quake, but she is holding back. She wants more than anything to figure it out—it is the one thing besides fire that she could use to her advantage—but there is no way to do it secretively. If she figures it out, Jake will know. She has spent a little time on it, holding her hand against the ground, but it continues to elude her.

Every time Jake sees her, he asks about it. And every time, she tells him she's been hard at work, but nothing is happening.

She looks over her shoulder at the white gown on the table. Another gift from Jake, with a card telling her she will join him tonight for dinner in the city. The citizens of Leucothea still think they are a couple, and Jake has demanded they keep up appearances. *The people really love you. It will work in my favor with the upcoming election.*

She has no choice but to join him. She'll wear the dress, smile for the cameras, play the part. She needs to remain confident, cool, calm ... and buy time until she figures out what to do.

And if he tries to kiss her again, she'll punch him.

Another large truck rumbles past her house. The past few days, there has been a lot of commotion around Jake's mansion. Vehicles driving up and down the driveway. Maia assumes it has something to do with her new estate, where they have already begun work. She asked that it be built on another property, but Jake has insisted it remain on his. Not that it will ever be finished … but it's proving to be a nice distraction. Jake's extravagant, peaceful estate has become filled with an incessant parade of workers, trucks, banging hammers, and chainsaws. The upheaval certainly makes it easier for Maia to work on her powers.

Later that night, she stands before the long mirror in her floor-length white gown. With her hair down, she looks *exactly* like the vision of herself from her old dreams. Her hand on her chest, she holds her pounamu. What she wouldn't give to put it on a proper flax cord. But it wouldn't bode well for her and her "partnership" with Jake to replace his fancy gold necklace.

Orson knocks at her door and she answers it, leaving her coat behind. They only ever go from heated cars to heated buildings anyway. Walking outside, she is surprised to see Jake's stretch limo waiting. Orson avoids eye contact as he holds open the car door, and she slides in next to Jake, who is dressed in his finest army uniform. Two guards are seated across from him, their guns on their laps. Maia rolls her eyes.

"You look stunning," Jake says.

"I know."

He laughs. "You're beginning to sound like me."

Maia forces a smile. He slides closer to her, and she nonchalantly inches away. "What's with the white dress?" she asks, looking out the window.

"Isn't this what you've always dreamed about?"

Alarmed, she turns toward him, and he reacts with a sly grin. She quickly looks away, trying to calm her nerves. "What do you mean?"

"Isn't this what all women want?" He leans in closer,

twisting one of her curls between his fingers. "To wear the white dress?"

She smiles, feigning laughter. "Aw, Jake. Are you proposing?"

He grazes his nose along her cheek, nestling into her. The guards watch, entertained, and she grits her teeth, glaring at them. She wants to claw their eyeballs out.

"No," Jake whispers, sliding away. "But we do make an amazing couple."

"In what way?" Maia snaps. "I *hate* you."

This makes him laugh—a hearty, gut-busting laugh. "Yes, there it is. *Finally.* Thank you. I think you've taken your poker face a little too far." When he looks at her, there is something sinister about his smile.

Maia's gut twists. Not right—something isn't right. She looks out the window. They are not driving *toward* the city but farther from it. She grabs the door, and both guards lift their guns.

She whirls toward Jake. His head is cocked to the side, watching her with amusement. *Always* with amusement. A line of cars follows closely behind them. "What's happening?" Maia asks.

Jake's face becomes very serious. "No more questions, Maia."

"Jake—"

He lunges, shoving her hard against the window with his hands around her throat. She clutches at them, gasping.

"I want to trust you," he whispers, tightening his grip. "I want to *so badly.*" He tenderly kisses her cheek, his lips lingering as she wheezes, and then he releases her, leaning back onto his seat.

Maia clings to the door, coughing and gasping for air.

Smoothing the wrinkles in his uniform, he clears his

throat. "But I can't—not yet." He picks a piece of imaginary fluff from his knee. "So, I have a little surprise for you."

A surprise? Maia struggles to regain her composure. She's not prepared for this. This is all happening so fast. She can't think clearly.

Their car drives up to a large field with something called a "helicopter" in the middle, its wide blades swinging. Maia gawks at it from her window. She's come across these strange machines from time to time, devoured by rust in old airports or smashed in the middle of roads. She's never seen one in working order—until now.

The two guards step from the car, quickly pulling Maia out. The swirling winds are freezing cold. The men lead her to the aircraft, holding her head down as they run beneath the blades.

Inside the loud cabin, Maia is terrified. She cannot fathom what Jake could have planned, but that terrible pit in her stomach has grown into a boulder. He hasn't engaged with the other cities yet; she knows this. She's overheard many conversations between him and his advisors—he won't start a war until he is president of Leucothea. He wants full credit for when they take over the Arctic, and the elections aren't for another six months.

She stares at him next to her, but he won't meet her gaze. The features of his face are cold, his eyes empty, as if possessed by a demon.

She looks out the window. Where would he be taking her? She scans the scenery below, astounded at how much ground they cover in such a short time, how quickly they pass mountains and lands that would take weeks to travel on foot. They are *flying*. She would be thrilled if she weren't so terrified.

The helicopter hovers along a cliff with scores of army vehicles, cars, and soldiers in combat gear awaiting below.

"Jake," Maia says with alarm, her voice pleading. "What is this?"

He looks at her very seriously. "A test."

"A *test*?"

"A small one," he says as they land, and he grabs her hand. "Now is your chance to prove your loyalty to me. I believe in you—I know you can do this. Prove to me that you are devoted to Leucothea, and then I can begin to trust you."

The door swings open, and a guard yanks Maia into the freezing cold, the erratic wind whipping around. Huddled into herself, she whirls in place, meeting the hardened glares of a hundred eyes. Guns pointed, the soldiers crouch behind barricades—watching. Waiting.

She should have known something like this would happen. She should have expected the worst from Jake. Why didn't she expect this? She should have expected this.

With a soldier on each side, they drag Maia to the cliff's edge. A modest town sits below, with about a hundred people standing in the streets looking up at her.

"No one has to die, Maia!" Jake yells over the wind.

She looks behind her, horrified. "I don't understand!"

"My men have told them to leave, that they are in grave danger, but they won't do it."

Maia shakes her head. "Danger?"

Jake smiles. "Yes. *You.*"

"What?!"

Jake backs away, palms up. "They won't leave. They will not obey Leucothea's orders. *Make* them."

"What do you expect *me* to do?"

"Up to you, really!" He shrugs as he continues toward a barrier next to the helicopter. "Something with the wind?

Not many trees around. I know you've got more to you than what you've let on. I *know* it. *Push* them out! Show me what those powers can do!"

Standing at the edge of the cliff, Maia finds it hard to breathe. She eyes the guns pointed at her, the soldiers hiding behind vehicles with doors open, ready to vacate.

"Maia?" Jake yells from behind his barricade. "That town is small—nothing compared to a large city. This should be an easy task for you."

Shivering cold, Maia looks around in a panic.

"Okay," Jake says, nodding at a large man standing next to a car. He is the only one not in a Leucothean uniform.

The man opens the door and pulls out a woman with a black bag over her head. He drags her before Maia and rips off the sack.

Renee. She is sobbing, black eyeliner running down her cheeks.

"Renee!" Maia screams. She lurches, but the guards hold her back.

"Maia! Help me!" Renee wails.

The man drags Renee toward the cliff's edge. He grips her arm as she frantically claws at his hand, her feet slipping over the ledge.

Maia turns toward Jake. "What do you *want*?!" she screeches.

"I'm not going to repeat myself," he says, annoyed. "You tell me that you're loyal to Leucothea. *Prove* it."

Maia turns toward the village, toward all those innocent people. Terrified men and women peer up at her, their sobbing children clinging to them. Jake and his men have placed themselves far enough away to be hidden from view. The villagers wouldn't be able to see them; they won't even know they're there.

They can only see Maia.

Lightheaded, she grows faint. Can't. *Can't.*

Renee continues to sob, and the man holding her pushes her. She shrieks as her feet slip from the cliff. Women cry out below, shielding their children's eyes.

Maia holds out her hands. "Stop! *Please!*"

The guard, enjoying the horror on Maia's face, pushes Renee again. Only this time, he releases his grip. Renee disappears over the side.

Maia screams, running to the edge. Renee lies motionless at the rocky bottom, eyes blank, staring up at the sky. Her body contorted, blood spills from her mouth.

Maia gasps, and for a moment, her heart stops beating. Gasping. *Gasping.* Heaving for breath, she digs her fingers into her palms, trembling with rage. The earth shakes in response. Light at first, it strengthens as she wails. Stones tumble from her feet down the side of the cliff, and the people cry out below, scattering across the streets.

"It's happening!" Jake shouts.

As Maia turns to face him, her vision turns red. All she can see is red: a bright and blinding, blood-curdling red. Agonizing pain shoots across her body, and a piercing ringing fills her ears.

Red. Ringing. Gasping for air. Searing pain.

Scores of people screaming.

Smoke ... There is so much smoke filling her lungs.

TWENTY

"Maia?"

Strange noises penetrate the darkness behind Maia's closed eyes. Feet shuffling against gravel. Orders being barked out. Children wailing. Women crying.

"Wake up, baby," Jake sings softly into her ear.

Someone holding a screaming infant is slowly passing before her. Its shriek comes from her right ... her front ... her left. Car doors are slamming shut. Murmuring and whimpering from both men and women.

Maia opens her eyes to a gravel road. Her legs and feet behind her, she has been dragged to the place she is now. Whoever is gripping her arms is hurting her. Her entire body aches—every muscle, every bone. Chills run up and down her skin like a fever, and she moans.

"Maia, I don't want you to miss this," Jake says. He grabs her hair and lifts her head, showing her the gruesome scene unfolding before them.

Armies. A parade of people forming lines, piling into large trucks. Billows of black smoke filling the sky from the burning buildings behind them. The villagers are down-trodden. Staring at Maia. *Glaring* at Maia.

"Remember, don't do anything stupid," Jake whispers, and then he stands, patting her head like a dog. "Yes, people! Take a good look. This is the woman who did this to you! She is a *monster*! Do not worry, all will be well. We will take care of you. We are taking you somewhere safe. We will give you food and shelter after this *vicious* attack! We are from Leucothea. Leucothea has saved you!"

Maia shakes her head as she sobs. "*No*," is all she can mutter, her voice hoarse. A handful of soldiers surround her, their guns pointed with fingers on triggers.

The villagers walking past glare at her, dust and ash smeared across their faces. As they willingly climb into the trucks, Jake's soldiers hand them blankets. Water. The people are scared, broken. They have lost everything.

They have no idea they have also just lost their freedom.

———

Maia awakens to another day in solitude. Another day in this brick room with no windows and a bed in the corner. Lying in the middle of the floor, she stares at the ceiling. She feels far away—she must be in Jake's underground bunker. She has spent an untold amount of time banging on the door. Screaming. Losing her mind.

But it's no use.

She should have jumped. Should have jumped off that cliff. Better yet, she should have destroyed Jake and all those soldiers around her. But then they would have shot her, Jake would have died a hero, and Leucothea's government would have continued on its mission.

She panicked ... froze. So caught off guard. Jake told her no one had to die. But he lied—*of course* he lied.

All she could see was red. The piercing ringing in her ears.

But now she remembers. Now she can see it all: the earthquakes, the fires, the wind. So many of her powers at once, used in a vicious act of terrorism so Jake could witness exactly what she could do.

Men, women, and children screaming, running for their lives. So much screaming.

Screaming.

Screaming.

Their cries still echo in her mind. Over and over and over again.

The door opens and closes again very quickly. She doesn't look; she knows exactly what just happened. Another bowl of food added to the collection of untouched dishes on the floor.

She had weeks to prepare. She should have known. But she was so focused on fooling Jake until she could figure out what to do. The entire time he was planning, plotting against her.

Always think of your opponent's next move.

The door opens again. This time it slams against the wall. Speak of the devil, Jake has just stepped inside her room. His hands on his hips, he peers down at her. "Why aren't you eating?"

Maia stares up at the ceiling, refusing to speak.

"*EAT!*" Jake picks up a bowl and throws it against the wall. The spoiled food slides down the brick.

She sighs, too exhausted to react.

He crouches next to her. "If you don't eat something, I

will have one of my doctors come in and hook you up to needles, and we will *force* food into you. Is that what you want?" He stands. "But you should know, those supplies are incredibly limited. We've taken them from the hospital, meaning some poor soul who actually *needs* them will die."

Maia closes her eyes.

"Sir?" A voice echoes from the hallway.

"Yes, do it."

The room fills with soldiers. They yank Maia from the ground and throw her onto the bed, strapping her down. A man rolls in a cart. Jake is standing behind him with his fist at his closed mouth, shaking his head. The doctor pulls out a large needle.

"No," Maia gasps, her voice broken.

The man glances back at Jake.

"Leave us," Jake says, and the room quickly empties. He stares down at her. "Don't look at me like that. You've done this to yourself." He sits on the edge of her bed, surveying the bowls of food on the floor. "You know Renee was a spy, don't you?" he finally says.

Maia refuses to speak.

He sighs, crossing his arms. "No, you don't. I know you don't. You assumed I had recording devices set up in the apartment. I know, Renee told me. But I didn't. I didn't need to. Renee told me everything. *Everything.* Every conversation. Every hope. Every dream. Every little thing you said to her, she ran straight back to me and told me. She was actually one of Claire's recruits. We hired her before you graduated from orientation."

Maia stares at the ceiling, shaking her head.

"So don't be sad about her death, Maia. She was a waste anyway." He stands. Glaring down at her, he grimaces. "Sort of like you. You're disgusting now; look at you. All helpless and strapped down. You could have been huge. You *should* have been my *wife*. You would have been celebrated as a goddess. Your name would have lived on in history books forever. But now ... now I'll never be able to trust you, and so, you've ruined *everything*." He turns away, sighing at the wall.

"You think I didn't know exactly what you were doing? You're a terrible liar." He peers at her from over his shoulder. "But I wanted to trust you, so I gave you a chance to prove to me that I could, and you have failed. You have failed on *so* many counts. Which is ... *disappointing*.

"So, this is it for you, I suppose." He looks around the room, his hands on his hips. "It's not ideal ... Certainly not the life *I* had planned for you, but you've left me no choice. I'll just leave you down here until I need you. And now that I know what makes you tick—*anger*, that's a good one—I'll just pull people as pawns until you break."

A tear slides down Maia's temple.

"Might need a few of them for Asiaq Bay, but we'll see. You always have the option to do as I say, and no one has to get hurt. Well, no one on *our* side." He leans across her, his hands on either side of her head. "But you need to tell me, *right now*, where *are* they?"

She glares at him. "*Who*."

"You know who. I gave you freedom, I was building you a *mansion* for fuck's sake, and you were sneaking around sending someone to warn your little tribe. They've cleared out, led by some native with long hair and Miguel. *Where* did they *go*?"

Maia holds back her smile. Miguel and Shinesho. The tribe has escaped. Miguel and the tribe are *safe*.

Jake lowers his face inches from hers. "*Tell me!*" He grabs her shoulder, ramming his fist into her ribs. She tries to recoil, gasping for air, but the straps hold her down. He turns and opens the door, seizing a gun from the guard. Trembling with rage, he pries open Maia's mouth and shoves the barrel down her throat. "*TELL ME!*"

Maia chokes on the cold metal. The pain is so sharp in her throat, but she doesn't care. She doesn't care that she can't breathe, that she might suffocate in this tiny brick room in Jake's underground bunker. The sense of relief she feels in this moment is overwhelmingly peaceful. Miguel and Tema and Chayanne and Shinesho—that tribe was Jake's only real leverage against her, and they have escaped.

She begins to grow faint. Let him kill her. Gagging, with tears flowing from her eyes, she glares up at him with every last ounce of hatred she has.

He comes to his senses and pulls the gun from her mouth, and she sucks in a desperate breath. Panting, he looks around, wiping beads of sweat from his reddened forehead. "Why don't you use your magic? It's because you're separated, isn't it? It *is*, isn't it? You have nothing if you don't have the elements."

Maia wheezes, the metallic taste of blood filling her mouth.

"Well, you better get used to it. Your days of luxury are over. I know you sent someone to warn your friends. I will comb through every worker here, interrogate them, and I will find out who. And when I do, you will both pay for this. I swear to God, Maia. And when I find your little tribe, they'll pay too." He stands back, straightening his shirt. "Until then, I'd like you to officially meet my friend here. He's been following you for a *long* time and has been dying to meet you."

Maia's stalker steps next to him and she flinches at the sight.

"This world is so big, yet so small," Jake says with a smile, smoothing his hair back. "This is Silas. And he knew Lucas."

Maia's eyes widen despite herself.

"Yes, there's a reaction. Silas fought with Lucas on the shores of South America for a spot on that ship you hid on. Actually, Silas already had a spot, and Lucas took it. He fought dirty, from what I've been told. Silas has spent *years* waiting to seek his revenge. Lucas may have won that battle, but now look where we are."

Maia remembers Lucas telling her about that fight, late one night while sitting on their island of plastic in the middle of the Pacific.

A week later, we left that man on shore, Lucas had told her. *I will never forget his face, bruised and broken, glaring at me ... Every night it haunts me still.*

Silas steps forward, and Jake holds him back. "Not yet. Let her sit here in the dark and think about her options."

Silas leers at her.

"Go," Jake says, and Silas leaves the room.

Jake sits beside her. Tilting his gaze, he caresses her cheek with his thumb. "I don't *want* to let him hurt you," he says, his voice alarmingly tender. "I can make it all go away. All you need to do is tell me who you sent and where your tribe is, and I will spare you the ruthless cruelty that Silas will be allowed to take out on you ... day after day after day. I'll eventually find your people anyway, I guarantee it. Don't make me find them myself." He softly kisses her forehead, whispering, "Please, don't be stupid." He hesitates, then slowly lowers his face to hers, eyeing her lips.

"Do it," Maia seethes. "I *dare* you."

He stands, smirking. "I told you there's a fine line," he says as he turns and exits the room, pulling the door closed. "Could be fun."

Maia's frustrated scream echoes against the brick, and she writhes within the straps. Jake slams the door shut, shrouding her in darkness.

TWENTY-ONE

"*Y*ou are my sunshine..."

There is nothing but a blanket of darkness around Maia. No longer bound to her bed, she has curled up into a corner, rocking back and forth and singing softly to herself.

"*My only ... sun ... shine...*"

Her bones dig into the cold cement. How long has it been since Jake had her untied? It was just after he threatened her. A few days? A week?

A long time. *Too* long.

Any moment, her door will open and Silas will exact his revenge for what Lucas did to him all those years ago. Jake thinks she knows where the tribe is, and if she doesn't give him what he wants, he'll allow Silas to torture her. Day after day after *day*...

"*Don't ... sunshine ... away.*" That's not how the song goes.

Rock. Rock. Dig. Rock.

She has had a lot of time to think, and she has finally come to a decision. It's not the greatest decision she's ever made, but it's the only one she has left. It is her final pawn.

Jake may have taken away every last piece of her, left her to rot in this cell underground with no trees, no wind, no water. But ... she still has *fire*.

She's tested it a few times now on her clothing. Watched a small flame ignite in the darkness—felt the burn, smelled the smoke, and then quickly smothered it between her palms.

Jake will stop at nothing to find Miguel and the tribe. They hold the power he so desperately needs to control Maia—to control the Arctic. And so, she has no choice but to *end* him, here and now. He and Silas will be coming any time. Jake will stand over her and demand an answer she doesn't have. Even if she did know who warned Miguel, she would rather die than tell Jake.

She has but one chance. If she does nothing at that moment, Jake will leave her with Silas, and then he will send his search parties out far and wide to find the tribe. And when he does find them, he will use them one by one as pawns to abuse Maia's power against more innocent people.

And so, she will burn this entire place to the ground, starting with Jake. While he is standing over her, she will light him ablaze. He will cry out in terror, and she will lift her hands to the sky, commanding the flames to rise. His soldiers will try to help him, but he will be untouchable. She'll quickly move on to Silas before he can escape, and then the bed, which will make for excellent kindling.

And as the black smoke fills the halls, she will walk from room to room, burning everyone and everything she sees. It won't be long before the entire bunker crumbles to ash inside the ground, most likely with her still inside. She knows this is a grave possibility, but it is the only way.

She will stop Jake once and for all. And then she and

this man she has been called to her entire life will burn ... until there is nothing left of them but ashes and a memory. Jake thinks he has taken everything, leaving her with no choice but to give him what he wants. But he has misjudged her.

And he will *burn* for his mistake.

Half asleep in her corner, Maia drifts in and out of an anxious slumber, always dreaming of Miguel. What she wouldn't give to talk to him, to see his face one last time. Hear his laugh. She really loved his laugh.

If only she could tell him goodbye, tell him how *much* she loved him. How every night, she has seen him in her dreams, held her hand to his cheek. She's never had long before the snow falling inside her cabin obscures him and her child from sight, but at least she has finally stopped screaming when she wakes.

Maia's door shakes back and forth, and she cries out. After so long in silence, the sudden noise has jolted her.

This is it. Dazed, she sits up and braces herself against her corner. But her head—it's spinning. The earth feels ... *uneven*. Is she dreaming?

The door keeps shaking. What are they up to? There is a murmuring of voices, like a scuffle is occurring outside her room. This isn't right—something isn't right. Maia strains her eyes against the blackness, watching the light beneath the door flicker from the movement of feet.

Jake has always had a guard unlock the cell for him. There has never been a struggle. Maybe she's still dreaming. So *disorientated*. She feels strange—this *all* feels strange.

A key enters the lock, followed by a loud click. The door swings open, flooding Maia's room with light. She holds out her hand, squinting. After so long in darkness, the light is like an assault.

A strange man steps inside. One of Jake's guards? Maia can make out the bright white star on his uniform, but she cannot see his face. Whomever this man is, he's definitely not Silas. She lifts her hand to light him ablaze, but something feels off. No, it's all *wrong*.

"In here!" the guard yells, startling her.

This is her only shot; the door to her cell has been left wide open. She tries to stand, but her legs give out. She can't mess this up, but this is the wrong guy. Where's Jake?! No. She's getting out of here—she'll start with the bed.

Desperate, she holds her hand out to the mattress as the guard rushes up to her. She pushes into the corner, screaming. The man reaches for her, and she closes her eyes, kicking him away. "No! *Stop!*" she yells.

"Look at me!" the man shouts, grunting against her kicks.

She glances at the bed. Nothing is happening ... She's too weak. Gasping, she keeps her hand held out, focusing with the last of her strength on the corner of the mattress. A small flame ignites.

Yes.

She lifts her palm to the ceiling, and new flames burst forth.

YES.

"Look at me, Maia!" the man shouts, shaking her.

She knows that voice. She looks at him, confused, but the figure is dark, the light behind him so bright. She rubs her eyes. His black hair is tied back into a long braid. He sets a staff on the ground next to him and his face comes into focus.

"*Shinesho?*" Maia whispers.

Smoke begins to fill her cell. Squinting at him against the light, she coughs.

Another man dressed in black runs into the room. His shoulders are broad. He is also in a Leucothean uniform and is wearing a fitted, black knitted hat. "We need to hurry, they are coming." His voice is hushed, his accent thick.

Maia *knows* that voice.

"What happened?!" He gestures toward the bed.

"I think *she* did that," Shinesho replies.

The man kneels by her side. Trembling, Maia reaches for his face.

Can't be.

All his dreadlocks are gone. She *is* still dreaming. But this is all so real. There are sounds of people struggling in the hallway. A gunshot fires. And then the ashes from the blazing bed drift around the room like snow. Tears flow down Maia's cheeks as she realizes ... it was never snow in her dreams—it was *ash*. It was always *ash* falling inside that cabin.

"Hello, little bird," he says, holding Maia's hand against his face.

Maia stares at him in awe. He's so *lifelike*. She strokes his cheek, his black knitted cap, his bare neck. "You're so *real*," she whispers.

"I swore to you," he says softly. "I swore to you I would find you."

Another gun fires in the hall, snapping Maia out of her daze.

"We have to go, Miguel," Shinesho whispers. "*Now*."

Maia pushes against the corner, staring at him in shock. "*Miguel*?!" she screams. She holds her hand against her mouth as her cries steal her breath. When she finally finds the strength to inhale, she doesn't recognize her own wail.

One of Jake's guards runs into the room, and Shinesho grabs his bo. Spinning around, he knocks the guard to the ground, then swipes a gun from his pants and shoots him. Maia recoils, her hands at her ears.

Another man from the tribe rushes in. Maia recognizes him too—Kaique, one of Shinesho's soldiers she met at the tribe. He is also dressed in a Leucothean uniform. He braces himself against the wall of growing flames and motions for them to follow. "Now, guys! Now, now, now!"

Miguel quickly gathers a trembling Maia into his arms. She buries her face in his chest and clutches for dear life as he races into the bright light of the hallway.

<hr />

Maia awakens a few times for brief stints. The ground beneath her is unsteady, rickety. The constant hum of a motor is so loud in the small space. Is she in the back of a truck? The air is cold, drafty. Whoever is around her is silent besides the odd sniffle or whisper or murmur.

Was it all a dream? She doesn't dare open her eyes. Because, what if? What if she opens her eyes to find it was some sort of delusion or hysteria from being stuck inside a black cell for days on end? What if she's still a prisoner in Jake's underground bunker, Silas still coming for her? She doesn't dare open her eyes. If it was all a dream, it would be unbearable, a form of torture far beyond anything Silas could inflict.

So, every time she wakes, she keeps her eyes closed and she whispers into the void, "Miguel?" And then she waits for a response, filled with dread.

But every time, the arms enclosed around her tighten, and he whispers, "I am here."

<hr />

The next time Maia stirs, she is no longer curled up in Miguel's arms but lying down. The ground beneath her doesn't move. It is hard, uneven. The sounds are different —smells too.

She hesitantly opens her eyes to the sloped ceiling of a small nylon tent, dimly lit in an early-evening light. She shifts in a sleeping bag, a woman's arm draped across her chest. As she turns to the person sleeping next to her, she draws a sharp breath.

Chayanne.

Tears fall onto her pillow as she reaches for Chayanne's cheek. She softly grazes it, unbelieving.

Chayanne awakens with a gasp. As she takes in Maia's face, her eyes well with tears, and the two women lean in, forehead to forehead. "Hi, sweet friend," Chayanne whispers, and Maia begins to sob. Chayanne sits up and pulls Maia into her, wrapping her arms around her. "Oh, Maia," she whispers as Maia cries. "My sweet, sweet, Maia. I am so sorry. We would have come sooner. We didn't know."

Maia closes her eyes, her chin quivering. "I can't believe you came," she finally manages to mutter, her voice broken. She looks at Chayanne. "You could have *died*."

Chayanne leans back with a sigh. "I wasn't there. We only had so much room, so Shinesho made me wait here with the others. I could have *killed* him for making me stay behind."

Maia strokes Chayanne's long black hair. "I can't believe you're here. Right here before me. I never—" She chokes on her words. "I never thought I'd see you again."

Chayanne quickly nods, tears falling. "Me too." She holds Maia's face. "Me too."

The tent's zipper slides open, and Miguel peers inside.

Maia is breathless, seeing him in the light of day. Just

like her dreams, his dreadlocks have been shaved off, his face more chiseled. Just like her dreams, he is more handsome than ever.

"I'll get you some food," Chayanne says quietly. She grabs Maia's cheeks and draws her in, kissing her forehead. "There's water in that canister behind you. *Drink*." She hands Maia the bottle and stands.

Maia nods. Watching Miguel, she absently places the canister beside her. He steps out of the tent as Chayanne leaves, then crouches back inside, zipping the doorway closed. Maia's heart skips a beat. She can't stop staring—it's like looking at a ghost. He crouches down and sits before her.

Reaching her hand to his face, she whispers, "Is it really you?" She holds his cheek, tears falling from her fluttering eyes.

He doesn't speak, his eyes glassy, and he nods ever so slightly. He pulls her hand from his cheek, repeatedly squeezing it as if he, too, needs reassurance that she is sitting before him—*safe*. Whole. He gently kisses the top of her hand. Visibly upset, his breathing is uneven, his lips lingering on her skin.

Maia lifts to her knees, and Miguel does the same. Pulling her into him, he wraps his heavy arms around her, and she buries her head in his chest. Memories from the last time she held him in her hut at the tribe come back to her. How excruciating it was to stand there and pretend like she understood as he told her he would no longer be joining them to Leucothea.

Somehow, they have found their way back inside each other's arms. She clutches at him, gasping against her sobs. She can't let go. Please don't make her let go.

After a while, he pulls away and looks her over, his

expression deeply concerned. He leans in, and for a moment, it seems he's going to kiss her. Maia's breath catches, but he stops, grabbing the steel canister at her side. Tenderly wiping the tears from her cheeks, he whispers, "Please," and hands her the water.

Maia sighs and sips from the container. Miguel sits and she does the same, and the two gaze at one another in silence.

"I was," Miguel begins to say, but he hesitates, struggling to hold his composure. Maia has never seen him in such a fragile state. "I was ... *so worried* about you," he finally says. "What happened up there?"

She closes her eyes, shaking her head. "I wouldn't know where to begin." But then, she does. She looks up at him, covering her mouth. "*Lucas,*" she whispers.

He turns away. "I know."

"You know?"

His throat bobs, but he doesn't say a word.

"I am so *sorry,*" she whispers.

"Yes," he says quietly, looking down. "I am too."

The two sit without speaking. For years, all Maia has ever wanted was to see him again, to hold him, to tell him everything. Now that they are here, she has no idea what to say. "Your hair," she finally mutters. "It's all gone."

For a while, he doesn't look at her. When he does, there is a profound sadness behind his eyes. "Yes," he says softly. "I was in mourning."

Maia swallows. "I am so sorry. The rapids were so treacherous. He injured his leg—"

The way Miguel looks at her silences her. "I cut my hair long before I learned about Lucas," he mutters.

Maia closes her eyes. *She* is the reason he cut his hair.

She peers up at him, lost for words. She knows she hurt

him, and now, he has chosen another. He's not wearing a ring, but this doesn't surprise her. It's an old tradition, one that she has only ever seen upheld in "the land of plenty," Leucothea. And while she has known about Miguel's new wife for some time now, she never thought she'd see him again. She was actually relieved to know that he had found someone new—someone he loved and who loved him in return. But now that Maia is sitting across from him and that "someone" will never be her, it feels nothing short of excruciating.

She looks around, unsure of what to say. Her tent is small, saturated in an old, musty smell. A few packs and supplies are piled in a corner. Her sleeping bag is next to what she can only assume is Chayanne's. There are soft murmurings of men and women outside her tent.

"Where are we?" she asks.

"Deep in the wilderness of the Old Alaska. There are a few dozen of us from the tribe. We are going to lay low for a while. Your absence will not go unnoticed, and we have a few injured."

"Injured? But not..."

"We lost a few."

"Oh, Miguel. I'm so sorry."

He nods, looking down. "Thank you. We were all fully aware of the risk."

"How did you..."

Miguel sighs. "Claire."

Maia gapes at him, stunned. "*Claire* warned you?"

"Yes. This is a surprise?"

"She wasn't exactly a friend of mine."

"She sent a messenger. Apparently, things had gone from bad to worse with the ... *situation* ... between you and Jake."

The way he looks at her makes her wonder what he knows. Does he know that she and Jake were romantic? That she lived on his property? Became a shell of the woman she once was? She can't bear the thought.

"She warned us that our community was in grave danger," Miguel continues. "Her message was very clear for us *not* to come for you, that it would be too dangerous. But we told her messenger there was no way we wouldn't. Somehow, she expected this and said if that was our reply, she would try to get us in and out hidden in the back of something called an 'S&R Truck.' With her authority, no one would search the vehicle or ask any questions. She sent her messenger back with strict instructions on where to meet and when. Gave us uniforms to wear. We got in with no problem, but getting you out didn't go as smoothly. Three of our men were shot; only one survived. We killed a few of Jake's men, injured more." He shakes his head. "I don't think Claire is safe. We pleaded with her to come with us, but she refused."

"No, I'm not surprised she wouldn't leave. Jake is her life," Maia says quietly. "And what about the tribe? Tema?" *Your wife?*

"Everyone is safe. We have cleared the grounds of our people and have them hidden until we sort something out. We won't go back there until this is dealt with ... Whatever that means."

"This is too dangerous," Maia says. "You *all* need to leave. *Now.* Just leave me here before anyone else gets hurt."

He shakes his head, and for a moment, it seems he wants to smile. "Maia, that will *never* happen."

"You don't understand. Jake won't stop searching for me, and when he finds me, he'll kill you—*all* of you."

"Do not worry about that right now. You need rest." He

grabs her hand. His face is pained—*angry*—as he surveys her state. "He hurt you."

"Not as much as he would've liked "

Miguel grimaces at her response. "But he knows ... about your powers."

"I tried ... I tried *so hard* to keep them hidden," she gasps. "But he knows. Miguel, you don't understand. The things he's planning ... He won't stop until he has me back in Leucothea."

"I won't let that happen."

"I wish it were that simple, but he is a very powerful man."

"Maybe. But *you* are a very powerful woman, yes? Much more powerful than him."

Maia gazes up at Miguel. He has always believed in her in a way that no one else has. "I can't believe," she whispers, "after everything that happened between us ... you still came for me."

He peers down at their hands, and his voice softens. "I swore to you I would."

Maia stares at his face, her hand within his, and she holds back her sob. After all this time, she has tried to convince herself that what they had was nothing. That she had let him go. Laid it to rest. But it was always profound, this connection between them. A force beyond them. And after all this time, it's still *here*. He's reserved—distant—but she can still feel it, the love between them. A tear falls down her cheek. "I can't begin to tell you how much I've missed you."

"Maia," he says tenderly, "it would *pale* in comparison."

She throws herself around him, and he holds her tight. Burying his face in her neck, he sighs.

TWENTY-TWO

Days pass, and Maia rests inside her little tent. Chayanne brings in buckets of hot water, helping Maia bathe and applying a traditional herbal balm on her cuts and bruises. She wraps Maia in warm clothes and thick blankets and braids back her hair. Miguel pops in from time to time, always bringing plates of food but never staying long. All the while Maia desperately tries to sleep, the exhaustion from her trauma with Jake hanging over her like a dense fog, but sleep does not come.

The late-spring days have once again become long, the nights increasingly short. Chayanne has given Maia a mask to wear over her eyes, but she cannot wear it. Every time she does, the darkness brings her back to that tiny cell underground. She wakes up screaming, ripping off her mask as flashbacks of Jake's quivering, angry face hangs over her. That rage. That horrifying, possessive look in his eyes.

I'm a jealous man, Maia. If I can't have you, no one can.

She can only imagine how furious Jake would be at this very moment. Obsessing over the fact that members of the tribe he had been searching for had not only infiltrated his land while he slept, but had also stolen his most prized possession. He would have footage from his cameras, and Maia knows he will be watching it ... over and over and over again, memorizing Miguel's face as he carried Maia away from the bunker.

There is an endless pit in Maia's stomach that no amount of food can satiate. A bottomless, swirling void of dread. She knows, without a single doubt in her mind, that Jake will not rest. Every minute she is sitting here, he will be planning, searching. He will destroy everything in his path, and every single person with her right now is in grave danger.

She has pleaded with Miguel, Shinesho, and Chayanne to leave her. She has begged them with tears streaming down her face to pack up immediately and get as far away from her as they can.

But they have refused. They have tried to soothe her with empty words. To assure her that they are safe, hidden deep within the wilderness. That they know this land. They have lookouts stationed.

But they don't know. They couldn't possibly know.

Nowhere is safe.

And so, Maia has no other option but to use this time to rest and regain her strength. To breathe and clear her mind. To come up with a plan. How do you stop such a force to be reckoned with? But is she not *also* a force to be reckoned with? Maia knows she and Jake must once again come face to face. Only this time, she will make sure she is good and ready.

A battle is coming.

209

Lying in her tent with Chayanne beside her, Maia stares at the forest debris on the other side of the nylon. She listens to the quiet murmurings outside, trying to pick out Miguel's voice from the rest. The time has come to talk to the tribe, tell them who she is and why Jake will be fighting so hard to get her back.

"Chayanne?" Maia turns to face her. "There is something I need to tell you ... about who I am."

Chayanne smiles. "I know."

Maia looks at her, a crease between her brow, and she sits up. "What do you know?"

"Miguel told us everything. He had to, to help us understand what was happening in Leucothea. Tema backed him, said she had been dreaming of you for years. We know who you are, Maia. We all know. We love you, and we support you."

Maia sighs in relief. "You *know*?"

"We know." Chayanne sits up. "And *you* need to know, there is not a soul at this camp who doesn't want to be here. We will do whatever it takes. We are in this together."

"You don't understand how dangerous this man is. The number of people supporting him, how vast his armies are."

"Maia? Good will prevail. We will figure out a way. There's always a way. Isn't that what you've always said?"

"There's always a way," Maia whispers.

Chayanne holds her hand. "We'll figure it out, I know we will."

"If anything were to happen to you, or to these men and women ... Or Tema."

"I have something for you," Chayanne says with a smile, and she reaches into her pocket. She pulls out a necklace braided from dried grass and hands it to Maia. "To replace the devil's chain around your neck."

"Oh, *Chayanne*." Maia takes it, running the smooth cord between her fingertips. "This is so thoughtful. Thank you."

Chayanne stands and holds out her hand. "I'm sick of being cooped up in here. Shall we take a walk?"

Maia nods. Yes, a walk. A walk would be good.

The two women step outside their tent, and a few men nod as they pass. Maia locks eyes with Miguel across the camp, talking to Shinesho next to a fire. He is quick to look away.

It has been a week since he carried Maia back to their hideaway in the woods, and over that time, he has stopped by her tent less and less. It's been *days* since he last visited her. Maia understands why, but it doesn't make it any easier. Every time that zipper slides down her doorway, she yearns to see his face, but more often than not, it is someone else.

As Chayanne and Maia walk through the woods, they are bathed in the sounds of nature. Chirping birds. Screeching insects. It feels like coming home; the sounds and the delicate presence of whispering trees seem to be the only things to soothe the gnawing ache inside Maia's heart.

"How are you feeling?" Chayanne asks.

Maia nods, looking down at the path. "I'm okay."

Chayanne halts in the middle of the trail, her hand on her hip.

Maia smiles. "Fair enough. It's tough ... being around him like this. He's so *distant*."

"Maia, you need to understand. When you left, it was like you died. Miguel was devastated. I didn't know him at the time." She scoffs, shaking her head. "Nor did I *want* to know him. The only impression I had was that he had left you in the wilderness before you showed up delirious on our grounds. But then he and I became friends. He opened up to me about how he felt about you, and it broke my heart. That man really loved you."

Maia nods, guilt stealing her words.

"His friendship with Shinesho was really good for him. Shinesho helped him mourn losing you. Miguel had to work really hard on letting you go. You understand that, don't you?"

"I do. I understand more than you know."

"I know you do, sweetheart." She links her arm through Maia's, and they continue their walk. "We've become close, Miguel and I. He's like a brother to me now. I really admire his strength. Before Claire's messengers came, it seemed like he had finally moved on with his life. He was talking about going to Leucothea to visit you and Lucas, which was a huge step for him.

"But then these strange men showed up on our grounds, and we came to discover that not only were we all in serious danger, but that you were being held captive, and that Lucas had *died* on your journey. Miguel had no time to come to terms with *any* of it. He became hyper-focused, working around the clock to take care of our community, making sure everyone was safe, and organizing our departure. I can't tell you how happy I am that you're here and safe with us, but ... oh, Maia. He seems so pained. Conflicted. I really think you two should talk. Get out anything lingering between you and move on. We can all feel the tension, and it's awful. There's no way either one of you will be able to focus with all this weighing you down."

"I know. You're right. I'll talk to him."

As the women arrive back at camp, Maia finds Miguel between the trees, chopping wood. He pauses, watching from over his shoulder as she walks toward him. She forces a smile and he does the same, and then he goes back to axing.

Her heart is racing. She's not ready for this, but someone has to say *something*. "I thought ... I thought maybe we could talk," she says as she approaches.

He stops, waiting for her to continue.

She blows out a long breath. Wrapping her arms around herself, she nervously shifts from foot to foot. "I don't know where to begin."

He grips his axe, peering down at the wood, then holds his breath and swings. The timber breaks in two, and he sighs. "You don't need to say anything. You don't need to worry about me," he grumbles as he picks up the pieces and tosses them into a pile.

"I'm ... I'm *not*."

"Then what's with the looks, Maia?" he snaps, placing another chunk of wood on the stump.

"What looks?"

"You are always looking at me so concerned. You don't need to be concerned about me. Or sad for me. Or whatever it is that you are. I've done just fine without you. I've..." He swings hard, and the wood splits. "I've moved on."

She swallows, pushing down her ache. "Yes, of course. I know that."

"*Do* you." He looks at her. His face appears as pained as it does angry. He picks up the timber and tosses it into the pile, then places another block on the stump. "Good." He strikes, and the wood fractures. He swings again and it snaps in two, tumbling across the dirt. He hangs his head. Sighing, he says quietly, "You left me no choice."

Maia closes her eyes. She thought she could do this, but she can't. She turns and walks away.

"Maia?" Miguel calls after her.

No. *Can't.*

TWENTY-THREE

Sitting along the banks of a stream, Maia dips her feet into the crystal blue waters. As her toes glide against the stones, the ripples from her legs glimmer in the afternoon light. She breathes sweet relief, a trace of herself awakening for the first time in years.

Separated from the natural elements for so long, it is no wonder she became lost in that city of lights. Surrounded by cement and towers of glass, her body malnourished from artificial food, she became a shell of the woman she once was. She had spent her entire life living among the trees, hunting her own food, and digging her toes into the earth. To be thrown into a deadened world wrapped in a façade of glittering lights ... She didn't stand a chance.

A gentle breeze carries the whispers of the trees, and she knows what she must do. Her heart aches for Miguel, but he has moved on with his life, and she must do the same. He has a family, his pregnant wife hidden away with the rest of the tribe. It would be wrong not to be happy for him. And she will be. She isn't yet, but she will. She *must*. He deserves that. She and Miguel are friends. *Buddies.*

She inwardly groans.

This dance of lies, they know it well.

It's the same battle they've been fighting from the beginning. Pretty much from the moment they met. They should be good at it by now.

She wades into the middle of the shallow stream and falls to her knees. How is she supposed to find the strength to let him go all over again? Sitting in the river's cool waters, she tips her head back, welcoming the sun's warm rays on her face. She will because she *must*.

A battle is looming.

From the moment Maia stood in the pouring rain on Jake's cliff, she has known without a shadow of a doubt why her destiny has called her to the Arctic. Why Jake feels so strongly that they've been drawn to one another.

I am the reason you have always felt called here.

He's not wrong.

Jake may be one of the most powerful men on Earth, but she *is* the Earth. He may be hell-bent on destroying her in his quest for *more*. He may have his armies, and he may have his weapons. He may have resurrected the technology of their ancestors.

But none of that has ever been able to withstand the weight of Mother Nature's wrath.

The weight of *her* wrath.

Like water, she is nurturing, and she is destructive. Her power is vast—unmatched by anything Jake's cronies can create in one of his labs. Only Maia has the potential to destroy Jake and his precious New System. He knows it. She knows it.

And like water, she will crush him with the weight of a thousand oceans.

She stands in the middle of the stream. Gazing up at the

swaying pines, she sweeps her hand across the sky, and every tree before her swoops to the ground. Unbreaking, they bow to her in reverence.

She dips her hands beneath the river, then lifts them up before her. With water streaming down her arms, she divides the shallow river down its center. It sweeps against its banks, forming walls on either side and exposing a wet riverbed. Maia steps down the barren center, and the trees one by one lift back to the sky.

She drops to her knees. Sinking her hands into the wet sand, she closes her eyes, thinking of all those innocent people living in the Arctic—both inside Leucothea and out. Somehow, she must stop Jake and his government, but how can she do that without harming its people?

She has come here to defend the Earth, but are humans not also part of the Earth? Do those people supporting Leucothea's New System deserve to die? To lose the life they have come so far to live? They don't know ... *Do* they? They couldn't possibly know the systems they support.

"What do I do?" she whispers. Breathing deep, she listens for the answer lying just beyond her thoughts.

And it comes to her, a soft, curling tendril of a whisper.

She is only as strong as her greatest weakness. She must learn to control her powers. She must learn to control her *temper* in the face of grave difficulty. Then, no matter what happens with this war—with *Jake*—she can never be used for evil again.

She needs to harness her powers—*all* of them. How can she make this ground move? When has it happened before?

Anger—that's a good one, Jake had said as he strapped her down and stood over her in his bunker.

She clenches her jaw, thinking of the misery he has inflicted, not only on her but on the scores of enslaved souls outside Leucothea's gates. The pain he intends to exact on the people she loves. The lies he's told. The greed he's fed. The burning oil. Burning, burning, *burning* into the skies of an overburdened atmosphere. She slams her fists into the wet riverbed, and the earth quakes in response. Clouds of birds burst from the trees, soaring high into the skies. She smiles. Yes, anger *is* a good one.

She thinks of Jake again, of his beloved New System and his deluded, monstrous city of lights, and she beats her fists into the earth. It trembles. She digs her knuckles into the wet sand, twisting as she pushes, and the riverbed's rocks clink against one another.

Clink. Clink. Clinkclinkclinkclink.

A twig snaps, and Maia looks up with a start.

Pushing through the tall weeds along the river's edge, stands Maia's tiger.

Gasping, Maia falls back onto her hands, and the river plummets from its walls. It surges across the drying channel and claps hard in the middle, blasting water into the sky. She braces herself against the sloshing river, squinting through the spray.

Can't be.

She stands, her heart pounding. Her tiger tilts his head as he looks at her, and she stumbles toward him, her feet slipping among the mossy stones. He steps into the river, slowly making his way toward her. Crouching down, she reaches out with a trembling hand, and he timidly sniffs in her direction, his white whiskers flickering. Then he bursts forward, nestling into her.

Running her fingers through his thick fur, she peers into his pale-yellow eyes. Such a *magnificent* creature. "You're still alive," she whispers, and she wraps her arms around him. "I'm so *glad* you're still alive." They lean in nose to nose, and Maia thinks of Huck, missing him so much it hurts. "Hey." She pulls away, sniffling. "I was too afraid to name you before, but you should have a name. Don't you think you should have a name?"

He sniffs around her face, and she smiles. "How about ... *Atlas*?"

The tiger nudges her in approval, and she giggles. "Okay, then. Your name shall be Atlas."

There is more rustling from the brush along the riverbank. Maia looks up as another tiger steps into the river. It's a female. Maia stands in shock.

Tigers don't travel in packs.

Downstream, another tiger steps out. And another. *Another.* Maia looks down at Atlas and she knows, these tigers have come together because of *her*.

She stands motionless in the middle of the stream as each tiger slowly makes its way toward her. She peers over her shoulder as more join from the other side, including two young cubs running ahead of their mother—one of them racing toward Maia. It's another female, splashing through the waters. Maia picks her up, and the cub burrows her head into Maia's neck.

As Maia makes her way back to camp with Atlas by her side, over a dozen tigers and two cubs now follow in a line behind her. The trees' whispers become louder with every step she takes.

Mother.

Mother.

Mother.

Observing the Earth's energy flowing up and down their trunks, Maia sighs. A great war may be building, but at this very moment, everything feels so ... *right*. She is exactly where she is meant to be. She was *always* where she was meant to be, as painful as it's been.

She holds her hands out to her sides, sweeping her fingers along branches, and she finally understands. That tree on Jake's property never betrayed her—it was the *catalyst* to open her eyes. Only because of that tree is she standing where she is today. Because of that tree, the people and the Arctic will stand a chance to rise against the New System's corruption.

She smiles. Once again, the darkest days of her life have carved the way to a new beginning.

As Maia enters the camp, the people rushing around take no notice of her. Heads down, they are busy preparing dinner. Two men are stripping and draining an elk hanging upside down from a tree. Others are standing around a table, cutting vegetation from the forest and throwing it in skillets to be cooked. A young man is kneeling next to a pit filled with wood and kindling beneath an old metal grate. Frustrated, he tries to start a fire, but the glint won't catch.

Maia steps from the tree line with Atlas beside her. One by one, the people freeze, staring at her tiger with their mouths agape. Kaique swipes his crossbow from a table and Maia lifts her hand, slowly shaking her head. He begrudgingly lowers it. Chayanne turns from speaking with a small group, and she covers her mouth. Miguel steps outside his tent, scanning the scene unfolding before him. He looks the least surprised, as if he knew all along that this was a matter of time.

Maia's tigers one by one step out from the trees, forming a line behind her until eventually, the tribe of humans stands on one side of the camp while Maia and her legion of tigers stand on the other. She lifts her palm to the sky, and the firepit roars to life. The young man next to it falls back-ward, inching away on his hands and feet.

The men and women gape between the blazing fire and the tigers and Maia, but her eyes remain fixed on Miguel's.

And for the first time since they've been reunited, he smiles.

———

Sitting around the fire, the tribe tries to eat, but there are now over a dozen large tigers lying around them, sniffing the air as the aromas of meat waft from plates. The two cubs are chasing each other around the camp, playfully biting and rolling around in the dirt. The people swap glances, tense and unsure.

Maia is the only one eating her dinner. "They aren't going to hurt you," she says as she tears off a piece of her steak. She offers it to Atlas, who tenderly nips it from her fingers with his front teeth.

No one says a word.

"I promise, they won't," Maia says, looking around.

"So..." a young man sitting across from her says. "It's true, what they've been saying about you."

She peers up at him. "It is."

"What do you want to do?" the young man asks.

Everyone looks at Maia.

For a moment, she is taken aback. "Well, I've had a lot of time to think about that," she says, glancing between each person. She stops when she reaches Shinesho. "Jake is preparing his army, and he plans to take over the entire Arctic. He'll be waging a war—and soon—starting with Asiaq Bay. It will be an ambush. His army will surround them, and they will take the city, its resources, and its people. I need to go there. Not only do they need to be warned, but I'd like to ask if they'd be willing to join us in stopping Leucothea."

"Not you," Miguel says from across the fire.

Maia shoots him a reproachful look. "What do you mean, *not* me? Of course me—"

"Jake will have eyes all over that city," Shinesho says. "If you go anywhere near it, he will be waiting."

"But that's not his land."

"Doesn't matter," Miguel says. "His biggest priority, besides finding *you*, will be stopping you from warning them. He'll have undercover spies stationed all over the place, guaranteed. If you go up there, he will have accomplished two goals."

"We will send a few of our finest," Kaique says. "Those who didn't sneak onto Jake's property, so he won't know their faces. They will warn the city and ask if they would be willing to join forces."

"Our small army has been preparing for a long time now," Shinesho says. "We've heard the rumors about Leucothea. I have no doubt Asiaq Bay will be the same, along with the Old Russia, although we won't have enough time to reach them. I'll have my messengers see if Asiaq Bay has the resources to contact them."

"We also thought we could send a few soldiers down to New Portland," Miguel says. "Jake isn't just a threat to the civilizations in the Arctic. We have friends in New Portland. I believe they will help us."

Maia nods. "That's a good idea. Let me go with you, I can help—"

"You cannot go with them," Shinesho says. "Your presence will be like a shining beacon to the mission, and it will most certainly fail."

Maia gawks at him from across the fire. This isn't going as planned.

"The only thing Jake cares about right now is finding *you*," Shinesho continues. "You must lay low, and we know exactly where you should go—a place where we can all gather to prepare for this war. It's the perfect location to train, and we believe it to be outside of Leucothea's vision. It's hidden between mountains, so we can easily have people on the lookout. But we need time: time to gather armies, make a plan, and prepare. The only way we can get that is by moving farther away from Leucothea, out of Jake's reach. And by keeping *you* hidden until we are ready. Chayanne and I will take you there, and we will prep the armies as they arrive. My soldiers just need a little more time to rest before we separate."

"But I have the power to help—"

"Yes," Shinesho says sternly, "and you still need to figure out how to harness that power on a much grander scale. Am I correct in that assumption?"

She crosses her arms, looking away. "You're not wrong," she mumbles.

Chayanne sits down beside her, softly rubbing her back.

"Maia," Miguel says. "We need to keep you safe. I won't let him find you. I won't let him take you from—"

Chayanne starts to cough, and Miguel shoots her a sharp look. "Sorry," she says. "I swallowed a bug! *Weird*." She glares at him.

"Maia?" Shinesho says. "You should be aware of what Jake has done."

Maia glances at those around her, but they shift their gazes to the ground. Even Chayanne refuses to make eye contact. Maia looks at Miguel. "What aren't you telling me?"

"Jake has already had scores of soldiers out looking for you," Miguel replies gravely. "And he has sent us a message."

"A *message*?"

"His men came to our village," Kaique says. "Truckloads of them. They've destroyed everything, Maia. Burned it all to the ground."

Maia stands. "*What*?!"

The tigers lift their heads.

"No one was there, but they are not fools," Miguel says. "They knew we were gone, but our lookouts watched from a distance. Jake would have known that too. It was a message, and one we've received loud and clear. He thinks he can threaten us, that we are small and insignificant compared to him. But if we can get these other cities to join us and give *you* time with your powers, we believe we'll have a shot at stopping him."

Maia sits down, her head in her hands. "He is such a *monster*." She looks up at Chayanne. "I am so sorry. Your home. Your beautiful, beautiful home."

"Don't be sorry," Chayanne says, but her gaze is pained. "This isn't your fault."

"It is, actually," Maia says.

"We've feared for a long time that Leucothea was a threat," Shinesho interjects, "but we couldn't be sure. It's only because of you that we now know what is going on up there. Now we can warn the other cities and join forces. If it weren't for you, we would have been blindsided, and Jake and his New System would have surely taken over. Now, we at least have a chance to stop him."

"And remember," Chayanne says, "we have something very powerful that Jake doesn't."

Maia peers at her over her shoulder, and Chayanne smiles. "*You*," she says tenderly.

Maia gazes around. Every person is now looking at her, nodding and humming their agreement.

"Maia," Shinesho says very seriously, "you know Leucothea. You know *Jake*. Do you have any information that can help us? Because you know as well as we do, you cannot kill a movement's leader and stop the movement. Even if we took down Jake, another general would rise in his place."

Maia sighs. "We have to destroy the illusion. I believe the people of Leucothea are good, but they are fooled. They have no idea what's happening behind the scenes or the deplorable situation they are supporting. They love their city, and they *adore* Jake. We have to shine a light on what their New System has been doing in the shadows, and allow the people to decide for themselves. If we don't, they will surely fight back, and there are too many of them. We need them on our side."

"How are we supposed to show a population of tens of thousands what the city has been doing?" Miguel asks.

"Could hijack one of their drones? They record things, right?" Shinesho asks Maia.

"Yes, but they work on a live feed."

The people stare blankly at her.

"The video they are recording is being played immediately on television screens in secured government offices back in the city," Maia says. "If we steal one of their drones, we would just be showing them in real-time exactly who and where we are. We need someone who has been trained to work with the technology to cut the feed and then record what we want it to."

"Anyone know how to work with drones?" Miguel asks.

They all glance between each other, shrugging.

"I bet they do up in Asiaq Bay," Kaique says. "Lots of people there. We'll see what they have to work with."

"So," Chayanne says, "the plan is to combine armies, surround Leucothea, and demand the current government step down."

"And show the people that we are on their side," Maia says. "That is *really* important."

"And if they still support Leucothea?" Chayanne asks.

"If the people decide to stand by their leaders, then we will have no choice but to go to war," Maia says. "I will have to use my powers to make up for our lack in numbers, which could be ... *catastrophic*. I really don't want to do that. But Leucothea cannot take over the only livable land left on Earth, supported by a legion of blind followers. They will destroy everything, and nothing and no one will stand a chance."

Chayanne asks, "What if we freed the enslaved people and offered them a chance to join us? They could infiltrate the city and tell the people of Leucothea what has been happening."

"Jake would know immediately," Maia says. "He has everything on watch. It would be a slaughter. Our only hope is to take him by surprise. They have a citywide celebration called Leucothea Day in a little over four months. They honor their armies on this day, so most of the soldiers will be inside the city. They'll still have their walls highly guarded, so only a select few of us should try to sneak in. Maybe in one of their S&R Trucks again?" She looks at Shinesho. "Are you still in contact with Claire's messenger?"

He nods. "I'll see what I can do."

"President Augustus always gives a speech at the end of the celebration," Maia continues. "The entire city will be watching on screens projected on the buildings. We'll switch the feed and play our footage. We'll show them everything. With everyone so distracted, it will be the perfect time to surround their encampments and free the people. The soldiers stationed there have guns, but there are a relatively small number of them compared to the prisoners they are guarding.

"With the added numbers of Asiaq Bay, New Portland, and hopefully some of the freed slaves, Leucothea's army will be outnumbered and the city surrounded. We'll cut their electricity after showing them our feed, and the precious system they love so much will come to a screeching halt. Their walls will be broken, their illusion shattered, and they will have no choice but to start over. Not only will the lives of thousands in Canada and Russia be spared, but so will their future generations."

"And ours," Chayanne says.

"That's an ideal situation," Shinesho says. "Things always go wrong. We'll need to prepare for every scenario."

"Of course," Maia says.

"And what if no one agrees to join our revolution?" Kaique asks. "What if it's just us? How is our tiny army supposed to stop a giant like Leucothea?"

Maia gazes at him. "You won't."

He looks at her, confused.

"*I* will," she says. "I have the power to destroy every-thing, which is why Jake is fighting so hard to find me."

"So why don't we just start with that?" he asks with nervous laughter.

Maia tilts her gaze. "Because I have the power to destroy *everything*. The laws of nature aren't specific." She looks at the faces around her. "And I am bound by those same laws. If I use an earthquake or fire or flood the city with a tsunami-like wall of water, these are forces that will destroy

everything and everyone in their path. And there are innocent people in that city."

There is silence as they digest the severity of her words.

"We will do everything we can to give these people a
chance," Chayanne says quietly beside her.

"And..." Shinesho peers around at the sleeping tigers, at
Atlas sprawled by Maia's feet. "We also have ... *tigers*? I
assume they will be coming with us to base camp?"

Maia smiles. "They will."

Shinesho's eyes widen, and he nods. "Okay, then."

The men and women chuckle. Shaking their heads, they
go back to eating their meals ... Everyone except Maia and
Miguel, who have locked eyes from across the fire.

"And after all that," Miguel says quietly, and the group
looks up from their plates, "you're going to walk straight
back to the man that wants to enslave you."

"I have no choice," Maia says.

"*Why*?"

"Because he is the reason I'm here."

TWENTY-FOUR

Time. Time is good.

Head down, Maia paces between the trees, her mind reeling like the forest floor beneath her, passing in a blur. Atlas is perched to the side, curiously watching her as a cub pounces on his flopping tail. He rests his head on the ground.

Yes, time. Time is precisely what they need. They don't have much, but it will have to be enough. Time to gather their armies and collect enough footage to show the citizens of Leucothea what's been happening behind the scenes. Time for Maia to harness her powers on a much grander scale. Time to make a plan of attack against Jake, whose presence still haunts her every waking moment like a black, foreboding fog.

And time for Maia and Miguel to mend the demons that plague them: *Lucas, wife, baby*. It's been nearly two weeks since he carried her back to this little camp in the dark night, and the two have barely spoken. Distant. So, so distant. But they are always watching each other. Everywhere Maia goes, she looks for Miguel over her shoulder.

Even if he isn't speaking to her, just knowing he's there is better than nothing at all. *Anything* is better than nothing at all.

She needs to talk to him, just get it over with—she'll do it tonight. She'll ask about his new life and this woman he has given his heart to. Maybe if she starts a dialogue, then this awful silence between the two of them can dissipate, and they can find a new normal—a less painful normal. And since he's clearly not going to do it, she will.

Back at camp, everyone is sitting quietly around the fire eating dinner. Miguel, Chayanne, and Maia are perched on a log next to one another, with Chayanne between Maia and Miguel. Now is the perfect time for Maia to say something. It's never going to get any easier, and maybe having Chayanne there will ease the awkwardness.

"So..." Maia says. She hesitates, her heart thundering, and her cheeks flush.

Both Chayanne and Miguel look at her, and she *immediately* regrets saying anything. What was she thinking? She's not ready for this.

Chayanne leans to her side, studying Maia.

"What's *up*, Maia?" Miguel asks, half-smiling.

"I ... I just wanted to say ... *congratulations*," Maia says definitively, lifting her chin. She can do this.

Chayanne's brow creases. She looks at Maia like she has grown horns out of her head. Entertained, she leans back, glancing between Maia and Miguel.

Miguel tilts his head. "*For...*"

Chayanne lifts her mug, taking a sip.

"Your marriage," Maia says, forcing a smile.

Chayanne chokes on her water, and snickers resound around the fire.

Maia's cheeks are ablaze. Why is everyone laughing? "*Why* is this funny?" She smacks Chayanne, who is now belting loud, exaggerated laughs.

Miguel has a sly, amused look on his face.

"Miguel is *not* married," Shinesho says coolly from across the fire.

Maia's mouth agape, she looks at Miguel. "Are you ... *expecting*?"

Chayanne falls backward off the log. Miguel closes his eyes, delicately shaking his head as Chayanne carries on in hysterics between them.

"*Chayanne!*" Shinesho hushes her.

"But I thought—I was told..." Maia stammers, her head spinning.

"Oh my *God*! Can you imagine?!" Chayanne climbs back onto her seat. "Mr. Unattainable Bachelor over here?"

More resounding chuckles, and Maia starts to sweat. She is so embarrassed. And relieved. And *confused*.

"Maia, who told you these things?" Miguel asks tenderly.

Shaking her head, she glares at the fire. "*Jake*." He is *such* an asshole.

"Probably knew it would upset you," Shinesho says quietly, arching his brow.

The tribe averts their eyes. So, the entire camp knows.

Maia peers back at Miguel, who has a sheepish grin on his face. He shakes his head again. "Not married. No babies."

"Not even *close*," Chayanne says, still chuckling. "Oh, Maia, I'm so glad you're back." She wraps her arm around her and they all share a laugh.

Maia smiles, but now she is even more confused. Why has he been so distant?

———

Much later that night, Maia finds Miguel alone by the fire, sitting on a log and sipping from a mug. Most of the camp has gone to sleep in their tents. Now is her chance.

He stands as soon as she sits.

Please don't walk away.

"Hot water?" He winks, dimple showing.

She beams up at him. "Please."

He pours her a mug, and they sit next to one another. "So," Miguel finally says. "*Wow*. I've apparently had quite the life since you've been gone."

Maia nods. "I guess Jake knew his audience."

"I guess so."

Chayanne walks up with a smile. She takes one look at the two of them and freezes. "*Nope*." She turns on a heel and heads back to her tent.

Miguel laughs. "I've really grown to love that woman."

"Yeah, she's the best."

They stare at the fire.

"So," Maia says. "*Not* married."

Miguel looks at her tenderly, resting his chin on his shoulder. He shakes his head.

"Are..." Maia hesitates. "Are you *with* someone?"

He bites his lip, gazing at her. He shakes his head again.

Maia is flooded with relief. "But ... you've been so *distant*."

He sighs and looks down at his mug. "When I lost my wife and girls, it was the worst thing to ever happen to me. That sort of pain ... My God, I wouldn't wish it on my worst enemy. It took me *years* to function as a normal person again." He thumbs the edge of his metal mug, hesitating. "And then I lost you." He looks at her for a moment, then turns his attention to the fire. "It was nowhere near the same pain as losing my girls ... but there were days ... there were days it felt pretty damn close."

Maia swallows hard, blinking back her tears.

"I bared myself to you, Maia. I *pleaded* with you. A love like that, in a world like this? But you had a choice to make, and you didn't choose me. I mourned you as if you had died. I buried you." He looks at her, his eyes glassy. "And now ... now it is like you are back from the dead. I am not trying to be distant." He sits up straight, clears his throat. "But I have accepted what has happened between us, and I've moved on."

She nods. *Worse*. This is so much worse than marriage. "Look." She stands to face him, but he won't meet her gaze. "I know I chose Lucas. But I was only trying ... I have *always* loved—"

"Maia, it's okay," he says, standing to face her. "You don't need to explain. That was a long time ago. I'm okay now. I'm ... I'm *glad* you chose him."

Lies.

"You and I are buddies, yes?" He forces a smile, and for a moment, Maia can see the wounded man Chayanne has been talking about. "Let's forget about what happened and move on. What's done is done. We have a war to prepare for."

Maia looks up at him. So much unspoken behind his eyes. He says he has let her go, but she doesn't believe him. She can feel it—right now, she can still feel it between them. What they had, it was never nothing.

He turns to walk away, and Maia throws her arms around him. "Please don't go," she begs into his back.

He turns, breaking her embrace, and he holds out his hand.

She angles her head. "*Miguel*."

"We are *friends*, yes?" He swallows hard, his face stern.

She looks down at his hand and sighs, shaking it. "Yes, Miguel. Friends."

As he walks away, she says quietly, "You said 'back.'"

He turns to face her, exasperated. "*What*?"

She steps toward him, wringing her hands. "Before we separated ... by the field with the caribou. You said there would never come a day when you wouldn't give up hope that I would find my way back to you."

Anger flashes across his face. "I can't believe you would bring that up."

"Did you not mean it?"

"I meant every word. I am happy that you are back with us. You *belong* with us."

"That's not what you meant, and you know it."

"Well, that was before."

"Before what?"

He takes a step closer, his face reddening. "Before you *left* to spend your life with my brother."

"But—"

"Things change. People change."

"*You've* changed," she mumbles.

"Yeah? *Good*," he growls. "Maybe next time, I'll know better." He turns to leave.

She grabs his hand. "What's *that* supposed to mean?!"

He breaks from her grasp. "You know exactly what it means," he says, and he walks away.

"You say you've moved on?" she yells at his back. "That

you have 'accepted' everything that has happened between us? You're a *liar*."

He stops in his tracks and marches back up to her. "Well, you told me you loved me, so that makes *two* liars standing here, Maia."

"I wasn't lying when I said that," she says, fighting tears. "I have *always* loved you."

"No. You don't get to say that to me—not anymore."

"You want to make it out like you're the victim here, Miguel? That I'm so heartless? Fine. You think I should have done something different? Well, get in line. You think I haven't hashed out every little thing that has happened between us? You think I haven't repeated every conversation and wondered what I could have done differently? You want to blame me—"

"I'm not blaming you, Maia. That's all on you. You are doing that to *yourself*."

"Your words ... you're so bitter." She looks at him, surprised. "Why are you so *angry*?!" she screams.

"*Why*? Why am I angry?!" he yells, eyes wide with his hands at his head. "You have *got* to be kidding me! You are the most infuriating woman I have *ever*..." He rants in Portuguese.

"*English*, Miguel."

His gaze turns cold. "I am angry because you have *no idea* how hard it was or how long it took for me to get over you. What it felt like to watch you walk away when you and I both knew—hell, we *all* knew, that you didn't love him like that. And then you come back into my life *so quickly,* and you want to pretend like nothing even happened! I am so sick of you always looking at me the way you do, always gazing at me from across the camp. You are *always looking* at me—"

"You're mad at me for looking at you?!"

"*Yes*! Yes, I am! Stop *looking* at me, Maia."

"Fine," she says. Crossing her arms, she stares at the ground. "I'll stop *looking* at you."

He lifts her chin, leaning so close they share a breath. "That's not what I mean, and *you* know it," he growls through his teeth.

Enraged, Maia fights the urge to grab his face and kiss him.

His eyes waver to her lips, and he quickly backs away. "And while we're talking about it, I'm also angry about Lucas."

"*Lucas*?"

"Yes, Lucas. You think you are the only one who lost him? You've had time to mourn, but I haven't. After all those years apart, I finally got him back in my life again, and now he's gone? Just like that—he's *gone*. I'm angry that I wasn't there for him when he was suffering. Or for *you*," he adds quietly, "for that matter."

She looks up at him in the fire's flickering light. All this time, all she's ever wanted was to be near him again, but she never thought it would be like this. She would give anything to hold him, but his walls are like a fortress.

Rubbing the back of his neck, he peers up at the sky and sighs. "Look, I am not trying to be distant. But these last few years have been..." His voice trails. When he gazes down at her, the look on his face crushes her. "I was so in love with you."

"*Was*?" she whispers, stepping closer to him.

He backs up. "Yes, Maia ... *was*," he says quietly, and then he turns and walks away.

This time, she doesn't try to stop him.

TWENTY-FIVE

Maia stumbles back to her tent, hollowed to her core. Chayanne is curled up under her sleeping bag. She rolls onto her back as Maia crawls onto the blankets next to her.

"Everything okay?" Chayanne asks at the ceiling.

"No," Maia grumbles.

Chayanne sighs. "He doesn't mean it."

"You heard."

"I think the entire Arctic heard."

"I've never seen him so angry. So cold. It doesn't matter what I do or say ... I think he hates me."

"He doesn't hate you."

Maia falls onto her back, covering her face with her hands. "Oh, Chayanne. What am I going to do?"

"A wise old woman once told me when someone is *that* angry, to remember that the only thing worse than hate is indifference."

Maia turns toward her. "So, you *do* think Miguel hates me."

"Of course not. But you have to remember, his father abandoned him when he was a child. His mother died, and then Lucas deserted him in the exact same way as his dad—in the middle of the night without saying a word. He lost his wife and both his little girls. And then he met you. You fell in love, despite everything you did to deny it was happening, and then *you* left him. That anger of his ... It's not all about you, but you must understand, his pain runs deep."

Maia closes her eyes.

"He still loves you, Maia. I have no doubt about that. But if there is one thing I've learned about Miguel since we've been friends, is that he needs to do things on his own time. Just leave him be. Don't force it. He'll come around."

"You think?" Maia looks at her.

Chayanne flips her head toward Maia and smiles. "I actually have no idea. That man has always been a mystery to me."

Maia laughs, looking back up at the tent's ceiling. "Awesome, Chayanne. *Comforting.* Thank you."

Chayanne pats Maia's knee and then rolls away, yawning. "Just give him time."

"Chayanne?"

"Yeah?"

"Why did you interrupt Miguel the other night at dinner? You pretended like you swallowed a bug, and you two ... shared a look?"

Chayanne rolls onto her back. "I didn't want him to lose his temper or say something he'd regret. I suppose I was being overprotective."

"Overprotective? Of me ... or him?"

Chayanne hesitates. "Him."

"Right."

"Just give him time, Maia. That's all I'm saying."

———

Another week passes, and the long summer days slowly soften the painful words hanging in the air between Maia and Miguel. They don't speak much, but they are always watching each other. It's like nothing else matters if Miguel's not around. Maia tries to respect his wishes and not always *look* at him, but almost every time she does, he is already watching her.

All she can think about is, he said *was*. He *was* in love with her, but now he is no longer. She doesn't believe him ... Or is it just that she can't? Chayanne said the only thing worse than hate is indifference. If he had no feelings for her, he would have no issue being friends. He would have no problem with her at all. But like Chayanne said, his pain runs deep. And Maia has no other option but to leave him be.

After spending most mornings hunting with Chayanne and helping the tribe prepare for the next leg of their journey, Maia spends her afternoons down by the river with her tigers. It would be the perfect time to practice her powers on a grand scale, but after a long conversation with Shinesho, she has agreed not to use them until they get to base camp, farther from Leucothea. The last thing they need is a signal to Jake and his men of her whereabouts.

Tonight is their group's final meal together until they reunite at their new camp in the mountains. Shinesho's men have healed and are ready to go. A small crew of his soldiers will head up to Asiaq Bay on horseback, another unit will head down to New Portland, and a few more will head back to the tribe for supplies and the rest of their army. All of these missions will take time, to not only prepare and gather the others but also to make sure they aren't being followed by any of Jake's men.

As Maia and Chayanne walk toward the tables to help with dinner, they pass the camp's makeshift showers. A blanket has been hung from a branch, with a small fire blazing on the other side, heating buckets of water. Maia slows. Miguel is behind that sheet, the silhouette of his body highlighted by the campfire's glow. She becomes transfixed, Chayanne's voice fading away.

Miguel bends over, dipping his cloth into a steaming bucket. He stands, wringing it out before him, and Maia runs into a large pile of stacked pots waiting to be divvied between the crews. The metal crashes across the dirt, and she loses her footing, stumbling and skipping across the pans.

Laughing, Chayanne clutches Maia's arm as she clears the rolling pots. "You okay there, soldier?"

Maia rubs the back of her neck, her cheeks on fire. "Yes, fine," she says quickly, wiping imaginary dirt from her top. She peers back at Miguel.

He has stepped out from behind the sheet, dripping wet with a towel around his chiseled waist. He tilts his head as they lock eyes from across the grounds, and a sly smile curves up from his mouth.

Maia whirls around, biting her lip. "Is ... *uh* ... Miguel going to New Portland? They know him there."

Chayanne raises her brow. "Shinesho asked the same thing."

"And?"

"And..." Chayanne says slowly, glancing between Maia

and Miguel. "Miguel insisted it wasn't necessary. He'll be coming with us."

"Why is that?" Maia asks in her most casual voice.

"Girl, you know why."

Maia peers back at him, but he's turned away. Shaking his head, his smile is wide.

"He's different around you," Chayanne says.

"What do you mean?" Maia faces forward, still catching her breath.

"He's normally proud and strong and a little egotistical at times, if I'm being completely honest. But around you," Chayanne continues, "he's sort of like a schoolboy."

"A schoolboy?"

"It's an old term." Chayanne shrugs. "He's lost his cocky arrogance ... I think you make him nervous." She smiles. "It's cute."

Maia and Chayanne have been trying to get the tribe's horses comfortable with the tigers being around, but they remain uneasy. Atlas sits next to Maia as she attempts once again to introduce him to her stallion. The large tiger yawns, white teeth glistening, and Maia's horse backs up, neighing and stomping his hooves.

"*Atlas!*" Maia chastises. "You're doing that on purpose!"

Miguel approaches, and both women watch from over their shoulders. "I am going for a walk," he says, looking at Maia. "Join me?"

Maia glances back at Chayanne, who is smirking at Miguel. "Go on," Chayanne says. "I've got this."

"Stay here," Maia says to Atlas. "You be *nice* to that horse."

Maia and Miguel walk along the trail in silence. Chayanne mentioned that Maia made Miguel nervous, but she, too, always finds her heart racing around this man.

Miguel stops walking. "I'm in hell," he says, and Maia turns to face him. "I can't stand this awkwardness between us. We have to move past this. You were right the other day, telling me I wasn't over it, but I am trying. Despite the way I've been acting, I want you to know that I am *really* happy you are here, back with us ... Back with me." He smiles. It is so good to see him smile. "I don't want to fight with you, Maia. Or not speak with you every day."

"I don't want that either."

"Okay, so we will be done now, yes? We are friends."

"Yes, of course. We will always be friends," Maia says with resignation. She gazes up at him, and he peers down at her with those gorgeous brown eyes that she loves so fiercely. This dance of lies, they know it well.

She makes to walk, but Miguel grabs her hand. When she faces him, he is quick to let go. "Did he ... *suffer* ... for long?" he asks.

Maia looks at her feet, her heart aching. "Not long. A few days," she says quietly.

"I'm sorry I wasn't there."

"Oh, Miguel. There would have been nothing you could have done."

"I know. But I'm still sorry."

"Me too."

They gaze at one another in silence. When Maia turns to continue on, Miguel doesn't join her. She keeps walking anyway.

"I lied to you," he says at her back, and she stops. "It's not ... *was*, Maia," he says softly, and she faces him again. "Not ... *was*," he says.

I know. She wants to respond, but the wounded look on his face has stolen her words.

"But I can't," he says. Shaking his head, he shrugs. "I'm sorry, Maia. I want to, but I can't."

Maia turns away. "I know that too," she says quietly.

TWENTY-SIX

This is a dream—an old one. Maia hasn't walked these woods since arriving in Leucothea.

She gazes up at the mammoth pines towering like skyscrapers, their peaks piercing the night sky. Only now, thick layers of snow do not coat their branches. There is no crystalline blanket of white beneath her bare feet.

The woods are burning.

The crackling fires slowly devouring them are deafening. The constellations beyond the trees' jagged tips have been obscured by heavy clouds of black smoke. Maia peers down at her feet. The forest floor is smoldering beneath her skin, but she cannot feel its burn.

A great horned owl soars above. Cutting through the dense clouds, the tips of his wings are on fire. He lands on a branch, glaring down at Maia with yellow eyes like saucers. He stares, and he burns. He knows—he has always known —and looking up at him, she knows too.

She steps into the woods, pulled by what she once believed to be a great unknowable force. It's the same force that has always called her. From her childhood in New

244

Zealand playing with a strange and foreign power, to this very moment as it reaches deep into her slumber, it has always been the same. The same calling. The same place.

The same man.

She brushes her fingertips against the orange coals gleaming on the trees, and an array of sparks rains to the ground. Her white dress drags against the burning earth, scattering embers as she walks. She knows this land; she knows it well. It's the same forest she has walked in her dreams for years.

And it is the exact same forest surrounding Jake's estate.

Trees pop and explode across the wilderness as the cries of a smoldering Earth surround her. Everywhere she looks, the blackened bodies of animals lie curled into themselves along the forest floor. Bodies of tigers. Bodies of people. Bodies of creatures with nowhere to run. Her heart aches, and she is breathless at the sight.

The outline of a man appears between the thick wafts of smoke, and Maia squints through the haze. As Jake draws near, the once subdued fires begin to rage. Maia cowers, backing up as he approaches, and his face appears through the flames.

Memories of their time together flash before her, and Maia's hands drop to her sides. She forgot how intoxicating his presence was. The way he'd look at her from across the room, how he'd hold her in his gaze. How they, too, seemed to dance across an intricate web of lies, delicately woven by both the light and the dark. She and Jake have always carried them both: the human vulnerability and the undeniable force of power. Drawn toward each other throughout their lifetimes, their two souls have always been linked.

I am the reason you have always felt called here.

He is the reason for her powers, for her incarnation into

this world. Something has drawn them together, building from the moment Maia was born. Every decision he has made to claw his way into his deadly position of power has only strengthened her own.

He is the reason.

She knows she will have to destroy him, and with that, she may also perish. Once her destiny is fulfilled, will there be anything left of her? For who is she without him? She is the Earth's only hope. He is its guaranteed destruction.

As Jake stands before her, Maia holds his cheek. As much as she abhors him, she is surprised to find she still cares for this man. The light cannot exist without the dark. Like them, the two are inextricably linked. Her heart breaks as she recalls the rage behind his eyes when she refused to give herself to him, the undeniable pain fueling his anger.

You and I ... We are meant to be together.

He reaches for her hand. As his fingers wrap around hers, she remembers the first time they held each other in the snowy hills outside his home. Back when he showed her the glittering lights of Leucothea. Back when she believed that he, too, carried light within his soul.

As Jake leads her through the crackling forest trail, in and out of burning fires, she does not struggle against him. They clear the tree line to the lookout above his property. Leucothea sits glittering on the cliff alongside them, and Maia can hear the life of thousands flourishing within. Glasses clinking. People laughing.

I am saving thousands of people's lives.

So many innocent people inside those gates. So many miserable people outside them. Most of this burning Earth has been deserted, but these few remaining civilizations in the Old Arctic are humanity's new beginning, its only hope.

But Leucothea is different. It is not humanity's new beginning; it is its hungry ghost.

Maia turns to find the ocean outside Leucothea replaced by vast deadlands, with towers of burning oil scattered like skeletons. A tear slides down her cheek as she and Jake watch scores of slaves struggling day in and day out to support the life inside Leucothea. Shuffling before her, their backs hunch under the weight of a life forced upon them, and they glare at her.

"Look," Jake whispers into her ear. "Look what we've created."

She looks at him. "*We?*"

He grabs her chin, directing her gaze toward a hilltop overlooking the sea of working bodies. Standing high up on the hill is Maia—alive, but dead inside. Watching over the slaves with eyes glazed over, she is a warning should they revolt. There are metal bands around her neck, her wrists, her ankles. A handful of soldiers stand around her, holding guns ready to fire. A pile of dead bodies has been stacked next to her, a warning should *she* revolt: Miguel, Chayanne, Shinesho, Tema.

"No one had to die," Jake says. "But I will not stop. I will not stop until I have you. You know it. I know it. You belong to *me*."

Maia turns toward him, and he grabs her arm. "And I am so close." He smiles, his dark eyes penetrating. High above the glistening city of lights and an ocean of heaving bodies, he whispers again, his grip on her arm tightening, "Can you feel me? I am *so close*."

Maia wakes up screaming, ripping off her mask and writhing against the grasp she can still feel on her arm.

"Maia?!" Chayanne sits up next to her. "Oh, honey. You're soaking wet."

Maia turns toward her, her mouth agape.

"What? What is it?" Chayanne wipes a strand of hair stuck to Maia's forehead.

Maia crawls out from her sleeping bag, standing. "I should have left," she says, her hands at her head. "I should have snuck away from here ... in the middle of the night when no one could stop me!"

Chayanne holds out her hand. "Maia, calm down."

"I have put you all in danger. Every day you stay with me is another day Jake's men are combing through these lands, looking for me, looking for *you*. And now we are all together, tied up in one big bow. I should have left! Why didn't I *leave*?"

"We've talked about this," Chayanne says sternly. "Because you know Jake would still try to find us. Whether we are together or not, he will be searching for us."

Maia can hear her, but she's not listening. "He studies people, Chayanne. He knows Shinesho's face ... Miguel's face. You could all die. I can't lose another person I love. I can't."

"You are not going to lose us."

"He'll use you. He'll use you to manipulate me. And then he'll kill you."

"Maia? *Stop*. We are in this together. Jake's decisions affect all of us, whether we live behind those walls or not. This is not just a battle of one—you know that. This is a battle for every person here, for every person who will come after us."

Maia sits across from her, and the two women lean in, forehead to forehead.

"Listen to those raindrops hitting our tent," Chayanne says softly. "Can you hear them?"

Maia nods.

"Each drop may not be powerful on its own, but combined, they have the strength to move mountains."

Maia sits back and sighs, looking at her dear friend.

"Yes, Jake and his New System are powerful," Chayanne continues, "but only if they keep us divided. United, we have the power to rise above. United, we can make a stand. You did not *start* this, Maia—none of us did. But I do believe we hold the power to end it."

Maia looks down. If only Chayanne knew the gravity of her words.

"We have a big day ahead of us," Chayanne says quietly. "Get some rest."

The following morning, their once bustling little camp is eerily empty, most of the crews having packed up the night before and left in the early-morning hours. This is it. Today, small covert missions are headed in opposite directions to Asiaq Bay, the tribe, and New Portland. And Maia, Miguel, Chayanne, and Shinesho will begin their journey to their new base camp in the mountains where, hopefully, the few remaining armies of North America will combine. How many will join them is yet to be seen, and they won't know for a few months. They can only hope for the best ... And prepare for the worst.

Maia is breaking apart her tent as Miguel approaches. "You okay?" he asks.

Chayanne quickly walks past, avoiding eye contact. Maia shakes her head. She told him.

Maia stands. "I am."

"Are you sure?"

She sighs. "I can't lose you, Miguel."

"You won't lose me."

She nods, looking around. He doesn't know. He doesn't know Jake like she does.

He walks up to her and pulls her into him. "I'm not going anywhere, okay?" he says softly, wrapping his heavy arms around her.

Maia embraces him, closing her eyes.

"We are taking you someplace safe," he says, resting his cheek on her head. "Hopefully, armies will be trickling in for months, depending on how our missions go. We will prepare the area, and we will come up with a plan. Okay? Just take it one day at a time. Don't worry."

"It's hard not to."

"I know." He squeezes her tighter. "But please, try," he whispers.

She pulls away, looking up at him with a sigh.

"Shinesho said it will take us a few weeks of intense travel to get there," he says. "You sure you are ready? We can always wait a little while."

"No, I'm ready. We have to move on—I can't sit here any longer."

"Okay," he says. "Stay here. I have something for you."

Maia waits. Gazing around at the tigers lying beside her broken-down tent, she smiles. The cubs are growing up so fast.

Miguel comes back with a wooden staff in hand.

"What do you have there?" Maia asks, her smile wide.

"I have been working on it for weeks. I wanted to make sure it was ready before our journey. Here." He hands it to her. "It is small, like you," he says with a wink.

She snatches it from him. "I'm not that small," she says. She holds the staff in her hands; it is the perfect weight and size. She beams up at him. "It's perfect, Miguel. Thank you."

He walks backward with his hands in his pockets. "But we need to practice again, yes? Can't have my wing-woman doing a piss-poor job at fighting."

She bites her lip. "I could still take you."

She catches his smile as he turns away. "Looking forward to it," he says over his shoulder.

Maia slides her foot into the stirrup and lifts herself onto her horse. She's been practicing riding him for weeks. What once started as an unsure and nervous endeavor for the both of them now feels like second nature. And her horse is finally used to Atlas's presence, which was a *long* process. Maia can tell he still doesn't like it, but he is at least comfortable enough to know that this large tiger walking beside them won't turn him into dinner.

Ahead of Maia, Chayanne, Shinesho, and Miguel await on their horses, along with fifteen tigers—a few more having joined their camp over the past few weeks.

The four follow the same rules as before: no talking while traveling, whispers and hand signals only. Although, this time, these rules are less to watch out for mobs, since the route is well known by Shinesho and has always remained relatively empty, and more to listen for drones. They've seen a few soaring high above them while they've been under a protective forest canopy, but the sightings have become less and less the farther out they travel.

Only once has one flown close enough for their crew to possibly be seen. The tigers were the first to sense it. They stopped along the trail, looking up at the sky. Then came the hum of a motor in the distance. The four travelers hopped off their horses and yanked them off the trail, forcing them to the ground. Then they crouched in the dense forest brush as the eerie hovercraft slowly flew among the trees. It stopped a few times, hovering in place as it scanned the woods, then continued on its way.

After it passed, they stood from the bushes, and all three gawked at Maia.

"Yeah," she said, shaking her head. "Creepy, right?"

Day after day becomes more of the same: setting up camp, taking turns hunting, searching for water, hiding traps. The four get along so well. Sitting around fires, they share quiet laughs and eat the food of the earth, surrounded by a chorus of wild nature. Maia and Chayanne cuddle together in their tent to stay warm on the cooler nights, while the men sleep in another tent next to them.

So far from Leucothea, in the middle of nowhere, it's almost like they are living the *actual* good life. It feels so right to be traveling through the forest again, bathed in the whispers of the trees, often with Miguel by Maia's side. The two have agreed the journey doesn't feel right without Lucas, but at least they now have Chayanne, Shinesho, and a legion of tigers alongside them.

With their horses walking next to each other along the long and winding road, the four share silent smiles between them. They are all trying, if only for brief moments, to forget that they are traveling to the grounds where they will prepare for a war. That Jake and his henchmen are on a massive manhunt, working around the clock with only one goal in mind.

Finding Maia.

TWENTY-SEVEN

Late at night, the four weary travelers sit around a crackling fire. Someone needs to check the traps, but no one has the energy. The summer "evenings" have been reduced to twilight for only a few hours, but it is still dark enough that whoever goes will need a flashlight. And so far, despite their deep hunger, there have been no volunteers.

Today has been a long day, with on-and-off-again drizzle, slick mud, and very little food. The air is muggy, and the relentless black flies seem to be gathering in swarms between the spells of rain. Every few kilometers, someone has cursed from a bite, and they are all *over it*.

As they sit in silence, Maia absently takes a sip from her mug of hot water. Her gaze drifts to Miguel, watching her from across the flames.

"Some things never change," he says, dimple showing.

She grins.

"What does that mean?" Chayanne asks.

"I've never seen anyone drink as much hot water as this one," Miguel says, nodding at Maia.

"It's the next best thing..." Maia begins.

"Since there is no tea," he says, and the two smile at one another.

Shinesho rolls his eyes. "Okay, *I'll* go check the traps. Where's the torch?"

"I think it's in my bag," Miguel says. "I'll go with you."

Shinesho steps away, and Miguel stands to follow. As he walks behind the women, he drags his fingertips across Maia's shoulders, and she peers up at him. Sometimes, the way he looks at her—he doesn't smile, his gaze strong.

"Girl, you two need to get a room," Chayanne mumbles as the men walk away.

"What does that mean?" Maia asks.

"Oh, it's just an *old* saying."

"*Meaning...*"

"Meaning when two people are into each other, they should go to a bedroom, and you know ... make *love*," she drawls.

"Oh." Maia tucks her hair behind her ear. "Well, I wouldn't turn *that* down."

Both women laugh.

"Speaking of," Chayanne says, leaning in, "I keep meaning to ask you. Are the rumors true?"

"What rumors?"

"About you and ... *Jake*? Were you two really together?"

Maia is shocked. It's a fact she was happy to forget and one she was hoping she'd never have to admit.

"I heard you two were quite the item..." Chayanne's voice trails off.

Miguel steps back into the fire's light, his eyes wide. Chayanne peers into her mug of water as if looking for something. "*Uh-oh,*" she mumbles into her cup.

"You ... and *Jake*?" Miguel asks. His voice is quiet, tense. He looks horrified—*angry*. Shinesho steps next to him.

Maia is taken aback. Suddenly everyone is looking at her.

"You *didn't*. Maia? Please, tell me you didn't," Miguel asks again, raising his voice.

"I better go check the traps," Shinesho says quickly.

"I'll go with." Chayanne jumps from her log, and the two disappear into the woods.

Miguel is staring at her. "*Maia*."

"I ... I—" Her mouth dries.

"Oh my *God*, I'm going to be sick."

"It wasn't like that! I had no idea he was so evil. He ... he seemed ... sweet."

"Sweet?! Are we talking about the same man?"

"Yes, we are talking about the same man."

"Oh, okay." He nods sarcastically, placing his fist under his chin. "So, the same man who punched you and kept you tied to a bed? *That* man? The same man who burned our village to the ground?!"

"I get it, Miguel."

"The man who has troops of armed soldiers out looking for us so he can murder *everyone* and then take you as prisoner?! The man hell-bent on destroying anything good left in the world?"

"I didn't know any of that then!"

"I feel sick. I'm going to be sick." His hands on his hips, he turns in place.

"You weren't there! You swore to me you would be there, but you never came! Lucas was dead, and I thought I would never see you again. I had nothing and no one!"

"So, you just crawl into the arms of the most dangerous man on the planet?!"

255

"I didn't know! Obviously, he didn't *lead* with that!"

"Couldn't you tell?! When he and Mario showed up at my cabin outside of LA, I *immediately* hated him. Such an arrogant *prick*."

"I was lost. My biggest dream come true had turned into my worst nightmare. My powers had disappeared…"

His face pulls into a grimace, and he nods. "So, why not take your mind off things and date a warmonger. Makes sense."

Maia drags a hand over her face. "That man … *saved* me from a horrific sentence at a labor camp. He never said a word about what he was doing behind closed doors. I found that out on my own, and as soon as I did, I broke it off."

Miguel continues turning in place. He buries his face in his hands, growling. "I just keep picturing you two together, and it makes me *sick*."

"Stop!"

He faces her. "Did you love him?"

Maia glares at him. "*Excuse* me?"

"Simple question."

"No, I didn't love him. We dated, Miguel. That's what single people do. I've heard you've done plenty of the same. Right? *Mr. Unattainable Bachelor*?"

"But you cared for him, yes?"

"Not that it's any of your business, but I did—for a time."

"And you are telling me you honestly didn't know what he was doing."

"*Of course* I didn't—who do you think I am?"

"You know? Sometimes I'm not so sure anymore."

Appalled, Maia's mouth drops open. "How could you say that?!"

Her tigers have all woken up. Uneasy, they begin pacing between the two of them.

"You know what, Maia? You're a coward. You knew you were making the wrong decision with Lucas, but you didn't want to be the one to blame for the fact that you and I had fallen in love. So, you blamed *me* for ruining everything, but it was you."

"Wait—*what*?!" She holds her head, whiplashed from the change in subject. "I didn't *blame* you—"

"You weren't in love with him and you knew it. You *knew* it! The way you looked at me on the river..." He shakes his head. "I have carried that look with me every day for nearly *two years*. But you turned your back on me. You turned your back on *us* and chose him anyway because you're a fucking coward, just like him." He chuckles, turning away. "You two deserved each other."

"How *dare* you talk about Lucas like that!"

He whirls on her. "Oh, give me a break! I loved him more than anyone! He's my brother and nothing will ever change that, even though he's done nothing but *hurt me* my entire life! It doesn't mean I can't point out his flaws, and it doesn't mean I won't point out yours either. I'm not afraid to hurt you by telling you the truth."

Maia holds back a sob. "I have told you, *repeatedly*, I was wrong. I love you. I have *always* loved you."

Miguel marches up to her and grabs her by the shoulders. "You're too late. You can't undo what you've done."

"*Why*?!" she screams, shoving him. "Why does it have to be that way? You call *me* a coward? *You're* the coward! Because I'm still here, standing before you, telling you that I love you. We can be together, but you keep *pushing* me away! So, what's your excuse?! I was trying to do what I thought was right. But you? You're just being an asshole, trying to hurt me back for hurting you. But at least I ... I wasn't *trying* to hurt you. I was trying to do *everything* in my power *not* to hurt you!"

"Bullshit! You were only trying not to hurt yourself!"

"I have told you, over and over again, how sorry I am. I can't say it any more. I won't. You don't want to forgive me? Fine. But this is on you," Maia says, tears streaming down her cheeks.

Miguel turns away, fists clenched.

"I know you still love me," she says between gasps. "Miguel? I can feel it. I know it's still there."

He turns toward her. "It was a mistake coming here. I should have gone to New Portland."

Maia holds her head. This has all gone so wrong. "You don't mean it."

He nods. "You know what? I should have never left New Portland in the first place."

Maia falls to her knees, sobbing.

Miguel looks pained by the sight of her, but he holds back. "I'll be gone by morning," he mumbles, and he disappears into the darkness.

TWENTY-EIGHT

Early the next morning, Maia sits alone by the fire. She didn't sleep last night. Chayanne and Shinesho came back shortly after Miguel stormed off, their faces contorted with worry. Chayanne sat with Maia, neither one speaking a word until eventually, Chayanne excused herself to bed. She knew better than to say anything.

Miguel didn't come back last night. Maia wants to believe he's still coming, but maybe he decided to leave right then and there. It would be stupid, but it wouldn't be the first time.

Glaring at the fire, Maia grimaces as Miguel's harsh words circle around her head. *Can't*. Can't fight for this anymore. He looked her dead in the eyes and called her a coward. Repeatedly.

Screw him.

Chayanne steps outside their tent and sits next to Maia with a sigh. "Did you get any sleep?"

"Nope."

"Would it help if I said he didn't mean it?"

"*Nope.*"

"What if I *know* he didn't—"

"Chayanne, I swear to God."

Chayanne sighs. Shaking her head, she says, "See? This is why sometimes a girl's gotta swallow a bug."

Maia can't help but smile, and she and Chayanne bump shoulders.

Miguel walks up to the camp, and Maia closes her eyes in relief. He looks tired, but at least he no longer appears angry. "Maia?" he says quietly.

She ignores him.

"*Por favor.*"

Chayanne elbows her, and her eyes flicker up to Miguel's.

He nods toward the trail. "Let's take a walk."

A few tigers get up, looking at her. She shakes her head. Atlas starts to follow anyway, and she snaps her fingers. "No. *Stay.*"

He plops his bum to the ground with a grumble.

Marching through the woods, Maia knows Miguel is behind her, but she doesn't look back.

"Maia."

She whirls toward him. "*What*, Miguel?"

"I'm sorry. That was awful, what I said last night."

Her eyes narrow. "Which part? Calling me a coward? *That* part? Or for questioning my character? Which is worse —*hmm*, I can't decide."

"I didn't mean it."

"You know what, Miguel? You want to sit on your high horse and judge me, fine. But you have no *idea* what I have been through these past few years."

"You're right. I don't. I can't begin to imagine how difficult it was up there for you. I had no right to say what I did, and I'm sorry."

Maia looks away, shaking her head.

"Maia," Miguel says quietly. He reaches for her and she shrugs him off. "All I've done from the moment you walked away is think of you. Miss you." He steps closer to her, cornering her between trees. "*Crave* you."

She meets his gaze.

"All I've *ever* wanted is to be with you," he says, "from the moment I met you. To love you and call you my own. The thought of that man's disgusting hands on you ... I lost my temper, and I'm sorry."

She shoves past him. "Whatever."

"Don't walk away from me."

"Screw you," she says over her shoulder.

He rushes behind her and grabs her arm, yanking her into him. "I don't want to fight with you," he says, his face inches from hers. "I am trying to tell you I'm sorry."

"Go to New Portland," she says, pushing away. "I'm sure your little friend Hannah would *love*—"

He seizes her hand and pulls her back into him, clutching her shoulders. His gaze is pained. "I'm not going anywhere," he says quietly, breathing hard. "I love you, Maia. I'm in love with you. And I'm sorry for hurting you." He hesitates, then he draws her into him and kisses her.

She shoves him, and he stumbles backward, surprised. He steps toward her again, and she grabs his shirt with both hands, pulling him into her and kissing him.

He doesn't waste a second. Lifting her from the ground, he carries her to a tree, pinning her against it. She wraps herself around him as they gasp between their kisses.

Shinesho whistles from a distance: their call to gather —nonemergency. They ignore it. How long has Maia yearned for this moment? She clutches at his shirt, *desperate* for him. For years, she feared she may never see him again, and now she is enclosed within his arms beneath the awning of the trees. And he is kissing her. Miguel is *kissing* her. And it is so much better than her memories.

Shinesho whistles again. This time, it is louder, longer. *Closer.*

Miguel stops, heaving out a sigh. Still holding Maia against the tree, his eyes are closed, his brow against hers.

"Guys?" Chayanne calls from a distance.

"Yeah," Miguel replies. "Be right there." He lowers Maia back to the ground.

Breathless, she straightens her clothes, and he does the same.

"You have no idea how *long...*" His voice trails as he looks her up and down. He fights a grin. "I mean ... *wow.*"

She smiles, slapping her hand against her mouth. *Wow, indeed.*

He changes the subject. "Are we okay?"

She nods, running a hand through her hair. "I'm okay. Are *you* okay?"

"I am now." He hesitates, then adds with a sigh, "I'd be better if I hadn't taught Shinesho how to whistle."

She laughs, and Miguel nods toward the trail. "We should go. Don't want to anger Princess Chayanne."

"Miguel?"

He stops, turning to face her.

"I love you too," she says quietly.

He smiles. "I know."

She beams at him, shaking her head.

He lifts her chin and kisses her. This time, it is soft, gentle. His lips feel so good against hers—like they were made for her. When he pulls away, it takes her a moment to open her eyes. When she does, the tender look on his face makes her heart melt.

Shinesho and Chayanne are crouched together along the dirt, laughing and playing with the growing cubs. Shinesho is the first to spot Maia as she and Miguel approach. "You okay?" he asks.

"Fine," Maia mumbles, nonchalantly scratching her neck.

Shinesho peers over her shoulder, raising his brow.

"Fine," Miguel says behind her.

"So, what do you want to do?" Shinesho asks. "I know you haven't slept, but are you two up for moving? We don't have to spend an entire day at it, but I think it would be wise to switch locations considering how ... *loud* ... we've been."

"And by 'we,' he means *you*," Chayanne grumbles, scowling at Miguel.

Miguel looks at Maia. "You up for that?"

She nods. "I am. I agree with Shinesho—we don't have the luxury to rest. We need to keep moving."

The four sluggish travelers and Maia's legion of tigers hit the road again, and the day passes in a hazy blur. Since they haven't seen a drone or another person in weeks, the rules on talking while traveling have eased, but mostly just between Chayanne and Shinesho, who have been leading the way. Maia and Miguel have been trailing quietly behind them, both exhausted and lost in their own worlds.

Maia bites her lip. *That kiss*—she can't stop thinking

about it. And every time she looks at Miguel, he smiles at her like he's doing the same. He moves his horse closer to hers, and they reach out to one another, holding hands as they travel side by side.

"I think we should start practicing our old bo routine at the next stop," he says, releasing her hand. "I'm still waiting for you to ... *take me*." His eyes flicker to hers before looking ahead, a sly grin tugging his lip.

Maia can't hold back her smile.

He nods ahead. "Have you noticed those two?"

Maia follows his gaze to Chayanne and Shinesho, speaking quietly between each other on their horses. She watches them ... The way Chayanne smiles. Shinesho too. Maia's eyes widen. "You think?"

Miguel tilts his gaze. "Not sure yet."

"Has Shinesho said anything?"

"Nah, we don't really talk about that stuff."

Maia rolls her eyes. "Sure you don't," she says with a wink.

Walking along the city streets, Maia peers down at her feet. The fiery wooded path in her dreams has been replaced by a blackened, scorched cement. Her white dress is gone too. She now wears a black uniform like that of a soldier, or a prisoner—or both.

She gazes up at the towering skyscrapers—all burning. She is in Leucothea. The black and white flags hanging from the buildings are ablaze, the storefronts' windows fracturing against the pressure. The structures' melting metal is oozing into the streets, coursing against the curbs in rivers.

Up ahead, Jake walks toward her in and out of the

clouds of smoke, the ashes of their burning city drifting like snow. The two meet in the middle of the road. Once again, he takes her hands within his own. Their destinies are linked like their fingers, now wrapped tightly around each other.

Jake's face, always so angry in Maia's dreams, now appears saddened. Like her, he is terrified. The illusion of his grand dream is collapsing around him, and it is only because of her.

Peering into his eyes, she can see what he is doing at this very moment while she sleeps. Sitting next to her old fireplace in his guest suite, he has destroyed everything in a fit of rage. The pictures have been torn from the walls. The furniture broken. Windows shattered. He glares at a stack of newspapers at his feet. The black-and-white photo on top is a picture of them. Smiling, Maia stands next to him in her black satin dress, her arm linked with his. For a moment, she looked happy.

So did he.

He lifts the paper before him. Glowering at Maia's smiling face, a hardened resentment fills his eyes. He crumples the photo with white-knuckled fists. And as he chucks it into the flames, the storefront windows shatter into the gloom. Maia cowers from the blast, but Jake does not release his grip. The glass floats weightlessly across the sky.

Maia has never been afraid of Jake. It is his power, what he can take from her—*who* he can take from her—that terrifies her. The heinous way he has figured out how to manipulate her to get what he wants.

Jake, too, is keenly aware of the power Maia holds, and it frightens him. He knows she will stop at nothing to take it all away, everything he has worked for his entire life, the grand vision he so strongly believes in. She has the power to destroy it all, and she is *so close*.

Only one of them will make it out of this war alive.

Or ... neither of them will.

Linked. Their souls are linked.

The burning city melts faster now, and the streets begin to flood. The hot liquid bleeding from the buckling buildings courses against their feet, rising rapidly up their legs. But the two remain in the middle of the street, bound to the place that has made them. Bound to one another.

The flowing metal quickly rises up Maia's chest and across her shoulders. Jake glares at her, his eyes cold as ice. A tear slips down her cheek, and she lifts her chin, the molten fluid splashing against it.

She can't escape. Jake's hands grip hers, pinning her in place. He watches as the torrent slowly overtakes her mouth. It reaches his chin and he lifts it, but he does not move.

It covers her nose.

Can't breathe. Can't ... *breathe*...

Jake's smiling face is the last thing she sees before the darkness swallows her whole.

Maia wakes up gasping. Drenched in sweat, she rips off her mask. Chayanne, now used to Maia's nightly terrors, wraps her arms around her and lays her back to the ground, holding her as she trembles.

Maia stares at the tent's ceiling, filled with dread. She and Jake were in a new location in her dreams—this isn't good. His presence continues to haunt her, but she now knows he is no longer out searching for her. Growing ever more frustrated with his failed mission to locate her, he has called back his men. Switched tactics. To what, she can't be sure, but there has been a definite shift—a *deadly* shift.

She can feel it in her bones.

Jake is more determined than ever to have her back in his grasp. Only now he knows he can never risk losing her to his enemies again. What was once a mission to keep her alive is no longer. Jake has made his decision.

He will find her.

And once he has her, he will kill her.

TWENTY-NINE

Traversing a valley between mountains, the four travelers and Maia's tigers are enclosed within a nourishing and protective cover of trees. Chayanne and Maia are next to one another, the two men in the lead.

Maia takes in their surroundings. There is something in the air—something feels different. Is this because of her nightmares? No ... no, there's something else. There's something very ... *peculiar* ... about these woods.

"So?" Chayanne asks Maia.

"So ... what?"

"What's the *gos*?"

"Huh?"

"What's the *haps*?" Chayanne asks with a quirky grin.

"Are you speaking English?"

Chayanne leans in, whispering, "What's been—"

"I told you, you don't have to whisper. They're not out looking for us anymore."

Chayanne sits up, annoyed. "WHAT'S BEEN GOING ON WITH YOU AND MIGUEL?" she yells.

THE ECHO OF A THOUSAND VOICES

Miguel and Shinesho peer over their shoulders. Chayanne waves at them with a wide smile. The men swap a glance, then turn back around, shaking their heads.

"*Nice*, Chayanne," Maia says, rolling her eyes.

"Tell me."

Maia shrugs. "Nothing."

"Maia, I *know*."

"*What*? Who told you?"

"Shinesho."

"Shinesho!?" Maia yells.

"Yes?" Shinesho asks.

Miguel looks back at Maia, and she flashes him a sly smile, shaking her head. She *knew* they talked.

"Nothing! Never mind," Chayanne says.

Both men face forward again. Shinesho mumbles something to Miguel, and they chuckle.

Maia looks at Chayanne. "Okay, so Miguel told Shinesho, and then Shinesho told you?"

Chayanne grins, nodding.

"There's a rumor mill, and we only have four people..." Maia says.

"It's not a rumor if it's true."

"Is that so?"

Chayanne shrugs.

"And why would Mr. Serious Shinesho be *gossiping*?" Maia asks, arching her brow. "*Pillow talk*, maybe?"

Chayanne smiles. "What?! No."

"Chayanne."

"I asked you first," Chayanne hisses, swatting the air.

"Okay. Miguel and I kissed."

Chayanne rolls her eyes. "I already knew that. And?"

"And ... that's it. It's only been a few days. We're not rushing it."

"*Rushing* it? You've already said you love each other."

Maia shrugs. "It's complicated."

Chayanne scoffs. "Only because you're *making* it complicated." She leans in. "How was the kiss?"

Maia tips her head back and sighs. She looks at her friend with a dreamy smile. "It was ... *unbelievable.*"

"Girl, I give you a few more days—a week *tops*—before you're doing more than just kissing."

"I'm not even sure I can wait *that* long."

"Well, when you do, we are happy to switch tent partners," Chayanne says, avoiding eye contact.

"I knew it!" Maia says. "When did this happen?!"

Chayanne smiles. "It's been a long time coming, I think. I've always had a thing for him, but he was so busy with the army. We never really had the opportunity to get to know each other. Apparently, he noticed me too but was too shy to approach me. But now that we are spending so much time together, it just *happened.*"

"Have you..."

Chayanne grins.

"Chayanne! When?!"

"When we go hunting or get water. Or when you and Miguel fight," she adds with a laugh. "You're *super* distracted then."

Maia gawks at her. "*Scandalous.*"

"Right?" Chayanne looks proud.

"Aw, Chayanne. I'm so happy for you."

"I'm happy for you too—*both* of you." She reaches out her hand.

Maia holds it. "Thanks, friend."

The trees' whispers intensify.

Mother.

Mother.

MotherMotherMotherMotherMother.

Maia slows her horse.

There is something about this land— about this spot in particular. It feels comforting, *familiar*, even though she's never been here before. The air around her shimmers, the trees' vibrant life highlighted in the sun. The Earth—it is speaking to her.

Pay attention.

Atlas has been walking before her, but he stops. He lifts his nose into the air, his whiskers flickering as he sniffs.

"Atlas?" Maia stops her horse, and Miguel and Shinesho turn to look at her.

Atlas tilts his head as he peers into the forest, and then he races between the trees.

"Atlas!" Maia yells.

The rest of the tigers stop and look up at Maia. Then, one by one, they step off the track to follow Atlas.

"Maia?" Chayanne whispers behind her. "What's happening?"

"I don't know," she says quietly, dismounting her horse, and she follows the felines into the woods.

It feels as though she's lifted a curtain and stepped inside a dream. She runs her fingers along the trees' ridged bark as she walks, and the birds' songs crescendo, filling the sky with a melodious symphony. Her hearing becomes hyper-focused, listening to the crisp *snap* of twigs and shattering of leaves beneath her boots. She inhales the rich scent of deep, misty earth, and she smiles.

This place.

She has been here before.

She follows the tigers weaving between the brush until she enters a small clearing. An abandoned, one-room church stands in the middle, highlighted in streams of light.

Half-devoured by the forest, it is smothered in vines and a thick carpet of moss, a patchwork of weeds pushing between its stones.

Maia walks up the cracked cement steps leading to the church's entry. A wooden frame is all that's left of the door, rotted into slivers hanging from the sides. She tears the thick cobwebs draped across the opening and steps inside.

The room is empty, save for small clusters of weeds growing up from the floorboards. The forest's thick webbing of vines has invaded the inside of the structure and now sprawl across the ceiling and down the walls. A half-dozen narrow windows line either side of the church, broken and covered in dust. An immense circular window covers nearly the entire back wall, with light streaming through what remains of its intricate mosaic of glasswork.

As Atlas pads across the room, an old vision comes flooding back to Maia. She's been here before—in her dreams—*many* times. That was years ago, back in New Zealand. Back when she thought tigers were extinct and that Leucothea was a land where all her dreams would come true. Back when she assumed the woman on the throne in the middle of this room was her *mother*.

But then she discovered, much to her own horror, that *she* was the one sitting on that throne. It was a version of herself she barely knew at the time and did everything in her power to hide. It was a version of herself that she now proudly embodies, more and more with each passing day.

Maia walks to the middle of the empty room, surrounded by weeds and pacing tigers. Everything is the same, but in her dream, there was a throne on the barren ground where she now stands, made of woven tree branches that towered into the sky.

She gazes around, her sigh echoing against the stone.

This is it. She knows it, feels it with every fiber of her being. This is where they will prepare their armies. This is where she will fully embody all she was ever meant to become. This will be her final resting place before her destiny is fulfilled—whatever that may be.

"Wow," Chayanne whispers.

Maia turns to find Miguel, Shinesho, and Chayanne have stepped inside the hall. Standing in a line, they gawk at the majestic old building.

Maia kneels. Sweeping aside clumps of dead leaves and broken stone, she places her hand against the floor. This is where the throne was—in her dreams. This is where it *should* be. She can feel its spirit like a ghost.

A piece of broken glass falls from a window, shattering on the ground. The four turn, watching in disbelief as a small vine slides along the window's ledge. It slithers down the wall, hesitating when it reaches the floor, then taps the ground, briefly hovering above it like a snake. Then it makes its way across the warped floorboards toward Maia.

The tip of another green vine peeks into the window behind it, and then it, too, carves its way down the wall's mossy stones. Another one enters behind it. And another. *Another.*

Chayanne cries out, jumping into Shinesho's arms as a large tree root snakes past her, shoving through clumps of dead leaves on the floor. More vines and roots slink through the old church's broken windows and holes in the ceiling. They glide down the walls and twist across the floor, all meeting in the middle where Maia still kneels.

She slowly stands, lifting her hand from the ground, and the foliage follows her command. Rising from the floor, they spiral around one another. Maia steps back with her hand on her chest, and the branches forge on. They tighten and weave, bending and curving and climbing on top of each other as they assemble the throne from her dreams.

Then they join as a single unit, corkscrewing toward the ceiling. They smash through the roof, raining dust and debris upon Maia. Towering high into the sky, the vines blossom into an immense tree. The branches simultaneously shoot out in myriad directions, with green leaves unfurling from their tips.

Maia steps back in awe. Breathless, she gapes at the living throne before her. Atlas nudges her leg, and she stumbles forward. Running her hand along the intricate weave, tears fall from her fluttering eyes. It's the *exact* same throne from her dreams—down to every last intricate detail.

She peers over her shoulder. Chayanne has covered her mouth, tears streaming down her cheeks. Shinesho is staring at Maia, paled and dumbfounded. She looks at Miguel, and he nods knowingly with a smile.

Maia turns back toward her throne and walks up the roots like steps, taking her place on the seat. Crossing her legs, she leans back, running her hand along the armrest's smooth, tightly woven branches, and Atlas curls up at her feet.

She gazes around the room, exhaling in relief.

For the first time in a long time, she feels like she's home.

———

Later that night, after the four have set up camp outside the old church, they sit in silence next to the fire. No one needed to discuss whether or not this is where they would stay. It's close enough to the spot Shinesho had pinned for their base camp, and no one can deny that this is where they belong.

Over the evening, they take turns bathing in a small inland lake not far from the church. Chayanne went first, then Shinesho. All the while, Maia and Miguel stare at one another from across the fire.

"So..." Chayanne breaks the silence, and she looks at Maia. "Do we need to make you a crown or something?"

Maia laughs. "God, no—no crown."

"But that was ... *uh*..." Shinesho stumbles on his words. "That was ... interesting ... or ... something."

"Now you can see what I've been talking about," Miguel says.

Shinesho nods, eyes wide, and Chayanne pokes his ribs.

"Do you want to talk about it?" Maia asks.

"I do," Shinesho says. "Sometime—not tonight. I think I need a minute."

Maia smiles. "Take your time."

"Okay, who's next to bathe?" Miguel asks.

"Either you or Maia," Chayanne says.

Miguel gazes at Maia, arching his brow. "Ladies first."

Maia stands, glancing at him sidelong as she grabs the lantern and her towel. She walks behind him, dragging her fingertips across his shoulders, then steps away from the fire's light. She does not look back.

As Maia wanders through the forest in the evening twilight, she keeps her lantern off. There is a full moon tonight, ducking in and out of large puffs of white clouds, highlighting the land in an enchanting silver hue. She sets the barren lantern next to a tree alongside the lake, taking it all in. Fireflies flicker between the pines, and a lazy fog has gathered in patches along the glassy waters. It all looks so *magical*.

After hanging her towel and clothing from a branch, she wades into the lake and dips below the water, blowing air as she swims. Breaking the surface, she tips her head back and sighs, gazing up at the sky. Her future may be uncertain, but in this one brief snapshot in time, life seems ... *perfect*.

There are new ripples in the water, coming from the shoreline behind her, and Maia's heart skips a beat. Tilting her head in his direction, she acknowledges his presence, but she doesn't turn around. She exhales a long, nervous breath, and as the ripples intensify, she slowly turns to face him.

Bathed in a chorus of chirping crickets and wood frogs, Maia and Miguel gaze at one another in the moonlight, neither one speaking a word. The luminescence highlights the contours of his face and the deep grooves of his muscles. He steps closer, his eyes never once leaving hers. The water laps across her shoulders.

She reaches out to him, placing her hand against his chest. His heart is pounding—he's nervous, but so is she. She's dreamed of this moment for so long. The few kisses they have shared have been passionate, rushed—*desperate*.

Now, they have all the time in the world.

He grazes the side of her face with his curled fist, and the water trickles down her cheek. He leans down, gently kissing every drop. His breath is hot against her skin and she closes her eyes, chills scattering across her body as his lips move farther down her neck.

Reaching below the water, he lifts her from the ground, and she wraps herself around him. He tightens his embrace, consuming her in his gaze. As he leans in, a spark flashes between them. They flinch, looking at one another in awe—just like the first time their hands met back in LA.

And then Maia grabs his face and kisses him.

With her lips against his, Miguel does not hold back. Ravenous, he devours her, and she moans against his kisses.

The water swirls around them as he caresses every curve of her body, his touch unleashing a wildfire within. She clutches at his back, dragging her fingers down his skin, and he growls her name into her neck.

"Take me," she gasps, holding his face to hers. "Take ... *all* ... of me," she whispers, brushing her lips against his.

Miguel doesn't speak, his breathing heavy. As he carries her toward the shore, she locks her legs around him, kissing down his neck. Across his shoulder. She tugs his ear with her teeth and his skin prickles. He gives her a reassuring squeeze, and she smiles.

Along the shore, Miguel holds on to her as he pulls her towel from the tree and lays it on the grass. He slowly lowers her to the ground, and they lie together in the moonlight, Maia enveloped beneath him. She presses her body against his, her heart beating wildly against him.

"Do you remember," he breathes, tenderly sweeping a curl from her face, "down by the field with the caribou ... I said there will *never* be another soul in this world who could ever love you as much as me?"

Maia softly nods.

He drops his forehead to hers. "You are my person, Maia."

She grabs his face, looking into his eyes as the fog rolls across them. "And you're mine."

———

Maia awakens on the floor in the old church, tangled between layers of sleeping bags and Miguel's arm beneath her neck. Birds line the shrubs and trees inside the room, chirping away, while sunlight pours through the windows alongside them. Yellow buds of unfurling flowers now hang from the sprawling branches of Maia's throne. She looks up at them in wonder.

They look like the wildflower from her dreams.

Miguel stirs. She reaches above her head, stretching long and grinning wide. Curled up beside him, she finds she fits perfectly inside his arms. She gazes up at him, and he peels one eye open, peering down at her. She shimmies up to his lips and kisses him, and he pulls her on top of him all over again.

This is how it goes. Every time they awaken, they make love—over and over and over again. All evening and all morning long, the old building echoes with Maia's giggles.

After a while, wafts of something delicious cooking on a fire float across them, and they decide it would be a good idea to get dressed and have something to eat.

As they stumble into the sun, they meet the amused eyes of Chayanne, sitting on a log beside the fire. She raises an eyebrow, a mischievous grin across her face.

"Good morning," Miguel says.

"Yes," Chayanne says, cocking her head. "It certainly is, isn't it?"

Maia laughs and sits beside her, laying her head on her shoulder.

Shinesho walks up, head down in all his seriousness. "Okay, I've mapped out the land. We need to clear some trees to make sure there is enough room for the armies as they arrive."

Everyone is quiet, staring at him.

"What?" he says.

Chayanne nods toward Maia and Miguel.

He rolls his eyes. "Yes, Miguel and Maia finally got it on. What am I supposed to say? *Congratulations*?"

They glance at one another and laugh.

Shinesho winks at Maia. "About time," he mumbles, shaking his head. "*Damn.*"

The next few days are like a dream, and Maia and Miguel are all smiles.

Jake may have immense armies preparing for war.

The world may be burning.

But Maia and Miguel are finally together.

THIRTY

Maia and Miguel stand apart, circling one another. He swings his staff, and she blocks his blow. He swipes it across her legs, and she jumps. Swing. Block. *Breathe.*

Shinesho walks past, shaking his head. "You're wasting your time."

Maia and Miguel both stop, lowering their bo.

"Excuse me?" Maia asks, panting.

Shinesho approaches them. "You're already good at fighting with your bo—really good." He looks at Maia. "But how likely is it that you'll be standing across from Jake and you'll both have a staff?"

Maia looks at Miguel, still catching her breath. "Not likely," she says.

"Right," Shinesho says. He grabs her bo and throws it to the ground. "You are only as good as your weakest link. We don't have much time. You don't need to practice this anymore." He takes the staff from Miguel and hands him a small stick. "You need to start working through worst-case scenarios."

"Okay?" Maia's statement comes out more of a question. She stares at the stick in Miguel's hand.

"You said Jake studied you, right?" Shinesho asks. "So, what does he know to be your greatest weakness?"

Maia nods at Miguel.

"Miguel?" Shinesho asks.

"Miguel, and the people I love. He'll be working very hard right now to not only get me back in Leucothea, but to take you all as prisoners."

"And Jake? What is his biggest weakness?" Shinesho asks.

Maia glances between the two men. "I am."

"See?" Miguel shakes his head. "This is why I don't like this plan. We are going to walk straight back into this walled city and deliver the one thing he wants most."

"I have to go, Miguel. We've *talked* about this. This will never end if I keep running from him."

"So let *us* kill him," Miguel says.

"And what, fuel their rage? Feed the vendetta? Another leader will take his place, and the search for me will continue. At least this way, we have a plan, we have my powers to fall back on, and we are doing it on *our* terms."

"She's right," Shinesho says to Miguel. "We need Maia there, as risky as it is." He turns to face her. "What can we count on with your powers? On a *grand* scale?"

"Fire, which I don't need to practice; I've got that one down. Wind too. Leucothea is next to the ocean, but I've never worked with massive bodies of water—only shallow ponds, rivers, and streams. I think our safest bet would be on earthquakes, wind, and fire. Those elements can level a city—and quickly."

"How are you with earthquakes?"

"Not great, but I haven't had much practice."

"Well, try to get in as much training as possible before the armies arrive. We're going to need this field to set up their camps, and I believe the less they know about your powers, the better. There is always the possibility of a bad egg."

"Meaning?"

"People can be greedy if they spy an opportunity. You never know. I would like to handle the armies if you are okay with that. It's what I do best."

"Sure," Maia says.

"Above all else, I need to keep you safe," he continues. "We can't do this without you. I need you to focus on your role in this war—this is of the utmost importance. Let me and Miguel and Chayanne handle the logistics and the armies."

Maia nods. "But the big decisions…"

"We will always consult you."

"Good."

"In the meantime, you two need to put down your staff and start practicing how you will react in worst-case situations." Shinesho taps the stick in Miguel's hand.

"Like, Jake has a knife?" Maia asks.

"No," Shinesho says. "I'm Jake." He grabs the stick and shoves the tip against Miguel's temple. He looks at Maia very seriously and says, "*Bang*."

"Close your eyes," Miguel whispers.

Maia closes them, and Miguel ties a blindfold around her head. He grabs her shoulders. "Breathe deep," he says, and she inhales. "You are no longer standing in the middle of this field. You are in your worst nightmare. Where are you?"

"I'm back in that cell underground. He has me tied down."

"Okay, now imagine every last detail. What does the room look like? What does *he* look like? What does it feel like to be there? Place yourself in this situation. What are you going to do?"

Miguel circles Maia all afternoon as they run through different scenarios, but they always get trapped on one.

"He has a gun to your head," Maia whispers, trembling. "If I don't destroy Asiaq Bay, he will pull the trigger."

"Maia? *Concentrate.* Either way, I die. You know this, yes? You won't use your powers to destroy thousands of innocent lives, so Jake will do whatever it takes to get the strongest reaction out of you to use them anyway. Either way, I will be dead. You must learn to control your powers so that thousands don't perish alongside me."

Maia is shaking her head.

"He is shoving the barrel against my head," Miguel continues. "He is *screaming* at you!"

"Wait—"

"BANG!" Miguel yells, and Maia jumps, her hand over her mouth.

Breathing hard, she continues shaking her head, and the ground begins to tremble.

"Maia? *Focus.*"

Maia gasps as terrifying visions fill her mind: Miguel falling to the ground, a pool of blood spilling from his head. The field where they stand continues to tremble, and the wind blows hard against them.

"Breathe deep, Maia. Don't resist the emotion—this will

only strengthen it. *Work* through it. *Feel* it. Look at me in your vision. I am dead on the ground."

"*Please,* stop."

"Jake is waiting. He's smiling. It's working—don't let it. Don't let all those innocent people die."

Maia takes a deep breath, continuing to envision her worst nightmare playing out before her. Standing on a cliff, she overlooks a city of thousands with Miguel dead next to her and Jake standing by her side. Her heart thumping, a tear slides out from under her mask.

"Breathe, Maia."

The ground continues to tremble.

"Okay," Miguel goes on, "Jake is dragging Tema before you. He has a knife to her throat."

"Just ... *wait* a minute! I need a break!"

"You're exhausted? *Too bad*! Imagine how it will feel when you're there! When everything has gone wrong, and Jake is slowly taking everyone from you! When you are over-looking a city with the lives of thousands in your hands."

"I can't do this!" Maia grabs her mask.

Miguel wraps his arms around her, holding her down. "*Breathe.*"

She cries out, and the earth violently shakes. Gale-force winds slam into them, and Miguel struggles to stay on his feet. "This is *your* power!" he yells over the wind. "This is *yours* to control! He can only take this from you if you allow it!"

Gasping, Maia considers his words. Should all their plans falter, and she finds herself back in Jake's grasp, he will take everything and everyone from her—whether she gives him what he wants or not. But she cannot allow him to take control of her powers—of her connection to the Earth. To *herself*. If he takes that, everyone loses.

She exhales through pursed lips, long and steady, envisioning an immense, wall-like fortress rising within. Slowly, the shuddering begins to calm, and the ground stills.

"*Magnífico*," Miguel says, and he releases his hold.

Maia slumps to the ground, hanging her head and catching her breath. When she removes her mask, Miguel is kneeling before her.

His smile is tender. "You did good."

"You can't come with me to Leucothea," she says.

Miguel laughs, tilting his gaze. "And what? I will just hide in the woods and play cards while you go to war? That will never happen."

"If you're not there, he won't have as much power over me. You don't need to be there."

"I *absolutely* need to be there. There is no way you'll walk back inside those gates without me beside you. We do this together."

Maia shakes her head, looking at the ground. "I don't like it."

"Maia?" Miguel lifts her chin. "He will only have that control over you if you *give* it to him. This is why we are preparing. I believe in you. I *know* you can do this. You will practice every day, you will master your powers, and we will win this war. But you can't do this alone. You know this, yes?"

She stares at the ground. She knows.

"And you need to be prepared for the worst," he says.

She looks up at him, tears spilling from her eyes. She knows this too.

———

Maia stands alone in the middle of the field. With eyes closed, she imagines Jake standing before her, his obsidian eyes peering deep into hers. Just like her dreams, her memory of him is vivid, the details of his face etched into her mind. Just like her nightmares, the burning buildings of Leucothea tower above them.

Jake steps closer to her, placing his hand against her heart. Tema's voice rings through her mind:

You are a powerful being, and *you are a human being.*

Maia is powerful, *and* she is human.

She glares up at Jake, and she knows what she must do. After weeks of practicing, the entire time focusing on controlling her powers—subduing them, pushing them down, holding them back—she has only experienced a few small victories. She has made some progress, but not nearly enough. At this point, should Jake capture her, she will most certainly fail. And people will die—*scores* of them.

This entire time, Maia has been concentrating on the fact that this monster wants to use her *powers* against her. She realizes now that her eyes have been fixated in the wrong direction. She remembers Shinesho's admonishment: *you are only as strong as your weakest link.*

It is her ability to love—her *humanity*—that is her greatest weakness. Jake knows this. He knows how to manipulate love to create pain.

And pain is powerful.

Maia's temper flairs. If Jake is successful, the amount of agony he will inflict on her will be enough to destroy worlds, and destroy worlds it will. The lives of countless innocent people and generations of their offspring all hinge on the outcome of this single war.

She has always understood that in fulfilling her destiny, a part of her must die, but she could never be sure which part. She now knows, it must be her humanity. It *must* be. She is far too dangerous to be played with like a toy, baited like a switch as a psychopath turns her powers off and on to destroy the lives of the majority in favor of the few.

It is the only way. The only way.

Keeping her eyes shut, she summons the energies of the Earth. They surge across the field, thrumming up from the ground and coursing through her veins. She clenches her fists as the burn spills into the last hollows of her soul. Holding on to the possibility of unforetold pain should Jake be successful, she allows it to wrap around her heart like a cloak of ice.

It is the only way.

Shinesho approaches. She can't see him, but she knows he's there. As he circles her, his feet shuffle against the blades of grass. "Ready?" he asks.

She peers up at him and nods.

He stops before her. "*Now.*"

She crouches to the ground, breathing deeply and spreading her fingers wide. The earth trembles from her touch.

"More," Shinesho says.

She digs her fingers into the dirt, and birds burst from the trees as the ground violently shakes.

"More!" he screams, his voice shaken as he wavers on his feet.

Maia slams her fist into the earth, and it jolts a forceful blow, knocking Shinesho onto his back. She stands, and the ground stills under her command. "Good?" she asks, breathless.

"Yeah," Shinesho says. Looking up at the sky, he smiles. "Good."

THIRTY-ONE

Lying on their backs, Maia and Miguel gaze up at the twisting branches of her living throne. A few fireflies blink and drift across the room, now darkened in the blue haze of twilight. A great horned owl has flown in through one of the church's windows, newly broken from Maia's quakes. It perches on a branch, its head on a swivel.

"That owl has been here a few times now," Miguel says.

"It has."

"Will you name this one too?"

Maia grins. She can't see Miguel's face, but she knows he is smirking. She lifts onto her elbow, and her smile fades.

He looks at her. "What is it?"

She runs her hand over his shaved head. "Will you grow it out again?"

"I'm not sure ... I don't think so. I think I look pretty fetching with it gone," he says with a wink.

"You do..." She tries to smile but swallows instead.

He tilts his gaze, a worried crease forming. "What are you not saying?"

"I..." She hesitates. "I have to go away for a while."

His features soften, and he sighs. "I know."

"Not ... *physically*."

"I know."

"How?"

He swipes her thick hair off her shoulder, then softly caresses her cheek. "I can already feel it ... *you* ... slipping away."

"It's the only way, Miguel. This is how it needs to be."

"Whatever you need to do, I support you."

"I'm not leaving you. I just ... I might be a little distant for a while."

"I understand."

She lays her head on his chest, listening as he fills his lungs with air. He slowly blows it out. "Will you come back to me?" he finally asks, his voice soft like a whisper.

She closes her eyes. "I hope so."

Running his fingertips up and down her arm, he says, "You will. I know you will."

She sits up again, gazing down at him. "And, what if I don't?"

He looks at her a long while, his eyes glassy. Finally, he says, "You have once. You will again."

———

Over the next month, Maia, Miguel, Shinesho, and Chayanne work tirelessly on combat training and how to tackle different scenarios should Jake be successful in capturing Maia. She sits blindfolded on a stump in the middle of the field while they take turns circling her and berating her with situations—horrific situations. All the while, she focuses on controlling her powers *and* her emotions. She makes decisions she doesn't want to make, some better than others, which they discuss later at length: which choices were clever, which were shortsighted, and which could be improved upon.

Maia is about to walk straight back into the welcoming arms of her worst enemy. A man who has spent every waking hour preparing for her capture. Every day, her powers grow. Every day, she becomes physically and mentally stronger. And every day, her instinct to fight slowly overpowers her fears. The small amount of innocence left in her has disappeared. War is so close she can smell it.

And she wants blood.

After a while, the crews from the tribe arrive, bringing tearful reunions and much-needed supplies. It is so good to see the chief and familiar faces from Maia's short time there. But now the people are unsure of how to act in her presence. Everyone looks at her differently. They can sense her power, they have heard the stories, and they have been prepared by their shaman. They try to act normal, but how can you not revere the woman sitting on a living throne of trees, surrounded by a legion of tigers?

Every day, as Maia practices combat, more and more people join in. Not only have her powers strengthened, but her body has as well. It's like she has become more than she is. Her muscles have superhuman strength, like what they used to say all humans could possess if only their minds would free them to do so.

Maia stands in the middle of the field, encircled by Shinesho and his troops. A soldier approaches from behind, and Maia turns to face him. The two fight. It doesn't last long before she twists his arm, then lifts and slams him to the ground. He waves his hand in a truce as he groans.

Behind Maia, another person approaches. She turns,

facing a woman. The two fight until the woman falls. Another warrior advances. They fight Maia, and the warrior falls. Another round, another fall. And another. As people limp off the field, Maia barely breaks a sweat. It's exhilarating. It's like her body knows, and she is *ready* for it.

Maia smiles at Shinesho, and he nods. The two battle it out for a while—the longest Maia fights with anyone—until he, too, falls. She steps next to him and offers her hand, helping him from the ground. He grimaces, rubbing his ribs.

"You okay?" she asks.

He nods but says nothing.

After that, no one wants to fight her anymore. She stands alone in the middle of the field, looking around. A large crowd has gathered, but no one dares enter the circle. She waits until, eventually, Shinesho says, "I'm sorry, Maia, but I think we're done."

Much later that night, Maia sits alone on her throne. The hall is filled with tigers curled between tree roots twisted along the ground. Miguel is sleeping on their bed tucked in a corner. Everyone is resting except Maia. She hasn't slept much lately—she doesn't seem to need much of it anymore. When she does, she often dreams of Jake, and the nightmares always end the same: standing in the burning streets of a melting Leucothea, Maia suffocates while Jake watches her drown.

What are these dreams trying to tell her? Can't breathe. Can't *ever* breathe.

The late summer heat has caused a lightning storm, and Maia's great hall fills with ceaseless flashes of light. It highlights the twisting vines lining the walls, which continued multiplying by the day. It's almost as if there is no building left, just a structure made of trees.

The magic of her living throne is evident to all who enter, but only Maia can see the glimmering sparks of blue light softly drifting from the branches' yellow flowers. It's like this tree has become a part of her. She listens to it breathe, filling her with a profound sense of peace.

The silent lightning continues. As Maia stares into the flickering weave of vines, she becomes lost in a meditative state, envisioning Jake sitting in his mansion high up on a hill. His face is highlighted in the streaks of light, and she knows in this very moment that she haunts him as much as he does her.

Autumn is fast approaching; Leucothea Day is near. They are running out of time. Should the separate missions be successful, their tiny militia hiding in the woods will be joined by the few known armies of North America. They'll create a sizable military, although it still won't match Leucothea's numbers or technology. But they hold an incredibly powerful war chip that Leucothea does not. They have Maia, who has the destructive strength of *ten* armies. She holds a power so fierce, it could destroy the city in minutes.

Yet, she is not indestructible. A single bullet could end her life, and then the possibility of a peaceful revolution will be left solely in the hands of Leucothea's people.

War ... It seems like such a primitive part of the past. What will come of this? Will Maia and her armies overtake Leucothea? Will this destroy the city? Will *Maia* destroy the city? Battles cannot be fought without loss. Will the people see what Maia and her tribe are trying to show them? And if she is left with no other option but to take Leucothea from them, will this not only breed *more* hatred? More leaders like Jake?

Jake—Maia dreads the moment they'll meet as much as

she craves it. Miguel keeps pressing her for a plan, but she doesn't have one. It is impossible to say how, but she knows an opportunity will present itself. Everything has been leading up to this, and there will be a moment—a single explosive moment—where Maia and Jake will hold each other's lives in their hands. Day in and day out, Maia tries to prepare herself for this moment, whatever it may be, but it is impossible to know. Jake has always held an inexplicable power over her. And despite all her visualizations and meditations, she knows what is about to come is something she will never be prepared for.

As time passes, more people arrive, and the few campfires around the grounds turn into dozens. Maia can't go anywhere without the soldiers stopping to stare at the magical woman who has started a war. It's unnerving. Conversations stop, work screeches to a halt, and the people watch her every move. Eventually, Maia decides to leave Miguel, Shinesho, and Chayanne to handle most things, and she retreats to her church.

Shinesho has confirmed that they still have Claire on their side, and they are currently working on setting up a Special Mission S&R Truck to sneak them back inside Leucothea's gates. Maia doesn't have the slightest clue as to why Claire has had such a change of heart or why she would risk her life to help them. Maia would give anything to talk to her, but the line of communication between Shinesho and Leucothea has remained top secret, and they have agreed it's best to keep it that way.

The military from New Portland has arrived, led by Andrew, the soldier who guarded Maia, Lucas, and Miguel when they stayed in their village a few years ago. Their numbers are half of what Miguel and Shinesho were expecting. New Portland's leader, along with the rest of their troops, has remained in New Portland should Leucothea's army counterattack.

The army general from Asiaq Bay has also arrived. She has brought a few soldiers—but no army.

Miguel and Shinesho bring the leaders to Maia. As the generals timidly step inside the hall, their eyes widen and their mouths fall open. It is truly a sight to behold. Maia's tigers pace the floors, stepping in and out of large roots, while Maia sits before them on her throne.

Andrew is the first to speak. "Maia, it is so good to see you again."

"And you," she says with a warm smile. "I'm only sorry it's not under happier circumstances."

He nods.

"I can't begin to thank you for joining us," Maia says.

"Of course. Had I known..." He hesitates, nervously eyeing an approaching tiger.

Maia snaps her fingers, and the tiger turns away.

Andrew exhales relief. "Had I known who you were..." He looks at her apologetically.

"What?"

"I would have been kinder to you."

"You were very kind to us, Andrew. Your community didn't have to let us in, but I will be forever grateful that you did. How is Thomas? His boots saved my life."

"He's well. I'll send your regards."

"Please do."

He takes off his hat. "I also wanted to give my condolences to you for Lucas. I was really sorry to hear of his passing."

Maia looks away. Even after all this time, a simple mention of his name still feels like a stab to her heart. When she finally looks back at him, she can only nod.

"Maia," Miguel says. "This is Uki. She is the army general of Asiaq Bay."

Uki steps forward. She looks like she's made of ice and steel. Her black hair is shaved short on the sides, a little longer on top. She has strong eyes and a sharp jaw, but her smile is warm and genuine. "It's a pleasure to finally meet you, Maia. We've heard so much about you."

"The pleasure is all mine," Maia says.

"I want to thank you for sending your soldiers to warn us about Leucothea," Uki says. "We've been aware of its threat for quite some time but were hoping our nations could maintain peace between us. Little did we know, Leucothea has been conspiring against us this entire time. We will be forever indebted to you, and will do everything in our power to be of service."

"Thank you," Maia says. "The addition of your armies will hopefully give us the advantage we need to avoid a war."

Uki nods.

"Speaking of," Maia says with a tilted gaze. "Where *are* your armies?"

"We will be deploying them in smaller units at separate times. Despite our best efforts to prevent it, we have received word that the New System has put our city under surveillance, so we didn't want to make any sudden moves to tip them off. Plus, we need to keep a portion of our army on our own land. The last thing we want is to leave our people unprotected."

Maia nods. "Of course. New Portland has done the same."

"We have also sent messengers to warn the Old Russia. It will take some time, so we can't count on them to join us."

Shinesho steps forward. "Asiaq Bay has gifted us with a few drones, so we are currently working on recording the material we need. The plan is to cut the electricity after we have shown the city our footage, which will kill the government's security cameras so they won't see us coming. Uki's army will surround the city—they have more soldiers and advanced armory—and my troops will join them. Andrew will split his military between the slave encampments and the power plants. Once his missions have been accomplished, they will join us in Leucothea."

Maia sits in silence as the small group fills her in on the upcoming battle plans, *dreading* her next question. Once they have finished, she asks Shinesho, "And who will be accompanying me inside the gates of Leucothea?"

"Me, Miguel, and Chayanne."

Maia closes her eyes, shaking her head. "No. Jake knows you—he knows your faces."

"He doesn't know Chayanne's. And he knows yours as well, doesn't he?"

Maia sighs in frustration. "I don't want you coming with me."

Miguel cuts in calmly. "We are the best team for this mission, and you know it. Shinesho and I are being taught how to hack the feed for the celebration projections. Jake doesn't know Chayanne, so she will be the perfect person to have your back in the city as you make your way toward the square. She and Shinesho are some of the toughest fighters I know—I trust them with my life. It would be a huge risk to send you in there with strangers. We *know* each other. There is no one better to accompany you than the three of us."

"And no one worse," Maia says. "You are my family. Jake

will be so happy to see us all together, I would be shocked if he wasn't there to *personally* open the gates for us."

"He won't know we're there; we are making sure of it," Shinesho says. "And the four of us will separate as soon as we enter the gates. We'll stay connected with radios and earpieces. Chayanne will be two steps behind you with your radios linked to mine and Miguel's, as well as Uki's and Andrew's. Miguel and I will head to another part of the city to work on the feed, and then we'll meet you both in the square. New Portland's army has given us bulletproof vests, and if anyone's radio is cut, we will all be alerted. If something happens to me, Miguel can step in—or vice versa. None of us will be 'together,' but we will all be connected and keeping an eye on one another."

Maia sighs, and she nods. This mission has always been risky. There is no "safe" way to go to war. And Miguel is right. There is no one she trusts more with her life than the three of them.

"And, what about Jake?" Andrew asks.

Maia peers up at him, her voice laden with ice. "Leave Jake to me."

THIRTY-TWO

Draped across her throne, Maia listens to Shinesho and Miguel whispering outside the building. They are debating like children, finally agreeing to play *Rock, Paper, Scissors* to decide who will be the one to tell her. Tell her what, though, they haven't said.

It is silent.

Shinesho pulls aside the vines hanging across the doorway, and Maia lifts her head. As he steps inside, she makes a mental note to give Miguel a hard time later. *Coward.*

Shinesho opens his mouth, hesitating, then closes it again. Maia sits up. Shinesho looks *nervous*. She has never seen Shinesho nervous before. "There is someone here to see you," he says quickly.

She slants her eyes. "Could you be more specific?"

"Before I bring him in, you need to know this man is on our side. Okay? He has already taken great risks to help us. He is here to *help*."

Maia straightens. Now *she's* the nervous one. "Okay?"

"Do you trust me?"

"With my life."

Shinesho steps to the side, and Maia stands in shock.

Behind Shinesho is President Augustus, Leucothea's beloved leader. Maia is frozen, unsure of what to do. She glares at Shinesho.

It's okay, he mouths.

The president walks inside the great hall, his eyes wide, and he removes his hat. Gazing around, a smile stretches across his weathered face. "So. The rumors are true."

Maia steps down from her throne, approaching him with a surprising amount of fury. He stumbles backward, nearly tripping over a root, and Shinesho slides between them, holding out his hand. Maia slows her pace.

"It's okay, Shinesho," President Augustus says, and Shinesho cautiously moves to the side.

Maia approaches. It's strange to be standing before this iconic man she has only ever seen on TV screens, billboards, and framed plaques. He is older than what he appears to be in pictures. His skin drapes beneath his neck, the hair on top of his head has thinned significantly, and his hardened belly extends beyond his pants.

"So, this is the young woman who has started a revolution," he says, straightening his top. He lifts his chin. "I recognize you from the papers."

"I was going to say the same to you," Maia says.

For a moment, there is silence.

"What are you *doing* here?" Maia finally says.

"I understand you want to remove Jake and his New System from Leucothea. Peaceably, if possible. I want to be of service in this regard. I have been helping Claire and Kaique arrange a truck to sneak you back into the city for Leucothea Day, but I needed to meet you before we went any further. I needed to ... see for myself." He turns behind him to Shinesho, who nods and exits the church.

Maia gawks at him, confused. The president of Leucothea wants to ... *help*?

"I have to say, this is pretty magnificent." He eyes Atlas, now standing next to Maia. "I was told about the tigers, but they disappeared the same time you did. Little did we know, they were all there to see you," he says with a chuckle.

"You and Claire have been working *together*? This *entire* time?"

"Not the entire time. Up until recently, Claire had always been on Jake's side."

Side?

"But then you came along, which changed everything. Maybe change is the wrong word—*accelerated*. I'm not sure if Claire was blind to who Jake was or if she just didn't *want* to see, but after you showed up, his voracious appetite for power went from greedy to downright deadly.

"As you know, Claire was the one who sent messengers to your tribe in hopes they would get you out of there. But when Shinesho reached out to her again with plans for a revolution, she knew she needed to go to higher ground for help. Jake had the entire city on lockdown after your capture." He lowers his gaze, clearing his throat. "After your *rescue*." He looks at her apologetically. "So, Claire needed someone with more authority to get an S&R Truck in without being searched."

"And that's you."

"That's pretty much *only* me now, besides Jake."

Maia nods, trying to take it all in. "Why are you doing this?"

"Because I want Leucothea to go back to what it was always intended to be, but I just can't seem to break this raging beast that keeps growing. Knowing how long I've been angry with Leucothea, Claire took the risk and approached me for help, and I'm glad she did."

"Angry? With *Leucothea*? But you're its leader."

"Was—I *was* its leader. Now, I'm just a face."

Maia shakes her head. "I don't understand."

"Humans ... At the end of the day, we're still animals. We need comfort. We need to feel safe. I wanted that for my people, but our budding city needed alternatives and fast. Our numbers were growing out of control. Things stopped working. Our resources couldn't keep up. Crime was on the rise, and people were going hungry. We needed help. The citizens were getting frustrated and angry. My most trusted advisors started to ... talk—to *others*, people who've traveled, followed their own laws. Last I knew, they called themselves 'pirates.' I wanted nothing to do with them. They're basically thugs of the sea."

Maia's mouth dries.

"I had originally banned them from Leucothea, but my advisors went behind my back and consulted with them anyway. They set up a line of communication with these ships and established a new trade route. Together, they came up with new solutions for our city, which were just old solutions—dated solutions—and my government rewarded those pirates handsomely. I agreed to go along with it all as a short-term measure until we could figure something else out. This new 'movement,' as they called it, got things up and running again. I knew their methods were dirty, but they worked. My city was in celebration, but they had no idea what we had done."

The president twists his hat in his grip. "I felt so ashamed, but I was at ease for the first time in years. That was my biggest mistake. I got comfortable."

Maia nods. "Please, sit." She leads him to a large root

lifted like a bench beside the windows, the vines draped across them tied to the side. They sit next to one another, looking out as a few soldiers pass by.

"Jake seemed to come from nowhere," Augustus continues, "and was voted in immediately. I later discovered that he had been on the scene from the beginning, and he used that charm of his to work his way up, and fast. Under his command as army general, the New System grew like a virus. They wanted to change everything to be as much like the old days as possible. They were bullies, more like a dictatorship than a democracy, but it was too late. They had already won the hearts of my people, and it wasn't long before the city had become the polar opposite of what it was intended to be.

"After most of the original government officials started disappearing in the middle of the night, the few remaining escaped the city pretty quickly. We had lost everything we had worked so hard for. But I was one of the 'lucky' ones. The people trusted me, so Jake kept me as president, but I was stripped of my power. I became a face. A fat, overfed face."

Augustus turns toward her. "Surely, you understand. You know Jake. He threatened my family, my loved ones, even their children. He threatened everything I loved. And the people in Leucothea seemed happy. I felt powerless. I knew if I spoke out, the only thing that would happen was I would get myself and my family killed, and the New System would continue without me. I ... I have *grandchildren*, Maia."

She looks up at him. "I understand."

"But then you came along," he says. "And you ... *you* changed everything."

"I haven't, though."

"You have. Look around. Look at all the people who have

gathered together. This would never have happened if it weren't for you."

Maia looks out the window at the people passing by.

"I want to be the trusted face you need to reach the people," Augustus says, and she looks at him in surprise. "Those are good people, Maia. And they trust me. I believe they will listen to me, and we can come to an arrangement without anyone getting hurt. I will be delivering my usual speech on Leucothea Day, but this year, I will tell my people what has been happening behind the scenes. I will tell them that the New System is a wolf in sheep's clothing and that wolf is hungry for more. I will show them everything and demand the current government step down. But should anything happen to me, I have given your men a prerecorded speech to play with the footage they've gathered."

"Should anything happen?"

"They will most certainly cut my feed—Jake won't let me talk for long once he hears what I've got to say. But he won't hurt me in front of the people, and I've got security guards I can trust. We have trained your men and have given them a device that will fit in their packs, so they can hijack the video from the square. This way, you'll still have control of the citywide projections, but the four of you won't have to be separated."

"But what about Jake's threats? What about your family?"

"We're moving them out. With the help of Shinesho and Claire, we'll be sneaking them out before my speech. Kaique and a few of Shinesho's soldiers will be waiting at a specified location in the woods outside of the gates to take them into hiding. I have the authority to make sure the trucks aren't searched. And it's only the two vehicles, mine going out and yours coming in, so it shouldn't raise any flags."

Maia sighs. "But what about *you*?"

He smiles at her tenderly. "Yes, and what about *you*?"

She nods. There isn't much to say. They both know they are risking their lives. "Thank you, President Augustus."

"Just Augustus. And thank *you*, Maia. I have hope again." He shakes his head. "It has been *so long* since I've had hope."

Maia places her hand on top of his, squeezing it. "Please, stay for dinner tonight?"

"I would love to, but I can't. I need to get back before too much time passes and people notice my absence."

"You're sure you weren't followed?"

"I haven't been followed."

Maia nods.

"I've also come with a warning," Augustus says gravely.

She looks at him, her nerves prickling. "Yes?"

He studies her face. "Please don't take this as disrespect, but do you think you are some sort of prophet?"

Maia is taken aback. "Of course not."

"But you believe you'll save the people."

"I *hope* I can."

He looks away.

"You think I'm foolish," Maia says.

"I think there have been numerous stories, spanning many lifetimes, of people who have tried to bring change or a message of hope. They've come under different names across varying cultures..."

"And?"

"And ... those people have generally not been well received."

"You think this is a suicide mission?"

"Risky, yes. Suicide, no. But you need to be mindful of your expectations. People can surprise you. They become entrenched in their own cultures and environments, and they don't always take lightly to change. They will find what-ever it takes to protect the status quo, especially if the message is coming from an outsider."

"But you aren't an outsider."

"I'm not, but *you* are. And I hear *concerns*," he says with hesitation, "that you may step in and talk to the people if you need to."

Miguel.

"I—I haven't decided yet. And I'm not an outsider, at least not to them. I'm a citizen. People know me."

"Maia, Jake has turned the entire city against you."

"*What?*"

"He has announced that you are a traitor. He's put a bounty on your capture, offering an enormous reward for anyone who can deliver you back to him. There were flyers all over the city."

Maia is speechless.

"I needed you to know this before walking back inside those gates. Not only will Jake be looking for you, but the damage he has caused by his propaganda has already been done, and anyone who recognizes you may turn on you. Those people you are risking your life to save? They now consider you their enemy."

Maia closes her eyes. *Of course.* "Have you told anyone this? Anyone here?" She peers up at him.

He shakes his head, confused. "No..."

"Don't. Please."

"And why is that?"

Maia gazes out the window and sighs. "My entire life, I've lived for a dream I've never understood. The only family I had—my grandfather—never understood it either." She smiles. "He gave me such a hard time. Spent years trying to talk me out of it. In the end, I left everything behind, risked

305

my life, risked *other* people's lives..." She turns to face him. "All for a relentless dream I couldn't understand. But now? Now I understand. I know why I'm here. And I know, beyond a shadow of a doubt, that I must go back to Leucothea. This war belongs to all of us, but ultimately, *I* must be the one to end this."

Augustus stands, and Maia joins him. "Just ... don't let them see your eyes," he says with a saddened smile. "You have unforgettable eyes."

Maia nods.

He puts his hat back on. "Ma'am."

She steps forward as he walks away. "See you on the other side?"

"Here's hoping," the president says, tapping the brim of his hat. He hesitates at the doorway, then turns to face her. "You won't destroy it all, will you? If everything goes pear-shaped?"

Maia sighs. "I don't know."

He looks down, nodding. Then he sweeps the vines aside and disappears behind them.

After he leaves, Maia turns toward her throne and reaches out her hand. A branch swings down and grabs hold. Together, with the root beneath her feet, the tree lifts her above the great hall, and she steps onto another branch extending far beyond the roof.

Campfires and tents sprawl in every direction. How many do they have in total gathered here today? Shinesho said that with Asiaq Bay's new arrivals, and the lookouts hidden in the mountains, they are a thousand strong.

As Maia walks farther out along the limb, the tigers form a line on the ground below. The men and women in the field slowly back up, and the crowd hushes in a wave.

"I want to thank you all," Maia shouts, "for joining me in

this great war against the wretchedness that has crawled from beneath the ashes! In the days to come, we will make history! From this moment forward, it is my fervent hope that with every step you take, you are comforted by the noble truth that you are changing the world! You are *saving* the world! This," Maia holds her hands above her, "is what *legends* are made of!"

The troops roar in applause, clapping their hands above their heads.

"From this moment forward, you will leave a lasting legacy, a unifying story of bravery that will be known by every child who will walk a better planet because of *you*! Look around! We are the descendants of a near-extinct humanity in a burning and destroyed world. We are the forgotten ones! From this point forward, we will no longer be silenced by the forces that try to subdue us! The authority of the few cannot squander the power of the majority! From this point forward, we will unite, and we will never again be forgotten!"

When the people cheer, the echo of a thousand voices reverberates across the mountains.

THIRTY-THREE

Today is the day.

It is early morning, and the few remaining soldiers outside Maia's church have been up for hours. They are busy, resolute, hushed. Maia lies on her side next to Miguel, tracing his tattoos with the tip of her finger. He is on his back, staring up at the vines as they listen to the quiet rustlings of the camp. Most of the soldiers left days ago. There is only the odd cough, the sporadic shuffle of feet, and the occasional soft murmuring as people pass outside their windows—now completely covered with foliage.

Miguel turns toward her. The look on his face reminds her of the moment they locked eyes from across that tent in New Portland under the glittering Christmas lights. That moment will be forever engrained in Maia's memory. It wasn't just the way he looked at her, but it was the way she understood everything he couldn't say from a single glance. It was a look of resolution. A look of acceptance of a situation that he somehow knew, even back then, had the power to break them. This morning, Miguel has that same look of sadness—of acceptance—that the harsh reality of life may once again tear them apart.

In a few hours, Maia, Miguel, Shinesho, and Chayanne will begin their trek through the wilderness toward an S&R Truck that will deliver them back to the eager claws of a deadly beast. By tonight, if all goes to plan, they will be walking the streets of Leucothea, the grave threat of war on the horizon.

Maia takes in Miguel's eyes, the shadow of a beard covering his dimple, the intricate design of the tribal tattoos on his arm. As if memorizing him for the last time, she studies every last detail.

There is a knock on the doorframe. "Miguel?" Shinesho calls from the other side of the vines.

Miguel closes his eyes. When he opens them again, a sheen of tears reflects back to her. He opens his mouth to speak, but she places her finger against his lips, shaking her head. The two lean in, their noses touching, and he wraps his arms around her, rolling her on top of him as they kiss.

"Just need your help with something," Shinesho says.

Maia buries her head in Miguel's neck, and he sighs. "Yes, mate. Coming."

She rolls onto her back, and Miguel kisses her one last time before leaving.

Blowing out a breath, she climbs to her feet and wanders to her uniform draped over her throne. Just like her vision where she stood above a burning Leucothea, everything she is about to wear is black: black socks, black boots, black cargo pants, black sleeveless top. She puts it all on, followed by her holster and gun. Her knife is wrapped in a sheath, tucked into her pants. She finishes by zipping up her black jacket with an extra-large hood that will easily drape over her face. To blend in with the festive crowds, Chayanne has painted a white star on the back of the coat. All four will be wearing the same.

Maia steps to a window, pulling back the vines. She taps a loose piece of broken glass, and it drops to the other side. Resting her head against the frame, she gazes across the large, empty spaces that once held people and fires and tents. The only remnants of life are now footprints in the dirt.

Chayanne steps inside the hall with her basket of breakfast, and her famous eggs cooked in willow bark over the fire. With a playful grin, she sets the goods down and reaches into her pocket.

"What are you up to?" Maia asks, smiling despite herself.

Chayanne pulls out a pair of black sunglasses and slides them on. The shades have a white star painted on the right lens. "Leucothea Day glasses. How do I look?"

Maia nods, impressed. "Like a proud citizen."

Chayanne takes them off and grabs her basket as she walks over to Maia. "They'll help us blend in, and they're perfect for covering your eyes." She hands a pair to Maia. "The star is painted with tiny dots, so you can still see through it."

"Perfect," Maia says. She puts them on, then drapes her hood over her head.

Chayanne nods in approval, looking her up and down. "Perfect indeed." She tucks Maia's greenstone necklace beneath her shirt. "The only thing you're missing is this." She lifts a bulletproof vest from the top of the basket. "I've painted a few things on it for you."

Maia takes it. "Oh, Chayanne."

"We would normally paint our horses, but since our horse is an S&R Truck, I decided to get creative," she says.

Maia holds it up, and Chayanne puts her arm around

her, pointing. "There's a horse, here, for a safe journey. A broken arrow, here, for a peaceful resolution. I've painted a tiger—symbolizing Atlas—for protection. I made that last one up," she says, her voice cracking, and she steps away, wiping her eyes.

Maia throws herself around her. "Thank you," she whispers.

Chayanne squeezes her arms. Turning, she says, "You'll need to wear it under your jacket. Let me help." She unzips Maia's hoodie and helps her into her vest.

It's much heavier than Maia expected. She pats it for reassurance, looking at Chayanne with uncertainty.

"It will block a bullet from here," Chayanne says, placing her hand over Maia's heart. "Unfortunately, your head and neck will still be exposed, but this is all we have."

Maia pats Chayanne's shoulders and chest, her eyes glazed with tears.

"I've got mine on already," Chayanne says softly. "Don't you worry about me."

Maia nods, and Chayanne helps her back into her jacket. When she zips it up, the black fabric covers the broken arrow on Maia's chest.

After breakfast, Maia sits on her throne with Atlas at her feet, and Chayanne props herself on the armrest behind her to braid back her hair. When she finishes, Maia leans between Chayanne's legs, and Chayanne wraps her arms around her.

And the two women sit in silence for a while.

As Maia, Miguel, Shinesho, and Chayanne begin their trek away from the camp, the tigers follow behind them.

Maia stops with a sigh, and the three turn to look at her. "I need a minute," she says quietly.

They peer at the tigers, then step to the side to wait by a tree.

Maia turns toward Atlas, faithfully standing by her side. She crouches down and holds his face between her hands. "You have been with me for so long, but you absolutely *cannot* come with me now."

He angles his head, and she runs her fingers through his fur. He touches his nose to hers, gathering her scent, and she closes her eyes. She can't believe this is happening; this is just like Huck. She was hoping she'd never have to go through this again.

She stands, and Atlas peers up at her, confused.

"You need to stay here, where it's safe," she says. "I will come back for you. I *swear*..." Her voice cracks. Can she make a promise she's not sure she can keep? "I will do *everything* I can to come back for you." She falls to her knees and throws her arms around the large tiger, and he burrows his head into her, knocking her to the ground. She laughs through her tears, and the rest of the tigers surround her.

As she walks backward down the road, she holds out her hand. "*Stay*," she says, her voice quivering.

The tigers line up. Unsure, they glance between Maia and Atlas, who is now standing before them. He steps forward.

"I will come back for you," Maia says. "I will *try*..." She shakes her head. "Just ... *stay*." She quickly turns away, wiping the tears from her cheeks.

And the four quietly continue on, leaving Maia's legion of tigers behind them.

As Maia, Miguel, Shinesho, and Chayanne traverse the deep, misty forests, they are silent. Resolute. They have a half-day hike to the spot where the truck and Kaique will be waiting, and so far, no one has said a word.

Maia focuses on her feet, running the lists on repeat in her mind. Miguel and Shinesho each have a pack of supplies to hack the projections, and they have been thoroughly trained by Asiaq Bay's most experienced technical gurus. They all have a small earpiece hidden in their ears. Their radios have been tried and tested, and then tested again. Vests are secured and hidden under their jackets. Guns are loaded. Knives tucked.

Maia has spent hours—*days*—preparing them for the chaos of Leucothea's city streets, running through every possible scenario she could think of. Thankfully, there will be no cars driving down the roads tonight—too many people. So, that's one less risk to worry about.

Maia peers at the others, but only Chayanne looks back at her. Both the men appear lost in thought. Miguel has that deep crease between his brow, the same look Lucas used to have when he was worried, and Maia focuses once again on her feet, running the lists from the top.

The trees still whisper as they pass, but this is the first time their murmurings do not bring Maia comfort. Despite repeated deep breaths, she cannot contain her nerves. This is it. It's happening. Over a thousand soldiers are now scattered across this land, all making their way toward Leucothea. *Maia* is making her way back to Leucothea— back to the place that once broke her. Back to the *man* who once broke her. The man who wants nothing more than to end her. Tonight is the night it will all go down. Tonight is the night everything will change.

Shinesho slows, his palm up, and they stop. Up ahead,

an S&R Truck sits in a wooded clearing. It's much smaller than Maia had imagined. It looks like a small delivery truck from the city. Shinesho glances between them and nods. They have agreed to approach the vehicle one at a time in case of an ambush or trap.

As the four separate, Miguel grabs Maia's hand, pulling her into him. His face is stern, his jaw clenched.

She shakes her head. "No, Miguel," she whispers. "No goodbyes. Not now—not ever."

He gazes down at her, and she peers up at him. He grabs her face and kisses her, and then he walks away.

"Miguel?" she whispers, and he looks back at her. *I love you*, she mouths.

He nods. *Me too*. And the two separate, crouching between the thick brush.

Shinesho hides behind a tree, peering at the truck. He whistles. The driver's door opens, and Kaique steps out, looking around. He nods, then whistles back.

The coast is clear.

Shinesho is the first to approach, and Kaique walks from the truck to greet him. Kaique is also dressed in black. His shirt has a white star embroidered on the right chest pocket, and a badge stating "Special Mission S&R Crew" is pinned to his top. Seeing the Leucothean uniform again sends shivers down Maia's spine.

The two men shake hands, and then Kaique swings open the back door. The old metal groans before it slams against the side of the truck. Miguel is the next to approach, followed by Chayanne. Kaique steps to the driver's side and turns on the ignition, and the vehicle roars to life. It's much louder than Maia expected. As she steps into the clearing, a thick cloud of black smoke pours from a silver tube extending from the truck's cargo area. Maia stares at it, unsure.

Sensing her uncertainty, Kaique whispers, "It's okay. It's not electric. She's an old girl." He holds out his hand and helps Maia inside.

The back of the truck is stacked with crates and piles of junk. Brooms. Buckets. Blankets. Rope.

Miguel, Chayanne, and Shinesho are already hidden behind a wall of boxes along the back. Maia crouches between the supplies until she reaches them, then she slides against the back wall next to Miguel. The four unfold a few large blankets to cover themselves while Kaique jumps inside and pulls a few boxes down, refilling the walkway. Then he closes the door, shrouding them in darkness.

As the truck idles, exhaust fumes fill the small cargo space. The smell is overwhelming, and Maia holds her hand over her mouth, suppressing a cough.

Miguel leans in, whispering, "Pull your hood over your nose."

She yanks her hood across her face, using the fabric like a mask, and the truck lurches forward. She reaches for Miguel, and he holds her hand against his chest.

Hours pass, although it feels much more like days, until eventually, the truck comes to a stop, its old brakes squealing. Why are they stopping? The back door swings open.

"Last stop before Leucothea," Kaique whispers. "If you need to relieve yourself, now is the time."

The four stand and the blankets drop to the ground.

Kaique moves a few crates to let them out. Shinesho and Miguel exit first, then hold out their hands to help the women. As Maia jumps from the vehicle, Kaique fills a hole in the truck with a pungent liquid from a red canister. She gazes around. They are surrounded by dense Alaskan wilderness, reminding her so much of her original journey to Leucothea.

Kaique looks incredibly nervous. "Be quick," he whispers, peering over his shoulder at the sky. *Drones*. He is looking for drones.

They scatter into the woods to relieve themselves and then hurry back inside the cargo area. This time, after Kaique closes the door, he fiddles with a metal lock on the other side. Maia is grateful she can't see the others' faces. Here they all are, corralled into a cage headed straight for the mouth of a monster.

Hours pass as the four huddle beneath the blankets. They are surrounded in darkness, with nothing but the deafening roar of the motor and the endless clattering of metal as the old truck hurtles down the rough and battered road. At times, they hit craters so deep, Maia is surprised the entire rig doesn't buckle at the seams.

As the vehicle slows, the long squeal of brakes pulls Maia from her anxiety-ridden daze, and they come to a stop. Her heart racing, she listens on a knife's edge, her eyes straining against the blackness.

A man's muffled voice sounds from outside, and Kaique is quick to respond. Maia strains to listen, but she cannot make out what they are saying over the rumbling motor. There is a long silence. The other man speaks again, his voice tense. More silence. Kaique responds. His reply is brief —annoyed. Maia's heart is in her throat, and she grips her gun.

As they wait, fumes once again fill the back of the truck. Maia grimaces, covering her mouth. Her throat tightens, and she curls into herself, pulling her hood over her face. She holds her breath, suppressing an intense urge to cough.

A loud bang slams into the side of the cargo area, startling them—like someone has struck it with an open palm. There is a sharp blow of a whistle, and their S&R Truck lurches forward.

Sighs of relief resound in the small space around Maia, and she releases her breath.

They are in.

THIRTY-FOUR

As the truck drives down an eerily smooth road, Maia listens to the rapid, shallow breathing of those around her. She keeps her hand inside her coat, gripping her gun.

After a painfully long few minutes, the truck slows once again to a stop. The engine turns off, but Kaique does not release his "coast is clear" whistle.

They wait.

The hum of a drone sounds above, and Maia's heart leaps into her throat. It hovers for a while, and then the sound fades. The lock on the cargo area moves, metal against metal, and then the doors swing open, flooding the back of the truck with light.

"All clear," Kaique says in a hushed voice. "Lots of drones around. *Hurry*."

The four quickly stand, sliding on their glasses and draping their hoods. One by one, they pile out of the truck. Maia recognizes the area as the loading docks from one of the larger S&R Warehouses. The smells of the cement city hit her, and she clutches at her chest. Scent can be funny that way—the power it has to slip you straight into a memory.

The four race between the truck and the warehouse and slip into an open doorway where Kaique is waiting, circling his hand to *hurry*. It is black inside. No one will be around tonight with the citywide celebrations. Most of Leucothea has the night off.

As Maia steps inside, she takes off her glasses and looks around. It feels so strange to be back inside this place. The last time she was here, she was loading her arms full of clothing—a gift from Jake. She was still reeling from Lucas's death and heartbroken over Miguel. She was suppressing her powers ... She was another person entirely.

"Maia?" a woman's voice whispers.

Maia recognizes it immediately, although she can't place where it came from. She looks around, and Claire steps forward, barely visible in the dark.

Maia approaches. Claire's cheeks are flushed; she looks nervous. She timidly extends her hand, and Maia holds it within hers.

"Thank you, Claire," Maia says quietly, "for everything you've done to help us. For saving my life."

Claire sighs. "I just wish..." She hesitates, sucking in her lips, and her eyes line with tears. "I just wish I would have stepped in sooner. I am *so sorry*, Maia."

Maia bows her head. "It's okay."

"I can't believe I stood by and did nothing for so long. I didn't know." Her voice breaks at the last word.

"I know you didn't."

Claire wraps her arms around her, and Maia closes her eyes in relief.

As Maia walks away, Claire says, "He's up to something."

Maia turns to face her. "What do you mean?"

"He pulled refugees from the camps. *Your* refugees. The people who watched you burn their homes to the ground. He's given them citizenship. Nice apartments, food, jobs. They'll all be at the celebrations tonight. I don't like it. Please, be careful."

Maia nods, swallowing hard. As she turns to leave, Claire whispers again. "Maia?"

She glances over her shoulder.

"Those are good people in there," Claire says.

Maia looks at her for a moment. "I know," she finally says, and then she walks away, joining the others now huddled in the dark. They have removed their glasses, and their eyes dart nervously around the large space.

"Okay, I'll lead the way," Maia whispers. "Just like we've planned. Keep a safe distance from one another, but don't let too many people shove between you. It gets hectic in there."

They nod.

"Once we get to the square, make sure you stay separated but can easily see one another," Maia continues. "Stay on the fringes, but within range of the stage in case President Augustus needs protection."

They put their sunglasses back on and drape their hoods over their faces.

"I'll go first," Maia says. "And remember, *don't* look up at the drones. The citizens don't even notice them."

As the four briskly walk from the warehouse with Maia in the lead, it doesn't take long to get to the busy inner-city streets. There are people everywhere, packed together like a herd of cattle, slowly making their way toward the square. In every direction Maia looks, there are throngs of people laughing, drinking, donning hats, and lighting small firecrackers. The atmosphere is loud, boisterous—perfect for a revolution. Maia glances behind her to Chayanne, who nods.

It feels so strange to be walking these familiar city streets. Maia recognizes a few people passing by—old workmates—but with her wide hood and glasses covering her eyes, they don't take notice of her.

The skies explode with fireworks, and countless drones zip down the road. The projections across the darkened towers switch to Jake's smiling face, and Maia's heart jolts, her body thrumming with nerves. The video shifts to President Augustus, then throngs of people cheering. Then their slogan, *Leucothea has saved you.* Footage from an earlier parade: their immense army marching down the streets, the adoring city applauding from the sides. Finally, the screens show Leucothea's beloved flag rippling in the wind.

"Slower, Maia," Chayanne says into Maia's earpiece. "I'm losing you."

Maia stops at the curb. A man passing by stares at her, and she looks at her feet.

"Cool glasses," he says as he passes.

"Thanks," she mumbles, still peering down at her boots. A half-folded flyer is stuck underneath. She reaches down and picks it up, peeling back the crinkled paper.

It's her. It's *Maia*—a close-up photo of her face.

"Okay, Maia. Keep moving," Chayanne says into her earpiece.

Maia is paralyzed. The flyer reads: "TRAITOR. Very dangerous. Do not approach. Substantial reward if located."

It's a cropped photo. Black dress. Jake's shoulder is cut off from the side. Maia is smiling.

For a moment, she looked happy.

"Maia?" Miguel's voice sounds through her earpiece, snapping her out of her daze. She crumples the paper into a ball, chucking it to the street as she crosses. She glances over her shoulder, locking eyes with Chayanne through the crowd. Chayanne nods, and Maia faces forward again.

She holds the button on her earpiece. "Everyone here?"

"Here," comes three separate responses.

As the skies darken, the streetlamps flicker on, and the projections continue around every corner until the four find themselves joining hundreds of citizens piling into the square. Groups of workers at each entrance are handing out small, unlit candles.

They separate within the crowd, and Maia makes her way along the back of the square to stand beneath the awning of a closed café. Large banners drape across the well-lit stage before her. Above it is a projection screen stretching many stories high, displaying Leucothea's rippling flag. To the right of the stage is a VIP section. Maia recognizes a few of the faces—she'll never forget them. It's just as Claire said: Maia's refugees, no doubt filled with abhorrent, fuming hatred for her.

Armed officers pile out before the stage, and the square's lights dim. The people begin lighting their candles. One after the next, the flames flicker in a wave across the crowd. This is Maia's third Leucothea Day, and she knows this is when President Augustus should be starting his speech. But so far, it is just a microphone on an empty stage.

Maia waits, anxiously watching the screens with the rest of the citizens. Something is wrong. President Augustus should be up there by now, but the screens continue to display the flag. The people are silent, holding their candles. Confused, they glance between one another. Maia stands on her toes, peering across the sea of heads at Miguel. He shrugs.

And then the crowd erupts into a deafening roar. Maia

whirls toward the stage, and her blood runs cold. Jake is walking across the platform, dressed in his finest army uniform. She clutches at her chest, her heart thrashing beneath it.

The citizens are delighted, cheering and waving their little black flags. Spotlights flood across Jake as he makes his way toward the microphone, and the immense screens project his smiling face.

The crowd goes wild, but Maia can no longer hear them. It's as if the city has fallen away, and her world dims to a muted haze, leaving behind only her and Jake. She wavers on her feet, gripping the wall behind her as she glares at the man who has made her—filled with anger. Resentment. Fear. But most unsettling of all … she is still drawn to him, his presence all-pervasive like a spell. Their connection is mythical, bound by some great unknowable force. Together, she and Jake hold the light and the dark. The yin and the yang. The beginning and the end.

Jake peers across the crowd, and Maia pulls her hood farther over her face, thankful for her glasses. He lifts his hands, and the people hush in a wave. "Thank you for joining me in this celebration of the greatest civilization on *Earth*!" he announces, and thousands cheer, holding their candles above their heads.

"Tonight is a very special night," he says with a smile. "Because President Augustus has asked *me* to deliver his opening speech!"

Maia's mouth dries. Something is definitely wrong. She peers through the crowd at Miguel, and he nods and slips off his pack. He'll have to hack the feed, *now*. She glances at Shinesho, whose gaze is focused downward. He must already be working on it. Jake continues speaking into the microphone. Whatever he has said, the crowd has roared in response. Maia looks for Chayanne, relieved when she spots her. Separate, but together. Everyone is still safe.

Jake smiles wide, nodding his head. Everything is happening in slow motion. Maia notes the line of armed guards both behind him on stage and before him on the ground. There are more at the entrances and interspersed throughout the crowd. Dozens of drones now hover above. There is a lot more security than usual tonight ... Or is it just that she's never noticed? She looks at the guards. They appear to be on high alert, their eyes darting back and forth as they scan the crowd. No, there is definitely more than usual.

Jake's microphone dies, and the projections around the square go dark. Miguel and Shinesho have hacked the feed. Maia releases her breath, unaware she had been holding it.

The darkness highlights the candles in the air. *"Oooo,"* the crowd sings in awe. It all appears magical, like it's part of Leucothea's plan. A few more drones join the others in the sky.

Standing in the shadows, Maia watches Jake's face. He looks angry, his eyes searching the crowd. She presses her back against the brick. There is something about his face. No, it doesn't appear angry. It's more ... *amused*.

President Augustus's face appears across the projections, and the people cheer in celebration. "My people!" He begins. "Thank you for coming together to honor this beautiful life we have in the greatest city in the world!" Cheers resound throughout Leucothea, and fireworks explode across the sky. Augustus's smile fades. "My beloved citizens, I have a grave announcement to make. Unfortunately, our city has been taken hostage by a government that does not have our best interests at heart..."

Across the crowd, flags and candles are lowered, and it

becomes eerily silent. The people stare at the screens, confused and murmuring amongst themselves.

While Augustus continues speaking, Maia keeps her eyes firmly planted on Jake. She expected him to be upset, angry even, but he almost looks pleased. His eyes continue searching the massive crowd before him.

He's looking for her.

She slinks deeper into the shadows.

"... built on the backs of slaves ... an illusion ... *lying* to you!" Augustus continues. Images flash of the camps of enslaved people. Of Jake's soldiers beating them. Screaming women. Crying children. Abhorrent living conditions. Animals climbing through black sludge.

The citizens gasp, covering their mouths and shaking their heads, and the video projections turn black. The New System has reclaimed the feed. Jake's face is once again projected on the screens across the city, and his scowl flips to a smile.

The crowd is silent. Shocked. They look up at him in disbelief, awaiting his response.

Maia looks for Miguel. Augustus's message wasn't finished. Can he or Shinesho hack the feed again? Her eyes dart back and forth across the spot where he was just standing.

He's gone.

Shinesho? Maia looks around. *Gone.* She steps away from the building, scouring the faces around her. Chayanne is still in her spot with her hand over her mouth, watching Jake. Maia stares at her, but she won't look. She clicks the button on her earpiece. "Chayanne?" She presses it again. And again. There's nothing.

Their radios have been cut.

Where was their alarm? There was supposed to be an alert if this happened.

"My fellow Leucotheans," Jake says, his voice solemn. "I understand you are upset, so I will show you the truth, and then *you* can decide for yourself." He blows out a breath, shaking his head. "There is no easy way to say this, but the time has come for you to know: your beloved President Augustus ... is a *traitor*."

The citizens gasp, covering their mouths.

"He has joined forces with *her*," Jake continues, and Maia's face appears across the vast metropolis, on every projection across every building.

Maia stares up at the screens, *horrified*, as they play footage from her burning the small community to the ground. The way they filmed it—the village appears ten times bigger than its actual size. Maia looks like she's alone, standing on the cliff in her white dress. The footage does not show the dozens of guns pointed at her back, nor does it show Renee's mangled corpse lying below. It plays closeups of terrified people running for their lives, screaming in horror while Maia inflicts round after round of mayhem. The earth quakes and the buildings burn, all the while Maia's eyes shimmer. Her head tips back, and she unleashes an other-worldly wail.

Horrified, the citizens cry out. Some turn away, shielding their eyes from the gruesome footage playing before them. Those sitting in the VIP section cover their mouths, their children sobbing as their frantic mothers rush to console them.

Jake continues, "This woman is a *monster*! She is a criminal, a danger to society, and she must be stopped! It is her desire to destroy Leucothea, just like she has done to this poor city you see burning on our screens. She is trying to take away everything we have worked so hard to create! And now you can see for yourself, President Augustus has been helping her!"

The projections switch to Maia and Leucothea's president from her camp. Zooming in through a broken window, it shows them speaking next to her throne.

There was a spy.

"This footage was taken just days ago from their secret hideaway in the woods. Leucothea, I would never lie to you, but Augustus has. He has been deceiving you for *years*! Look! He is the one who does not have your best interests at heart!"

The people in the crowd begin to shout. Booing, they throw garbage at the screens.

Maia searches again for Miguel and Shinesho. She spots Chayanne and mouths, *Miguel? Shinesho?*

Chayanne looks around in a panic. She doesn't know. She points at her earpiece.

Maia shakes her head. *Dead.*

This is all falling apart. Miguel, Shinesho, and Augustus are missing. Augustus's video has been intercepted, and Jake has turned Leucothea against them. The electricity should be cut. Their armies should be here by now. *Where are their armies?*

"Look what this woman has done to these innocent people!" Jake yells.

The screens show Maia being held by armed officers while Jake helps the refugees limp from their burning homes. He's hugging them, handing them water and blankets. The footage pans across the wreckage, and the citizens cover their mouths, their eyes filled with fear.

And then they become angry—*infuriated*—pointing and shouting at the screens.

"Thankfully, we were there to stop her before she viciously murdered them all! But our beloved president ... My fellow citizens, he has been working with her this entire time. Do not be fooled! All those atrocities Augustus has shown you are *his* doing, and we have been trying to stop him!"

Panicked, Maia continues searching for Miguel and Shinesho but to no avail. She nods at Chayanne. They need to meet behind the square, come up with a new plan.

A man from the VIP section shouts into a microphone, pointing at the screens, "That was my home! That woman destroyed *everything*!"

Maia keeps her head down as she weaves through the crowd.

"She's dangerous!" another woman yells. "She's the *devil*!"

"Freak!"

"Monster!"

The projections show two of Jake's henchmen dragging a man dressed in black on stage with a sack over his head. Jake rips off the bag, revealing a badly beaten Miguel beneath.

Maia halts, whirling toward the stage with her hand over her mouth. Thick blood oozes from Miguel's lip. His nose. An open gash on the top of his head.

"This man is her co-conspirator!" Jake yells, throwing down the sack. "He tried to ruin our celebrations tonight by showing you these horrible lies. He has tried to turn you against *me* so that *he* could take over our city!"

The people around Maia shake their heads.

"How *dare* this bounder try to take what is rightfully ours!" Jake yells, pointing at Miguel.

"Traitor!" the man beside Maia yells.

"Bounder!" screams the woman behind her.

Jake grabs the microphone from its stand and walks along the edge of the stage. "Now you can see exactly why I've been working so hard to protect you. Why I have been creating such a large army. Why we have these walls and these cameras and these drones. It's so we can stop *bounders* like *him*! We have permitted these evil people to come inside our gates and have *allowed* them to play their silly video so that you could finally know the truth about our president. If you ever had a single doubt in your mind, now you know. I am a man of my people. I will always protect you. I will *never* lie to you!"

The crowds cheer across the city, clapping and waving their flags.

Jake holds up his hand. "Rest assured, we now have these people in our custody, and justice *will* be served. But Maia—that *monstrous* woman—is still out there, hiding like a coward while we hold her people captive."

Maia glares at him. Breathing deep to control her temper, she digs her nails into her palms. The citywide projections once again display her face with the word TRAITOR flashing below it.

"As rightful citizens of Leucothea, it is your duty to keep your eyes peeled. If you see her, wave down a drone, but *do not* approach her! I promise you, she won't stay hidden for long. And Maia?" Jake peers into the camera, and the screens show his face. "We know you are watching. Your mission has failed. Now, please, enough with the silly games. Turn yourself in, and let us get back to our celebrations."

The citizens look around, heaving their fists into the air. "Turn yourself in!" they shout.

"Monster!"

"Coward!"

Miguel glances at Maia, then quickly looks away. He shakes his head ever so slightly. *Don't.*

"In the meantime…" Jake flicks out a switchblade, lifting it above him. The lights glimmer off the metal, and the crowd roars with applause. "Shall we show Maia exactly what we do with traitors like him?" he yells into the microphone.

"Kill him!"

"*Bounder!*"

Stomping their feet, the citizens drag their thumbs across their necks, demanding an execution.

Maia is breathless, knocked around by the heaving bodies beside her. She grips her gun inside her coat, but she can't use it. She'd have to lift it above the crowd to aim and would be spotted immediately by the drones. She's surrounded by Jake's guards. She'd be shot in the head within seconds, and Miguel would still die.

The henchmen force Miguel to his knees. They yank his head back and lift his chin. Jake approaches as the crowd cheers him on, and he digs the tip of his knife into Miguel's throat.

This is it. This is the moment. She didn't know how it would happen or when, but she knew she'd recognize it when it came. And this is it.

Miguel's blood flows down the blade and the crowd thunders in delight.

"Stop!" Maia screams.

The people look back at her in surprise.

"Stop!" Maia screams again. "*I'm here.*" She takes off her glasses and throws them to the ground, then rips back her hood.

The citizens scream, forming a wide circle as they shove and push away. They wave their arms for the drones. "Here!"

More shouting, "She's here!"

Jake lowers his knife, and he walks toward the edge of the stage.

The drones flick on their searchlights, scanning the crowd. The circle of people widens as they stumble to distance themselves while dozens of lights flood across Maia at once.

Jake stares at her in disbelief.

She lifts her chin. "Don't hurt him. It's me you want."

He tilts his head as he glares at her from across the crowd, and a sinister grin spreads wide across his face.

THIRTY-FIVE

The panicked crowd continues to shove away from Maia as a fury of armed officers close in. They surround her, the extended barrels of their guns pointed at her head. She never once takes her eyes off Jake.

He stares back at her, *delighted*. "Everyone move away," he says calmly into the microphone. "Don't touch her."

The crowd continues to back up, their faces contorted with anger. They yell and throw things. Food. Cups. Wads of paper. "Monster!" they shout. "Traitor!"

"Maia, *run*!" Miguel screams.

The soldier next to him punches him hard across his face, and he slumps to the ground. Maia forces herself not to react.

Jake's henchmen close in. "Hands in the air!" they shout, and she lifts them. She and Jake continue to glare at one another as the men grab her, aggressively twisting her hands behind her back and cuffing them. They pat her down, removing both her knife and her gun. They lift the weapons triumphantly into the air, and the crowd roars in applause as if she didn't just *let* them take them.

As the soldiers lead Maia through the separating crowd, the once adoring citizens—those who loved her and smiled at her and held open her doors—now scream in her face. They yell, their faces red. They spit. They shake their fists as they shriek in disgust.

Maia pays them no mind. She keeps her focus solely on Jake, now eyeing her like prey.

The soldiers drag her up the stairs and onto the stage past Miguel.

"Oh, Miguel," she whispers.

Hunched over with blood oozing from his mouth, he gazes up at Maia with broken eyes.

Jake doesn't hesitate to grab her. Pulling her into him, he whispers, "Maia, so nice to see you again."

She glares at him. "Touch him again, and I destroy everything."

He cocks his head, suppressing a laugh.

"Let him go. *Now*," she growls.

He smiles at the crowd, casually pushing the microphone away. "And *why* would I do that?" he snarls through his teeth.

"Do it now, or I destroy it all."

His eyes narrow. "You wouldn't."

She breathes deep, and the earth begins to tremble.

The crowd panics, and Jake holds out his hand. "Okay."

She continues.

"*Stop*," he says quietly.

She lifts her chin, and the ground calms.

"I can't just let him loose," he says under his breath.

"Drop him on the other side of the gates."

Jake looks at her, considering, and he sighs. "Fine." He waves his hand at his men, and they drag a barely conscious

Miguel from the stage. The crowd boos, garbage skidding across the platform.

Maia looks at Chayanne, with Shinesho now standing behind her. Maia nods in Miguel's direction. *Follow them.*

Chayanne shakes her head.

Maia's eyes widen, glaring at her. Chayanne whispers to Shinesho, and the two begin making their way out of the crowd.

"This monster has joined forces with our enemy, Asiaq Bay," Jake says into the microphone, "and they have led a *pathetic* little army of bounders from across North America!" He laughs, and the crowd howls in response. "How dare they think they can take everything we have for their own!" he yells, and the citizens throw more litter at Maia.

"My people!" He lifts his hand and his adoring crowd silences. "War is on our doorstep, but do not be afraid! Our mighty walls are secure, and our vast army is protecting you! Leucothea will *always* protect you!"

The screens across the buildings show armies fighting outside the gates. Those are *Maia's* men and women. The footage is real.

"Their pathetic little militia is *nothing* compared to our mighty forces! Look! Watch as they fall!" He lifts his hand toward the projection screens, and his delighted flock applauds in approval.

"My fellow citizens," Jake addresses the crowd, his voice solemn. "What shall you have me do with this *vile* woman?"

"Save us!"

"Finish her!"

"Kill her!"

The guards on either side of Maia force her to her knees and the crowd roars, cheering and screaming and waving their flags. They begin chanting in unison, "Fin-ish her! Fin-ish her!"

Maia sneers across their disgusting faces with contempt. She tried All she wanted was to help them—to show them the truth—and now they want her dead. This place is nothing but a virus. A dangerous, life-sucking disease that will only continue to breed more of itself.

A guard wipes Miguel's blood from Jake's blade and hands it back to him. Jake holds it up like a trophy, and the crowd goes *wild*. Like animals, they demand Maia's blood. Spotlights crisscross the sky—an impressive show to delight the masses.

This is why she is here. This is the moment she knew would present itself, and she knows what she must do. Her armies are battling outside the city, but they are outnumbered—they'll never reach the gates. President Augustus is likely dead. The citizens have been lied to, yet again. Maia's mission has failed, her message fallen on deaf ears.

It is just as Jake said: the people of Leucothea have sided with him.

If Maia doesn't do something now—something catastrophic—she will die, her armies will fall, and this will all be for nothing. She closes her eyes, blowing out a steady breath, and allows the darkness to take her over.

Kneeling in the middle of Leucothea with Jake by her side, Maia is the epicenter of destruction. And she has been left with no choice but to destroy it. Right here. Right now. She will wreak havoc on this land until her troops can break the gates. She glares up at Jake, meeting his piercing gaze. And amid the chaos, she will *end* him.

Screaming at her, the crowd chucks their trash and shakes their fists, their faces contorted and ugly with rage. She scowls, her temper flaring. Disgusting creatures, the lot of them. Wads of paper ricochet off her, tumbling across the stage, and anger surges through her veins.

She quickly searches the horde, ensuring that Chayanne and Shinesho have left. She spots Chayanne in the shadows along a back wall, aiming her pistol at Jake. Light glints off the metal as she lifts her gun higher, and a henchman to her left aims his own.

Maia chokes, losing her focus. "*No!*" she screams.

His gun fires, and Chayanne drops. The people around her shriek and scatter.

A piercing ringing fills Maia's ears and she doubles over, gasping for air, her vision a blinding red.

All those evenings on her throne, she has done nothing but prepare herself for this moment. For the grave possibility that everything could fall apart.

She will not lose her cool.

Hyper-focused, Maia opens her eyes. *Breathe out.*

She blows through pursed lips. Gale winds gather at her command, swirling around the square.

Maia closes her eyes again. *Breathe in.*

The ground teeters—violent and sharp. The crowd separates, screaming, and mayhem breaks loose.

"Somebody stop her!" Jake screams from behind.

Maia opens her eyes and climbs to her feet as the land continues to tremble. The guard next to her wavers as he reaches for her, his arms circling at his sides.

Breathing hard through a clenched jaw, Maia nods once. The earth lifts and drops, and the people before her simultaneously fall to the ground. She peers over her shoulder at Jake and his soldiers, now stunned and lying on their backs, and she smiles.

Broken glass rains from the buildings above, shattering like bombs across the pavement. The throngs of people cry out, trampling over one another in a panic. Lit candles lie abandoned in the litter, and small fires ignite. Heaving for air, Maia glances between each one, fueling them. Their flames rise high into the sky.

A few guards help Jake to his feet, but they hesitate to approach her. A bullet slams into her vest. And another. Maia stumbles backward.

Filled with rage, she dips her chin, and the earth jolts again. The crowds tumble back to the ground. More brick and glass and debris fall from above, and the panicked citizens scatter and scream. Fires rage, black smoke billowing into the sky.

Leucothea is buckling.

Maia prepares herself for another earth-shattering blow. This one is going to be catastrophic. This one will *level* them. Another bullet whizzes past her head. She breathes deep, readying herself, and a soldier throws himself against her. They fly off the stage and roll across the pavement.

Winded, Maia lies with her cheek to the ground as countless feet trample around her. Her leg—something is happening with her leg. She looks back at the needle in her thigh as the guard injects the last of the solution.

She gasps as an icy pain surges through her veins, and she is swallowed in darkness.

THIRTY-SIX

When Maia awakens, she finds herself back on the couch in Jake's living room. Her hands are still cuffed, and she is surrounded by henchmen. Guns pointed, ready to shoot. Her vision is blurred, her stomach twisting in knots.

Jake is sitting on a chair across from her, glaring at her with his fist at his chin. His eyes are cold, his jaw clenched. There is banging outside his living room windows, hammers against nails.

She rolls to her side and buries her face into the cushion, moaning. Head is throbbing. Stomach clenched. Earth spinning. She coughs until she gags. *Poison.* So much poison in her veins.

"Try anything, and you're dead," Jake says dryly.

She sucks in a breath, struggling to breathe through the pain.

"I mean it, Maia. The slightest tremble, and you'll have a bullet in your brain."

"Why wait?" she mumbles into the couch. "Why not do it back at the square after you drugged me?" She twists her head to look at him. His face spins from left to right. Left to right. She closes her eyes, swallowing the bile rising from her throat.

"Because my people were afraid and hurt. I told them to go home. Or to the hospital. Firetrucks and emergency crews needed to tend to the ... *situation* ... you created."

Maia writhes into herself, suppressing her scream. There are razor blades in her bloodstream. After a moment, the pain passes, and she exhales relief.

"Tonight, we finish this," Jake says, and Maia peers at him with one eye. One eye is better.

He looks her up and down. "It's not exactly how I pictured it." He shakes his head, his face contorted with disgust. "You're so pathetic right now. You look like shit. Hardly a fight worth showcasing for the world to see, but showcase it, I will." He stands and walks to a window, pulling the curtain back with the tip of his finger. "Nearly there. Do you have the camera set up and ready to go?"

"We do, sir."

"Good. The quicker we get this over with, the better," he says without turning around.

Maia briefly surveys the room, the soldiers covered from head to toe in army gear. She spots Claire in the corner and quickly looks away.

"Stand her up," Jake says, and two soldiers rush to her side, lifting her by her arms.

She wavers, struggling to find the strength to stand. It takes everything in her not to buckle at the knees.

Jake turns to face her, and he glares at her with a hatred so pure that it freezes her blood. He walks up to her, his eyes quivering. "After all this time, how could you believe me to be so *stupid*." He backhands her and her world spins, her mouth filling with blood. "You think I didn't know what you were up to?!" He grabs her face, forcing her to look at him. "You think I didn't have my *own* spies?" he sneers. "That I didn't know about the S&R Truck sneaking you back in here? Oh, I knew. I knew the entire time. And I *knew* you would come back to me."

He leans in, his nose against hers. "I told you from the beginning," he says quietly, seething with rage, "you belong to *me*. But if I can't have you—Maia—*no one can*." When he releases her head, it hangs from her body, blood and drool spilling from her mouth. "And tonight," he says, backing away and straightening his top, "I will execute you. The entire city will be watching, *celebrating*, and then I will send the video, along with the footage of all your dead soldiers, to the other cities as a warning. Leucothea is, and always will be, the *only* world power. Not even a monster like you can stop us."

Maia looks at her feet, swallowing hard. The ground has finally stopped spinning, but she needs time. She needs to *think*. Grimacing, she moans, and more blood dribbles from her mouth.

"Put her down," Jake says. "This is disgusting. How much did you give her?"

"Everything in the syringe, sir."

"*Christ.*"

They drop Maia back to the couch, and she closes her eyes. She needs these drugs to wear off; she is powerless with this poison in her system.

Time passes as the banging outside continues, and Maia lies on the couch. How much time has passed is impossible to say. A few hours? Drifting in and out of a mindless daze, she tries to think of a plan, but she can't focus. Her vision keeps fading back to her and Jake standing on that stage in Leucothea Square. Those brainwashed worshipers chanting his name and waving their flags.

"Maia?"

She opens her eyes to Jake, patting her cheek. "Wake up, baby. Your gallows await." He pulls her up by the shoulders, and her head flops to the side.

Her mouth dry, she croaks, "You're going to *hang* me?"

"For the whole world to see," he says proudly as he lifts her to her feet. "Take her."

His soldiers grab her arms, and she wavers, unsteady. The drugs are still in her system, but now they are mild. Subdued. No longer angry or sick, she can finally think, but she doesn't have much time.

As the men push her toward the hallway, she locks eyes with Claire, sitting on a chair against the wall. Claire's gaze flickers to a corner of the ceiling. Maia looks up to a small black device: one of Jake's precious cameras. She glances back at Claire, whose eyes repeatedly dart to the corner.

Why would Claire want Maia to notice that? Why would Claire want her to ... *The feed*. Their original plan had always revolved around hacking the video feed to show the citizens the truth.

Maia's vision comes flooding back to her of Jake waving on stage, the people cheering his name. She always thought *she* was Jake's greatest weakness, but she was wrong. It's his city. His reputation. His precarious level of power over the masses—and it all hinges on an illusion. Without it, he is nothing.

Maia can't be entirely sure if this is what Claire is alluding to, but it is her only option. She might still have a chance.

But she needs to stay in the living room.

The guards lead her toward the hallway. She can no

longer count on her powers. Jake's soldiers are following her every move and will shoot her dead in an instant. But she can still fight.

And she is much stronger than Jake.

"You're going to hang a drugged, defenseless woman?" she says to him from over her shoulder. "Way to go, *brave soldier*."

Jake grabs a vase from a table and smashes it against the ledge. "Drop her," he says, and his soldiers release their grips, quickly stepping away. Jake doesn't waste a second in shoving Maia to the ground.

She rolls onto her cuffed arms as he jumps on top of her. Grabbing her hair, he yanks her chin to the ceiling and shoves the ragged glass beneath. "You are such a *nightmare*," he growls, the sharp crystal digging into her throat. "I should just kill you right here and now."

"Sir? Sir, you don't want to do that. You wanted us to film—"

He lifts off her, chucking the shard to the side. "You're right," he says, straightening his uniform. "Don't want to waste a good show."

The guards lift her by her shoulders as Jake walks away.

"Why don't you fight me like a man?" Maia yells at his back.

He sighs in annoyance and turns to face her.

She tilts her head. "You think you're such a big hero? *How*? By having your men drug me and then string a rope around my neck while you stand by and watch like the coward that you are?"

He steps toward her, breathing hard.

"Your grandchildren will ask, 'Grandpa, how did you take down the most dangerous woman in the world?' And you'll say, 'Oh, I drugged her and hung her while she was completely defenseless.'" She glares at him, her eyes wide in mockery. "Wow. *What a star.*"

Jake pulls his gun from its holster, pointing the barrel at her face. "Would you prefer I shoot you?"

She gazes at him seductively. "Fight me, Jake. Right here. Right now. No guns, no powers. Just you and me."

He glares at her, a smile tugging, and he lowers his gun. "You want to *fight* me?"

She nods.

"Hand-to-hand combat. With *me*. The army general of the most powerful nation in the world."

Maia laughs. "You keep saying that as if it's some big accomplishment. This world is empty—"

Jake backhands her, and the soldiers drop her to the ground, laughing.

"Is this really how you want this to go?" Jake asks while she gasps at his feet. "Me beating you to death?"

"It's not a fair fight when I'm in *cuffs*, Jake," she mumbles at the floor, licking the blood from her lip.

There is silence. Maia sits back on her heels, peering up at him, and he stares at her, considering. "Uncuff her."

She suppresses her smile. Such a fragile ego.

"Sir, I don't trust this."

"What is she going to do, kill me while you all sit back and watch? If she does anything stupid, you have my permission to shoot her. Uncuff her. *Now*."

The soldier beside her pulls the keys from his pocket, releasing the harsh metal around her wrists. Maia quickly stands, backing into the couch, and the guards on either side of her step away, pointing their guns.

"I'm going to appease this dying wish of yours," Jake says, approaching her. He caresses her cheek with the back of his hand. "I'll fight you. No guns, no knives, no magic. But

I must warn you: even the *slightest* use of your powers and my men have full authority to shoot you. Understand?"

Maia nods.

"*Okay*." He shrugs.

Maia backs into the living room, and Jake follows like a hungry bull. He kicks the coffee table out of the way, and his men push back the couches. They look excited—every last one of them.

"But once I knock you out," Jake continues, looking her up and down, "I'm still going to hang you from my gallows. It feels a bit too barbaric to beat you to death—not really my style."

Maia rolls her eyes. "But it's your style to beat those slaves of yours out in the fields? Some of them to death? Men, women, children ... all the same."

Jake removes his jacket, and a guard quickly takes it. "Well, *I* don't, no. I have soldiers to do that," he says as he unbuttons his sleeves, rolling them to his elbows.

Maia smiles. *Check.*

The two circle one another. Jake reaches for her head and she veers away. She's fast, but not nearly as quick as she used to be. Those drugs must still be in her system.

Jake swings, but misses. She swings and he ducks. He grabs her arm and throws her into the wall. Her head slams against it and she stumbles back, stunned. His drugs are *definitely* still in her system.

She turns as he charges and she eludes his embrace, running across the floor. They face one another, panting.

"Sure you want to do this?" Jake asks. "A hanging would be so much easier on you."

"Sure *you* still want to lie to your people?" Maia asks. "What will you tell them when Augustus is dead, and I'm dead ... and yet, your fields are still filled with slaves?

Sooner or later, they're going to figure out that all that footage we played them tonight is of crimes *you're* committing. They're going to know that you've lied to them this entire time. What will they think of you then?"

Jake grins. "That's the beauty of it all—they *don't* think. They are the perfect sheeple: lazy and *stupid*." He screams as he charges, and she braces herself as he slams into her. They tumble across the floor. Jake climbs on top of her and grips her throat. His soldiers close in, watching with amusement as she claws at his hands.

"Sir—" a soldier says.

"I'm not going to *kill* her," Jake seethes through clenched teeth. "I'm just going to knock the bitch out."

Memories of her and Lucas's combat training in LA come back to her. She throws her feet onto Jake's shoulders, lifting her hips and hugging his arms, bending his elbows backward. He cries out as she arches against him, and his soldiers rip her off, throwing her across the room. She slams into a shelf, shattering glass across the floor.

Breathless on all fours, she wipes the blood now trickling from her brow. "Is this..." She coughs, wheezing. "Is this a fight between you and me? Or me ... and your *cronies*?"

Jake sits on the ground, rubbing his elbows. "Can't fight if my arms are broken."

"Fair is fair," Maia gasps. "I would win."

"Win what, Maia? This is a lose-lose battle for you. No matter what happens, you are dead tonight."

She smiles. "I don't think so."

His eyes narrow.

A man runs into the living room, looking around in a panic. He lifts his gun and shoots the camera in the corner, then drops his pistol to the ground. He leans forward, panting with his hands on his knees.

"What the *fuck*?" Jake says as he stands.

"Sir," the man says, breathless. "*Hacked* ... They hacked your cameras. The entire city ... *entire* ... *city* ... just watched you ... call ... them..."

The color drains from Jake's face. "*Sheeple*."

Checkmate.

Jake screams with rage. He swipes the gun from the floor and turns toward Maia, shooting her.

THIRTY-SEVEN

L ying on her back, Maia gasps for air. She pats her chest, then looks at her hands. No blood? She pats and checks again. *No blood.* She still has her vest on. Jake shot her at nearly point-blank. That force ... It feels like her ribs are broken. She wheezes, struggling to take a breath.

Jake is still screaming, and he chucks something at a window, shattering the glass. People shuffle around her as she stares at the ceiling in a state of shock.

"*Why* is she not dead?!" Jake shouts.

A soldier leans down and unzips her jacket. "Bulletproof vest, sir."

It is silent, and then Jake starts to laugh. His soldiers join him. Chuckling, they sound nervous. One steps next to her, pointing his pistol in her face. "Want me to?"

"No! No, no, no. Get away from her. I'm glad she's still alive. I really need to stop shooting people when I'm angry," Jake says with a sigh. "Get her up. And get those cuffs back on. I'm tired of fighting."

The soldiers yank Maia from the ground and set her on

a chair, cuffing her hands behind her. She doesn't have the strength to fight back. She and Jake gaze at one another from across the room, both exhausted. Maia has never seen him look so disheveled.

His face softens. "I have to say, I'm a little relieved." He scratches the back of his neck. "Now I can still execute you for the cameras." He looks at his advisors, who have stepped inside the room. "So? What's next? The citizens will be angry."

"This will hurt your approval ratings," one of them says, and Maia stares at them, her mouth dropping open.

"I'm a politician," Jake says. "Politicians say and do stupid things all the time. Get someone to write up an apology speech and I'll deliver it tonight, right before I execute her."

"I'm on it," one of them says.

"Really work on the angle that this is *her* fault," Jake calls after him. "I'm the hero."

"Of course, sir."

He sighs, visibly shaken. "And somebody figure out how the hell my personal video got hacked. Don't bother me with the details. Just find whoever screwed up and shoot them," he says, rubbing his temples.

The men excuse themselves, and Maia looks at him in shock.

"Close your mouth, Maia," Jake says. "You think you've hurt me—and you have, no question—but I'll claw my way out of it. I always do. Hell, I'll probably end up even more popular. But you..." He wags his finger at her, shaking his head. "I don't know how you pulled that one off, but that was ballsy. And you'll pay for it. *Dearly*."

"I've got nothing left, Jake."

"Oh, but you do." He looks back at the soldiers behind

him and nods. They leave the room. "I have a surprise for you," he says.

Maia closes her eyes. *Miguel*

"Someone get me a washrag and a coffee," Jake calls over his shoulder. "I have a speech to prepare for."

Maia's heart is pounding. Without opening her eyes, she says, "I'm not sure why I trusted you. You swore he would be let out of the gates."

"Who—*Miguel*? He was."

When Maia looks at him, the smile on his face crushes her. "And?" she whispers.

"This isn't about Miguel. I've been saving this surprise for a ... *special* occasion."

Maia stares at him, terrified.

"You're going to cooperate with me from this point forward, Maia. I guarantee it."

Jake stands as the soldiers drag in a prisoner, holding him by his arms. The man doesn't appear conscious. His head hangs from his bony frame and his ratted, long brown hair blends with his beard. Maia can't see his face, but she certainly doesn't know this man. His atrocious state makes her grimace.

Jake's face is twisted in disgust, and a soldier hands him a glove. "Make him stand," he says as he slides it on.

One of the soldiers knees the man, and they lift him onto his *one* remaining leg. Jake grabs his hair with his gloved hand and pulls back his head.

Maia stands.

Can't be.

He has looked at her in a hundred different ways, in a hundred different places. From the basement of a pirate ship. An island made of trash. The bottom of an umiak.

Never. *Never* has he looked at her like this. His brown eyes lock onto hers, and a tear traces down his sunken cheek.

Maia steps forward, and the guards grab her arms. "*Lucas*?" she whispers, unbelieving.

"Maia," he says with a broken voice.

The sound of his voice startles her, like she has awoken from a dream. "*LUCAS*!?" she screams, and she lunges. The soldiers hold her back and force her into the chair. "Lucas!" she shrieks, and the men grunt, holding her down as she arches her back in hysterics.

"Maia!" Lucas yells.

"Get him out of here," Jake says.

"No! *Please*!" Maia twists within the soldiers' grasps. "Jake, please!? *Lucas*? LUCAS!"

"Maia!" Lucas shouts from the hallway.

The men pile on top of her, and a strange noise escapes her lips—something between a desperate gasp and a wail—and the earth begins to tremble.

"Okay, knock her out again," Jake says.

The soldiers shove a wet cloth over her face, smothering her until she blacks out.

When she awakens, she is back on the couch with a splitting headache like a fracture to the skull. Claire is sitting in a chair across from her; a gun in one hand, head cupped in the other. Her eyes are closed.

"Lucas?!" Maia tries to scream, but her voice is muffled. A twisted cloth has been tied across her mouth.

"*Shhh*," Claire says, briefly placing her hand on Maia's leg before quickly removing it.

Maia surveys the room. Only a few guards remain, but there are a lot of voices coming from the gallows outside. Maia's hands are still cuffed, and there is now a rope binding her feet. She peers back at Claire.

Claire briefly shakes her head and nods ever so slightly at the guards. She can't say anything. The look on her face makes Maia's heart sink.

Defeat.

Jake walks back into the room, and Claire straightens as he approaches. He peers at her from the corner of his eye, holding out his hand. "If I didn't know any better," he says, and she gives him the gun, "I would say you two were sharing a moment."

"Don't be ridiculous," Claire says, rolling her eyes.

"Sir, we're on in five," a man says from behind Maia.

Jake nods. "Give us a minute." He looks around. "Everyone out."

The room empties, and Jake sits before Maia. He leans back, scratching his temple with the tip of his gun. "Yeah ... so, Lucas is ... *not* dead."

Maia glares at him, her eyes overflowing with tears. This entire time. All their dates and dinners ... and Lucas was rotting in a cell on the same property.

Jake glances up at her. "I was expecting you to yell, but you can't." His eyes narrow, considering. "Yes, I think I like it better this way—you not speaking." He lays the gun in his lap, watching her. "So, I have to keep this short since I'm going to execute you in a few minutes. Obviously, Lucas was still alive when you arrived."

Maia's stomach churns. She's going to throw up.

"*Barely* alive, but alive nonetheless. I thought..." Jake hesitates, looking at the ceiling. "I thought it could work in my favor to save him. Maybe it could have been a gift for you?" He looks at her, his brow raised. "Or used as a bargaining chip. Either way, I had a feeling it would be worth my while." He rubs his chin in thought. "Took a lot to save him. Like ... *a lot*. It was expensive—definitely more work than we would have ever put into a normal nameless migrant. But now you can understand why I let Miguel go; I knew I still had Lucas. I could have used him before, but I still had plenty of chips on the table. I wanted to save him. But now," he says with a shrug. "Now, you've only got minutes to live, so I don't need him anymore."

Maia closes her eyes, her tears disappearing into the cloth across her face.

The cool tip of Jake's pistol lifts her chin, and she opens her eyes to Jake leaning toward her. "So, here's the deal. I swore to you that I'd let Miguel go, and I did. I didn't have to, but I did. Because I am a man of my word."

Maia tilts her head, glaring at him.

"Now, now. I may have told a fib or two, but if I tell you I'm going to do something in a verbal agreement, I will not break that bond. So, this is what you're going to do, and I will let Lucas live. You're going to stand before the cameras and admit that this was all a setup against me. All lies. You're going to confirm everything I've told my people in the square, and then you're going to *allow* me to hang you—no games, *no* powers. You do this, and I swear to you—you have my *word*—Lucas will be released from this city in complete freedom. I will also leave Miguel and your tribe alone.

"OR!" He leans back into his chair, shrugging. "You can continue to fight the inevitable, and I'll hang Lucas alongside you. Better yet, I'll have Silas torture him until he dies. Then, I will find Miguel and your tribe, and I will hang them in the gallows next to you and Lucas's decaying bodies."

Maia sighs. So many scenarios ... Days, weeks, months, she spent preparing for every possible situation she could think of.

Never could she have prepared for this.

"Okay," Jake says, and he pulls the cloth from her mouth. "Do we have a deal? You leave this world in peace, your precious loved ones will be left alone, and Lucas is released from Leucothea alive."

"Can I have a moment with him?" she croaks.

Jake laughs. "I think you're overestimating my kindness here, Maia. No, you can't have a *moment* with him. Besides, he's not in the house anymore, and we don't have time."

"Sir?" a man says from behind Maia. His voice is tense, and a few soldiers fill the room. Claire steps in behind them.

"One minute," Jake snaps without looking. He keeps his focus on Maia, arching his brow. "Deal?"

She hesitates.

"Your mission has failed, Maia. It's over. The least you can do before you die is save your friends—especially the one we've got tied up just outside the house."

"How do I know you won't hang him after I'm gone?"

"You don't. You're just going to have to trust me. But I can promise you, you making this deal with me is the *only* shot you have at keeping him alive. Otherwise, you'll listen to his last choking breaths beside you as you hang."

"Let him out of the gates first."

"Again, overestimating. *Way* too much overestimating. You have no bargaining chips here."

"Sir?"

Jake sighs in annoyance, and he looks up.

"Sir, the alarms are going off. There are intruders outside the property. We need to keep you indoors until we get it sorted."

"Intruders. Who?"

"We can't be sure yet. Our security cameras have been cut."

The lights flicker, then the room is shrouded in darkness. Jake pounces on top of Maia, shoving his gun into her neck. "Make one move, and I swear to God, I'll torture him in front of you," he growls.

"Sir?"

"Just give it a minute. I have a backup," Jake snaps.

A few lights flicker on, but not all of them, casting strange shadows across the room. Jake climbs off Maia. "What have you done?"

She shrugs. "This isn't me."

"Yeah, right." He looks around the room. "Well, don't just stand there!" he yells at the soldiers. "Take care of them! You've got guns! Use them!"

The room clears out. Jake grabs Claire as she passes. "Not you. You're useless with a gun."

Claire glances at Maia and walks back to her chair in the corner.

Jake paces before Maia. "*You*. This is all you, isn't it?"

Maia doesn't speak.

"Forget the deal. Whatever you've got going on out there, it's not going to save you, nor will it save what I'm about to do to Lucas. I'm going to kill that son-of-a-bitch the second I get my hands on him. I'm going to kill them *all*." He sets his gun aside and kneels before Maia, leaning just inches from her face. "My advisors thought it would be best to execute you by firing squad, but I wanted a hanging. Do you want to know *why*?" he sneers.

"I'd rather not," she mumbles.

He laughs. "I've been watching you." He cocks his head, his black eyes burrowing into hers. "I know your powers take it out of you. Every. Last. *Drop*." He taps his fingers against her chest. "Your heart pounds. Your breathing is always ... *labored*—more so the longer you do it."

He straddles her with his forearm across her chest,

shoving her into the couch. "*That's* why I'm going to hang you. I'm going to take the one thing you need to fight back, and then I will watch as your life slowly drains out of you. And you'll be *completely* defenseless." He pulls a needle from his pocket.

Maia screams, thrashing against him, and he presses his legs around her, pushing her farther into the cushions. As he fumbles with the needle, Claire slowly walks up behind him, holding a lamp high above her head.

Jake puts the needle's cap between his teeth and rips off the lid, spitting it to the floor. "Stop moving!" he screams.

Claire slams the lamp's base against his head, and he flops to the side. Maia gasps and Claire drops the fixture, backing up with her hand over her mouth.

Maia stares at his motionless body beside her, terrified to take a breath. "Is he ... dead?" she whispers.

Claire rolls him onto the ground and checks his pulse. She hangs her head, sighing relief. "No."

"The needle," Maia whispers. "Inject him with the needle!"

Claire tenderly wipes the blood from his brow. "He's already passed out," she says quietly, smoothing back his hair.

"Where is his gun?" Maia asks, looking around.

"I ... I don't know." Claire glances at Maia over her shoulder. "I can't shoot him, Maia. I won't."

"Will you get me out of these cuffs?"

Claire nods, and she searches Jake's pockets.

"Hurry!" Maia says. She spots the keys on a shelf in the corner. "Over there!" She nods.

Claire races to the shelf, then rushes back and kneels before Maia, who leans to her side to expose her cuffs. As

Claire fumbles with the keys, Maia glances between the doors and Jake's legs on the floor. His foot twitches.

"*Hurry*," Maia whispers.

"There are so many keys. I can't find the right one!"

Jake's foot twitches again, and Maia's heart twists inside her chest.

Hurry.

THIRTY-EIGHT

Claire rummages through the keys, the metal *clinking* together. Maia glances back at the doors —still closed.

Claire gasps. "Found it!"

There is a loud *thud*, like someone has punched Claire in the back. And then another. Maia peers over her shoulder as the smile fades from Claire's face. Jake's bloody hand reaches around her arm, and he pulls himself up from the ground.

Claire continues to stare at Maia, a look of horror across her face. Jake delivers another sharp blow to her back, and Claire jerks forward, a deep crease between her brow.

"Claire?" Maia whispers.

Jake leans on the couch next to them, rubbing the gash on his head. Claire's lips part, and she fingers the blood spilling from her mouth. She holds her hand before her, then looks at Maia one last time before slumping to the ground.

"*NO!*" Maia screams. She thrashes, kicking Jake off the couch. "You *monster!*"

Jake yanks his knife from Claire's back and falls onto the carpet. "Traitorous bitch," he gasps. He drops his bloody switchblade beside him, sighing at the ceiling.

Maia stands to run, forgetting her legs are bound. She trips over Claire's lifeless body and flips onto her back, inching away from the pool of blood soaking into the carpet.

A soldier rushes into the room and scans the gruesome scene before him: Jake lying on the floor with blood dripping down his face, Claire's dead body next to him.

"*What*?" Jake asks, annoyed.

"Sir, things aren't going well. They are ramming down the gates."

"Who are *they*?!"

"Can't be sure. It's dark, and our cameras are dead. But there seem to be a lot of them. They're armed. And there are … there are *tigers* circling the property."

Maia looks up.

Enraged, Jake screams at the ceiling. He climbs to his feet, looking around. "All right, grab some men. This ends now."

The guard disappears for a moment, then comes back in with a few soldiers and one of Jake's most trusted advisors. Jake grabs the needle from the carpet and caps it, then chucks it at him. "Drug her before she does anything stupid."

"NO!" Maia yells. Within seconds, Jake's soldiers are holding her down as his advisor pinches her arm. "No…" she whispers, and her entire body relaxes. Melts into the ground. They leave her lying on her back, and she gazes around the room, subdued. She feels … *euphoric*. They're underwater. The furniture ripples and a few air bubbles escape her mouth. Jake and his men appear in a circle above, watching her. And ... and now they have bodies like little cherub angels.

"What did you give her?" Jake asks.

"Different stuff from before. Didn't want to knock her out."

"Is she..."

"High as a kite, sir."

"I'd say so." He watches her for a moment, smirking, and then he flies away. "Take her outside," he says from a distance. "We do this now."

Someone lifts Maia from the ground and drapes her over his shoulder. As he carries her across the room, she stares at the man walking behind her. He looks like Miguel. No, it's definitely Lucas. She shakes her head. That's not Lucas! This man has two legs, and Lucas has three. Or is it one? She starts to giggle, and Lucas looks at her strangely. She wants to reach for him, but she can't find her arms. Where did they go?

Outside, the soldier drops Maia onto the lawn as pops and bangs explode across the property.

"*Oooooo*," Maia sings, and she rubs her cheek against the grass. There's a familiar scent in the breeze. She knows that scent. It must be Huck. He's finally come to visit? That's so nice.

"You—get her to the gallows," Jake shouts. "The rest of you prepare my bunker. Go! Now!"

A soldier lifts her over his shoulder, and the horizon seesaws back and forth. He stops, placing her on a wooden stool in the grass. "Stand here. Can you do that?" he asks her.

She nods, looking at him. Wait, this man isn't Lucas. Her aquatic world is fading as reality slowly settles back in.

There's a strange sensation around her neck—thick, heavy. She looks around, confused, sniffing into the air. She knows that scent. *That scent.* "Atlas?" she calls out, and her guard looks up at her.

That's when she realizes she's at the gallows—a simple wooden setup in Jake's backyard. Her hands and feet are still bound, and there's a rope around her neck. People are crying out in the distance. They are yelling. Angry. Maybe a kilometer down the road? They must be by her old guest suite.

Jake screams at the soldier next to her to check it out. The guard runs off, leaving the two of them alone. Jake walks away from a tripod with a black box on top, its red light lit—he's recording. He marches up to her with a gun in his hand, and she looks around in a panic.

As he stands before her, an undeniable look of anguish crosses his face. "Could have been you and me, Maia," he says quietly. "It *should* have been..." He turns away, shaking his head and sighing heavily.

She tries to concentrate on the rope above her, struggling to conjure a flame. But the drugs in her system—they've muddled her mind. She can't *focus.*

Jake turns to face her, and his saddened features harden. He points at her. "You—*you* did this."

"Jake, wait—"

He kicks the stool beneath her. The pressure around her neck, the pain, the immense force behind her eyes—it's *excruciating.* She thrashes her feet as Jake watches, and the earth begins to shudder. He braces himself against the tremors, but keeps his focus fixed on her.

The ground slowly stills, and Jake smiles. He was expecting this. Maia can't fuel a quake. Can't feed a fire. No wind. The more she uses her powers, the faster her heart will pound, and the quicker she'll suffocate.

This is the moment her dreams have been warning her about. So many nightmares she's had where Jake held her beneath the torrent of a melting Leucothea. Watched as she suffocated. Stared at her with that same look of resentment as her life drained away by the second.

Can't breathe. Can't *ever* breathe.

Something races from the shadows across the lawn. Jake turns as Atlas slams into him, and Maia's world begins to fade.

Another tiger approaches. Sniffing the air, it flinches as Maia thrashes. A tear slips down Maia's cheek, and she relaxes, going against every inclination she has to struggle. The tiger positions itself beneath her, and she places her feet on its back. She stands, wavering, and the noose loosens enough for her to wheeze in a breath.

She can't find her balance with her legs bound—she needs her hands. Grimacing, she leans back, hanging long enough to loop her cuffed hands beneath her feet. She can barely get them through; the cuffs cut into her skin. Crossing her hands to her front, she stands back on the tiger and grips the rope above her head. Pulling herself up, she gasps in a desperate breath. Jake is screaming from the lawn behind her as she loosens the noose, and then she tears the rope from her neck and drops to the ground.

Lying in the grass, she coughs, wheezing for breath. She whispers, "Thank you," to the large tiger beside her, her voice broken. "*Thank you.*"

A gun fires and the tiger falls by Maia's side. Anger surges through her, and she sits up. Jake's soldier is back, cautiously crossing the lawn with a pistol in his hand. She searches the grass for Jake's gun. The soldier shoots again, the bullet grazing her shoulder. She growls through gritted teeth. Her fingers land on the cold metal of a pistol and she lifts it, firing several rounds. The man drops to the ground.

She drapes herself across her dead tiger. "I'm *so* sorry," she whispers, burying her face into its fur.

The soldier groans from the lawn. She lifts her head, glaring where he lies. Ripping the rope from her feet, she stands and stumbles toward the guard with Jake's gun in her hand. He's alive—barely. She shoots him several more times.

Bang, bang, bang, bang.

She turns toward Jake, lying alone on the grass behind the gallows. Atlas is gone.

This ends *now.*

She staggers toward him with her gun pointed, her finger hovering above the trigger. It's so dark in this part of the yard. The electricity is still out, but one end of Jake's mansion is on fire, highlighting the lawn in waves.

Jake lifts his head from the grass, then lays it back down again, laughing. "You're still alive," he mumbles. "*Of course* you're still alive."

Maia takes in his injuries, flickering in the fire's light, and she swallows hard. His right arm is mauled, along with a portion of his neck and shoulder. Blood trickles from his mouth, his mangled throat dark and glossy. He has a gun in his left hand, now resting on his chest, rapidly rising and falling with his shallow breath.

"Where's my tiger?" Maia asks as she approaches.

"Don't know," he croaks.

"Did you shoot him?"

"Hard to pull a gun from your back when you've got a five-hundred-pound tiger on top of you."

For a while, there is only the sound of gunshots resounding across the property. Maia glances across the yard for any other soldiers. She and Jake are alone, the tigers dispersed into the woods. Clouds of smoke waft across them.

"You know..." Jake sputters blood as he coughs. "I was only trying to scare you ... with Silas. I would have never let him hurt you."

Maia scoffs. "No, you wanted to do that all on your own."

He casts her a sidelong glance, considering, and he nods. "I suppose I did." He grimaces, suppressing a cough, and then he glances between her and her gun. "Just do it already," he gasps. "Do it ... before I do."

She glares at him, breathing hard. Her finger on the trigger, she tightens her grip, and the fire behind her grows.

He watches her, waiting, and then he chuckles, looking back at the sky. "Why ... are you fighting for these people anyway?" Blood trickles from his mouth, and he swallows. "It was only hours ago ... they wanted you dead."

"A wise old woman once told me an ancient word for human. Do you know what it means?"

"Virus," Jake coughs, spattering blood across the grass.

"No. *Animated Earth*."

"But ... you're Mother Nature. Humans ... have always ... destroyed you."

"Not always. And not anymore." She focuses her aim. "Now, it is only *you*. And you were wrong."

He glares at her. "About *what*."

"*Everything*."

He lifts his pistol, pointing it at her, and she pulls her trigger. The bullet lands between his eyes.

That's for Lucas.

She shoots him again for Miguel. Again for Chayanne. For Claire. She shoots him for every soul he's destroyed and for every life that he's taken. She pulls the trigger until her gun is empty and then she drops to her knees beside him, her pistol sliding from her hand into the splattered blades of grass.

THIRTY-NINE

Maia catches her breath as black smoke drifts across her.

One explosive moment. She knew there would be one explosive moment where she and Jake would hold the other's life in their hands. Guns pointed, they had the power to take the other's last breath. She knew it was coming. She had prepared herself. For months, she had yearned for nothing more than her moment to end him. But she hesitated—they both did. She's surprised at how long she wavered. How long her finger sat unmoving on the trigger.

And now, it's over. He is finally gone. She thought she would be happy. She should feel relieved.

So why does it feel like a part of her is missing?

She glares at him. Just like her dreams, his face appears in and out of clouds of smoke. Only now, it is broken, lifeless, covered in blood. Looking at him, she finds her soul no longer fills with dread.

Now, she is only resentful.

More gunshots sound from the other side of the house,

snapping her out of her daze. She peers over her shoulder at Jake's mansion. The fire is devouring the far east side. The rest of it is still black, filling with smoke. It won't be long before the entire thing is burning to the ground.

And that's when it hits her—*Lucas*.

Jake said he wasn't inside, but she doesn't believe that for a second. She pries the gun from his bloody fingers, and she stumbles to her feet. Sprinting across the lawn, she looks for soldiers, then leans against the back of the house. Clutching her pistol before her, she gathers her wits. Her hands are still bound with cuffs—she needs those keys.

She peers around the corner to an empty yard, then races along the side of the house. As she rounds the corner to the driveway, she nearly drops her gun. The once glistening city of lights in the background is now dark, with countless columns of smoke rising into the early-morning skies.

Leucothea has been devastated. Whatever happened down there was not just Maia's doing. It looks like a war has broken through the gates.

Strange people have gathered along the driveway and front yard. Some have guns—others have bats or knives or wooden spikes. They've all stopped to look at her. They're not soldiers, hers or Leucothea's. Are they citizens? No, their clothing is tattered. Dirty. Held together in patches. Some of them are not wearing shoes.

They're Leucothea's slaves.

Maia approaches. "Where are Jake's soldiers?"

"They've fled," a young man says.

"Cowards," Maia mumbles. She tucks her pistol into her pants and turns toward the house. Its front doors have been left wide open. She runs up the granite steps and peers inside. Black smoke curls in waves across the ceiling—she doesn't have long.

She runs into the living room, hesitating at the couch with her hand on her chest. When she crosses to the other side, Claire is still lying there, face down in a pool of blood.

Maia kneels beside her, hanging her head. Grimacing, she rolls Claire over and gently sweeps a hand across her eyes, closing them. She pulls the keys from Claire's grasp and fumbles through them, her fingers slick with blood. When she finds the right one, she unlocks her cuffs and sets them beside her. Wiping the hair from Claire's face, she whispers, "I'm *so* sorry. I'll come back for you."

She stands. Where to start? Racing across the living room, she heads toward the hallway along the west side of the house. So many rooms down there.

"Lucas!" she screams. Sprinting down the corridor, she peers inside the different doors, her eyes burning from the smoke. Most rooms are empty, save for a few dead bodies sprawled across the floors. It's so hard to see. She runs to each one, flipping them over. "Lucas?!" None of them are him, but she does find Silas—dead. She fights the urge to shoot him again.

Where would Jake keep someone as important as Lucas? She turns toward the closed door at the end of the hallway.

His office.

She rushes up to it, jiggles the knob. Locked. "Lucas!" She pounds on the door. Placing her head against the wood, she can hear coughing on the other side. "Stay away from the door!" she screams, and she stands back, aiming her pistol above the knob. She shoots, then kicks it open. More smoke barrels in. Choking, she looks around in a panic. The fire is spreading quickly now.

In a dark corner of the room, a body lie curled on the floor. She runs up to it.

Lucas. He's passed out, his hands and mouth bound with tape.

"Lucas! Wake up!" she screams, and she pulls the tape from his face. He moans, but he doesn't come to. She shakes him. "Lucas! *Please*! Please, wake up!"

But he won't. She tears the tape from around his hands, then drags him toward the door. He flips his head from side to side, mumbling.

"Lucas!" Maia screams. "Please, wake *up*!"

Another man runs into the room and she pivots, swiping the gun from her pants.

"Don't shoot!" the man shouts, coughing.

His face comes into focus. "Shinesho!" she screams. "It's *Lucas*!"

"*What*?!"

"Help me!"

Lucas is now waking, coughing and gasping for air. Maia and Shinesho drape his arms across their shoulders, and together, the three head down the hallway. The fire is devouring the walls, obscuring the front door.

"Turn around!" Shinesho yells.

They stumble back to Jake's office. Shinesho leaves Lucas with Maia, and he grabs a chair, smashing it against a window. He climbs into the bushes outside, then holds out his hands to help Lucas and Maia. Together, they drag Lucas across the lawn away from the fire.

"Stay with him," Maia says to Shinesho, and she runs toward the front of the house.

"Where are you going?!" he screams after her.

"I have to get Claire!"

"Maia, *no*!"

Maia runs up the front steps, shielding her face against the raging fire now spilling from the doors. She'll have to find another way in.

Shinesho pulls her back. "Maia, you can't! You'll never make it out!"

"I have to get her out of there! I promised!"

"She's already burning! She's *gone*! Leave her!"

Maia screams as she breaks from his grasp, glaring up at Jake's mansion. Everything this house represents. All the lies. The heartache. He has taken so much from her. He has taken so much from them *all*.

She turns toward Shinesho as the events of the evening come back to her, and she covers her mouth.

"What?" he asks. "What is it?"

"*Chayanne*. Oh my God, Shinesho," she says, shaking her head.

"No, it's okay. It's okay!" he yells. "She's alive!"

"What?!"

"She's wounded—they shot her shoulder. She dropped to the ground so that no one else could shoot. A doctor in the crowd helped us, took Chayanne back to her apartment. She and a friend are taking care of her."

Maia is laughing. Crying. Overcome with relief. "She's alive?! Chayanne is *alive*?"

Shinesho nods with a wide grin. "She's alive."

"And Miguel?" Maia asks, still smiling. "Where is he? You followed him … right?" The look on Shinesho's face makes her heart sink. "Shinesho?!" she shouts over the fire. "You followed him—*right*?"

He looks down at her with glassy eyes, breathing hard. "Jake's soldiers threw him in a truck," he says. "I couldn't keep up. The crowds were so dense, and then they drove to the back roads. They … they were too fast."

Maia is staring at him, shaking her head. "So … you don't know? Or do you?" That look on his face. "Why?! *Why* are you looking at me like that?"

He takes a breath. "Our men found him." His voice is so shaken that Maia covers her mouth. "He was left outside the city gates, badly beaten. He was still alive, but it didn't look good. They took him to a hospital in the city."

"What do you mean, 'it didn't look good.' What does that *mean*?!" Maia shrieks over the roar of the fire.

"It means what it means, Maia!" He looks at his feet, shaking his head.

"Why!? *Why* do you keep shaking your head? Stop *doing* that!" she screams, shoving him. "Why do you keep doing that!"

"Because I don't know!" Shinesho yells. "I don't know if they could…" Hanging his head, he begins to sob. "If they could … save him," he gasps.

Clenching her fists, Maia turns toward the house. She doubles over, wailing at the ground. The winds pick up, and Shinesho backs away, covering his face against the swirling red embers.

Shrieking, Maia lifts her bloody hands before her, causing a fireball to explode from the back of the house. The roof caves in and the windows explode, shattering glass across her feet. A crowd gathers behind her, watching in horror as she cries out and the fires rage. They cover their faces, backing up, their bodies covered in layers of gray.

With tears streaming down her face, Maia keeps her trembling hands held out, fueling the flames devouring Jake's mansion. Thick clouds of black smoke devour the sky, and the last of the roof caves in, enveloping Maia in a wave of ash. The fire is so hot, but she doesn't back away.

Let it burn.

Let it *all* burn.

She'll gut the place. Hollow it until there's nothing left. Nothing but smoldering embers and the echoes of a memory.

That's when she notices the blood. Her hands, they are covered in it. Jake's blood. Claire's blood. Her tiger's blood. She releases her breath and lowers her hands, glancing between them. So ... much ... *blood*.

No more. *Please*, no more.

Sniffling, she turns to the people behind her. They look at her, unsure, and slowly back away. Some are citizens, she can tell that as much. They're the same faces that had surrounded her in the square, demanding Jake drag a knife across her throat. They called her a monster, a traitor, a danger to society.

Another explosion mushrooms behind Maia, and she stumbles forward in a stupor. The crowd separates, and she zigzags between them, heading toward the cliff.

When she reaches the edge, she crumbles into a heap on the ground, gazing through the blades of grass at the city below. It looks like a shell. No electricity, no laughing, no glasses *clinking*, no 'thriving.' Parts of the metropolis are burning, some of the high-rises toppled from Maia's quakes.

Like her, the city has been gutted.

This war is over; she knows it from the depths of her soul. She rolls onto her back. The last of the night's stars peek in and out of clouds of smoke as embers and ash rain down upon them.

It is over.

Her rage now dissipated, she feels indescribably hollow. Something has left her—she can feel it in her bones, but she can't decipher what *it* is. Something is slipping from her grasp as surely as her past burns beside her, and Leucothea's walls crumble before her.

When she lifts herself from the ground, the sharp pain from her gunshot wound pierces through her arm. A large crowd has gathered around her. They look down at her, uncertain, their faces streaked with blood and ash and war.

A tiger makes his way toward her, limping, his head covered in blood. The crowd separates, stumbling over themselves to get away, and Maia gasps.

Atlas.

She opens her arms, and he gallops into them, burrowing his nose into her shoulder. She grimaces from the pain and buries her face into his fur, sobbing. "You're still alive," she whispers. "I'm so glad you're still alive."

A voice calls her name. She looks up, searching the faces. The blaze is so bright behind the mass of people that it's hard to see. Did she just hear her name? Someone has called her name.

Shinesho breaks through the bodies with Lucas leaning against him, his arm across his shoulder.

"Maia," Lucas whispers.

Maia's heart catches in her throat, and she grapples to her feet. Weeping, she races across the lawn and throws herself around him. Her sobs steal her breath as years of buried ache surge through her like a tidal wave, and she embraces her love brought back from the dead.

"*Meu Deus,*" he whispers as he holds her, trembling and unsteady. "Oh, my darling."

She helps him lower to the grass. "Is it really you?" she whispers, cupping the side of his emaciated face. Just skin over bones, he is nearly unrecognizable. But his eyes. His eyes are still the same. "I can't believe it's you," she says. "I thought you were dead. They told me you were dead."

He holds her cheek, wiping her tears with his thumb. "I know they did."

"Oh, Lucas!" She wraps her arms around him. "I am so sorry," she gasps between her sobs. "I am *so so* sorry."

"Don't be sorry," he whispers as he holds her. "As sinister as Jake's intentions were, he is the only reason I'm still alive. I owe that man my life."

Maia sits back, stunned.

All the darkness. And all the light.

Lucas tenderly caresses the side of her cheek, taking in every last inch of her, and then he leans in and kisses her. She kisses him back before pulling away, her fingers at her lips.

He studies her reaction for a moment, and then he peers down at his hands, nodding. "You are with Miguel," he says softly.

"Lucas," she begins, but the look on his face silences her.

"It's okay," he says. "I have had a lot of time to come to terms with this. And it's okay."

She gazes at him, lost for words.

"You *should* be with him," he says. "You should. What I said back on the river ... I meant every word. You and I?" He grabs her hand, holding it between his. "You and I were perfect for each other ... *for a time*. And we saved each other, didn't we? Many times over, we saved each other."

She nods.

"But we were never meant to *stay* together, as much as I wanted that."

"I wanted that too."

"I know you did. And we gave it a fair fight."

"I love you, Lucas. I love you in a way that I'll never love another. But that love isn't—"

"I know. And you deserve to have that sort of love. We both do."

Maia nods, holding her breath against her tears, and Lucas squeezes her hand. "You'll always have a piece of me," he whispers. "My little stowaway."

Maia's hand flies to her mouth, and Lucas pulls her into him, holding her as she cries. And that's where they stay, embracing high upon a cliff with the dark and broken city of Leucothea sprawling before them.

And the last of Jake's mansion crumbles to the ground.

FORTY

"I'm sorry, ma'am, but this is as far as I can go," Orson says. He slows the car to a stop, then turns in his seat to face her.

Maia stares up at the gates through her window.

Welcome to Leucothea.

How many times has she sat before these very same gates, inside this very same car, with Jake's hand in hers? Never could she have imagined she would sit before them like this.

Jake is dead, his life taken from him by a single shot from the barrel of his own gun. His precious New System has fallen overnight. And now Leucothea's mighty gates, a glittering crown of national pride, have been left wide open, the bodies of its sworn protectors strewn across the road.

"That's okay," Shinesho says from beside her. "We can walk from here."

"It's just straight down there. Can't miss it," Orson says.

Maia glares down the desolate road leading into the city. It looks surprisingly peaceful after a night of rioting and war. Her armies and many of Leucothea's citizens are now resting after working all morning gathering their deceased and treating the injured. Jake's soldiers, however, still lie dead in the streets, a ghastly reminder of the events that took place only a few short hours ago.

"Maia?" Shinesho asks, snapping her out of her daze.

She shakes her head. "Yes, right. It would probably help if I opened the door." She reaches to Orson, and he holds her hand. "What will you do?" she asks him.

"The same as everyone else, I suppose. Rebuild from the ashes."

Maia nods, and she opens the door. "Thank you," she says.

She pulls her hand, but Orson maintains his grip. "No, Miss Maia," he says quietly. "Thank *you*."

They smile at one another, and then Maia and Shinesho step out onto the road.

They were the last to leave Jake's property—or what was left of it. Those who knew how to drive gathered the injured and took them into the city for treatment. Lucas was one of them, unable to walk and suffering from smoke inhalation, severe malnutrition, and dehydration. Shortly afterward, a few ambulances arrived to treat the less critically injured, including Maia, whose gunshot graze on her arm has since been cleaned and stitched together.

Shinesho and Maia walk side by side down the destroyed streets of Leucothea in silence. It looks like a warzone. Most of the buildings are intact, although some have crumbled completely from the blow of Maia's quakes, their brick and glass and metal spilling like guts into the deserted city streets. The fires left over from the night are still smoldering with fading wisps of smoke. There are dead bodies on the road—mostly Jake's soldiers—next to paper and litter and debris tumbling across the broken glass.

Maia slows. Picking up a flyer, she finds half her face staring back at her, the word "Traitor" torn away from beneath. Only her eyes remain. One blue, one green—both glaring. She lets the photo hang by her side, and it slips from her fingers.

"How far?" she whispers.

"About a twenty-minute walk," Shinesho says.

She exhales a nervous breath, and he softly rubs her back. She looks up at him. "And you know where he'll be? Once we get there?"

He nods, short and quick.

They face forward again. Three Leucotheans are sweeping glass outside a dark bakery. They stop when they see Maia, and they step one by one to the curb, removing their hats. They each give a solemn nod as she and Shinesho pass.

Down the road, a woman wails over a dead body in the street—one of Jake's fallen soldiers. He looks young. Innocent. The woman's cries echo off the dark buildings, sending shivers down Maia's spine. A few older men kneel beside him, their eyes bloodshot and swollen, and they roll the young man onto a blanket. The woman drapes herself across him, screaming. Maia covers her mouth as they pass.

There can be no war without loss.

"Shall I tell you what happened last night?" Shinesho says quietly beside her.

Maia balks. "I'm not sure I can handle anymore right now."

"Please, Maia. I'm terrified."

She nods. Maybe talking will be good. It's a bit of a hike to the hospital, and they need the distraction. They both know Maia may soon become like the woman behind them, clinging to the body of a man she once loved.

Shinesho begins with Leucothea Square, after the New System had recovered the feed. The crowds around him were too rowdy, so he decided to hide along a back wall to work on claiming it back. It wasn't until he saw Miguel being dragged on stage that he realized how bad things had gotten. He found Chayanne, who whispered to him to follow the soldiers who had taken Miguel. He didn't know Chayanne's plans to shoot Jake—he didn't even hear the gunshots or the people screaming. He just ran as fast as he could to keep up with the truck.

After losing Miguel, he headed back to the square to find Chayanne being carried out by a doctor and her friend. The crowds were too thick and the hospital too far, so the doctor offered to take Chayanne back to her apartment a block away. That's where they were when Maia's first earthquake struck. Shinesho knew she was in trouble, so he raced back to the square, but Jake and his men had already taken her away. The citizens were angry. Terrified. Claire and a few of Jake's men were standing on the stage surrounded by guards, trying to calm the crowds and order them back to their homes.

Claire spotted Shinesho immediately and met him behind the stage. She told him Augustus and his family never escaped. Someone had tipped them off before they tried anything, and they went into hiding somewhere in the city. She told him Maia was to be hanged at Jake's house, which would be filmed and shown across all the homes in Leucothea.

"I wanted Claire to sneak me back into Jake's property to save you, but she refused. We knew it would be suicide. With our armies not yet combined outside the gates, we needed the backup of the citizens. You were knocked out, so we still had time. That's when Claire told me how comfortable Jake was in his home, ran his mouth all the time saying incriminating things that could be used against him. We decided to hack his video feed from inside the house. Claire would link it to me in the city, and we would wait for him to say something we could use. With you there, Claire said it wouldn't take long. So, I went back to the doctor's apartment and recorded the footage from inside Jake's living room." He shakes his head. "Maia, it was horrifying, watching that. I think it may haunt me for the rest of my life."

"You and me both," she says quietly.

"You were passed out for a while, so I worked on getting our radios back up and running with our armies outside the gates and was able to hold them off from cutting the electricity until I got what we needed."

Reaching the top of a small hill, Maia grabs Shinesho's arm. A large crowd has gathered before a building just a few blocks away. It looks like the hospital. They pick up their pace.

"Shinesho?" Maia says, not taking her eyes off the crowd. "Keep talking. *Please*, keep talking."

"I knew the moment you figured it out," he says. "The entire time you were in that living room, you never looked up at the camera in the corner. Not once. When Jake's men started dragging you away, I knew we were out of time, and I began to panic. But then your eyes flickered up to the camera, and I swear you looked right at me. It wasn't long before you got Jake to agree to his lies. Once he called his people stupid and lazy, I blasted the entire thing on a repeat feed into every home in the city. It just played over and over and *over* again.

"The citizens filled the streets, rioting. That's when I ordered our armies to cut the power. But then President Augustus addressed his people in the square. He told them everything—who you are and the truth behind Jake's government. He united them in a way I didn't think possible. Many of Leucothea's soldiers joined us. The others either hid or fled. We opened the gates to our armies, which had tripled in number with the freed slaves."

His voice trails off as they approach the large crowd, gathered before a tall brick building three stories high. *Hospital of Leucothea* is sprawled across the front, and a line of soldiers blocks the doors. A man is standing on a chair behind them, palms up toward the crowd. "We need to make space! Please be patient! You *will* be seen! If you are looking for a loved one, please go to the tent…"

Maia looks at Shinesho, and he grabs her shoulders, yelling above the mob. "Straight through the doors, up the stairs to the right! He should be somewhere on the second floor! I'll be right behind—"

But Maia is already shoving her way through the crowd. She smashes into the line of soldiers at the doors, unfazed by their pointed guns. They shove her to the ground, struggling to hold her down as she screams.

"Let her go!" another one shouts. "Don't you see who that is?" The soldiers look at her, then quickly back away.

One helps her to her feet. "Sorry, ma'am."

They allow Maia to pass between them, and she runs through the broken glass doors.

Inside, it is mayhem. There are people everywhere. Crying. Shouting. Nurses exasperated, leaning over wailing victims with arms outstretched. The injured line the walls and the floors and the stairs, their wounds wrapped with cloth, some soaked with blood. Maia takes the stairs to the second floor, sprinting up them two by two, and runs screaming down the hallway. "*Miguel*?!"

The floor is poorly lit, but they still have some electricity.

It must be coming from whatever Jake had alluded to as "backup." Like the first level, the wounded are in beds lining every square inch of these halls.

Maia races in and out of each room, checking every bed, desperate and sick with dread. "Miguel!" she screams. She runs to the other side of the hallway. There are doors everywhere, each open to surgeries crowded with people. "Miguel?!" she screeches. She runs back into the hall and slams into a nurse. They skid across the tiles.

"I'm so sorry," Maia mumbles from the ground. She sits up, rubbing the back of her head. "Have you seen a man with tattoos? Big man. Shaved head. Tattoos down both his arms."

"You're ... you're *her*," the nurse stammers, climbing to her feet and backing away. "You're ... that woman."

More people gather around, staring at Maia as she sits on the ground with her back hunched, her legs splayed out before her. "Please, I'm trying to find someone very important," she mumbles, catching her breath.

Another nurse approaches, and she helps Maia to her feet. "I know the man you are looking for," the woman quietly says, still holding on to Maia. "I'll take you to him. Excuse us!" she yells at the crowd around them. "Out of the way, please!" She leads Maia down the hallway to the very last room, stopping just outside it. "We've done everything we can—"

Maia bursts through the door. The room is dark, the only light coming from a single window on the back wall. It takes her eyes a moment to adjust. There is a man on the bed in the corner, covered in bandages and surrounded by blinking monitors with repetitive short *beeps*. Cords. There are so many cords coming out of his body. This is a mistake —that isn't Miguel.

"Ma'am, this must be a mistake," Maia says, but then she covers her mouth. The cords, they are attached to his arms ... arms with intricately designed tribal tattoos. So many nights Maia laid next to him, memorizing every last detail of those tattoos—every curve and every line. She memorized every last line.

She steps forward, her eyes fluttering with tears, and she slowly releases her breath. This strong, beautiful man ... left for dead, every last piece of him broken. Wrapping her trembling hands around his, she takes in the severity of his wounds. His eyes are swollen shut. Purple. There are stitches across his brow. His head wrapped in layers of gauze. Chest bandaged. Leg in a cast, elevated from his bed by a rope from the ceiling.

Maia delicately places her lips on his, careful to avoid a cut held together with tape, and her tears fall onto his ghostly skin. Sniffling, she delicately pats each one dry. She pulls a chair as close as she can, resting her cheek on his bed.

Behind her, the door opens and softly latches shut. She glances over her shoulder. The horrified look across Shinesho's face makes her quickly turn away. He crosses to the other side of Miguel's bed. His jaw clenched, he struggles to hold back his sob. Maia can't look at him. So, they sit together in silence, listening to the beeping of the monitor and Miguel's strained, shallow breaths.

Hours later, a soft moan escapes Miguel's lips, and Maia lifts her head with a start. He struggles to open his eyes, now swollen into slits. He turns to look at her. It takes a minute for him to focus, but when he does, the features of his face soften.

"Hello ... *little bird*," he croaks.

Maia smiles through her tears. "Hello, my love."

"You're alive," he gasps.

"*Shhh*, try not to talk."

He takes in the cuts on her lip and across her brow, then the red and purple bruising stretched across her neck, and his breath quickens. He closes his eyes, a tear escaping. "Is it over?"

She softly caresses the side of his cheek. "It's over," she whispers.

He sighs, and then he slips into a deep sleep.

Miguel spends the next few days drifting in and out of consciousness. Maia spends a lot of time sleeping next to him, repeatedly asking when she wakes when Chayanne will be well enough to visit.

Any day now, Shinesho keeps saying.

Miguel was thankfully awake for Lucas's first visit. Maia stood sobbing in the hallway, watching through the glass in the door as the two brothers had a long and tearful reunion.

Lucas is now using crutches to help him get around, made by a young woman who works for the hospital. With his hair cut and his beard gone, he looks more like himself, although he still has a lot of weight to gain.

Maia has stopped by Lucas's room every day for a visit. The last time she did, however, she quickly backed out before he could see her. The woman who made his crutches was sitting beside his bed, and they were speaking very closely to one another. Maia watched for a moment from the shadows of the hallway. The way Lucas looked at that woman, the way she made him smile ... Maia remembered when she used to make him smile like that.

And as she made her way back to Miguel's room, she

was filled with relief. Lucas is okay. Lucas will *continue* to be okay. He'll do just fine here in Leucothea.

———

Soon, Miguel's room becomes an endless parade of visitors, and he is up and smiling. Most of the tribe's soldiers stop by. They are heading home, although a few will come back with horses for those who are still healing. They have also happily reported that many of Maia's tigers have been spotted in the woods outside the city, much to her relief. The soldiers tried approaching the large cats, but they wanted nothing to do with the strange humans.

President Augustus visits, along with Andrew and Uki, whose armies have been helping with the cleanup efforts around the city. But the time has come to go home. Leucothea will always have allies with New Portland and Asiaq Bay, although with the New System gone, they will hopefully never need them.

"I'll never be able to thank you enough," Maia says to them. "I don't know what we would have done without you."

"No, thank *you*, Maia," Uki says. "Our cities, our families, our homes ... We are all safer now because of you."

"It wasn't just me. This war was fought and won by the collective hands of thousands. We each played a part."

"Yes, but it all started with *you*," Andrew says with a smile.

"Indeed," President Augustus says, and Maia graciously shakes their hands. The generals excuse themselves, leaving Maia alone with the president, his two armed guards outside the door.

"I'm sorry for not being with you in the square," Augustus says, "but our mission had been compromised, and it became far too dangerous for my family. Jake's men were hiding along our exit, waiting for us to escape. We would have been slaughtered."

"Please, don't be sorry. You did the right thing. And we were prepared. We had our backup video, which..." Maia hesitates, shuddering. "Which got the ball rolling, I suppose."

They share a pained chuckle.

"What about the formerly enslaved people? Where are they now?" Maia asks.

"Some have joined Leucothea to help rebuild. Many have left. There's a rumor they have been taken in by Asiaq Bay."

"And Leucothea?" Maia asks. "How bad is the damage?"

Augustus sighs through his nose. "It's significant," he says. "There's a lot of work to be done. But this is our chance to start over," he adds, "and do it the right way."

"I'm sorry I caused so much destruction. I just didn't see any other way."

"No need to be sorry. You did what you had to. We wouldn't be standing here today if you hadn't intervened."

She nods. "And our spy?"

"We'll be conducting an investigation, but considering how many people we combined from different lands, and now that they've all dispersed ... I'm not sure we'll ever know."

"Right."

"I want you to know we will be having a citywide memorial for Claire, who played such a dangerous and instrumental role in this revolution," Augustus says. "The people of Leucothea have always loved her, and she will be sorely missed. We will rename our university after her so that the future inhabitants of this city will forever know her name. She will never be forgotten."

"She would have really loved that," Maia breathes.

"We're going to put Leucothea back together again, Maia, the way it was always meant to be. We would be honored if you would join us. I have come to understand that Leucothea is where you have always felt called. With your help, we can make it the city you've always dreamed of."

Maia gazes at Miguel sleeping. "No," she says, shaking her head. "Thank you, but I know exactly where I belong. And it's not here."

Augustus nods, and then he peers behind her with a smile.

Maia turns to find Shinesho walking into the room with Chayanne behind him, her arm in a sling.

Maia rushes up to her, and the two women hug. Maia pulls back with tears in her eyes, inspecting Chayanne's shoulder. "All in one piece?" she whispers.

Chayanne smiles, and she cups Maia's cheek. "Mostly."

Maia hugs her again. "Oh, Chayanne, I'm so glad you're okay."

"I'm glad you're okay, too, sweet friend," Chayanne whispers, and she pulls away, looking Maia over. She grimaces at the dark bruising on Maia's face and across her neck, and she shakes her head. "I could dig him up and kill him all over again."

"He burned with the house," Maia says. "There's nothing left of him."

"Yeah?" Chayanne's brow raises. "Good," she says, and she walks up to Miguel. "He's going to be okay?"

"He'll be okay," Maia says. She steps beside Chayanne

and wraps her arms around her, and they both gaze down at him.

Chayanne sighs, and she turns toward Maia. Sweeping a curl from her face, she says, "Can we go home now?"

Maia smiles. "Yes, please."

President Augustus walks up to them. "Sorry to interrupt, but I'd better be going. Maia, you always have a place here should you ever change your mind."

"Thank you."

He turns to leave, then hesitates, eyeing Maia's face. "Huh," he says, pulling out his spectacles.

Maia holds her cheeks. "What?"

He peers at her through his glasses. "It's just ... I never noticed your freckles. With all the photos I've seen, I could have sworn." He waves his hand. "Anyway, I'm an old man. What do I know?"

Chayanne grabs Maia's shoulder and looks for herself. She smiles. "Well, would you look at that?"

Maia steps to a mirror, leaning in close. Her freckles, just a few of them, have reappeared and now scatter across her cheeks.

FORTY-ONE

After another week, Miguel and their few remaining injured agree they have healed enough to travel back to the tribe. It took a few men to help Miguel onto his horse with his leg in a cast, but he was so hell-bent on leaving that he couldn't be stopped.

Maia leads her horse beside his, and the two reach out to one another. "Ready?" she asks.

"More than," he says with a grin, dimple showing. His black knitted cap is covering the stitches on his head, and his face is no longer swollen, but there is still heavy bruising around both his eyes.

Maia looks at him and smiles. He is as handsome as ever.

Chayanne and Shinesho both guide their horses next to them. "Let's get this show on the road," Chayanne says. "I'm hungry."

"You just ate," Shinesho says.

She shoots him a look. "For *real* food. I can't stand this dehydrated goop. *Just add water*? What the hell is that?"

Miguel hushes her. "Good *God*, Chayanne."

"What?"

Maia laughs, and she catches Lucas's gaze. Standing by the hospital doors next to President Augustus, he tilts his head, and the two smile fondly at one another. Add this to the arsenal of looks Lucas has given her over the years—there have been many. This one is new. More than acceptance, it is a loving farewell.

Lucas told Maia and Miguel a few days ago that he's actually really happy to stay here, to be a part of the city's mass rebuilding. Purpose. His life has a purpose he can believe in. And he has promised to visit them at the tribe early next spring.

And as Maia turns her horse, Lucas's lady friend steps next to him, holding his hand.

President Augustus has kindly supplied their small crew with the food and equipment needed for their trip back home. Although, Maia had to elbow Chayanne when she turned her nose up at the food.

"Is there anything else we can do to help you?" Augustus asks. "We can send trucks with supplies."

"No, thank you," Shinesho says. "You'll need all hands on deck here. We'll be okay."

"At least take one of our solar-powered S&R Trucks," Augustus says. "We already have one of our largest rigs waiting for you at the gates, fully stocked from our warehouses. I insist."

"Thank you, sir."

"We have also sent soldiers ahead of you along the road leading out of Leucothea, and they have broken up the roadblocks and thugs. Most of those people were working hand in hand with Jake anyway, so their incentive to stay is no longer there."

"We really appreciate that," Chayanne says, and Augustus nods.

Their small group waves goodbye, and then they begin their journey down the long road leading out of the city. Large banners still hanging from Leucothea Day are being pulled down, Jake's face rippling as the posters fall. The citizens have gathered in large groups, cleaning the streets and sweeping the glass. Some small businesses are open, with people embracing in their doorways, and small food stands for the workers have been set up on the sidewalks.

There is something in the air this morning. Like the dawn of a new day, the city feels like a different place entirely. And yet, it is still Leucothea. Black flags with a single white star still hang from storefronts and windows. Its citizens are still proud to call this place their home—now more than ever. Their tribulations have united them.

As Maia and her crew travel down the city streets, the people walk out to greet them. Some are waving. Clapping. Others nod in acknowledgment. Not everyone is happy, Maia notes as she catches a few icy glares, which is to be expected. Leucothea will have its fair share of problems as the city rebuilds, but Maia knows without a doubt that they will build something better from the ashes.

A small child runs into the street toward Maia, giggling with her red curls flowing behind her. Maia stops her horse.

Can it be?

As the little girl approaches, Maia's vision fades, and she notes the child's straight brown hair and thick fringe. The girl stands before Maia, looking up at her with wide brown eyes, and she offers her a yellow wildflower.

Maia leans down and takes it. "Thank you, darling," she says, and the child grins, showing off her missing front teeth.

A woman runs out and picks the youngster up, placing her on her hip. She flashes Maia an apologetic smile, and then she turns and walks away. The child wraps her arms around her mother's neck and tenderly kisses her cheek.

Maia sits back on her horse, twirling the flower between her fingertips, watching them.

Arriving back at the tribe, Maia finds Tema waiting at the gates. The huge grin across her face causes her skin to wrinkle like fans from her eyes.

"Is this our welcome committee?" Maia calls from her horse.

"I knew you were coming," Tema says with that same gorgeous chuckle Maia has always loved.

Maia stops her horse and jumps off, running toward Tema's open arms.

"My sweet Anâna," Tema whispers as they hug. "Welcome *home*." She pulls away, gazing up at Maia with tears in her eyes, and then she looks behind her as Shinesho, Chayanne, and Miguel approach. She puts her hand over her heart, sighing in relief. "Thank you for bringing back my family." The smile fades from her face. "*Oh*! Oh my!"

Maia peers behind her as over a half dozen tigers enter the property, including Atlas. "Yes," she says. "We've brought a few extras."

Tema leans in with a childlike smile, whispering, "Truth be told, I've always wanted to be a crazy cat lady."

Maia laughs, and then Tema hobbles up to the others, hugging each one as they dismount their horse. With tears in her eyes, she kisses them, holding their faces and squeezing their cheeks. Unsurprisingly, her hug lingers when she reaches Miguel, and he smiles at Maia, shaking his head. Once satisfied, Tema shuffles back to Maia and links their arms. "Come, child. Let's get some food in that belly."

As the two walk through the grounds, Maia holds her hand against her chest. The place is unrecognizable. Jake's men have destroyed everything. But, like Leucothea, the tribe has banded together and is already hard at work rebuilding.

Maia stops before her old hut. Only a bathtub remains in the middle of the charred heap, but there are already a few blades of green grass peeking from the ashes.

And just then, a butterfly floats past.

Months pass and Maia has still not had a single dream. No more prophetic nightmares. No more waking up screaming, drenched in a cold sweat. Every day, she settles softly into this new life of hers. And every day, she feels her powers diminish a little more. The trees' whispers have become so hushed. Even in the quietest hours of the night, she can barely hear them.

Maia lies in bed, pulling the covers to her chin. Her and Miguel's new place is basic—*bare-bones*, Miguel has called it —essentially four walls and a roof, with a kitchen, a fire-place, and a few pieces of furniture that have either been distributed from their S&R Truck or made by Miguel. Supplies are limited, and the tribe has been working around the clock to ensure everyone is sheltered before winter.

Maia doesn't mind. This place is theirs and theirs alone. They have their entire lives to build it up.

To her, it is perfect.

"Shall I make us a fire?" Miguel mumbles beside her. Half-asleep, he drapes his arm across her.

She nods. "I'll make us some tea."

Walking past a mirror on the wall, Maia halts, then slowly backs up until she faces her reflection. She leans in, her brow creased. New auburn waves now blend with her red curls. She sweeps her fingertips across her freckled cheeks and stands back.

Huh.

"I didn't want to say anything," Miguel says, crouching beside the fireplace.

"When did you notice?"

"I've seen a little each day for a few weeks now. Small changes here and there. I wasn't sure if it'd upset you."

"I suppose I don't look in a mirror often."

"*Does* it upset you?"

Maia tilts her gaze. "I wouldn't say it upsets me. It's just … different."

"I like it," he says, gazing at her from over his shoulder. "I think you look more like … *you.*"

She backs away from the mirror. It *is* nice to have her freckles back. She pulls her hair into a messy bun. Miguel's right; she does look more like herself.

He sighs, frustrated. The kindling won't catch. "Maia, can you?"

She absently lifts her hand as she heads toward the kitchen, and then she stops, turning in place to peer behind her. Miguel sits waiting, the dark pit still barren. They look at one another, confused. She faces the fireplace and raises both hands. Nothing happens. Scrutinizing her palms, she flips them front to back. They feel oddly empty. Not empty, but *light.* She looks up at Miguel.

He smiles, raising his brow. "No?"

She gazes back at her hands. "I guess not."

———

Walking alone through the wild forest, Maia brushes her fingertips against the trees. She gazes up at the ancient pines, straining to hear their whispers ... but they are silent.

Are they silent? Or is it just that she can no longer hear them?

She turns in place and closes her eyes, tilting her face toward the sun streaming through the branches. Standing among these gentle giants feels different. It feels ... it feels unlike anything she has ever known. She opens her eyes, her heart aching, and she knows.

It is over.

Stepping before the broad base of a tree, she presses her hands against its mossy bark. She listens, awaiting a sound she fears may never come. A tear escapes, and she bites her lip, holding back her sob. She can no longer hear it breathe. There are no whispers of *Mother*.

She hangs her head. Is it really over? For so long, she knew a part of her would die at the end of this journey, although she could never be sure which part. She drops her head against the trunk, wrapping her arms around it. "I can't hear you, old friend," she whispers, "but I know you're still speaking. If I could just ... if I could just hear you one last time?"

She looks up. Listening. Waiting.

But there is silence.

She falls to her knees, and she knows what she must do. Breathing deep, she spreads her fingers wide across the dirt and presses them into the ground. She gasps, feeling the last traces of her powers slowly drain back into the earth. She scours the forest floor, searching for that familiar spark of life.

Searching. Searching. *Searching.* She glances back and forth.

It's gone.

Is it gone? Or is it just that she can no longer see it?

She hangs her head, remembering all those years she spent denying who she was—*hiding* who she was. Anchored by shame, she couldn't understand that those whispers inside her heart were there for a reason. All those years, they were only trying to lead her to the life she was always meant to live.

Her mother's voice rings through her memory: *Trust the gut pull you feel and follow it above all else.*

Maia couldn't understand. Couldn't *see.* And the journey here was *so painful*; it broke her, took everything she had. But the life awaiting on the other side has given it back tenfold.

The journey was necessary.

The journey is *always* necessary.

Collapsing onto her side, she presses her cheek against the forest floor and drags her fingers along the dirt. "I am ... *animated Earth,*" she whispers, and a tear falls onto the ground.

Bathed in the sun's soft glow, she closes her eyes, observing behind closed lids its flickering rays. She doesn't need to *see* to feel its power. Steadfast, it is always there.

This ending has paved the way for a new beginning. Death can be so misunderstood—not only in the loss of a physical bond, but more often than not, the loss of an emotional one: the ending of a relationship, a way of life, a dream. One of Maia's most painful lessons since embarking on this journey has been learning that a majority of her grief has come, not from the loss itself, but from her refusal to let go.

Death allows new life to unfurl from the ashes. Maia doesn't know what her future holds, but she knows without a doubt that she is exactly where she is meant to be. Her destiny fulfilled; she has arrived at the life patiently waiting for her on the other side.

Rolling onto her back, she gazes at the sky and holds her pounamu against her chest. The unfurling of a fern. A new beginning.

A mighty breeze swirls through the dense forest of pines, swaying the trees' jagged tips, and Maia smiles. She doesn't need to see the spirit of the Earth to know it's there.

It always has been, and it always will be.

FORTY-TWO

Walking through the grounds of the tribe, Maia passes familiar faces, people she now calls family, and they nod at one another with a smile. Everyone is off in different directions, busy preparing for their big celebration tonight for the spring equinox.

Maia wanders past a group of men and women working on constructing a large warehouse at the very back of their community area. Leucothea has sent at least a dozen large trucks over the winter filled to the brim with clothing, food, furniture, and medical supplies. With everyone's houses and cupboards fully stocked, Maia has told President Augustus they don't need any more trucks, but he keeps sending them anyway. So, they have decided to build a storehouse for extras. They live off the land, so they don't need much. But still, it's nice not to worry if someone needs something.

They once again have a large building for their army—led by Shinesho. Unfortunately, they'll always need to be prepared; people are still people. There are still bounders out there, dark souls with bad intentions, so Maia and

Miguel continue to practice their bo routine a few times a week.

Surprisingly, Maia's tigers are still hanging around—something she was not expecting once her powers had disappeared—but Atlas is the only one who remains by her side. The rest of the felines now cling to Tema, who has decidedly dubbed herself "Queen of the Jungle." The name hasn't caught on with the community, much to Tema's disappointment, but the old woman keeps trying.

A gaggle of children is playing in the field, running circles around Tema. As she chuckles, her hunched shoulders bounce up and down. Chayanne is standing next to her. She catches Maia watching from a distance. The two friends wave at one another, and Maia smiles with a sigh.

She is finally *home*. She can only hope that wherever her grandpa is, he can see her now—her mum too. And that they are resting peacefully, knowing she has found her place in the world.

She thinks of Huck, and a small ache flutters within. He'd be getting on in years by now, but he should still have a few good ones left. She hopes he is happy back in New Zealand with Collin and Sarah. She smiles, imagining him sleeping on their old wooden porch, his precious stick by his side and her little black fantail perching on the fence.

Heading toward home, Maia passes a field where Shinesho and Miguel are prepping meat from their morning hunt. Miguel laughs at something Shinesho has said, shaking his head. She gazes at him from across the grounds, clutching her pounamu.

She knew. From the moment she met him, she knew. And while their journey hasn't been easy, they have finally arrived. Maia's ending has become her and Miguel's new beginning.

Later that night, the celebrations have begun. Maia stares at the fire, transfixed by the repetitive banging of the drums. Tema sits down next to her, placing her arthritic hand upon Maia's leg. She leans in, whispering, "Everything okay?"

Maia forces a smile. "Fine."

Tema looks up at her, clicking her tongue. "Rubbish. What's weighing you down, child?"

Maia sighs. She can't keep anything from the old shaman. "I guess I'm confused."

"About?"

"I used to have this nightmare. For years, I was haunted by this terrifying vision of me standing on a cliff—*Jake's* cliff —overlooking Leucothea. And every time, I would burn the city to the ground. But now it's all over, and it never came to pass. I'm worried it's because it still awaits me in the future."

"It doesn't."

"But why would it haunt me for so long and not come true?"

"Because you, my sweet child, are not a robot."

Maia waits.

Tema turns her attention to the flames. "Our destinies are not set in stone. We have free will; we are continually evolving entities. That vision of yours was a grave possibility, but somewhere along the journey, you diverged down a different path. You changed."

Maia gazes back at the fire, Tema's words soaking in.

"Did the opportunity present itself?" Tema asks. "Did you find yourself standing on that cliff with the chance to burn Leucothea to the ground?"

"I did," Maia says. "I would be lying if I said I didn't think about it. *Many* times. But I couldn't."

"Exactly. From the very beginning, you fought to give those people a chance to avoid a war—even after they had turned against you. You could have destroyed it all. But you didn't. That, my darling, is true power. That is mercy."

"But I *did* almost destroy it all, when I was standing in the square."

"But you *didn't*. And when you had another opportunity on that cliff, you *still* didn't. Did you?"

"No."

"At the end of the day, how many opportunities did you have to walk to that cliff and burn that city to the ground?"

"Many."

Tema gazes up at her. "You, my darling, were an incredibly powerful being. But in the end, it was your *humanity* that saved them."

FORTY-THREE

Maia shoves aside the wooden stool, its legs groaning against the wet floor. Having already experienced this dream hundreds of times, she waits for it, nodding with a smile as the child's giggle echoes across the empty bar.

There it is.

The child's chubby feet patter in and out of small puddles, and then she runs out the front door.

Walking outside, Maia braces herself against the blinding glow of the sun. With its warm rays on her outstretched hand, she squints across the blue sky. The city streets are no longer drowned and empty, but *busy*, with an endless parade of people passing in every direction. Black and white flags now hang from entryways, and explosions of yellow flowers drape from window boxes.

As Maia wanders down the middle of the street, she prepares herself to step over a flopping fish—the same fish she has always crossed.

But it's not there.

The child rushes across the road, her laughter echoing

in blissful, repeated waves, and runs down the same narrow alley. Maia follows.

As the two weave through the corridors, what was once wet, soiled brick is now dry—almost glittering in the midday sun. Maia turns a corner, surprised to find not her New Zealand cabin at the end of the long alleyway, but her and Miguel's new house. The child is on the front porch, twisting the front doorknob. She swings the door open and slips inside.

As Maia makes her way toward the home, people gather along the sides of the street, each holding a bright yellow wildflower before them. She recognizes some of their faces—people both dead and alive. There are coworkers from her factory here, along with some of Jake's soldiers. Orson. Dawn. President Augustus. Claire. They line the thoroughfare and lean from windows, every single one of them smiling. And then they toss their flowers onto the road.

Maia gasps, bathed in an ocean of yellow, and the alley becomes a carpet of flowers. She holds out her hands. What was once flakes of snow are now yellow petals. She grins as the velvety blossoms caress her skin. It is all so lifelike. *So beautiful.*

The child's laughter pulls Maia's attention back to the home. She makes her way up the wooden steps and pushes open the door to find the little girl at the fireplace next to Miguel. He kneels beside the child, and she wraps her fingers around his, beaming at him.

The girl turns toward Maia and smiles, her chubby cheeks rounded beneath her crystal blue eyes. "Mum!" she yells, and she rushes up to her.

Maia lifts the child from the ground. The girl hugs her and kisses her cheek, and Maia looks at her in awe.

Never once has Maia held her, all those nights, all those years. Never once had they embraced.

Miguel approaches, and he wraps his arms around them. "*Família*," he whispers.

Family.

Maia wakes with a start.

Miguel sits up next to her. "Oh, my love. Your nightmares are back."

Maia places her hand against her belly, bathed in silver moonlight shining through their window. "No, quite the opposite." She faces him, her smile as wide as the sky. "I'm pregnant."

It doesn't take long for word to spread, and the tribe's women flock to Maia's side. They say it takes a village to raise a child, and Maia cannot be more grateful that she belongs to such a loving and supportive community. It's like she is suddenly surrounded by twenty Temas—although Tema has become particularly overprotective. Any day now, Maia expects to open her door to find the old shaman on her front porch, waving the other women back with a stick.

"They may say they're aunties," Tema told Maia sternly one day, "but I'm the only one who matters. I have first dibs."

"Of course, Tema," Maia said, rubbing the worried old woman's shoulders.

Chayanne stood behind Tema, shaking her head and pointing a thumb to herself.

Maia could only smile. This poor child is going to be smothered by women.

Lying on the couch with Miguel kneeling beside her, Maia beams as he wraps his large hands around her small growing belly, telling their baby stories about how he and Maia met. Tales of their adventures in the woods and the treacherous Great War in Leucothea. About brave Uncle Lucas, and the child's two older sisters, who are always watching over them.

Maia has never seen this side of Miguel before. There is so much hope in his eyes. He is so proud as he walks around the community. The first few weeks after discovering he would be a father again, he stopped everyone he passed to tell them the news, sometimes the same people many times a day. He bends over backward taking care of Maia, working around the clock to make sure their home, now fully furnished with rooms and doors, is stocked and ready for their new arrival, who is still not due for months.

A knock sounds at their front door.

"It's open!" Maia yells.

Chayanne pops her head in. "A truck has arrived from Leucothea. There is someone here to see you, Maia."

Approaching the gates, Maia spots Lucas leaning against the hood of a black pickup truck, his crutches propped beside him.

Maia can't hold back her grin. "Did you miss me?" she says as she approaches.

"Always." With his weight returned and his hair trimmed into short curls, he looks exactly like the Lucas Maia has always known and loved.

She throws her arms around him, and the two embrace. "I've missed you," she says, and she steps back to hold his face.

He grabs her hand, kissing the top. "Me too, darling."

"So, to what do we owe this pleasure?"

"The driver from your last S&R Truck delivery told me the news, and I wanted to come and personally congratulate you and Miguel," he says, looking her over. He angles his head with a smile.

"What?"

"It's just..." He takes in her freckles, her thick head of auburn waves. "You look like the young woman I found hiding in the basement of my ship." He shrugs with a grin. "Minus the belly." He looks over her shoulder, and his smile widens.

Maia turns as Miguel approaches, and she steps to the side as the brothers hug, slapping each other's backs and speaking Portuguese.

Miguel grabs Lucas's face and kisses his cheek. "My brother," he says. "I hope you are staying a while. Did you come on your own?"

"No," Lucas says, and his gaze flickers to Maia. "There is someone I would like you to officially meet." He turns toward the truck and waves. The driver's side door opens, and the woman who made his crutches steps out. "This is Emma," Lucas says as she approaches. "I know you met her briefly back at the hospital as a nurse, but..." He looks at her with an adoring smile. "She's not just a nurse. She is someone very special to me, and it is important that she meet my family."

Maia and Miguel both step forward, embracing Lucas's new love. "Emma," Maia says. "It's so nice to see you again."

As Miguel and Emma talk, Lucas and Maia smile at one another, and she remembers his words on Jake's cliff.

You deserve to have that sort of love. We both do.

Maia sighs. Lucas has found love, and she couldn't be happier for him. She knew it wouldn't be long—any woman would be lucky to have him. And she and Lucas are family; they will always be a part of each other's lives. Because of what they've been through, they will love each other in a way like no other, even though that love has changed.

Lucas will always be Maia's Brazilian pirate, and she will always be the stowaway who saved his life.

A bark sounds from inside the truck's cabin, and Maia's eyes widen. "Lucas! Did you get a dog?!"

"Not exactly," he says with a cheeky grin.

"Sounds like a dog." As Maia makes toward the truck, Lucas reaches out to stop her.

Her brow twitches. The bark sounds again and she peers up at the vehicle. *That bark*. She can't see through the windshield—only a bright sky reflecting behind the trees—but there is something moving on the other side of the glass.

She looks back at Lucas. "What's going on?"

Emma and Miguel stop talking.

Lucas holds Maia's hand within his. "I was informed that the New System had been in contact with my ship. So, I took the opportunity last fall and reached out to an old friend."

Maia shakes her head. "An old friend ... *Davies*?"

"He confirmed there was indeed a frequent visitor to the docks the last time they stopped by New Zealand. A visitor looking specifically for *you*."

Maia swallows, her heart racing. "A ... *visitor*."

Lucas smiles. "Davies is a staunch man of his word. Seeing how he never fulfilled his promise to your father to deliver you safely to North America, I was able to pull a few strings."

Emma walks to the passenger side door and opens it. "Come on, boy," she sings, patting her thighs.

Maia steps forward, her hand on her chest, and Miguel walks up next to her. She looks back at Lucas, still leaning against the hood, and he nods knowingly with a smile.

"Maia," Miguel says beside her, and she turns as a large black dog jumps from the truck onto the dirt.

She gasps and clutches at Miguel, her knees buckling. He wraps his arms around her and slowly lowers her to the ground.

He's an old boy now—his black face dusted with white, but he still has an undeniable pep in his step.

Huck lifts his nose into the air, sniffing. When he spots Maia, he cocks his head to the side. His tail slowly flops back and forth, and he whimpers. Maia covers her mouth, trembling as she sobs.

Huck sprints toward her and she opens her arms. He barrels into her, attacking her with kisses and wagging his tail, whimpering as Maia cries.

"Is it really you?" She wraps her arms around him, burying her face into his thick fur.

Unable to contain his excitement, Huck races in a circle around the truck. Maia glances back at Lucas. His arm around a now sniffling Emma, he smiles through his tears.

Huck rushes back to Maia, kissing her, and she laughs at the sky. Miguel kneels next to them and Huck sits, lifting his paw. Miguel laughs, shaking it. "It's nice to finally meet you, old boy." He wraps his arm around Maia, his lips lingering as he kisses the top of her head.

Huck races into the woods. They wait, listening to the crunching leaves and cracking twigs, until the old dog comes back a minute later, dragging a broken tree branch three times his size behind him.

Maia and Miguel laugh, and she looks up at him. "Is this *real*?! Please tell me I'm not dreaming."

He smiles, tenderly wiping her tears. "You, my love, are *not* dreaming."

She climbs to her feet. Emma knowingly steps to the

side as Maia races up to Lucas, sobbing as they embrace against the truck's wide hood. "Thank you, Lucas. Thank you *so much*."

"I'd do it a hundred times over again just to see that smile," he whispers.

A few hours later, Miguel is cooking lunch over an open fire while Lucas, Emma, and the chief talk at a picnic table. During his stay a few years back, Lucas loved chatting with the chief. Now that Lucas is one of President Augustus's main advisors, there is much to speak about.

Maia lies on a blanket in the sun with her head resting on a sleeping Atlas, who has been surprisingly tolerant of her old dog constantly dropping slobbery sticks by his side.

She gasps, perching onto her elbow. Her hand on her belly, she feels movement beneath the surface. "Miguel," she whispers, looking up at him with her mouth agape.

Miguel drops his tongs, rushing to her side.

"Here," she says, guiding his hand to the spot. They wait.

The baby moves again, and Miguel's eyes widen. "That's ... that's our *baby*."

She smiles. "That's our baby."

Always an opportunist, Huck wanders up, smothering Maia with kisses. She rolls onto her back laughing, gazing up at a furry black tail waving stark against a deep blue sky.

ACKNOWLEDGMENTS

All my love goes out to my husband, Rich. Despite having written another hundred thousand words, I am at a loss at how to describe how grateful I am for your enduring love, support, and listening ear. Thank you for believing in me. For understanding and loving me through this beautiful madness of being an author. For the days I became so obsessed with this story that I couldn't pull myself away. I will love you forever, and when forever is over...

To my father, Phil, and stepmother, Bonnie. There is no love and support like that of parents. Thank you for being mine.

To Amanda Hughes at Haint Blue Creative, for being my friend, my confidant, and editor. I will spend the rest of my life writing books just to read your comments.

To Elizabeth Packman—the yin to my yang. Oh, the hours and hours and hours we've spent discussing book matters, and anything and everything in between. Thank you for being such an incredible friend.

To the following beautiful souls: Molly, Ellie, Shandra, Amira, and Jesse Packman. You are each such a light in my life. Thank you.

To my fantastic team of BETA readers representing New Zealand, Canada, Sweden, and the United States: Caroline Ansley, Barbara Semenick-Watt, Amira Hilmy, Laura Cox, Elizabeth Packman, and MJ Carstarphen. Working with you has been a privilege and a joy. Your dedication, input, and honest opinions have made *Voices* a better story. Thank you, thank you, *thank you*.

To my incredibly talented cover designer, Murphy Rae, for yet another spectacular cover.

Last but not least, I thank you, dear reader, from the bottom of my heart, for giving this new author a chance.

ABOUT THE AUTHOR

Jillian Webster is the author of the climate fiction trilogy *The Forgotten Ones* and *Scared to Life: A Memoir*. Originally from Michigan, Jillian now lives in New Zealand with her husband and dog. When she's not writing, she enjoys nature walks, yoga, and cooking.

For more information, please visit www.jillianwebster.com

Connect with the author:

facebook.com/websterjillian

instagram.com/authorjillianwebster

Made in the USA
Monee, IL
08 August 2022